MW00627098

THE GIRL IN THE PEACH TREE

MICHELLE OUCHAREK-DEO

THE GIRL IN THE PEACH TREE

MICHELLE OUCHAREK-DEO

The Vinho Verde Trilogy
A crisp green wine filled with surprises.

❦

Book I

LIVE AND GROW
PRESS
Port Coquitlam

All rights reserved. Published by Live and Grow Press.

This book is a work of fiction. Any references to real people, real places or real events are used fictionally. Other names, characters, places and events are products of the author's imagination, and any resemblance to actual events or places or persons, living or dead is entirely coincidental.

Copyright 2nd Ed. © 2021 Michelle Oucharek-Deo

No part of this publication may be reproduced, stored in a retrieval system, or transmitted in any form or by any means, electronic, mechanical, photocopying, recording, or otherwise without written permission of the publisher. For information regarding permission, contact liveandgrowpress@gmail.com

Oucharek-Deo, Michelle B. 1969-

Oucharek-Deo, Michelle, author
The girl in the peach tree / Michelle Oucharek-Deo.

ISBN 978-1-988348-09-4 (paperback)
ISBN 978-1-988348-08-7 (html)
ISBN 978-1-988348-06-3 (hardcover)

Printed in the USA
First edition 2016
Book Cover Design by Nada Orlic

In loving memory of Emil and Jeanette Oucharek.
You lived a life of love, faith, and courage
and taught me how to do the same.
I will always love you Mom and Dad.

Table of Contents

Prologue		1
1.	The Night Before	5
2.	My 'Not' Wedding Day	10
3.	Puddle Jumping to Portugal	19
4.	Finding Athena	28
5.	A Lesson in Boarding and Life	41
6.	Changing World	49
7.	Who's Going to Portugal?	63
8.	Two Hours	72
9.	Lisbon	80
10.	The First Supper	93
11.	Confidence	102
12.	The Letter	111
13.	Maple Seeds from Home	125
14.	The Road to Somewhere	139
15.	Netuno	146
16.	Excited	154
17.	Maggie, Me, and the Goat	166
18.	Writing it Out	180
19.	Intentions	189
20.	Reflections	195
21.	I am Beautiful	206
22.	Who's the Sous Chef?	209
23.	Peach Pie	213
24.	Facing the Bread	218
25.	Tasting a Future	222
26.	The Date	231
27.	Silves	242
28.	Crushed Grapes	249
29.	A Hint of Haiku	262
30.	Happy Day, Sad Day	271
31.	What's up Dalley?	284

32. Avó's Letter   292
33. More Truth   304
34. Yesterday and Today   315
35. Walk and Talk   327
36. Crashing Waves   339
37. I Promise   351
38. Calling Home   359
39. A Day Off   366
40. Cake Chaos   372
41. What's in a Charm?   388
42. The Candle Lady   403
43. The Dam Breaks   411
44. Convergence   424
45. The Handkerchief   442
Epilogue   454

Acknowledgements   456
Barefoot in the Dirt, Book II Preview   459
Author's Note   467

Prologue

So WHERE DO I START in this tale of food, photos, a cancelled wedding, a handsome man, a beautiful rival, and—well, me? Throw in a widow, one divorcée, a traveler's journal, and you've got the makings for quite an adventure. I guess the beginning would be a good place.

My name is Maya Wells. I grew up in a little town called Peachland.

Peachland is right in the heart of the Okanagan Valley, an area in Canada filled with grapevines, fruit trees, and some of the most beautiful rolling hills you could ever see.

It was my father's dream to own a vineyard, and when I was almost four he purchased his dream plus a small peach orchard. He moved our little family out of town and into the hills. One of the best things I remember about that move was that my dad smiled a lot more. I think my mom was happier there too. At least that's what my dad told me. I saw her more often and sometimes she would even come down from her room to have lunch with us. As the years passed, I wasn't quite sure what was wrong with her, but I knew she wasn't like the other moms I met at school. I learned that there were black days and grey days in our house, and that the only yellow days were the ones I created.

I took refuge from the heaviness that hung over my home by running through the orchard and playing games in the vines that created my perfect kingdom. I was able to leave my childhood worries at the vineyard entrance and walk the property like a sentry protecting her land.

In my sentry days, there were times when I took my dad's globe out to my favorite peach tree and balanced precariously on the limbs, holding on with one hand and spinning the globe with the other. I remember the squeak it used to make when it turned. Then in a single motion I could stop the world with one finger, and wherever it landed would become the destination for my next imaginary journey. My adventures took me to Greece and Bali, Antarctica and Peru. When I was in that tree, I had the courage to go anywhere and be anyone. I was almost free.

When I was eight my world came to a crashing halt. My dad sold the ground from under my feet. I had to give up my kingdom, my refuge. He might as well have chopped down my peach tree with me in it.

We had to move back into town as there were no longer any grey days in the Wells' household—the black monster that had darkened our lives when I was so little was back, and it was now uglier than ever.

I had to become a grown-up Maya, watching out for my sister Jordan when my dad was busy with Mom and all of her appointments. There was no longer room for imagination, just practicality.

The only good thing that came out of the move was my friendship with Beth. I remember that first day at the new school, eating lunch by myself when she sat down and gave me half of her chocolate chip cookie. She didn't say anything to me—she just sat there and smiled. As our friendship grew she had a funny way of figuring out exactly what I needed. Once in a while we would steal away to one of the local orchards on our bikes and then run through the trees. I often lived from bike ride to bike ride, waiting for our next visit.

By the time I was in high school though, I had erased the remaining whimsy and play out of my life and had blown the last bits of yellow days onto the floor. I had altered my retreat pattern from orchard escapes to following rules, and the only place where I trusted dealing with my thoughts was in my journal. That was until the summer of grade twelve, when it felt like real life flanked me on all sides, and I couldn't even trust my own words. I went on to university, where I received an unremarkable education.

In my last year I met Steven, who was finishing his engineering degree. At first, I was grateful for his rigid schedules and particular behaviors. He made life easy for me. I never had to make any decisions. I could always predict where we would go and what we would eat. He never challenged me, and I never challenged myself. It was perfect, but I was withering inside. After graduation I found a job at a local sprinkler company. I was twenty-two, and it was a good life—or so I kept telling myself. I decided that safe was best. Dreaming was too painful, and imagining something better for my heart was not possible. Somewhere along the way though, taking the safe path became dangerous to me and my soul. I began to feel like I was losing things I didn't even know I wanted.

This tale starts when I was twenty-five and drowning in a life that I had created, grasping for a branch to hold on to.

The Night Before

Maya

IT WAS LATE AND ALL the lights were out in the house. I knew that I should have been sleeping, but my heart raced uncontrollably and I felt sick to my stomach. I got up and started pacing, tears brimming in my eyes. I felt anxious like my head was going to explode.

I kept asking myself the same questions: "What if I don't want to go back East? What if I'm finished with school? What if I have other things that I want to do?"

By midnight, the feeling of panic had seeped into my muscles. One by one, every fiber of my being started to scream. After an hour of that muscle-wrenching, heart-hurting exercise, I realized I was in the middle of a full-blown panic attack. I'd had a similar experience during exams, years ago, when I'd thought I was having a heart attack. I remembered calling my dad, who had walked me through it with ease. Later when I'd pressed him for more information about why he was able to help me so easily, he looked at me surprised saying, "Maya, your mom has been having them for years! Don't you remember?"

"No! I don't," I mumbled, feeling confused.

I decided then that I never wanted to have another panic attack again. I guess my ego allowed me to believe I had that kind of power, and maybe I did for a little while—until *that* night; the night before my wedding.

After catching my breath, I realized I was not dying. And then it hit me, "I don't love Steven. I never have."

It was that simple. The panic was gone, replaced with a mixed bag of guilt, fear, and a dash of relief.

"What have I done? It's now twelve hours before the wedding, and I can't marry him. What the hell am I going to do?" I asked myself.

By then it was sometime around 3:00 a.m. I quietly crept upstairs from the basement toward my parents' room. Standing in the doorway I watched them sleeping peacefully, side-by-side.

My mother turned over, and her eyes fluttered opened. She had always been a light sleeper, but to me it felt like she had not been sleeping at all. She sat up in the darkened room. I said nothing. She turned on the light, and then nudged my father. He rolled over, looked at the two of us, and he too sat straight up in bed. We all stared at one another for what seemed to be an eternity. I breathed in, and then on the exhale exclaimed, "I can't marry him!" The level of resolve in my voice surprised even me.

My parents waited for a moment before speaking. They looked at one another, and then at me. My dad paused, opened his mouth, and said, "Then don't." He didn't ask me a single question. He just told me it was late and that he had to make some calls.

He added, "You have one to make too, and you need to do it *now.*"

It was a long night that bled into the morning. Steven came over, and there were tears—lots of them—but not from me, though I wish they had been. It would have been much easier, but I guess I deserved that. I should have figured it out long before. But I had convinced myself that Steven was the safest route: no drama, no trauma. Our lives would be predictable and safe.

As we sat, he cried and tried to convince me we could work things out. But the more he talked, the more I knew I was done, and I just had to walk away.

Around 6:00 a.m. my dad came in. He took Steven by the arm and led him out of the den. Steven's best friend, Roger, had received a text from Jordan, telling him that the wedding was off. He'd arrived at our house angry and looking for a fight.

I heard some scuffling and swearing coming from the other room. "Steven, what the hell is going on? Was Jordan's text true? Did she *really* call the wedding off ?" he asked with anger spilling over into the space where I sat.

Steven replied with a simple, "Yes, Roger. We need to go *now*. Please get me out of here."

I could hear my dad's voice when he said, "Steven I'm really sorry. Please let us know if …"

Sounding irritated and broken, Steven interrupted, "Thank you, Mr. Wells. There is nothing that *you* can do."

I could hear Roger cursing my name as he walked out of the house and down the driveway. He and I had never gotten along. He'd told Steven from the beginning that I was not the right girl for him. Maybe we all should have listened.

I sat shaking, not knowing where my next breath was going to come from. Beth had just arrived and wanted to see me. I didn't want to see anyone, but at least I knew that she wouldn't give me a hard time. She was one of those friends who just knew when to be there, when to not say a word, and when to go. She was now a school teacher and loved her job. I envied how life looked so easy for her and I sometimes wished that I could just borrow her joy for a few days. She always laughed when I said that. She was the only one who knew how unhappy I was. Funny though, she never tried to change my mind about things; she just reminded me that I always had a choice. "It might not be easy," she would say, "but there's always another path."

Beth walked into the den with a pot of tea and two cups. "Come on," she said. "Come with me." She pointed to the two quilts that were on the couch and motioned for me to grab them. We snuck out through the back door, and into the garden.

The garden … was beautiful. It had been *de-wedding-ed*. I'm not sure if that is a word, but that's what it looked like. No more lace, ribbons, or fancy chairs. She smiled as I looked around. A week's worth of decorations and hard work were all gone, except for the twinkly lights that had been left hanging around the gazebo. I looked at them and smiled; having the lights was comforting.

"Do you want me to turn them off?" she asked softly. "No, the lights are good," I responded in a whisper.

"That's funny. That's what your mom said. She and I figured that you might need your garden back as soon as possible. We know that you have been spending a lot of time here lately. We spent most of the morning taking things down."

My eyes filled with tears as I asked her, "You did this for me, you and my mom?"

"Are you okay?" Beth asked.

"I don't know? I don't know anything right now." The words sprang from my lips.

"Maya? Did you make a mistake? Do you want to marry Steven?"

"NO!" I blurted out quickly. "That much I am clear about. I know I can't marry him! What I don't understand is how it got this far?"

"You mean with Steven?"

"With Steven—with my life—all of it. I'm twenty-five and lost. I don't want…" Beth interrupted me as she reached out and grabbed my hand. My tears welled up again, and my voice broke as I said, "I want a different life. I don't want this one. I've never wanted any of this. I want to be happy, like you are." I squeezed her hand and continued, "I have screwed everything up."

We made our way over to the twinkly gazebo and sat down. Wrapping ourselves up in the quilts, we sipped hot tea and talked for hours as my mom slipped to and from the kitchen making sure that the pot was always hot and full. She said nothing but smiled at us both. After she'd left the third pot, I called out to her, "Mom, you know I love you, right?"

She turned to me, "Yes Maya. I love you, too."

Beth and I sat quietly, finishing our tea until the sun started making its way around to the backyard.

"I'm going home to get cleaned up, make some calls, and then I will come back and see what I can do to help," Beth said simply. She had organized so much, and now she was dismantling it all too. She slipped out the gate, and I snuck back into the house.

The kitchen, although full, was strangely quiet. Making my way upstairs, I found my room thankfully empty. My wedding dress hung from the closet door tinged with the grey of my decision. I stepped into the bathroom and stared at myself in the mirror. I had no idea who was looking back at me, but I didn't like the person that I saw.

My 'Not' Wedding Day

Maya

AFTER A LONG, HOT SHOWER, I dressed and then made my way down the stairs. My heart beat frantically as I landed on the last step, slumping down, not knowing if I could face everyone. Then I heard voices coming from the kitchen.

To be more specific, I heard Jordan yelling, "Does she have any idea what she's done? Did you see Steven when he left? Mom, it was awful! He was absolutely broken. And I thought Roger was going to hit her. Dad had to physically hold him back. If it was me, I would have let him punch her right in the face!"

"Jordan, please. That's enough." Mom tried to settle her down. "She just didn't know."

"Didn't know? Didn't know *what*? That she didn't love him? That she wasn't ready to get married?" Silence hung in the air, and then she continued, "How could she *not* know until the night before the wedding? She is so self-absorbed! She is such a coward. I'm ashamed to call her my sister."

I was thankful that I was sitting on the bottom stair as Jordan's words hit me like a fist in my chest, leaving me winded and emotionally empty.

"Jordan!" Grandma Stella shouted with a quick command and greater force than my mom could ever rally. "That is enough! How dare you accuse your sister of being a coward? You have no idea the strength it takes to do the right thing in a situation like this. Do you think this was easy for her?

Do you think she doesn't know the impact this has had on everyone? It would have been far worse for her to marry Steven today, and then two or five years down the road realize that she had to leave him, but wouldn't or couldn't!"

She was right. It would have been *far* worse to marry Steven. But the truth was, Jordan was right too. I should have known, but I wasn't looking hard enough.

I knew that I couldn't sit on the stairs forever, so I shuffled my feet, and silence fell over the kitchen again. My mom popped her head around the corner and asked quietly, "Hi Maya. How are you feeling? Did you have a good shower?"

"Yes, it was fine. I guess I better get in there." I smiled weakly, and then stood up.

"How long have you been sitting here?"

"*Long enough*," I responded with a little sarcasm. "Mom, can I ask you a question?" I whispered.

"Yes," she answered simply.

"How do you know when you're really in love?"

She paused briefly and then spoke directly into my ear, "If you have to ask, then you're not." Then she took my arm and pulled me forward and said, "It'll be okay."

"Really? When?" Surprisingly, my weak smile began to feel a little stronger with her holding my arm.

"Well, honestly, not now, but it will. I'm living proof that things can get better, even when it feels like everything is falling apart."

Our eyes met briefly and in that second it felt like she almost understood me.

I stepped into the kitchen, walked over to the sink, and started to fill the kettle. I really didn't need another cup of tea but going through the process was a routine that gave me great comfort. It was something that I had done as far back as I could remember. It had always been my job. Dad would ask me to put the kettle on any time things were a little tense with my mom. It wasn't until years later I realized that having me make the tea gave him an excuse to send me out of earshot, as he thought the kitchen was far enough away from their bedroom that I could not hear the crying. It wasn't.

Good or bad, I always put it in a pretty pot for her and left it outside her door. Once in a while she would invite me in to have a cup with her, but that only happened on her good days. I loved those days. With her quiet voice, she would ask me if I had two cups. The truth was, I always had two cups on the tray, hoping she would invite me in. On those rare days when she did, we would cuddle on the bed and look out through her window over the orchard. Sometimes in the summer she would ask me to open the window and we would share the scent of the ripening peaches, winding their way up into her room.

But that last summer at the vineyard she never invited me for a single cup of tea. We left after the harvest that year. I'm not sure if things improved for her after we sold the vineyard, but my dad said it was easier— easier on him and on her—and that she was getting the help she needed.

When we'd first left, I knew my silence worried my dad. He'd tried to talk to me, but I was stubborn and refused to have any kind of conversation about it. Soon, Jordan's and my mom's needs outweighed my own and I discovered that answering him was easier on both of us, so I just started talking again and pretended I was fine.

In reality though, I felt like a cracked teapot that you might find in a second-hand store. I looked usable at first glance, but the fissures were undetectable. Only if you'd tested me out would you have discovered my weaknesses. I kept myself on the shelf for a long time, not taking any risks.

The cold water flowed over my hand, coaxing me back into the present. As I stood at the counter, I could feel Jordan's eyes burning into my back. I couldn't look at her, but I had to say something.

I opened my mouth and the words fell into the sink with a clatter, "Jordan, just say what you have to say."

There was a pause in the room and I heard Grandma Stella take in a breath, as if she was going to cut Jordan off; but I didn't give her a chance. I whipped around and yelled, "Just say it to my face!"

Jordan looked at me and shrieked, "You are a selfish coward and what you have done to Steven, Mom, Dad, me, and the whole family is horrible. Really Maya? The night before the wedding? Could you have picked a worse time? Well, yes. I guess you could have run out on him at the ceremony today. I am so tired of the fake persona that you put on. Nothing is ever real. Honestly, I can't imagine what he saw in you in the first place. You have always gotten your way your whole life. So nice, so kind, never getting mad, always doing the right thing. I'm sick of it!"

She turned to march out of the room.

"You're right," I said, without missing a beat. She turned back around to face me. My words had rendered her speechless. While I still had the courage, I continued, "Jordan, the bottom line is that you're right." My voice shook with the truth.

Her mouth dropped open with surprise, but she pulled her thoughts together, shrugged her shoulders, walked over to the sink, and took the kettle out of my hands.

"Maybe it's my turn to make the tea," she said quietly, pushing me out of the way.

I smiled and then realized for the first time that maybe Jordan was not as oblivious as she presented.

The next sound we heard was the doorbell. I took a deep breath and got ready to face the next wave of my non-wedding day. To describe all that happened over the next six hours as a series of waves crashing down around me would be an understatement. Honestly, it was more like sitting in the middle of an afternoon squall while tied to a rock, only able to catch a breath every few minutes.

I lost track of the number of visitors after the fifth Ding-Dong! Family and friends, asking questions, sharing thoughts, it all blurred together. I was exhausted.

Steven called on the hour, trying to convince me we could postpone, elope, or wait. He kept telling me he loved me, no matter what.

I didn't want to talk to him, but my dad continued to hand me the phone, saying that it was my responsibility. The conversations were pretty much the same, until the last one.

"Maya, it's not too late," Steven whispered with desperation. "We can work this out. We can throw things together in the next few hours. Everything is ready to go," he said pleading with me.

I knew it was time to end it. "No Steven, we can't!"

He grasped for answers, asking, "What did I do wrong?" His sadness was palpable.

"Steven," I said, keeping my voice still and cool, "You didn't do anything. It was me. I haven't been honest with you."

"Is there someone else?"

I laughed out loud as the thought was so ridiculous. I would never have cheated on him. I would never cheat on anyone. He appeared to have misunderstood my laugh, and now sounded even more wounded.

"Oh," he responded with dejection.

"There's no one else. It's just me. I'm not happy with anything in my life. I need something different, and marrying you is not the answer. It's not fair to you, or to me."

I could feel something change on the other end of the line and I knew I had said the wrong thing. Steven flipped from dejection to white hot anger in an instant. His sadness had been incinerated with my last statement. For the next few seconds, all I could do was listen.

"Fair to you!!!?" he yelled with a piercing pitch. "Are you fuckin' kidding me, Maya?"

I had never heard Steven swear before, so I knew we had just ventured into a land that I had no directions for.

"You just cancelled our wedding, destroyed my future plans, embarrassed me in front of everyone we love, and stole three years of my life, and this is not fair to *you*?" His anger now oozed through the lines. There was no way to avoid it, so I just sat back and let it cover me completely.

There was a small break in his rant, so I took my opportunity between his angry breaths.

"Steven, clearly no matter what I say to you, it will be the wrong answer. The only thing that I know for sure is that we are not getting married today. We are never getting married. I don't love you." The clarity of the words rang clean like a bell, struck in an empty hall.

Then all I heard was a *click*. I knew there was no going back.

I could hardly look up when my mom came in and told me Aunt Olive had arrived and wanted to see me. I smiled and was thankful for the distraction.

My great-aunt Olive had been married for 53 years and her husband had died just over a year ago. She is the oddest woman I have ever known, but we invited her to every family event because she kept things interesting.

She made me laugh, and she always incited some sort of rebellion during an evening. I nodded my head in agreement, letting my mom know that it was okay to show her in. She walked into the room with determination and I sensed that she had something important to tell me. Before we could even start that conversation though, I found myself staring at the sparkly, shockingly pink dress she was wearing. I couldn't help but laugh.

"Well don't look so surprised!" she exclaimed, "I bought this dress especially for today and I wanted to get some wear out of it. Meeting you here is just as good as at the wedding, don't you think?"

"I love it!" I told her. "You would have been the belle of the ball and outshone even the bride."

"Good lord. Is it that garish?" she asked, as she broke into chuckles. "No, Aunt Olive. It is perfect—just like you!" I said, getting up and giving her a big hug.

"Perfect? Did you hit your head?" Then she handed me a little gift bag covered in ribbons and bows.

"Aunt Olive, the wedding has been cancelled. Please take this back?" I said, pushing the bag toward her.

"Oh, Maya. I'm old, but I'm not stupid! This is not a wedding gift." Her voice was so resolute that I had to believe her. I smiled as she always had a way of shifting a moment. "It's a gift of bravery."

"Bravery? What do you mean?" I asked.

She leaned in so no one else could hear her, and then whispered, "I know what people think of me, that I'm a little strange, always doing things differently. But I have to tell you that it doesn't matter what other people think of you. You have to stand up for who you are. I'm so proud of you. I wish I'd had the courage to stop *my* wedding! Oh, what a miserable life I've had, and it was all my fault," she said, laughing. Then she puckered her lips, as if recalling a bad taste in her mouth, and said, "I made the best of things though, most of the time. But I made his life miserable too. He loved, but I could never love him back. I liked him well enough, but I could never give him what he needed. And he never really knew how to make me happy, so we existed—fifty-three years of existing. Now for the first time in my life, I'm happy."

"How did you do it for fifty-three years?" I asked, almost afraid of the answer.

"Count yourself lucky you'll never have to find out." She paused, and then said, "You look exhausted Maya. Get ready to escape. I have a plan." She left me alone in the living room with my thoughts and the ribbon-clad bag.

It was not long before I heard Grandma Stella yelling from the kitchen, "Olive, what the hell are you doing? Get your hands out of the cake!"

"Well, what are they going to do with it? Save it for the anniversary? This is delicious! Thank you, Maya."

The momentary confusion allowed me to steal away up to my room without anyone noticing. I was thankful for her in every way.

I locked the door, sat on the floor, and then opened the bag. Inside was a little velvet box and in the box lay a simple, tear-shaped diamond pendant. It was exquisite. It almost didn't look real, but I knew Aunt Olive and her love of fine jewelry. I lifted the pendant by its delicate chain and held my breath as the afternoon sun shone through my window and hit the diamond, casting a myriad of speckled colors over my arms and onto the walls. My room was filled with dancing light, and momentarily, my heart smiled as I felt a flash of freedom. I looked into the box and noticed a little scrap of paper tucked into the bottom.

My Dear Maya,

This is a Tear of Bravery. When we embark upon our true journey, there is both tremendous heartache and joy. Our bodies give us the gift of tears so that we can shed the heartache and share the joy when the time is right. Be brave and let yourself cry. Then stop crying and get on with it.

Love, Aunt Olive

PS: Don't wear this today—it might freak a few people out. PPS: When you are ready, your adventure will come to you.

Holding the teardrop in my hand, I grabbed a blanket off the bed, closed my eyes, and let my rhythmic sobs soothe me to sleep.

Puddle Jumping to Portugal

Maya

How could I figure anything out when it felt like every breath I took was weighted with the painful truth that I had no idea what to do next? I felt numb and panicked, heavy and wrinkled, and yet I knew in the deepest part of me I had done the right thing by stopping the wedding.

I touched the teardrop that hung around my neck and the words fell from my lips, "I don't feel brave, just tired."

For too long I had told my heart what to feel and how to act. I manipulated every emotion, and I was in control. I didn't want that anymore, but I wasn't sure I could do the real life piece either. It hurt too much. It felt like one part of me was lost, and another part had punched its way into a whole new mess.

"Good, bad, or ugly, this is my life now," I said, completing my thoughts out loud.

I stopped talking and listened to the drumming of the spring rain on the gazebo roof. It was steady and rhythmic; it was the only sound that gave me solace.

Judith

I made my way to the front door with a spring in my step that I had not felt for many years.

When Beth entered she wrapped her arms around me, smiling, knowing I was feeling better. She had been the one friend in Maya's life who knew all about the depressed demons that lived in the Wells' household, yet she had never been scared away by them. She was a remarkable child and grew into an amazing woman.

"Where is she?" Beth asked, with an unexpected spark of excitement.

"She's in the garden again. Maybe you can get her out of the house? I'm really worried about her." I shivered, knowing I was about Maya's age when the depression first took hold of me. I was determined not to let my daughter walk that same path. I had always dreamed there would come a time when Maya could turn to me for help and I would be the mom I'd always wanted to be. I felt I was ready, but it was going to take some time for Maya to trust that I could do my job. Although it was a little late in her life, she still needed me, and I knew I could help if she let me.

Beth's smile was calming, and her voice reassured me. "For sure, Mrs. Wells," she said, bringing me back to our conversation. "I've been worried about her, too. She has refused to go anywhere with me for the past four weeks. But today, I have a plan she cannot refuse. Maya!" she yelled through the open kitchen window. "Get in here. We're going out!"

Maya

When I heard Beth call my name, I reluctantly opened my eyes and saw her standing in the window, waving for me to come in.

I whispered quietly to myself, "I can't say *no* again, for both our sakes. Just stand up Maya, pull your shoulders back, and run."

As I made my way through the rain, I tried to jump over a puddle and misjudged its size, stumbling forward and causing the mud-filled water to bounce up and decorate my favorite fleece pants and give me a new set of dark brown freckles.

When I came through the sliding glass door, I caught sight of myself in the mirror. I had to stop and look. I'd ceased doing my hair since my wedding day and allowed it to develop into an abandoned nest; a true reflection of the crumpled spirit that was living within me.

"I cannot live like this anymore," I exclaimed at the Maya who stood looking back at me in the mirror.

Before I could give it another thought, Beth jumped into the mudroom. "Hey. Got plans for today?" she asked with a mischievous tone, not stopping to hear a response. "Excellent! I thought we would head over to the mall to do some shopping, or at least …"

She paused and stared at me, laughed out loud, and then said, "Pick you up a hair brush?" She reached for a clump of mud caught in my hair, then opened the door and threw it back into the puddle outside.

I smiled at her, and said sarcastically, "Thanks. That would be lovely."

"No problem. Wash your face. Change your clothes. Get your coat on, and let's go. Oh, yeah. I think you might need some new slippers, too!"

I looked down and saw my old slippers covered in mud and grime. Laughter was the only appropriate response. I really was a sight!

She gave me a moment to change and then took me by the arm, running me out the door.

As Beth and I settled into the car, I saw my mom watching us from the front window. A large smile broke across her face and she held up her hand, indicating for us to wait. In a flash, she came running out into the rain in her bare feet holding two oversized bags. I had never seen her move that fast before.

I rolled down the window and yelled to her, "Mom, what are you doing? You have no shoes on."

She laughed saying, "I know. Isn't it great?"

The rain was falling so hard I could hardly hear her. "Can you stop by the mall in Kelowna and return these?" she yelled, pushing the bags through the open window and onto my lap. "They're from that special kitchen store. I can't remember the name, but it's on the receipt in the bag. I paid for it in cash, so just keep the money and do something fun with it this afternoon!" She leaned in through the open window and put her hand on my cheek. "Have fun and laugh lots! I love you Maya."

I was filled with an odd sense of relief as I watched her stand in the rain, happiness radiating from her smile.

As we drove off, I turned around and saw her walk over to the closest puddle and jump straight in! She hopped up and down two more times, laughed, and then ran back into the house. My dad had been telling me for the last couple of months that she had been doing better, but I wouldn't allow myself to believe it until that very moment. It felt good to see her happy. I never dreamed that it could ever happen.

"So where are we going first?" I asked, curiously.

Beth smiled. "Well, let's start at the mall in Kelowna, and then we'll figure things out from there."

We drove quietly along 97 North, listening to the rhythm of the wipers swishing back and forth. Beth whispered to me, "Hey Maya. Do you want to take the back roads through the orchard grove? It may take a little bit longer, but ..."

"Yes, that would be perfect. It's been a long time since we've been down there." She knew I loved the old roads, and like me, I think she sensed that if I didn't turn things around soon my mom might drag me to see her psychiatrist.

As the late spring rain fell hard in the orchards, I rolled the window down and leaned my head out. I saw and smelled the beautiful blossoms on the trees. It would only be a matter of days before the last of the pink puffs fell and the trees started living in green again. I smiled, closed my eyes, and allowed the rain to continue cleansing.

It was only when I could feel the tires leave the peaceful dirt that I opened my eyes again and found us back on the highway. I pulled my body back into the car, dripping and loving it.

"You looked relaxed, almost happy," Beth sighed with satisfaction.

"I am. I couldn't have asked for anything more today." My tears took over where the rain left off. "Beth, when we were growing up, why did you like me?"

She smirked a little. "Strange adventures!" she exclaimed. "It was like you looked at the world through translucent glass. Nothing was quite clear, but I could still see it and I wanted to see what you saw. Everyone else thought you were extremely practical, but I saw a courageous adventurer in you. When we first met you were so quiet, but I always felt like you wanted to say something. I remember the day when I suggested we ride our bikes over to the local orchard and your face lit up like a Christmas tree. From then on, the only time I saw you truly happy was when we were there.

"As we got older though, those days became fewer, and you smiled less. It wasn't until I was about fourteen that I found out from my parents that before you moved, you and your family had owned a vineyard and a peach orchard. I couldn't understand why you hadn't told me, but I figured that one day you would, when you were ready. Then came our last year of high school. You were so quiet and I worried that the orchard adventurer had been swallowed up by your mom's depression and ceased to exist."

Her voice wavered. "There were moments when I just wanted to shake you, but then I looked deep into your eyes and I knew you were still in there fighting to keep my Maya alive. As you got older, you learned to cope a little better and to hide things with more ease. There was even a time when you almost fooled me—almost," she said winking.

My cheeks were now stained with tears, as the story brought me back to those days when my old friend knew just what I needed. And after almost twenty years, she still did. "Thank you for never giving up on me," I stammered. "For believing in me when no one else even knew they had to. For lending me your courage when I had none of my own." My voice cracked as I uttered the words.

"Oh, Maya. You've always had courage. Your Aunt Olive couldn't have been more right when she talked about how much courage it took to stop the wedding and a marriage that wasn't supposed to be." She pointed to my Tear of Bravery and touched it gently. "It really is stunning," she said, looking quickly from the stone back to the road.

I paused for a moment and sat with my thoughts, then began, "There were times I wished that you *would* have yelled or shook me; that someone would have done something. I guess part of the problem was that I did a pretty good job of convincing people that I felt fine, but the pain of growing up in a house with a depressed parent left me on the brink of my own depression for years. There were a few times when it felt like I was going crazy. I was so scared I was going to become my mother that I did anything I could to be *everything* she was not."

With my truthful words, Beth started crying so hard that she had to pull over. We held each other until the tears stopped and all the tissues were gone.

"Well," she said, "I guess cancelling the wedding was one way of letting everyone know that a new Maya was taking over; one that even *you* had not had the pleasure of meeting yet." We both laughed. "I'm really glad you let go of Steven. I never thought he was the right person for you."

"Why didn't you ever say anything?"

"What could I say?"

"Yes, I guess you're right. I probably wouldn't have listened."

After a few more laughs and random tears, we got back on the road, ready for a new kind of adventure. We pulled into the mall parking lot and each grabbed a bag and ran. We had the whole day ahead of us and decided that our first stop was to be the kitchen store.

As we came in from the rain my curiosity got the better of me. "Beth, what is this stuff anyway?"

"I don't know," she replied, peeking in her bag. She then closed it quickly, not wanting me to look inside. "Maya, I think it was supposed to be a wedding present."

Reluctantly, I looked in the bag. "Yes, it was," I said, grimacing. "It's a teapot and cups from the china pattern I picked out." My grimace then turned into a smile, "I never wanted to get a pattern, but Steven insisted. He always insisted on things. He said that we needed to get one. So, we came in here and I picked out the ugliest one I could find. It was chunky and nasty, some '70s throwback theme. Steven didn't like it, but I kept telling him it was perfect. As insistent as he was about most things, he did want to make me happy, so when I told him I loved it, he gave in." I paused, and then peered into the bag again as I continued, "My mom was pretty smart though; at least she knew which pieces to get me."

Beth looked at the teapot and cups and agreed that they were awful. We looped our arms together and walked into the store. As we entered, I saw the lady who had helped Steven and me pick out the pattern. She was at the cash desk, finishing with another customer. Beth motioned to take the bags, but I shook my head. "No, I want to take care of this,"

I said firmly. As we approached the counter, the lady smiled at me with recognition.

"Why, hello? How was the wedding?"

I put the bags on the counter with a clunk. "There was no wedding," I stated simply.

"Oh! I'm really sorry. I hope that everyone is okay. Did you set another date?" she asked with a mixture of concern and curiosity.

I looked at Beth and motioned for her to take over, as the question became too much for me and I could feel myself getting angry.

"Thank you," Beth said kindly, nudging me out of the way. "That is so thoughtful of you to be concerned. But no, the wedding was cancelled. We are just returning a few gifts that were bought here." Her words were spoken in her best stern teacher voice.

The lady peered over at me, clearly nosiness taking over curiosity. It looked as if she was going to ask another question, when Beth suddenly intervened, "Maya, why don't you fill out one of those entry forms on the counter. One for each of us. It looks like we could win a trip to Portugal!" I wasn't going to argue, as the wedding talk had deflated the previous laughing moments. I felt so resentful. During the transaction, the sales lady babbled on, talking about what a shame it was that the wedding had been cancelled. Then I cracked. I couldn't stand it any longer. I looked up from my entry form and yelled right at the clerk. "Frankly, it was me. I didn't love him. I never loved him. I simply woke up in the middle of the night, twelve hours before the wedding, and I realized I could not marry him."

Everyone in the store froze. The lady returned the cash to Beth, and without skipping a beat blurted, "Well, I see that you two are filling out the entry forms for the contest to Portugal. When you're done, just drop the entries into the box at the front of the store. *Maybe you'll have better luck,*" she quipped under her breath.

Beth pushed me along to the front door, grabbing the entries out of my hand. "Who knows? Portugal could be fun!" she exclaimed, and then she dropped the slips into the box and pulled me out of the store.

The teapot and four cups rendered us $338.54. With it raining heavily outside, and a dark mood cloaking the moment, Beth asked if I wanted to spend the rest of the day in the spa. I agreed, and we entered the palm tree laden establishment, leaving behind brief thoughts of Portugal, strewn on the mall floor.

4

Finding Athena

Maya

"GET UP! YOU'RE GOING TO BE LATE."

I was surprised by his tone and level of irritation. My dad was an even-tempered man and rarely got angry, but there was something different that morning. He was clearly done with me. He was done with all the moping and sitting around I'd been doing since cancelling the wedding.

"Maya, this trip is exactly what you need! Now it's time to deal with all of this and move on. You have a flight to catch and you will be on that plane." He paused for a moment, and his face changed, looking softer and more like himself. "It has been three months since you cancelled the wedding, and you survived; somehow we all survived. You have a chance to start over, meet some *new* people, and find what you're really looking for." He stopped and cleared his throat. "By the way, your mother and I have decided that after you leave we are turning your room into a workout space."

My jaw dropped. I couldn't believe that they were kicking me out of my room so that they could start exercising. It's not like I didn't want them to get healthy, but in my room?

"Don't look so surprised. You're not the only one that wants to make some changes in your life. Anyways, you're twenty-five years old and we love you, but we need you out of the house."

My eyes popped open and panic began to seep in.

"Oh Maya, relax! When you get back, you can stay in the guest room for a few weeks while you find a place to live. Now get ready. I'm leaving for the airport in thirty minutes." He closed the door firmly behind him.

As I lay there, I could feel the sunlight streaming through the window, like the day was already laughing at me. I threw the covers over my head, trying to pretend that the last two decades, five years, three months, and sixty seconds had not just happened, but the warmth of the morning sun beating down on my duvet started to suffocate me and I knew I had to face it all.

When I was finally forced to peek out and breathe in some fresh air again, I realized it was August, I had no one in my life, no place of my own and no real career. But, I *did* have a plane ticket to Portugal.

I shook my head and took a deep breath. *Everything is going to change; it has to. I have to find the real Maya Wells! Maybe she's in Portugal. She clearly is not in Peachland—not the Maya that I want to be anymore, that's for damn sure!*

I got out of bed and looked out the window. *I guess things could be worse. I could not have a plane ticket to Portugal, and I could be married right now. Did I just say that? It's funny when I think about the wedding and Steven. It makes me happy and sad at the same time. Happy that I had the courage to stop it, and sad because of all the chaos that I created. But if I were really honest, I'd say mostly happy.*

The weeks had limped by since finding out about the contest and I had done little to prepare for the trip. I guess fear of the unknown was still a theme to be tackled in my life. I packed hastily, and before doing up my luggage I squished my special tea and the rest of my chocolate bars into an outside pocket.

"Maya, it's time," Mom said quietly as she knocked on the door. "Your dad is waiting." I grabbed my bags and said goodbye to my room and my old life.

Dad threw the luggage in the trunk. He hated being late, and without a word we headed off to the local airport. He was quiet the whole way, which I was thankful for as I was tired of feeling like I had to say sorry yet again for the mess I had made out of everything. His impatience quickly dissipated though, and was replaced with a smile as we drove up to the drop-off point. We had made it just in time for me to catch my flight to Vancouver. He stopped, but left the engine running. Clearly, he had no intention of parking. He stepped out of the car, lifted my luggage to the curb, and gave me a hug goodbye. He said only three words, "Find some joy."

I stood on the curb secretly terrified, not sure I could venture out on my own, but there was no turning back. I put one foot in front of the other and made my way to the gate.

When I arrived in Vancouver I scanned the terminal, yearning for a cup of tea to settle my nerves, but somehow continued on, finding my way to Portugal Air. There was already a line forming so I hustled over and waited not-so-patiently. The woman who checked me in when I got to the front of the line was beautiful. She smiled kindly as she looked at my ticket and pointed to the sign beside us indicating that First Class tickets had priority boarding.

Really? First Class, I thought. I didn't feel First Class—old jeans and ugly shoes, but I did have my cool Paris purse that I'd found in a second-hand shop back home. It was at least a start.

The woman handed me my boarding pass. "Enjoy your flight, and may you find everything you're looking for in Portugal." I handed her my suitcase and took a second step into a journey that would unknowingly change my life beyond, forever.

I made it through security with little problem, except that when they searched my purse, they discovered part of my chocolate bar collection!

The security officer looked at me curiously and asked, "Are you planning on selling these?" The next thing I knew, my heart started to race, and I stumbled over my words. "Oh no, they're, um, uh for me," I stammered with embarrassment. Chocolate had always been a stress reliever, and I did not want to get caught without something to turn to on my journey. Just in case.

She shook her head and a note of humor landed on her lips. "You know, they do have chocolate bars in Europe."

I shrugged apologetically and then laughed nervously. "Thank you. I'll keep that in mind." As I put my purse back together, my stomach began to grumble reminding me I had not eaten since the night before when Beth and I had gone out to celebrate my upcoming adventure. She'd been excited for me, asking me more questions than I had answers for, and I remembered every word:

"Maya, so do you have everything packed?" She asked, bubbling at the seams. "No, I don't. I'm not sure what I should bring."

"Maya, you've had weeks to get yourself ready. How much more time do you need?"

"What if I can't do this? What if I get lost? What if no one likes me?"

"Maya, this is not high school. You're going to be with a group of grown-ups having the time of your life: drinking wine, eating, and taking photos. You just have to start living. You took your first step with getting rid of Steven, and now it's time to take the next one. Show me, your mom, your dad, Steven, but

more than anyone, show yourself that you made the right choice, and that you can build your life any way you want."

She sounded so convincing, I could almost believe her.

"Oh, by the way, thank you for helping me set up my classroom this week. My grade ones are going to love the travel corner. Make sure you start sending me stuff as soon as you get to your first destination. I want that wall filled with postcards for when you come back and meet my class at the end of September. Little kids love special guests." She was filled with enough excitement to render my nervous thoughts null and void for the time being.

I paused again, looking at her, and then jumped in:

"Do you love it?" I asked.

"Love what?"

"Teaching."

"Yes, with all my heart. I remember my first practicum. Do you remember that? I was so nervous that I threw up all night before my first day of teaching. You came over in the morning and brought me some special tea, and told me how lucky those little kids were to be meeting me and that I was a special gift to each one of them. We hugged, and then you sent me on my way. And since then, you've always come to visit me before my first day of school. I love teaching because there are so many possibilities. A great teacher can bring out the best in someone and can help them discover parts about themselves that were a mystery before. I have also learned that teaching is a gift I give to myself every day."

"Someday I'll find the thing that I love, too."

"And when you do, I'll be there, somehow, some way, like you were there for me." As she dropped me off at the house, she asked me one more question:

"Hey who's going to bring me my special tea this year on the first day of school?" I smiled and waved goodbye.

The security officer tapped my shoulder. "Miss, are you alright?"

"Yes, thank you," I smiled while repacking the last of the chocolate bars and made my way over to the closest kiosk to pick up a snack and a cup of tea. I watched the young man pour the extra hot water over my tea bag just as I had asked; then he carefully placed the lid on the cup and pointed to the cardboard sleeves, shaking his head.

When I took my first sip it was almost too hot even for me, but the cup heated my hand and my heart and I felt a familiar sense of calm that made me smile. As I walked down to the gate, I passed by one of the newsstands and thought about picking up something to read. I entered and made my way to the magazine rack at the back of the shop and plopped my bags on the floor while holding tightly onto my tea. I didn't see anything at first except for a few tabloids. While I flipped through a magazine, I couldn't help but wonder, *who writes this stuff?* It was so awful how people's lives could be exploited. They were just people—actors and rock stars, but in the end, just people. I put the magazine back on the rack, thankful that I was no rock star.

As I was about to leave, I saw a beautiful series of colorful books on the bottom shelf. Almost immediately I recognized that they weren't just any books, they were hard-covered journals.

I picked up a few of the glittery ones and paused, remembering my journaling days. When I was in high school my journal had been one of the only things that kept me sane, so why did I stop writing?

I shook my head and continued searching through the shelf, and then I saw it. It was kind of old looking, as if many people had picked it up, but it had never found its home. It was solid and heavy, and I had no idea how I was going to get it into my purse, but it was perfect. On the front it was titled *EXPLORATIONS: A Traveler's Journey.*

Inside was thick paper, separated into three sections, just aching to be written on. On the very last page was an old-fashioned envelope, the kind with string wrapped around paper circles. It was ideal for simple-found treasures. I held the journal tightly to my chest and knew it was mine.

My new story was already starting to write itself. I gathered my things and walked over to the cashier. Something sparkly on the counter caught my eye. It was the most amazing pen covered in aqua-colored beads and sequins, with little flecks of gold holding each bead in place. I picked it up and could feel the weight of the pen. It was superb and when I held it, I started to laugh.

The cashier looked at me with kindness and spoke very softly, "Oh, I'm so sorry, but that pen is not for sale. It was a gift from a friend of mine. I just use it for my paperwork here."

I gently released the pen, letting it roll from my fingertips onto the counter. "Just the journal, please."

We finished the transaction and I left the store feeling both happy and a little sad. My newly found treasure had not quite found its way into my purse when I heard someone calling out. "Miss! Miss!" I ignored the voice at first, not realizing that it was calling out to me. That was, until I felt a hand on my shoulder and jumped.

"Excuse me, Miss!! Sorry to startle you," the voice said, sounding out of breath.

I turned around to see the cashier. "Yes? Did I forget something?"

She paused, and with a beautiful smile responded, "Yes, you did—your pen."

She handed me a missing part of my world. I didn't know what to say at first, but finally sputtered, "I can't."

"Yes you can," she said, her eyes shining like the gift she'd given me. "In life there are moments when you just have to say yes, and thank you. This is one of those moments."

With true gratitude I whispered, "Yes and thank you."

Carefully, I put my pen and journal away and headed quickly down to the gate, excited about the feeling that flowed through me. It felt like if anyone touched me in that moment, they would be able to feel me spark.

After arriving at the gate, I sat down and threw my things over three small seats. It was so unlike me, but during the previous months my search for the new me had uncovered a disorganized Maya that I was not a bit comfortable with. I had hoped I could keep a few parts of my old organized self during the first part of the process, but on that day, my only goal was to not lose my passport or my boarding pass.

I opened my purse and slowly pulled out my new journal and pen and then randomly shrieked, surprising even myself. If anyone had been watching me, they might have thought me crazy. Holding my pen, I was taken aback by the overall impact it had on me as it lay in my palm.

When I was young, I used to name everything on our property—every tree and every vine. They were all my friends. In that moment I knew my pen and journal needed to be named. I contemplated briefly and then it came to me. My journal would be named Christopher, after Saint Christopher, the Patron Saint of Travelers. Grandma Stella used to wear a St. Christopher's medal. I remember her telling me the story about how he would help people cross raging rivers during long journeys so they could continue on their paths. I thought that was more than appropriate for where I was in my world. And the pen, well I needed a name that could hold strength, wisdom, and spirit. I took a sip of my tea and closed my eyes, holding my pen tightly in my hand. Then it came to me—Athena, the Greek goddess of Wisdom and War. What more could I ask for than to be protected by a combination of faith and myth, coming together through my heart and my writing?

I unscrewed the lid of Athena and placed half of her in my purse, not wanting to take any chance of losing her.

Holding Christopher tightly in my arms, I felt thankful we had found one another. He gave me a sense of—joy? I wasn't sure. What was joy? The only definition that I had for joy was one I had written years ago on an assignment when I was in grade ten English. I thought the teacher was trying to torture me by assigning the word *joy*. My classmates got words like suffering and sadness. Those would have been easy for me, but *joy*? I'd worked for days staring at a blank page of paper. It only needed to be a few lines, but it just wouldn't come to me. In the end I gave up trying so hard and wrote the first thing that came to my mind.

I got an A on the definition and never thought about it again, until that moment.

I took another sip of tea and gently opened Christopher, and in my very best handwriting wrote his name, my name, the date, and a title: *The Beginning*. I wrote to St. Christopher asking him to keep me safe on my journey. Then I began to write:

> *August 18th (Sitting in the airport)*
>
> *I think I will start with my definition of Joy that I wrote in Grade 10. How did it go?*
>
> *'Joy to me would be a sparkly feeling that would start in my toes and melt into my muscles, then travel straight through to my eyelashes, making me almost shine. Yes that would be my joy.'*
>
> *I have to tell you this is one of the most amazing moments I have ever had in my life. She just gave it to me, this pen I'm writing with. I know it sounds silly to be getting all weird about a pen, but honestly if you could see it and feel it, you would understand! It is sparkly and pretty and so special. It is everything I want to be. Her name is Athena, goddess of Wisdom and War. I had to name her—she was calling out for it.*

Crazy I know, but when I get a chance, I'll photo-graph her and put a picture in here for you.

I can't believe how long it has been since I felt really special. My heart has been waiting a long time. Thank you cashier girl. Thank you SPARKLY PEN. Thank you Christopher. We are going to be good friends. I can just tell.

I had wanted my first entry to be all profound, but I guess all you get is me. We are in this adventure together now. Hot Tea. Take a sip!! Ah now that is fantastic. Deep breath.

Maya where did you go? Where have you been all these years? I guess lost in a world of have-to's and should-haves. What do you want Maya? Well let me try and answer that:

I want to dance until the sun rises,

I want to laugh until my sides hurt,

I want to hold hands with someone I love ...

I want to cry without explaining why,

I want to wake each morning and when I look in the mirror, like the person I see ...

I want to spend my days creating something beauti-ful and fill my nights with joy and passion, and then the next day ...

I want to do it in reverse.

I want the grown-up life of the girl in the peach tree.

Is that too much to ask for?

As I wrote the last word a soft accented male voice came over the speaker announcing that they were starting to board First Class.

Write in you soon.
Maya

I placed Athena and Christopher on the seat beside me and rooted around in my purse, looking for the lid. Frustration took over and I started pulling things out, unable to find her other half.

The second announcement came. There was that voice again: "Second call for all First Class passengers bound for Lisbon, Portugal, with a stop-over in Montreal. Please be sure to have your passport and boarding pass ready. Thank you."

While frantically searching for the lid, I lifted my purse and forgot about the tea that was precariously balanced on the arm rest. Instant chaos filled my world as the thermal cup tipped over, soaking all my belongings, and burning my hand.

"Ow! Of course this would happen!" I yelled at myself.

Everything went flying and I found myself on the airport floor in the midst of a pile of tissues and napkins, trying to clean up yet another mess. Tears welled in my eyes, but I pushed them back. As I tried to clean up, I heard a voice—the same one from the announcements.

"*Scuse?*" he said gently to me.

I looked up and was taken by his beauty and sense of calm. His kind smile took my breath away. I must have been staring at him for a moment too long, as he started to laugh.

"Are you alright, Miss?" His accent was enchanting, his voice filled with concern. "I thought that you might need a few towels," he said handing me the cloths. Our fingers touched and a warm surge flowed through me.

"Uhm …" I couldn't find any words beyond, 'yes and thank you.'

He nodded and smirked, possibly laughing at my inability to speak. "I have to go and help the other passengers. Will you be alright?" he said with compassion in his eyes.

I nodded again, not so convincingly.

"Don't worry, I won't leave without you." He laughed again and started to walk away, "Oh what's your name?"

"Maya, Maya Wells," I stuttered.

I smiled and pushed back the hair that was now hanging in my face and watched him walk back to the desk. He turned ever so subtly back in my direction. Our eyes met and locked momentarily, creating a world of questions within me that ached to be answered. Our gaze was broken just as quietly as it had formed and I could feel a crimson blush fill my cheeks.

After gathering my things and my random thoughts, I stood up. I was the last passenger and the flight attendant motioned for me to hurry.

"Miss, we have to go." I handed her my crumpled and soggy boarding pass. "Passport too please," she asked with a hint of irritation.

"I know it's in here somewhere." I was filled with embarrassment and frustration as everything was not where it was supposed to be. "Oh! Here it is!"

"Thank you, Miss Wells, now *please* hurry."

I scuttled down the ramp with a feeling of both freedom and fear running through my veins. I knew I had to make a choice right then and there. There was no going back to the old Maya if I got on that plane. I would have to leave everything behind. I had lived my life according to what I'd thought everyone wanted me to be and it turned out I'd been wrong. In reality, nobody wanted anything from me except honesty. There was no one left to blame for the situation I found myself in but me. I didn't know who I was, but at least I had figured out who I wasn't.

Now with freedom taking over fear, I smiled and took my last first step.

A Lesson in Boarding and Life

Maya

THE STAIRCASE LOOKED LIKE ONE that you would have seen in an old movie, spiraling up to the second floor, with music playing lightly in the background. When I arrived at the top of the stairs, I was greeted by another beautiful flight attendant. Her smile reminded me that my only job was to leave Peachland behind, at least for four weeks.

I put my purse away and settled in. I could hardly believe how roomy the seats were. Each one was equipped with a kick-out foot rest and a large screen with a wide variety of movies. There were even little drapes that you could pull between yourself and the person you were sitting next to. It was kind of lavish and exciting all at the same time. It made me curious about our hosts and what Netuno was going to be like.

"Excuse me, Miss," I asked an attendant as she walked by.

"Yes, Miss Wells; please call me Joana. How can I help you?"

"Do you know anything about Netuno Wineries?"

"Well, I'm not from that region, but I know the vineyard and olive orchards have been owned and run by the same family for generations. They have made wine for many years, but have only started selling it commercially in the last two decades. The two brothers who own the vineyard took over for their father, who passed away several years ago. I really don't know a lot more than that. You should speak to Cristiano, one of our other flight attendants. He grew up in the area and knows most of the people who work there. I'll let him know that you were asking. Is there anything else I can help you with?"

"Yes, thank you. Do you know if there is anyone sitting beside me for the flight to Montreal?"

"Yes, but your seat mate has yet to sign in. We know that her connecting flight arrived on time, but we may have to leave without her."

"Oh, that would be awful," I responded, then quietly thanked God that was not me.

"Don't worry, Miss Wells. We will do one last check at the gate before we take off. I'll send an attendant down right now."

Suddenly my early morning waking washed over me like a wave. I pulled out my phone, plugged myself in, and let my music do all the work.

Cristiano

When Joana came down the staircase looking for me, I was standing at the back finalizing some paperwork before the flight.

"Cristiano, how was your time off in Vancouver? Sorry to hear that it was cut short, but it was very kind of you to take the flight for Bernard. I heard he came down with food poisoning."

I smiled knowing that Bernard owed me big time. "Oh yes, it came on quite suddenly, but I'm sure he will be up and flying in the next few days." My explanation sounded almost believable.

"Well, thank you again for coming in. It would have been almost impossible to manage this flight short-handed, especially with all the Netuno contest winners in First Class."

She stared at me and smiled like she wanted to ask me something else, but had decided against it. Joana had wanted me to take her out a few months back, but I had made it a policy never to date any of the women I worked with. I let the pilots make all of *those* mistakes. I only dated women I met when I was traveling abroad. It was easier that way, no strings, no attachments, just a few laughs. I stood uncomfortably waiting for the awkward moment to pass.

"Oh, Cristiano, after reviewing the passenger manifest, I noticed we're missing one of the Netuno people. She is supposed to be upstairs right now."

My chest tightened and a strange feeling came over me. My thoughts turned to the tea girl.

"Is it Miss Wells?" I asked holding my breath.

"No, Miss Wells is already on board and seated."

My imagination wandered briefly about my tea girl and our first encounter. I just couldn't get her out of my mind.

"Cristiano? CRISTIANO!"

"Yes, yes, sorry, just a little distracted. I'll run back to the gate to see if the missing passenger has arrived," I said trying to sound focused, but my thoughts continued to wander up to First Class. As I ran down the boarding ramp I felt a sense of elation, like the day I rode my first big wave. I was so excited that *she* was on the plane. She was beautiful and messy and there was just something about her: natural, real. I did a quick check in the waiting area and found it empty, but I could hear someone yelling from down the hall. A woman came running towards me, screaming at the top of her lungs.

"Wait, wait! I'm going to Portugal—wait for me," she bellowed across the room.

I started to laugh. "Are you our missing First Class passenger?" I asked with a little sarcasm in my voice.

"Yes." She took a deep breath, and then let it out slowly. "My name is Dalley Price, and who are you?" she asked leaning in close to me.

"My name is Cristiano. I will be one of your flight attendants for the trip," I responded, while strategically backing away from her.

"Nice to meet you, Cristiano." She held out her hand, changing her strategy.

"Well it's nice to meet you Miss Price. But let's save the rest of the hellos for the long flight." I checked her passport and boarding pass and ushered her through the gate. "Please head down the ramp. Ines will be waiting for you at the plane. Can you let her know that I will be right behind you?"

"Will do," she said in a suggestive voice. "What did you say your name was?"

"Please hurry Miss Price."

"Thank you, Cristiano." She smiled, winked at me, then ran up the ramp.

I took one last look around and scanned the seating area where *she* had been sitting when I first saw her. I broke into a smile as I thought about her kneeling on the floor, mopping up her mess with the towels I'd given her. As I turned to head back towards the plane, I saw something glitter on her seat. I walked over and found an old looking book, and a very sparkly pen that was missing a lid. I opened the book and inside the front cover it read, *Maya, August 18th. The Beginning. Christopher* and in tiny little handwriting were the words:

St. Christopher please keep me safe on my journey.

The book wasn't a book at all, but a journal, her journal. I knew it had to be hers. I held it tightly, grabbed the pen, and ran to catch the plane.

As I jumped on board I had to attend to all of my duties, so I tucked her things away into my seat pocket, knowing I would give them back to her after we settled into the flight. During the take-off procedures, I had difficulty staying focused. Silva, one of the other attendants, noticed I was dropping things and bumping into people.

"Cristiano, are you okay? You don't seem yourself."

"I'm not," I muttered, then shook my head. It was like trying to shake a fog out of my brain. She looked alarmed but said nothing.

"Don't worry, Silva, I'm not sick, just a little distracted. After we finish the safety checks, I'll take a few minutes and pull myself together."

"Yes, that sounds like a good idea. Do you want me to let Joana and Ines know?"

"No, I'll be fine," I said, convincing myself and Silva for at least the moment.

"Well then, let's get this plane into the air." Silva had always been easy to talk to, and she had never asked anything of me during the years that we had flown together. She was a young widowed mother who lived with her parents and always maintained one primary goal: to get home safely to her son.

I nodded, indicating I was ready to go. "Oh, I almost forgot," she added. "Joana asked me to tell you that a passenger upstairs wanted to speak with you about Netuno Wineries. She told her you would be the right person to talk to."

"Who was it?"

"Ah, Miss Wells. She's seated in 6A."

My heart flung against my ribs. She just kept popping up into my world.

I felt so drawn to her, yet I had no idea why.

I walked through all the safety procedures with agonizing precision, then went back to my seat. As I settled in, I struggled with the decision of whether I should read the journal or not. I couldn't figure out what was stopping me from running up the stairs and giving it back to her? Nothing—everything. I just wanted to know more about her, and her journal was right there.

An image of Avó, my dad's mother, flashed strongly in my mind. I had lived with her for most of my life, and she had the strangest ability to just look at me and activate my conscience. It was both effective and equally irritating.

I looked out the window and asked Avó under my breath, "What should I do? Read it or leave it?"

I had not visited Avó in two years, but I knew that during my next trip back to Portugal, I had to see her. For months I had been feeling that somehow she needed me or I needed her. I couldn't tell the difference. Years ago, when I'd left our little cottage just outside of the Netuno grounds and moved to Lisbon, I'd pushed Avó's voice out of my head, not wanting to deal with the memories of my parents' death and the sadness that had continued to weigh me down after so many years. I had been back to see her briefly once or twice, but with my careless lifestyle I mostly stayed away. I was ashamed of who I had become.

I had been on a path of pure selfish behavior with little concern for my heart or mind. I'd met a few women who'd tried to *save me* from myself and give me what *they thought* I needed to heal, but I didn't even know myself. As much love as Avó had given me over the years, there was always a ragged-edged hole in my heart. I ached for it to become even a little bit smaller, but feared if it ever closed completely, that I would forget them and forget how to love altogether. I was stuck somewhere between fear and pain.

As I pondered my past, I grasped her journal tighter and noticed the edges around my gaping hole felt less jagged. *How could that be possible? What was it about this woman this that smoothed the edges that had been cutting me up inside for years?* I needed to know. I wanted my Avó sitting beside me, helping me find the right answer.

Then I heard it. Avó's voice, 'Take a chance, Cristiano. The world is not as black and white as you have always thought.'

My heart raced, and suddenly I felt driven to know what made Maya different from everyone else. Pausing, I listened closely for any other comments or objections from the voice and then opened the journal. I reread the title written in her hand, tracing her name with my finger. M-A-Y-A. I could feel her energy radiating from the page. "She wrote this today." I inhaled a mixture of trepidation and excitement, holding on to my breath.

> *... I want to hold hands with someone I love ... I want to cry without explaining why ...*
> *I want to wake each morning and when I look in the mirror, like the person who I see ...*
> *... Is that too much to ask for?*

"No, Maya. I don't think it's too much to ask at all."

My hands trembled as I closed her journal, not sure which way to look or what to do next. Maya's words, her thoughts, her heart—it was my heart. It was a picture of a world I did not even know I needed, until that moment. It was only then I realized I'd been so caught up in my thoughts, that I'd missed part of the departure routine. Silva and the other flight attendants had covered for me and started preparing for the drink service. "Where did you come from, Maya Wells?"

A strange stillness took over me and I imagined I was sitting at Avó's kitchen table. I could hear the grinding wheel as she made flour for the bread. It was rhythmic and slow. That's how she dealt with everything, every sorrow, every joy. She believed all answers revealed themselves through silence, contemplation—and bread making.

It became clear to me what I needed to do besides making a loaf of bread. I tore a piece of paper from the back of her journal, held her pen tightly in my hand, and began.

Dear Maya,
In life sometimes we have moments that change us …

When I finished, I tucked the note into the journal and planned to drop it off, along with a hot cup of tea. I realized though that there was something missing. I needed to show her another side of myself, so I turned to the last page of her journal. I had to trust that she would find my heart when the time was right.

Changing World

Maya

EYES SHUT, OBOE PENETRATING MY mind with its clear and concise sound, my heartbeat slowed and I allowed myself to fall into the music.

I remembered the first time I'd heard the oboe. I was eleven. Dad had sent me to music camp for two weeks in the summer. I'd met a four-teen-year-old girl who carved her own reeds; she was amazing. I remember going to hear her play. Every note had such intention and filled my heart with music. I'd wished my piano playing had that depth, but sadly, I was never able to release myself to the music, so it stayed on the page, never truly connecting with anyone, including myself. But that was then, who knows …

There was a bump and then a tumble, and my eyes flashed open. Suddenly a whirlwind flew to the top of the stairs and sprang into First Class. I had to laugh out loud. She had this fabulous raven hair with a streak of fuchsia running down the side, and her laugh rang out over the music that I was listening to. I took the headphones off so that I could hear what was going on. As she walked down the aisle, she looked at her ticket, and then stopped right in front of me.

"Hi, it looks like you're stuck with me for the flight," she laughed as she twirled and sat down beside me. "I'm so excited. I've always wanted to go to Portugal. I've traveled a lot, but never made my way over there." She was in her early 30s, in fabulous shape, and electric by nature. "I won this contest to go to Portugal for this cooking and photo thing for a month. I love photography, but I cannot cook worth a damn. It should be good though. I convinced my boss back home that I would write an article about Portugal and send pictures and make a working holiday of it. I'm a journalist; always looking for a great story," she said sighing briefly. "Oh, I'm so sorry, I didn't even introduce myself. I'm Dalley Price, and you are?"

"Ah … I'm Maya Wells." I found myself struggling for my name while caught in her whirlwind. I had never met anyone quite like her in my life.

"Maya, what a beautiful name."

"Thank you," I responded feeling a little awkward.

"Why are you going to Portugal?"

"Funny thing, I'm one of the winners too."

Dalley squealed. "Oooh! That is so cool. Well, it is meant to be. We are on our way to one of the most beautiful places in the world and ready to have the adventure of a lifetime!" she exclaimed.

"Yes, we are going on an adventure, that's for sure. It's like a new beginning," I responded thoughtfully. Then suddenly a wave of nausea rushed through me. Adventure, new beginning …

"Oh no, Christopher! Where is he?" I gasped in horror, then grabbed my purse from under the seat, and emptied it out over the two of us. As I stared at the pile of papers and personal documents strewn across our laps, the only thing I found was Athena's lid, lonely and needing the rest of her. Somehow, I must have left them both behind, lying on an airport seat without a purpose or a home.

"Where is what? Who?" Dalley asked with a raised eyebrow.

I took a breath and tried to explain without sounding like a lunatic. "Christopher and Athena—my new journal and pen." I smiled weakly then clenched my fist and pushed it into my stomach trying to lessen the sick feeling. I had just lost a part of myself and there was nothing I could do to get it back.

"That must be *some* journal." She leaned into me. "Or maybe it's what is inside that's so valuable," she teased. She tapped my leg with her hand, trying to be supportive. When I looked down, I had to smirk as her nails were covered in bright blue polish with sparkly gems. Her fingers glimmered like Athena—then my tears fell.

Once I stopped crying, I realized we were in the air, but my words were still lost to me.

"Oh Maya, *everything* happens for a reason." She winked and then gave me a little jab in the ribs with her elbow.

"Is it that simple? *Everything* happens for a reason?" I asked wiping my tear-stained face with my hand.

"Yes, it does!" She took a tissue from her purse and finished the job. "Think about where you are, what you are doing, and what has brought you to this exact place in time."

She was right. I was on my way to Portugal, starting a new life whether Christopher and Athena were with me or not. I took a deep breath and smiled. She looked at me and said, "I think this is going to be a trip that could change *all* our lives."

"What do you mean by *all*?"

She looked surprised. "Oh, didn't you know? There are six other contest winners besides us. Five of us are on the flight right now. The other three will be joining us in Montreal. It is going to be pretty exciting."

"What do you mean by exciting?" I asked with trepidation.

"Well because of my connections at the paper, I was able to find out a little bit about everyone who is coming," she said in a very quiet voice.

"You did background checks on everyone?" I asked, feeling slightly uncomfortable.

"Well, I figured if I'm going to spend a month with all of you, I wanted to know more about what I was getting myself into. It should be a lot of fun," she said, laughing off my concern.

"So you researched *everyone*?" My concern turned to curiosity when I thought about myself and my uninteresting life.

"Yes," she chuckled.

"What did you find out about me? I really haven't done very much in my life."

"Do you really want to know?" she said leaning in.

"Yes, I do, as long as you're willing to answer my questions about *your* life."

"I'm an open book," she quipped. She reached down into her bag and pulled out a purple file. "This is you," she said, holding the file up and waving it in my face. "So what do you want to know about Miss Maya Wells?"

"Everything," I responded, feeling my nerves start to tingle. "I've been off the social grid for months. I can't imagine where I would pop up."

"Well, when I Googled you, the first thing that came up was your engagement announcement from over two years ago."

I almost choked when I heard that was the first thing to come up. Dalley saw me freeze and stopped for a second.

"Are you okay?"

"Yes, go on," I said with exasperation, wishing that my damn non-wedding would just disappear.

"Well, the next thing I checked for was recent marriage announcements in accordance with the wedding dates. When I couldn't find anything, I figured if you were on your way to Portugal, something must have happened. So I started doing a little digging. It was very interesting. I discovered that you had called the wedding off the night before your big day, and when I looked up your ex-fiancé, I noticed that he had set up a Facebook page recounting the entire event, allowing the public to post comments about you …"

My jaw hit the floor.

"You didn't know?" she guessed by looking at my face.

My jaw went from loose to tight and my eyes narrowed as I processed the information. I quickly shook off the angry feeling and laughed. "That's fantastic; I didn't know he had it in him. I am surprised though, that no one told me. What kind of things were people saying?" I asked screwing up my face, waiting for the worst.

"Well let's just say, you didn't have too many fans. There were a few people who chirped in and tried to give a different perspective, but they got shut down pretty quickly."

I looked out the window and pondered the information she had given me. "It's funny though. I guess in the end I screwed him again because I never even knew he was trying to get back at me." We both had a laugh.

Our conversation was interrupted by an announcement that our layover in Montreal would be extended and our arrival time in Lisbon would now be 9:03 a.m. August the 19th.

I was already exhausted and could not imagine what I was going to look like at the end of the journey, but honestly I didn't care. I had a month in Portugal coming my way, and I was not trying to impress anyone. As the flight leveled off, and the seat belt sign went out, my tea-burnt hand began to throb. Dalley noticed me cradling it. "Wow that looks painful!

I'll call the flight attendant to bring you some ice." As we waited, we talked about the trip. It felt like the first day of school when you don't know anyone and the first person that you meet ends up becoming your best friend. During our conversation, pieces of information shifted into place in my tired brain. *If Dalley had done all that research about me before coming on the trip, then it only stood to reason that she knew exactly who I was when she stepped into First Class. That meant that her whole introduction with me had been a big act.*

"Dalley, you knew exactly who I was when you stepped on to this plane.

"Oh, you got me Maya," she said with a smirk, neither confirming nor denying my comment.

"I would have thought that after discovering me as the *wedding monster* you would have wanted to sit as far away from me as possible!" I teased with a little bit of unease.

"It was quite the opposite, Maya. I knew I *had* to sit beside you. I have to be truthful though; I went a little deeper into your history than with some of the other contestants and found out that your family used to own a vineyard."

"Yes, that was a long time ago. We moved when I was eight, but I don't like to talk about it." The words fell quickly from my lips as I looked away.

"Well, between your connection to the vineyards and the fact that you called your wedding off the night before it happened, I knew I *had* to meet you," she said nonchalantly. "No more secrets, I promise," she said ending the conversation abruptly.

Then I saw him. My heart skipped. "It's him!" I tried to whisper to Dalley, trying to contain my excitement.

"Who's 'him'?"

"I met him out at the gate when I spilled my tea," I babbled. "It was really strange, but I think we had a moment …"

"Oh!" she exclaimed far too loudly. "Yes having a moment with him would be excellent. He *is* very helpful. He's the one who made sure I got on the plane." As he approached us, he avoided making eye contact with me and my heart sank.

"Hello, Miss Price. I see that you are settling into your flight nicely." His liquid tone melted me into my seat. "You pushed your call button." He pointed to the flashing light. "Is there something I can help you with?" He smiled casually at Dalley. I felt like I wanted to disappear.

"My friend here had an accident earlier and injured her hand when a cup of hot tea fell on her." She told the story to him, turning it into a grand drama knowing full well he knew exactly who I was and what had happened.

I briefly drifted in thought, trying to figure out how I could have been so delusional to think he would have noticed me before. Dalley elbowed me back into the present and when I went to ask her why, he was staring at me. His face had intensified and was filled with concern. He reached across her and took my hand gently; my heart and skin came alive. I was without words.

"Oh Miss Wells, that looks so painful. What can I get you? Some ice perhaps?"

"Ice would be great," I bumbled.

"I'll be right back," he said sounding flustered. Then he ran down the aisle and out of my sight.

Dalley started to laugh, "Maya, I have no doubt that there was *some* sort of a moment between the two of you earlier. Look at him; he doesn't know where he's going."

"What are you talking about? He was just concerned about my hand," I said weakly, hoping to myself she was right.

"No, *that* was not just concern. That was definitely something else. Oh this flight may turn out to be even *more* interesting than I thought. Switch places with me quickly," she said clapping her hands together and crawling over top of me.

Cristiano made his way back to us swiftly. He took my hand again, checking it, like it could be broken. He placed the ice ever so gently on the burn and laid my hand back down on my lap. "Miss Wells, let me know if you need anything, I mean *anything* else." He said the last words leaning into me so closely that I could feel the warmth of his breath on my neck.

Dalley laughed harder this time and I had to admit his concern did appear to go above that of a flight attendant and passenger relationship.

"What can I get you ladies to drink?" he asked.

Dalley jumped in. "Oh let's see. It's before noon, so I'll say, a Caesar. I had one for the first time when I came up here to Canada a couple months ago. I love that drink. Do you have any pickled beans?"

"No, just celery." A smile formed on his lips.

"Oh, that will have to do for now," she said, waving her hands around pretending like it was the end of the world.

"And you Miss Wells? What can I get you besides the ice?" His toned changed. I blushed. "Ah nothing right now thanks."

"I'll be right back, Miss Price," he said while he continued to stare at me.

"Oh, just call me Dalley!" she yelled as he turned and walked away. "Well, it was like I wasn't even here. He has it bad for you."

"Don't be ridiculous, we only met for a minute," I rebutted her chatter.

"Sometimes that's all it takes."

Cristiano returned with the drink cart and made Dalley's Caesar, then handed me a cup of tea. "I thought you might enjoy this," he said simply.

Smiling I took a sip of the tea and was momentarily lost in its warmth. It was perfect. Before I looked up again, he knelt down and whispered into my ear. "I believe these are yours." He then placed Christopher and Athena on my lap.

"Actually, can I have a Scotch please?" I asked, looking directly into his eyes.

"Like I said, you can have *anything* you like," he responded, and then touched my cheek. My heart almost stopped. He made my drink, placed it on my tray, and walked away.

Dalley laughed and shook her head at the movie moment.

"I didn't even say thank you," I mumbled as I grabbed the glass and swallowed. The liquid burned as it went down.

My hand quivered as I touched the journal, I could almost feel a buzz coming from inside the front cover. Intrigued by the physical sensation, I opened Christopher and found a note neatly folded in half, just waiting to be opened.

Dear Maya,

In life sometimes we have moments that change us. We don't know why or how, but they do. When I saw you kneeling there with your things all over the floor, you smiled. I'm not sure if you were smiling at yourself, or at the world, but it made me smile too.

When I went back to find our missing passenger, I looked over to where you had been sitting and found your journal and pen.

Please don't be upset with me or think I am strange, but I read your entry. It was so beautiful. I didn't want it to end. I loved the way you described your feelings about what you want for yourself in the world, it was so honest.

There was something about your writing that made me feel like you were talking to me. When we were at the gate, I looked back at you. You were looking at me too. I know it was only for a moment, but it felt like something happened, we happened. I had to take a chance to see if it was as real as it felt.

So here I am, I guess I should tell you a little something about myself. My name is Cristiano Lazaro. I am a flight attendant and based out of Lisbon, but grew up outside of the city with family, my grandmother. I call her Avó. She is a very special woman.

I could not just let you go. I had to say hello. I will be back in Portugal again in a week. I know that you are staying at Netuno Wineries as one of the contest winners. The flight attendants let me know you had some questions. I would be happy to help you in any way I can.

May I call on you while you are staying at Netuno? PS. I found Athena too. She is very beautiful, just like you. I will understand if you are not able to meet. I think though, that you will like me.

If 'Yes,' please, come to the front kitchen down in Economy after you have read this note. If 'No,' I will take your absence as your answer, and I will request a flight change in Montreal, so you will not have to feel awkward during the rest of your flight to Portugal.

Yours, Cristiano

"Wow, he is very convincing," Dalley said peeking over my shoulder.

"This can't be real. Things like this don't happen," I stammered. "At least not to me."

"What do you mean?" Dalley asked. "It's happening right now. Do you think a chance like this comes along every day? A gorgeous man, obviously hard working and kind, has just offered you a chance for an adventure in a foreign country. No rules. You get to be anybody you want. Maya, take a chance."

A bead of sweat developed on my forehead—not one of my most attractive features, but one that had been with me since I was little. It happened whenever my body decided I was beyond nervous and moving into anxious. "I can't do this, can I? I've never done anything like this before. What if he's awful? What if he's …" My question trailed off.

"What if, what if—is this the way you've been living your whole life?" she challenged me.

"Actually—yes!" I paused for a long moment. "But, you're right. No more what ifs."

Dalley gave me a pat of encouragement on the shoulder as I got up from my seat and made my way to the stairs. I took the rail with my good hand and balanced the ice on the other. I hung on so tightly my knuckles turned white. I made it to the bottom of the stairs and looked around for the kitchen. It only took a moment and then I saw him. My heart didn't stop this time but beat faster as I walked towards him. I almost forgot to breathe. I was sure he could hear my heart, as the sound almost deafened me. "How's the hand?" he asked casually, but I noticed he was tapping his foot.

"Oh the ice is helping, thank you. I may need some more though as it seems to be melting."

"No problem. I will make sure you have enough for the rest of the flight." The two of us stood a few feet apart, as we began our first dance.

"I was worried I might miss the plane. After I finished cleaning up it was just me and the other flight attendant," I said making conversation.

Cristiano's face changed. He looked into my eyes and spoke clearly to me. "I would never have let the plane leave without you."

We continued our dance taking a step closer to one another. "I found your note. It was a lovely surprise." I paused, my eyes cast down as I spoke, and then I felt his warm finger under my chin. His touch was like coming home. I lifted my head and looked at him. This time he stared at me beaming, not having to say a word. "If you still want to call me when we get to Portugal, I would love that," I said trying to sound casual, but feeling like I'd failed miserably.

His smile broadened and he walked past me, brushing my shoulder with his chest ever so gently. "I look forward to it. Hey, I have a break during the layover in Montreal. Would you like to get something to eat?"

My eyes and heart smiled at the same time. "Yes, that would be perfect," I responded, biting my lip on one side.

"Until Montreal then," he paused. "Oh, I wrote something else for you in your journal. Did you find it yet?" He walked away, not giving me a chance to answer.

I stood in the little kitchen alone, yet not alone. I wasn't sure what I felt.

It was a mixture of excitement and nerves, relief and jubilation.

As I reached the top of the stairs I noticed Dalley on the edge of her seat.

"What did he say to you? You look very flushed," she said analyzing my face.

"Just give me a second," I exhaled while sitting down. I scooped up Christopher and flipped through him searching for the note, but couldn't find a thing.

"What are you looking for?" Dalley asked.

"He told me he wrote something else, but that I had to find it."

She held out her hand for Christopher. I reluctantly passed him over. "Don't read my entry okay?"

"What do you take me for? That's private. But if I left *this* task to you we'd be here all day." She flipped through the journal twice, then gave it back. "Try the last page," she said sounding pleased with herself.

My heart pounded with excitement as I opened it. I looked down and there written in his hand, were three neatly scripted lines.

Heart Stopping Seeing you there
Knowing I had one chance …
One chance for you to be part of my world

Dalley couldn't take it any longer and peered over my shoulder to read what had riveted me. "Very nice," she chirped. "It looks like he is more than just a pretty face."

I laughed out loud and closed my journal. We sat quietly, neither knowing what to do next.

"I'm going to take a little rest," I sighed and yawned. "That Scotch is no longer making me feel courageous, but a little woozy."

"Oh sure. I'll fill you in later on all the other winners." Dalley pulled out her computer and began typing away madly.

I closed my eyes, hoping that a restful slumber would come quickly, but the harder I tried to relax the more activated my mind became. It had been a day filled with making and recalling memories, both warm and painful. When I gave up trying to sleep, I opened my eyes and realized I was still holding Christopher and Athena tightly in my arms. I needed to write.

Later on the Plane (the 18th)
I can hardly believe I almost lost you both. The thought of losing you before I even got to know you is too much.

How much is too much for one person to take? I don't know. I'm not saying that I was on the edge of losing my mind or anything when you went missing, but the sadness was so instant, it took me back to all my losses and failures and my tears just fell.

But there is no reason to cry anymore is there? You are back in my arms, gifted to me by a new light in my life. I have only just met him, but what else could I call him?

Cristiano is this amazing creature. I know that sounds weird but, he's more than ... more than what? I don't know. I guess only time will tell.

Talking about that, what do you think? I'm not sure how I am supposed to be feeling. It's both strange and exciting all at the same time.

He found you both and brought you back to me. Then he wrote me the most beautiful letter. He read you, but somehow that is okay. I'm not sure why, but it is.

He doesn't even know me, or maybe he knows me better than I do. Why would he think I am 'that' girl? I have never been 'that' girl. I have so many questions and no answers. Funny though, most of the questions are about me.

I need a distraction. Dalley is my best bet to get through the next five hours. Sorry friends, but you are going to have to wait. Thanks for being there when I needed you.

Maya

7

Who's Going to Portugal?

Maya

"Dalley, you ready to share?"

"I thought you were taking some down time?"

"No! My brain keeps running in circles. I need a distraction."

"Oh, so you came to me? I'm hurt. Well, not really," she teased. "I always find it flattering when people use me as a distraction. Okay so here it goes. There are eight winners in total, all women—half from the U.S. and half from Canada."

"Why do you think they chose a kitchen store in my area?" I asked.

"The wine country up there is beautiful. Maybe it has something to do with several of the wineries that are launching new product internationally in the next few months," she responded, offering a reasonable explanation.

"How do you know so much about Okanagan wineries? Have you been?"

"Research Maya, that's all. I haven't been stalking you in your hometown. It's wine country. I mean, look at you; your family used to own a vineyard," she noted bringing up my history again.

"I told you I was eight when they sold the vineyard. I know very little about making wine, except what kind of watering system works best to keep the grapes growing," I said flatly.

"Oh yeah, that's right. You work for a sprinkler company." I looked at her with surprise trying to remember when I had told her about where I worked. She continued. "Well, either way, it looks like they wanted to gather all different kinds of people. When we stop in Montreal, we will be picking up three more winners. They are all from back east: Montreal, New York, and Illinois."

She went into her bag and pulled out six more color-coded folders. "Let's see where we should start." She tapped her finger on the red file.

"Ah yes, Maggie from Vancouver, BC. Maggie is a forty-eight-year-old widow who stays at home with her kids. She has twin boys who will be graduating from high school next June. She had been a teacher but gave up her career to raise her children and be a stay-at-home mom. Her husband died about five years ago after a quick and nasty battle with cancer."

Maggie's story made me feel really sad; the death of her husband, the giving up of a career, and soon the graduation of her children. What would she be left with? "Where is she?" I asked.

"She's sitting one seat over. She has on an olive-green sweater and a beautiful scarf." Dalley pointed towards a woman who had the most genuine smile.

"She looks so happy. How is that possible?"

"Maya, I don't ask why or how, I just research the facts," she said shaking her head.

"How did you gather the information about everyone?" I asked with growing discomfort.

"Oh Maya, I didn't break into any files. Really, I just did some searches online and a little old-fashioned detective work. I can stop if you want?" She shrugged her shoulders like she didn't care.

"No, but I do want to discover *some* things for myself," I answered with reluctance.

She paused. "I would appreciate it if you didn't mention the color-coded files and research to anyone. I don't want them to feel uncomfortable."

Black was next: Jade from Montreal. "Jade is twenty years old and works for her father. She is the daughter of a very wealthy and powerful international investor and landowner. I found pictures of her in the society pages in Montreal and New York. It looks like she has done some modeling too. She is stunning, but from the comments I read in the society pages, not very pleasant to be around."

I ran my hand through my flat, dull hair. "I'm not sure anyone has ever used stunning to describe me before." I was resigned to my plain and ordinary look.

Dalley stared. "Are you always this hard on yourself?"

"What do you mean?" I responded, trying to make it sound like I didn't understand what she was talking about. She dropped the topic and went back to her sleuthing. Opening the file, I saw a young woman who could rival any runway model. She was just as striking as Dalley had noted.

"She will be boarding in Montreal," she said with an ominous tone, intimating that somehow Jade's presence could be trouble for all of us.

She grabbed the yellow file. "And then there is Josie, a sixty-four-year old recently-divorced woman. I found her *really* interesting. She had only been married for about two years when her third husband filed for divorce, just a year ago. The public papers noted adultery. She's up from Arizona and is on the plane with us. She has three grown children from her first marriage and two grandchildren."

"Divorced three times? This is going to be interesting," I mused.

"Yes, and she has traveled all over the world. I read that she likes to dance and have a *very* good time. Let's move on to orange now. Petra is forty-one, a successful executive who owns her own advertising agency in New York City with her husband. High stress, high action, big money, no down time, and no kids. She'll meet us in Montreal."

"Sounds like a very busy woman. I've always wanted to visit New York."

She looked over the list. "So let's see, that's you and me, Maggie, Jade, Josie, and Petra. That leaves Ellen and Sachi. Ellen is a part-time, stay-at-home mom who also works in a diamond mine up in the North West Territories. I'm not exactly sure what she does, as her work files were tightly secured. Her father was First Nations, her mother Caucasian. She grew up off reserve but kept close ties to the community until she married. She has two kids in elementary school. They are away at camp while she is here in Portugal."

The uncomfortable feeling started to creep back again, so I sat and partially listened as Dalley launched into the last story.

"Just one more," she continued, with what sounded like too much eagerness in her voice. "Sachi. Sachi is twenty-five like you and works in Chicago and is a bit of a mystery. She moved from Japan when she was a child due to some health problem. It had something to do with her blood and the family thought that they could get more of what she needed in the U.S. The family is wealthy, old Japanese money. Her father travels back and forth to Japan frequently."

"Dalley, how did you find out about her health stuff?"

"You don't really want to know, do you?" she asked frankly.

"No, I don't," I said, squirming in my seat.

Dalley continued before I could stop her. "Her family is very old fashioned in some ways. Her father is in the high-tech industry and owns several of his own companies. Sachi is an only child and works as a structural engineer at her father's friend's firm. She is extremely intelligent and graduated from the best schools. I had a hard time finding her on any kind of social media sites though. She keeps completely off the radar.

"Well it looks like we have quite the mix. It's going to be a lot of fun," she said, closing the files and putting everything away.

"I guess there really are no secrets in our lives anymore," I expressed uneasily. She smiled at me crookedly. "The only thing I need now is a file on you," I said trying to put myself at ease with a little humor.

"Well, I'm an open book. Ask and I'll tell you anything—almost."

"Almost?" I tapped her on the leg as she had done to me earlier.

"Almost," she responded slyly.

"Okay then, are you married?"

"No, not on your life. I have no interest in that institution," she said with a shudder.

"Boyfriend?" I smiled.

"Several," she answered coyly.

"Hobbies?" I asked, starting to have some fun again.

"Hey wait, this is way more than I know about you," she complained.

"I'm not so sure about that Dalley. Hobbies?"

"I knit and rock climb," she bantered.

"Knitting and rock-climbing? Are you joking?" I asked, not believing her.

"No seriously, I like to knit. I find it relaxing. I used it as a way to tick my mom off when I was a kid."

It was obvious I was not the only one who had difficult memories about their mother, but she didn't drop a beat and continued.

"During my holidays, I go climbing anywhere I can. It's taken me all over the world, and I've met some of the most athletic and flexible men you could ever imagine." She winked back at me.

"You are hilarious," I laughed feeling more at ease with her story telling.

"Why thank you, Maya," she said with pride.

"Now here are some more serious questions. What led you in the direction to become a journalist?"

"Hmm, tough question; can I take a pass?" I shook my head.

"Journalism kind of fell into my lap, or one might say I bumped into it. When I was twenty-two, I graduated from university with a Bachelor of Arts in History. Not exactly the degree that was going to pay off my student loans. I had no idea what I wanted to do and decided the best way to figure things out was to go traveling. While I was away, I stopped in Fiji and spent two weeks there. One night while I was at a celebration, we started drinking grog, made from kava root. It tasted horrible, and everyone at the party started doing some crazy things. I met this man in his late thirties. He and I sparked. I mean literally we almost fell into the fire. I had never connected with anyone like that. He was a journalist on holiday—a working holiday, as he told me that he was always working, always looking for that next big story. We spent the next two weeks together day and night."

"So what happened next?" I asked, dying to find out.

Dalley's face softened, and I saw a sadness flash across her face momentarily.

"Nothing really. The two weeks faded into a memory even before I got onto the plane," she said trying to end the conversation.

"You lie!! You mean you never saw him again?" I responded with shock.

"No, no need," she answered indifferently. "Our meeting was not about *being together forever*. It was about finding ourselves, I think. Once we had done that, saying goodbye was not that hard."

Studying her face, her words and her voice appeared incongruent.

"If that was the case then, what did *you* find out about yourself?"

"I found out I had a knack for getting people to tell me their stories, and that journalism was one way I could let people know what I really thought. So, I cut my trip short, went home, and got a job at a newspaper. I also learned that you couldn't just talk about doing something, you had to get out there and make it happen."

"Dalley, what do you think *he* found?" I asked digging a little deeper. "I'm not sure, but when he took me to the airport on my last day, he grabbed me and held my face close to his, studying every part of me. Then he pushed his lips hard on mine and kissed me passionately like it was the last time he would see me—and it was. I remember him getting into a cab and mouthing the words 'thank you,' as he drove away. I thought about it for a long time, trying to figure out what he was thanking me for. The best I could imagine was the passion and the laughter. We were good together in every way. I don't think I've ever met anyone who made me laugh so much." Her loud silence confirmed that the conversation about her love life was over.

"So, ten years later, do you still like being a journalist?" I asked with some curiosity.

"Yes, essentially I am my own boss in most ways. The paper pays my expenses and I get to travel sometimes, and recently the editorial I write got picked up by a few more online papers."

"Wow Dalley, that's awesome. I would love to read it one day!"

"Enough about me! Let's go meet the other ladies," she said, changing the subject.

She stood up and made an announcement: "Hi, I'm Dalley and this is Maya. We are two of the contest winners who are going to Portugal—to Netuno Wineries. I thought that we all might have a drink together and get this party started."

Maggie and Ellen smiled and waved quietly from their seats, but Josie got up and made her way over towards us.

"Thank God! Let me move over to sit with you two," she bellowed loudly, then plunked down in the open seat across from us. Dalley pushed the attendant button and within moments Cristiano came walking down the aisle. I blushed as he approached and could feel my heart start to race again. "What can I do for you Miss Price, oh sorry, Dalley?"

"Cristiano, we need a bottle of champagne and five glasses.

"Yes, I have just the thing for you," he answered, then quickly set off down the stairs, soon returning with everything we needed and more.

He brought back an open bottle of champagne, five glasses, and a tray of snacks, then poured the bubbly and handed each of us a glass. Before he handed me mine, he paused. The delay was long enough for the others to notice and gave them reason to use it as a topic of conversation after the second bottle of champagne had been opened.

With another full glass in her hand, and with all the introductions and start-up complete, Josie turned to me and in a loud booming voice asked, "So Maya, what was all *that* about with the flight attendant?"

The other women chimed in asking questions like we were all back in high school. I laughed at the thought, as high school was never like that for me. I was not one of the beautiful people, and back then someone like Cristiano would never have even looked at me. The chatter and questions were embarrassing, and I blushed as Dalley told the story of how we'd met.

That afternoon was one of the best I'd ever had. As we began flying over Ontario, I think it was Josie who took out her camera and started taking candid shots. It didn't take long for the rest of us to join in and before we knew it, we had five very happy shutterbugs taking pictures of everything. It was both silly and wonderful. It came as a surprise when I heard the announcement that we would be landing in Montreal soon. The second leg of my journey had gone by so quickly. Dalley and I continued to laugh until the plane rolled to a stop. It wasn't until then I realized what a great job she had done in distracting me.

As I began to gather my things, I looked down at myself and noticed I was covered in tea stains and remnants of our morning snack. "How can I meet him looking like this?" I shuddered.

Dalley went into her large purse and pulled out a clean, white t-shirt and tossed it onto my lap. "Why don't you freshen up somewhere?"

I smiled, grateful that someone else was a little more organized than I was. As I tucked the t-shirt into my purse, I pulled out Christopher and Athena, not sure what I should do with them during the layover and my date. I held them tightly in my arms.

"Maya, I can watch over them if you like. I'm just going to sit and drink most of the time anyway. I'll keep them safe. Lord knows I don't want you to lose them again." She shoved me out of my seat. "Have fun," she said laughing, like she was sending me off to my first day of school.

Two Hours

Maya

WALKING DOWN THE RAMP, I realized quickly my needs outweighed my wants, and I *needed* to find a place to pee. I looked around and found a bathroom that was close to where Cristiano had asked me to meet him, but the line was so long I worried I might miss him if I didn't stay. So I stood and waited, not so patiently. I thought briefly about running. Running away? Running around? I wasn't quite sure. But in the end I decided that no matter what happened, or how nervous I felt, I was going on that date. I leaned in awkwardly against a post and hoped that when he saw me, he would think I looked really relaxed. My stomach flipped and I started to sweat. It had been years since I'd been on a real date. "Breathe in and out," I said, trying to calm down, hoping I wouldn't faint.

"Maya," he said my name quietly.

I looked up and my heart opened to a world I didn't even know existed. He had changed into his street clothes: a basic white t-shirt and worn out jeans. We would look like twins once I changed.

He took my good hand and we started to walk through the airport. My heart fluttered as his grip was firm and gentle all at the same time. I trusted his hand.

"What do you want to do?" he asked.

Jokingly I answered, "A shower would be nice." Without hesitation he took a quick right turn and then a left, and brought me to a small hallway. He pulled out his security badge and clicked us through a locked door to a set of stairs. As we climbed, he placed his other hand ever so gently on the small of my back. It felt like his fingers could melt my skin. Although a part of me knew that this was all crazy, I wasn't nervous anymore, just puzzled. We walked into a very simple room that had a shower and some benches. He let go of my hand and threw me a towel from the shelf.

"Take your time, we're in no rush." The words rolled from his lips and his accent warmed me like liquid honey.

"Are you sure this is okay? I mean me taking a shower here?"

"Trust me."

I smiled.

His eyes flickered with pleasure. I put my purse down on the bench and walked towards the stall.

"Thank you. This is exactly what I needed."

"I guessed correctly then."

He walked towards me and my heart jumped. It was as if he could read me from the inside out. Then he turned and sat down on the bench, watching me closely as I went into the shower. I undressed slowly and hung my clothes on the outer door. I could see him through the modeled glass, sitting on the bench and waiting patiently, rocking ever so slightly with his arms outstretched behind him. I could hear him humming an unfamiliar tune. It was beautiful.

I stepped into the shower and turned on the water. It felt like an invitation of warmth to my skin. Within moments, I became so relaxed that I forgot about my burnt hand and when the hot water touched it, I yelped out in pain. Cristiano knocked on the outer change-room door.

"Are you alright? What happened?" he asked with concern.

"No, I'm fine. I just forgot about my hand and ran it under the hot water directly."

"Do you need any help?" he asked open-endedly. His tone had shifted and became more playful.

I wasn't absolutely sure what kind of help he was offering, but if I was correct in my assumption, I wasn't ready for *that* kind of an adventure.

"No, thanks. I can manage for now," I said, letting out a nervous giggle.

When I turned off the water, the room was silent. I began toweling off, but soon realized that my clean shirt was in my purse on the bench. I stood wrapped in a towel trying to figure out what I should do next. Then I took a deep breath and came out of the stall. Cristiano looked up at me smiling. "Are you looking for this?" he said holding up my purse. He walked over very slowly with it in one hand and an extra towel in the other.

"Thank you," was all I could say. I turned to walk back to the stall, but could feel his hand on my shoulder. I stopped. He took a step closer. I could feel his breath on my neck and he began gently wiping the beads of water off of my quivering body. It was enchanting. He was enchanting. Then as I was just about ready to turn around, the door opened, and someone walked in. We all froze. Cristiano's laugh broke the awkward moment. I quickly made my way back into the stall, with embarrassment cascading through my veins. I listened as he spoke in Portuguese. I guessed they must have been colleagues, as the conversation was relaxed and filled with laughter. I had no idea what they were saying, but I decided it was best if I didn't know. I dressed slowly and finger brushed my hair. When I came back out of the stall, the fellow was gone, and Cristiano was smiling broadly. I allowed a little grin to form on my lips and reached down to touch my pendant, realizing that courage was all that mattered, right then and there.

He waited for me patiently as I finished getting ready. Then he took my hand and led me back through the maze of hallways.

"What would you like to do?" he asked again.

"Whatever you like," I said, feeling shy and not sure what to do next. My confidence wavered and I started to wonder why he really wanted to be with me. His pace slowed to match my own.

"Maya, if you want to go back to the gate, we can. I'm sorry if I have upset you. I was too forward." I stared at his crinkled face. His eyes were filled with concern and compassion. I slipped my hand from his and fixed the one piece of hair that had fallen into my eyes.

"No, leave it," he insisted. "I like the way it falls across your face."

"Cristiano, I'm not sure …" I sputtered. His eyes fell. I had to tell him how I felt. I didn't want to be that other Maya ever again. I had to be honest. "I've never met anyone like you before. I'm not sure what to do or say. I'm nervous, not because you have done anything wrong, but because you have done so many things that feel so right, but—can you slow things down, for just a minute or two and let me catch up?"

He looked up, and appeared to be comforted by my words, as the wrinkles became smooth and he leaned in a little closer.

"Well then, let's start from the beginning. Come, let's share a meal."

"That sounds lovely," I sighed with relief. We walked side by side through the busy airport until we found ourselves in a quiet little lounge. It was quaint and very rustic, like someone's living room. We sunk into some comfy chairs, each of us taking a deep breath. When the waiter came over and asked what we wanted, my French response was both smooth and natural. It surprised me a little as it had been some time since I'd spoken the language. Cristiano smirked and gestured for me to continue.

What should have been awkward for me wasn't. What would have been hard for me in the past was easy. I kicked off my shoes, and curled up in the chair. We ate and shared stories and enjoyed two hours of laughter and questions. It was a good beginning. Then, while in the midst of his next story, his watch alarm went off.

"Maya, we need to get back. We board in about thirty minutes," he said simply. "Thank you for saying yes. It has been a wonderful afternoon, *every* part of it."

Taking his hand, I leaned in and whispered, "Yes, the meal *was* a perfect place to start."

We both laughed. Then he interlaced his fingers through mine and tightened his grip. "I want you to know that nothing like this has ever happened to me before," he shared cautiously.

His watch alarm rang again, and he looked at me with squinted eyes. It appeared he was trying to tell me that we had to hurry. "Thank goodness I have my running shoes on today," I joked. We took off, racing through the long hallways, and dodging around all the travelers. When we arrived at the gate, he stroked my face gently, and then slipped away through another door. I stood and touched my cheek tracing my skin where his fingers had touched me.

"Maya!" Dalley hollered across the room as she ran towards me. My trance was broken, and I looked up smiling, excited to see my new friend.

"So?" she asked, with a million questions hidden in that one word. "How was your date?"

In response, I beamed, but saved my story for later.

"I'm glad," she said reading my smile. "You deserve it."

The side door opened and Cristiano stepped out, dressed in his uniform. My heart leapt. He smiled at me and then joined his colleagues. I looked back to see Maggie, Josie, and Ellen walking arm and arm, their new friendship overflowing with laughter. They joined us in line, recalling their feeble attempts to speak French during the layover and how much they enjoyed their first order of poutine. They all knew about my date and eagerly waited for me to share details. I gave them a shortened version, starting with the scene of me leaning up against the post, and finishing with the two of us running through the airport trying to make it back in time. I even surprised myself by including the shower scene.

"Steamy!" Josie blurted out. "Now that is the way to start an adventure. It reminds me of this trip I took to Brazil, many years ago …"

I sighed happily as she told her story. I knew that the warmth I felt inside was not just about Cristiano but about taking chances, laughing, making new friends, and drinking champagne 35,000 feet in the air. I thought about my dad and sent him a quick text:

In Montreal waiting with some new friends to board my flight for Lisbon. Thanks for the seeds of joy, they are already starting to grow. Love you.

The call for First Class passengers blared over the speakers, alerting us to start moving towards the desk. As we stood in line, two other women joined us, both holding U.S. passports. One wore a tailored suit and spectacular heels. The other, a slight woman of Asian descent who stood quietly holding her documents. Dalley poked me, whispering, "The tall one is Petra and I am guessing the other one must be Sachi."

"She is a structural engineer?" I had met many of Steven's friends and could not imagine how this young woman would ever fit in with that crowd.

Dalley turned around and spontaneously introduced us as the other contest winners. "Well that only leaves one," Dalley mused to the group.

"One what?" Petra inquired.

"One more of us."

We stood and chatted for a minute as the flight attendants checked in several other passengers.

I was the first to see her, and then all the other eyes in the gate followed. Her picture in the file didn't do her justice. She wasn't just stunning, she was *exquisite*. Dalley smirked and said quietly in my ear, "This is going to be fun." Then turned in her direction.

"Are you the other Netuno Winery contest winner?" she asked in an overly friendly voice.

"Why? Who wants to know?" Jade answered very rudely. We were all taken aback by her response, except Dalley, who seemed to revel in Jade's offensive tone.

With a big sticky smile, Dalley countered, "We are the other contest winners. You are the last of our travel gang! I'm so excited," she yipped, sending the ooze of her enthusiasm spraying all over Jade's Prada bag.

"Oh," she said with disgust. Dalley had *niced* her into muteness and then invited her to have a drink with us on the plane. Jade however, was less than impressed with Dalley's forced community spirit. It appeared that nothing was of any interest to her. That was—until she saw Cristiano.

He happened to be looking our way. I'm not sure if he was looking at me, or at her, but she noticed him, and I noticed her. I could feel a warm flush run through me, as I saw her tracking him. I'm not sure what happened next, but in a flash I found myself standing directly in her line of sight.

"Excuse me!" Jade screeched, as I interrupted her hunt.

"Oh, no problem. You can go next in line. I'm in no rush," I said pretending not to understand which *excuse me* she had hurled in my direction. She craned her head trying to catch another glimpse of him, but

I took a step farther to the right obscuring her complete line of vision. Dalley laughed and Jade stood firm. My action had broken her hunt altogether. She was not pleased, but I was.

Jade's anger was black and intense. She brushed by, knocking me off balance for a second, cut to the front of the line, and stomped up the ramp like a child who had just lost her piece of candy. There was a stifled laugh from our group and then Dalley spoke up with an enthusiastic voice, "Oh, this is getting good already. A little drama and we haven't even taken off yet."

Josie interrupted with a yell, "Will someone grab their camera? Let's take a group shot." One of the attendants saw what we were trying to do, gathered us together, snapped a few pictures and shooed us up the ramp.

My phone buzzed. It was a text from my dad:

Love you. Proud of you. Take care of your Joy.

I smiled, turned my phone off, and stepped onto the plane.

Lisbon

Maya

Our flight to Lisbon was long and filled with laughter. Christopher and Athena were returned to me, and Petra, our new friend from New York, shared stories about her life in advertising. Sachi was a good listener and Jade, well, she avoided us altogether and gave the flight attendants a hard time about everything.

Throughout the flight, Cristiano and I stole a few moments away from his duties, talking about life and ourselves. It was fun and spontaneous. I felt like a teenager at summer camp, sneaking away to meet a boy down by the lake.

When Cristiano came by to see me before we landed, I was nervous about when and how we were going to meet again. I tried to act casually but when I asked him, it came out awkwardly. "Cristiano, I was going through my itinerary and noticed that we are in Lisbon for Saturday and most of Sunday. Do you have any plans?"

He knelt down and took my hand. "Oh Maya, you're so funny," he said smirking. "I just have Saturday night in town and then fly out again in the morning. I'll be back mid-week but have a few personal things to take care of. I was hoping we could spend next Saturday evening together, as I fly out again on Sunday."

"That would be wonderful," I said with relief, thankful that he had already started to think about being with me. I paused, wishing I could see him sooner than the following Saturday.

"I wonder what my first week at Netuno is going to be like?" I asked changing the subject.

He smiled and nodded his head. "I know that you are going to have a memorable time. Puro, the manager of the inn, is an old friend of mine. He will take good care of you. The seat belt sign went on. "I have to go, but I will see you before you leave."

Dalley started to laugh as Cristiano walked away. "What are you laughing about?" I asked.

"What am I laughing about? The two of you. It's like watching two swooning birds, diving and catching flight, bumping into one another and then starting all over again. I can't say I've ever seen anything like it. It is a true romance in the making," she said, cooing and making kissing sounds.

"Oh, it's not like that," I protested weakly.

"Yes Maya, it is," she stated, not leaving any room for rebuttal.

I shook my head and held Christopher close to my chest, knowing that Dalley was more right than wrong, and the only evidence of that strange and wonderful day was being held in my arms.

The plane landed smoothly, and Cristiano came quickly over to our seat. With a hushed voice he asked me if my friends and I would like to come out that night for a little live music.

My heart leapt and I squealed, "Yes, that would be great. I'm not sure who all can come though."

Cristiano looked at me and studied my face carefully. "Oh, just as long as *you* are there."

Dalley rolled her eyes, but I didn't mind.

"I will reserve a table for you and your friends for 9:00 p.m. Just give the front man your name when you arrive." He smiled and then handed me a slip of paper. I nodded my head in agreement, as my words seemed to stall at my lips. Then I opened the note and on it was the name and address of the club. I looked up and he smiled again.

"I will see you soon Maya."

Taking the paper, I carefully tucked it away in my purse.

"Sounds like fun. A little live music, a few drinks, and a room full of Portuguese men? What more could I want?" Dalley sparkled with mischief.

"Nothing, absolutely nothing," I said still swooning from the idea I was going to see him again that night. We had a few minutes before getting off the plane so I thought I would read the last journal entry I'd written while we were flying.

August 18th (Back on the plane, Lisbon here I come)

It's late, is it the 19th now? I don't know anymore. I've been traveling for hours and so much has happened that it almost feels like a dream. How can one person's world stay the same for so long and then in less than a day, everything turns upside down?

The plane is quiet right now. Our ladies finished three more bottles of champagne within the first hour of the flight. Josie, Maggie, and Ellen are asleep and Dalley is on her way. Petra is working on her computer, Sachi is reading, and well, Jade, actually I don't care. She's not very likable.

Anyway, Cristiano and I were able to steal a few moments tonight on the flight. He talked about Lisbon and his home village where he grew up. It sounds so beautiful. He mentioned that his parents died when he was little and that he was raised by his grand-mother. His eyes looked so sad when he talked about them. Anyways ...

I'm not sure about much right now but it does feel like I am digging my way out of a pile of muck; surfacing from years of my sorrow. Whose sorrow? I don't know. I guess I still have some work to do? It's time for a cup of tea? Oh I'm feeling a little tired, maybe a few hours of sleep wouldn't be the worst thing. Good night or good morning friend. I'll talk to you tomorrow.

Maya

After our group cleared customs, we made our way through the halls and headed towards baggage pick-up. A limo driver with a sign that read 'Netuno Winery Contest Winners' was waiting for us near the carousel.

When I saw him wave the sign again, the reality hit me that I was standing in an airport in Portugal, and free to become the real Maya—whoever that was.

As I walked out into the mid-morning sun, the warm dry air took me by surprise. I took in a deep breath. It smelled like home.

Everyone walked briskly behind the limo driver, chatting about all the sights and sounds. In broken English the driver began to speak: "Welcome to Portugal. My name is Francesco. Do not worry about your luggage. It will be brought to the hotel. If you have any questions, or if there is anything I can do for you ladies, please call me anytime," he said, then handed each of us his card.

As I stepped into the limo, I could hardly believe the size of it. It was one of those SUV vehicles that celebrities use. I paused briefly, thinking about the limo that had been booked for the wedding. I had never wanted a limo, but Steven insisted. Then I felt a bump from behind and was brought back from my memory.

"Hey, Maya! Where did you go?" Dalley asked as she climbed over me to get to the window seat.

"Nowhere really. I was just thinking that I could do with another shower." Laughter erupted in the limo, as the shower story from Montreal still shone as a highlight in our escapades so far.

The limo ride to the hotel was short, but fun. Francesco dropped us off and we headed into the lobby. Surprisingly, there was no one there to greet us from Netuno, just a welcome sign instructing us to register at the front desk.

Dalley and Josie sprinted over to the counter first to let them know we had arrived. "Ola!" Josie said with enthusiasm, and then struggled to find the next phrase. "We are the *competição vencedores em relação a Netuno Vinícolas*," she finished in her best broken Portuguese. "Oh, I am so rusty," she complained.

"Josie, it's like riding a bike, but I wouldn't worry too much. As long as you can order wine for us, we'll be fine," Dalley chuckled.

The young man at the front desk smiled and responded with excitement.

"Oh yes, yes, *bem-vindo*. Welcome. We have been waiting for you. We have all your rooms ready and are so pleased to be hosting you before you go to Netuno tomorrow. We hope you had a smooth flight and will enjoy your stay in Portugal. We have four rooms for you to share. You will be staying just one night with us." The young man laid out two keys for each room.

Everyone quickly made their decisions about who they would stay with and took keys from the desk accordingly. No one made eye contact with Jade except Sachi, who took the remaining two keys and gestured to Jade that maybe they could share. Jade walked up to her and roughly pulled the key out of her hand and stormed off.

"Sachi you didn't have to do that," I said feeling responsible for things starting off poorly with Jade.

"It is no problem," she said quietly. "I need a room and so does she." Sachi smiled respectfully, collecting her things.

Dalley jumped around the lobby with our keys. "What time do we need to be at the club tonight?" she asked in a booming voice for all to hear.

"Are we going out tonight?" Josie stepped in.

"Yes, Cristiano invited us out to a local club to hear some live music," I responded with a little blush in my cheek. "He said we should be there around 9:00 p.m."

Maggie chimed in, "Oh that sounds exciting. My boys aren't going to believe that their mother is going to a club her first night in Portugal. They think I'm so square."

"Well it's almost 11:00 now," Dalley interrupted. "That means there is lots of time to explore the city. Let's all meet back here for supper."

Everyone agreed and began finding their way through the ancient hotel towards their rooms. Everything was so authentic, right down to the rustic doorknobs.

"Dalley, I know you want to go exploring, so why don't you go without me? I'm going to take a little rest," I said, feeling exhausted.

"Are you kidding me, Maya? There's so much to do. Anyways, it will mess you up if you sleep right now," she said challenging me with her experienced travel logic.

She unlocked the door to our room, and there sitting on the table was the largest gift basket I had ever seen. She walked over and then started poking around through the contents.

"Wow that is spectacular! It's so colorful and *big!*" I gushed.

"Maya, I hate to burst your bubble, but did you look in the basket?" she asked as she held up a can of sardines and some herbs.

I walked over and found a wide variety of foods: fresh, canned, and dried. Dalley asked, "What are we supposed to do with this stuff? Besides the wine of course." She grabbed both bottles and tucked them under her arms.

"I guess it's a gift for us to share? Use?" I answered with a degree of confusion.

"Well then, let's start with the wine!"

"And what about the spices, and the dried cod?" I exclaimed, starting to laugh.

"You're right. That *is* some gift basket. Is there a note somewhere in the groceries?" she teased.

"*Yes* there's one here," I said shaking it in her direction.

Hello Ladies Bem-vindo to Portugal,

We assume you enjoyed your flights and that you are settling into your temporary rooms. We can only imagine how curious you are to learn where your hosts are.

We are busy getting ready for your arrival tomorrow evening, but have a little challenge for you to complete in the meantime.

In the basket before you, are a series of ingredients; all are flavors of Portugal. We have booked off the small kitchen in the hotel for you ladies to begin your culinary adventure. Today, the only rule is that you need to use at least two ingredients from the basket when making the supper dish you are going to create. We have included a little spending money for anything else you might need.

The kitchen will be open to you from 12:00 p.m. on. You have until 8:00 p.m. to have your dish ready. You can work in a group, or on your own, whichever you prefer. Be creative, use your imagination, take a picture or two, but most of all have fun. The hotel Chef will be joining you at 8:00 p.m. sharp to taste your creations.

See you tomorrow afternoon, Adeus

Mateus and Reinaldo Chavis, Netuno Wineries

"Well, this is interesting," Dalley said with fake enthusiasm.

Standing in the middle of the room, I wasn't sure what to think, but my mind started to click. "We can do this. This *does* sound like fun!" I exclaimed. "Dalley, get the guidebook out of my purse. We have some work to do."

"Why? I don't want to work. I want to go shopping," she whined.

"Well, you're in luck then. We *need* to go shopping."

"That's not the kind of shopping I wanted to do," she pouted. "Maya, can't we take a break for a few minutes? You were just telling me how tired you are." She tried one last weak attempt at changing my mind.

"No time for being tired anymore. We have a job to do," I said, now filled with anticipation around our first challenge.

"Okay, you're in charge," she said, laughing as she let me take over the supper project.

"First, get everything out of the basket and lay it out on the bed," I instructed, with a plan in mind.

"Maya, what are we looking for?" she asked, now starting to come around and sounding keener.

After surveying the contents the only item I knew *anything* about was the dried fish. I had remembered a lesson from my grade five socials class explaining how the pioneers used to use salt to dry the fish, and if you soaked it in milk for long enough it would extract the salt. "We need milk!" I yelled. "Grab the fish! We have to start right now because it takes a long time."

"A long time for what?" Dalley questioned.

"We have to soak the fish in milk, to extract the salt." I replied with confidence.

Dalley looked at me like I had become unspun, but that wasn't it. It felt like a switch had been thrown and I was actually coming *back* to life. I was excited. I was happy. I had a chance to do something adventurous, to create something. *Creating something? Was that it? Was that one of the missing pieces?* Many years ago, I stopped creating. I stopped writing and I stopped living.

Then without another moment of hesitation, I yelled at the top of my lungs, "Not anymore!!!" Dalley jumped as I stated my personal intention.

She laughed a little nervously, and then yelled in partnership. "Well damn straight, not anymore!" She had no idea what I was talking about, but joined in none the less.

I grabbed the packet of money and the cod and marched out the door. "Let's go shopping! But first to the kitchen," I yelled over my shoulder.

Dalley ran behind me as I led the way. We were the first ones to arrive. The chef spoke sparingly to us but knew who we were. When I asked for milk, he did not look surprised, but pleased that we were getting started. He showed us to our cooking station and raised a hand, ushering for us to begin. Dalley pulled her camera from her bag.

"We should document our first food adventure together," she said with no room for questions, and then took a shot of me pouring thick, farm milk over the cod.

Then we raced off to find a taxi and make our way to some kind of market. As we ran outside we saw Ellen, Maggie, and Josie speeding off in style. It looked like Francesco's card had come in handy for them.

I looked at Dalley and made a declaration, "We are going to create something remarkable today, or at least try." I sighed with fresh confidence.

"I'm in. I'll do the photos if you do the cooking," she said, throwing her arm around me.

We jumped into a waiting taxi and sped off. Dalley had her electronic translator with her and typed in, *fresh fruit and bread.* It came up as *frutos do mar, legumes, pão.* She tried to explain to the taxi driver where we wanted to go. "To the market, *frutos do mar, legumes, pão,*" she said slowly and loudly like he was deaf.

He smiled, parroting back the word "*pão*" to us. Then he turned on the radio and drove until we reached the outskirts of town. Suddenly, he stopped and then pointed to an area over a hill. "*Pão,*" he said. Then he motioned for us to get out. We climbed out of the taxi and shut the door. When we turned around, he was already halfway down the dirt road, music blaring, and dust billowing behind his vehicle.

"Uhm, where did he say to go?" I asked with unease.

"He pointed that way, over the hill. Maya what have you gotten me into?" she said half-jokingly.

As we climbed, both of us laughed and she teased me about the potential of having to walk back to the hotel. But there on the other side of the hill nestled between a few houses was a quaint little farmers' market. We walked down the slope, instantly taken in by the beauty and the scents of the space. There were colors everywhere and so many people talking. It was electric.

"We need to make a plan Dalley."

"Yes, I know," she smirked. "Two questions though: What are we making for supper? And how are we going to get back?"

"I'm not going to worry about the getting-back part right now."

"Lead the way then, Miss Maya. What do we need?"

"Let's sit down for a minute and figure out the menu." We found a bench and got to work on what we had to do. "Well, we only have a couple of hours to prepare, so we need something simple that includes cod."

Dalley pulled out her phone to see if she could connect to a network. "Excellent! We have access," she said, typing, 'Simple Portuguese Cod Recipes.' "Here we go—Portuguese Seafood Stew?"

"I've never made stew before. Have you?" I said feeling a little nervous.

"No, I told you, I don't cook, *ever*."

"Ever? And you entered the contest? Why?" I teased.

"A chance to win a trip to Portugal?" she answered, looking at me like I should have figured that one out sooner. "But cooking can't be that hard. We'll be fine."

"Well, what ingredients do we need for the stew?" I asked trying to clarify things for us.

Dalley recited the ingredients back to me. "Potatoes, olive oil, tomatoes, chili flakes, onion, bay leaf, green pepper, garlic, white wine, mussels, cod, and cilantro."

"So I guess the question is—what wasn't in the basket?" I pondered.

"I don't know. I wasn't paying too much attention after I realized there was no chocolate," she quipped.

"Okay then." I thought back to the basket and all the ingredients that were laid out on the bed. "I know we need potatoes, tomatoes, green peppers, mussels and cilantro; maybe a bay leaf," I added.

"Oh, make sure we have some fresh bread too. That way if all goes wrong, at least the chef has something to eat," she quipped, looking on the bright side of our potential culinary disaster.

"Good idea. I'll get the seafood and the bread if you can pick up the veggies. Let's split up."

"Meet you back here in thirty minutes," Dalley yelled as she pulled out her camera and melted into the crowd.

My time in the market was extraordinary. I felt like I had been transported back in time and was on a secret mission. I made it back to the meeting spot with just a minute to spare. "Dalley, did you get everything we need?"

"Yes, *I* did. What about you?" she responded, sounding proud of herself.

"Oh, I found this wonderful fishing family who sold me the mussels, and this interesting woman who gave me her last loaf of bread."

"She just gave it to you?" Dalley asked slightly perplexed. "Tell me more."

"After picking up the mussels, I walked around the market looking for bread, but everyone seemed to be sold out. I went back to the family and asked about finding some *pão*. They laughed and pointed me in the direction of an older woman sitting by herself at a card table. She only had one loaf left, but they encouraged me to go visit her. In fact, they physically pushed me in her direction. I was concerned that the loaf might be stale or something, but when I stood at the table, the scent of the bread was so inviting I could hardly believe it had not been sold. She picked up the loaf like it was a child, wrapped it in a cloth, and laid it in my arms. Our conversation was filled with only gestures and she wore the most intricately embroidered handkerchief I had ever seen. I handed her several euros to cover the cost of the bread, but she gently tucked it back into my hand."

"Yes, Maya that does sound a little odd. But right now, I think the only thing we should be concerned about is how we are going to get back to the hotel," she said, scratching her head, trying to figure out an answer.

We stood for a few minutes, bewildered about what to do next. But before we had a chance to even start making a plan, over the hill popped our taxi driver. He smiled and waved to us. We excitedly ran up the hill, laden with all of our new-found treasures of Portugal, and thankful for his return.

"I love this place," said Dalley with enthusiasm. "There are surprises around every corner."

"I wouldn't want to be anywhere else right now," I stated simply.

Excited and exhausted, it was mid-afternoon by the time we arrived back at the hotel and we both needed to rest. Dalley ran the food into the kitchen while I made my way upstairs.

I entered the room, slipped off my tired feet, and collapsed on the bed.

I heard the door open and close, and Dalley dropped down beside me.

The last thing I remembered was asking her to set the alarm for 5:00 p.m.

10

The First Supper

Maya

"MAYA, GET UP, IT'S AFTER 6:00!" Dalley's voice boomed, waking me from a colorful dream.

I sat up, my heart pounding in my ears. "We're late! Didn't you set the alarm?" I screeched.

"I thought you set it," she said, hiding her head under the pillow. "Come on Dalley, we've got five minutes to get down to that kitchen and start prepping." Within moments our room was a whirlwind of clothes and makeup everywhere. Dalley opened her suitcase and threw me a shirt.

"Hey Maya, you should wear this. It would look great on you."

"No thank you. It looks a little sparkly for me."

"Live a little, have some fun! You're more sparkly than you think. What about Athena?"

"She's a pen, not an article of clothing!"

"Yes, I know," she retorted. "But can you imagine wearing a shirt that is *like* Athena? You would be able to shimmer your way into any man's heart. You *are* going to see him tonight. Did you forget?"

I took the shirt and slipped it on reluctantly, but reluctant or not there was no time to change. I was set in sparkles. She blasted her crazy hair with spray and yelled: "It's 6:15, grab the basket and let's go!"

With wings on our feet, we ran down the hallway—two crazy women on a mission. When we arrived in the kitchen, things were well underway. Maggie, Ellen, and Josie were almost finished creating their dishes. They had completed two different kinds of casseroles and had made their own rolls. Petra, on the other hand, had made a simple plate of cold meats and cheeses, including pieces of the salted cod straight from the basket. Everything was done, and she was sitting at her clean cooking station, drinking a glass of wine, enjoying all the other food prep chaos. Sachi was on the other side of the kitchen working in her own corner, cooking up a storm. The scent that drifted over in our direction made all our mouths water.

Looking over at Petra, I asked, "What is she making over there? It smells amazing."

"Oh, you should have seen her an hour or two ago. She has been at it all afternoon. She is our secret chef," she laughed.

Josie yelled across the kitchen, "What happened to the two of you? *We've* been slaving away in here for hours."

Ellen and Maggie rolled their eyes at one another and took the last of the buns out of the oven. "*Now* can we please have a glass of wine?" Maggie asked, pretending to be exasperated by Josie, the keeper of the bottle. Josie nodded and poured each of them a glass.

Dalley yelled back, "Oh, Maya took us on an adventure, and almost got us kidnapped by a taxi driver. It was very exciting."

"You're ridiculous," I said laughing at Dalley. Then I quickly looked over to Josie and the other ladies. "When we got back from shopping, we went for a rest, and forgot to set the alarm.

"Dalley, we have just over an hour to prepare. How did that happen?" I exclaimed with panic.

Dalley and I catapulted into emergency mode. We talked little and worked hard, cutting, chopping, and slicing. Everyone else who had finished up before us set the tone for the evening and started the party early. The space was filled with laughter and sprinkled with new memories of food, wine, and friends.

As the minutes ticked by, Dalley and I followed the recipe that she'd found online for the Seafood Stew. When it was close to 8:00 p.m., we thought we should taste the results of our afternoon adventure. We grabbed a spoon and plunged in.

"You know Maya, it's not half bad. It's not good, but it's not half bad!" she said with encouragement. I took a second bite and knew she was on the mark with her assessment about the 'not good' part and hoped there was enough edible food made by everyone else to replace our first attempt at stew.

Still wrapped in a simple cloth of questions and kindness, I unwrapped the bread and picked up a knife. When I cut the first slice, the room went silent for me; the aroma was intoxicating. I had to have a piece right then. I took a large bite and the taste and texture of the bread was like nothing I had ever eaten before. It danced through my taste buds and invited me in, and when I swallowed, it became a part of me. It reminded me of the first time I saw the peach blossoms in the fields when I was a little girl.

"Maya, are you all right?" Dalley said, loudly enough to startle me out of my contemplation.

"You have to try this bread! It's like nothing I've ever eaten before. I know it sounds crazy, but I'm serious."

"What are you talking about? What's so great about the bread?" she said with skepticism in her voice.

I handed her a slice and with emphasis said, "Taste it."

She bit into the bread, but nothing appeared to happen to her.

"Yes, Maya, it's delicious, but it's just bread," she responded with a head shake and a pat on my shoulder.

"Just bread? Are you kidding me?" This is the most amazing food I've ever eaten. It's life altering," I stated, finishing my bread defense.

"Maya, you haven't eaten all day, and I think that anything would taste good to you right about now," she said trying to bring a little sanity back into the conversation.

I sat confused, but was not going to argue with her about a loaf of bread. As the clock ticked closer to 8:00, Jade stomped into the kitchen like an angry child ready to throw a tantrum. Then she made her way over to an empty station and slammed her open basket down on the counter.

Maggie looked around at our group, took a deep breath and walked over to Jade's station. "It's nice to see you Jade. I hope you had a good afternoon," she offered with kindness.

Jade's response though was less than enthusiastic. "Good? I wouldn't say *that* after suffering through *their* idea of First Class for six and a half hours, and then getting shoved into a run-down, garish SUV limo made for a very good afternoon. And to top it off, they expect me to share a room and cook my own meal tonight? They have got to be joking." She spat out her words, vibrating with disdain.

Maggie turned and walked back to Josie. "Wow!" she said quietly. I wasn't sure who the next comment was meant for, but she said it loudly enough for all of us to hear. "For someone so beautiful, she can be very ugly." Shortly after Jade's grand rant, the chef entered his kitchen. He said little at first, but sauntered around the stations, surveying all that had been happening in his absence.

His eyes twinkled as he spoke in English with a thick Portuguese accent. "I'm hungry. What's for supper?" He laughed, and then went straight to work. Most of us had no idea what to expect, except for Sachi. Her station was now clean, and her dishes were plated and ready to be tasted.

He started with Josie, Maggie, and Ellen. They were laughing when he approached and Josie handed him a glass of wine before he began. The chef took two bites of each casserole, ate one bun, and then smiled at the three who were eagerly awaiting his comments.

"Thank you. Your dishes are filled with experience and heart. The bun has good texture. Truly an excellent effort. Are there any photos?" The trio looked at each other. They clearly had gotten caught up in their food adventure and never thought about taking any pictures of the process.

"Oh not another thought ladies," he said, noticing the concern that crossed their faces. "Good job. Tastes like *mamãe* used to make." He winked at Josie and she blushed. "What was one of your special ingredients that you used from the basket?"

All three chimed in at the same time. "Cinnamon."

"Hmm? Very interesting," he pondered.

The chef nodded and headed over to Petra. He smiled and took a bite of cheese and picked up the cod, then placed it back on the plate. "I am glad you're here in Portugal. My friends over at Netuno have lots of work to do with you," he laughed.

She nodded and drank her wine. "I have many talents, but when it comes to food, I choose to let others shine. But I am willing to learn," she said, then lifted her glass to thank the chef.

He made his way over to our station and greeted us with a simple smile. "Stew and bread—a staple on any Portuguese table. Did you take any photos?"

Dalley pulled out her laptop, plugged in her camera, and within minutes was able to play a slide show of our afternoon.

"You will have to teach me how to do that," he said with great interest. Then he tasted the stew. He pursed his lips slightly. "I'm pleased that you soaked the cod. It was a good start," he said, with a little wince. Then he took two sips of wine and continued. "What were *your* special ingredients?"

I paused for a moment and thought about the day. Then I answered carefully, "Besides the cod—friendship." Dalley looked over and smiled at me. I thought I saw a look of surprise flash across her face.

The chef on the other hand, laughed, and then slapped me on the shoulder. "Friendship makes everything taste better, even salty cod." He picked up a slice of bread and took a bite. His face broadened into a large smile, which then changed into a look of curiosity. He stared at me quizzically. "Where did you get this bread?"

"From a market outside of town. I met an elderly woman who gave me her last loaf."

"Did she say anything?"

"No, she just smiled and handed me the bread. She didn't even want to take my money. It is the most amazing bread I have ever eaten. After the first piece, I found it difficult to stop."

He nodded his head like he knew what I was talking about. "You are a *very* lucky young woman." Then he moved on without any further explanation.

As he walked towards Sachi's station, his demeanor changed. He took on a serious look responding to her professional presentation. He tasted each of her dishes carefully and then asked her where she had studied.

"I have not gone to cooking school, I was taught at home," she said quietly. "I would like to meet your mother then," he said impressed.

"My mother did not teach me to cook," she responded with a degree of stiffness.

The chef shifted his focus back to the food. "The two dishes that you created clearly were developed from your imagination and food experience. The layers of flavors in your stew, the marinade on your meat—everything was cooked perfectly. I will let Gervais know you are coming. He is the chef at Netuno and will be very excited to meet you." He took one more look around the kitchen, resting his eyes on the final station. Jade stood scowling beside her basket. He scowled back at her, and then turned away without a word.

With his attention now focused on the rest of us he raised his arms and clapped. "Congratulations! My friends at Netuno will be so pleased with how well you have done. Please enjoy each of the dishes that your friends have made, except maybe *the fish*," he said picking up Petra's dried cod. "... and maybe the stew," he said pointing towards our pot. "I will see you all at 8:30 a.m., as I will be preparing something special for your morning meal."

Josie piped in, "8:30? What are you trying to do to me?"

"Miss Josie, if you have a complaint come see me after the supper service. I will address it at that time," he said with great innuendo.

"Promise?"

"Come see me when the kitchen closes after midnight." Josie winked.

After the chef and Josie booked their complaint session, it was time for supper. Everyone shared their food dishes except Dalley and me: we hid ours in the sink so we would not have to subject anyone to our creation. I watched Sachi walk over to Jade and offer her a plate of food. Jade didn't say thank you, but she did take the plate. I admired Sachi for holding out an olive branch to her. I wasn't sure I would have had that kind of compassion.

The rest of us talked and laughed. It was like we had known each other our whole lives.

"Well aren't we the most unlikely crew," Petra commented. "They couldn't have drawn the names of eight more *different* people if they had tried. Kind of makes you wonder doesn't it?"

"New Yorkers are so paranoid!" Josie chimed in.

"Not paranoid," Petra retorted. "I just work in an industry that manipulates everything you eat, drink, and have fun with. It's in my nature to be suspicious." Everyone burst into laughter. "But seriously, what do you think this whole contest is all about? Is it just marketing?"

"Why does it have to be about anything? Why can't it be just what it is?" I said, surprising myself with the comment.

"You're right, Maya. Life doesn't always have an ulterior motive," Petra responded with a shoulder shrug and sip of wine.

Ellen spoke up. "Well it doesn't matter to me why we are here. I am just glad that we are. I have never been on a holiday by myself, and even if I had to go back tomorrow, it would have all been worth it. Not that I want to go back tomorrow," she said clarifying her last comment as she finished her glass of wine.

As I enjoyed my last spoonful of Sachi's amazing stew and the final bite of bread from my loaf, I felt I could do or be anything that I wanted. Glancing down at my watch it was now after 9:30. My mind clicked and then stopped short. "Oh no! I'm late," I shrieked.

"Late for what?" Maggie asked, and then tapped her head as she too remembered. "Oh the night club! I'm so sorry, Maya! We just got carried away."

"Cristiano! I forgot him. How could I forget?" I exclaimed in panic. I could feel a swell of tears rising up, fighting to be released.

"We're not *that* late. Relax," said Dalley. "That man is not going to kick you to the curb for being a little late. You would have to do something far worse than that. Okay everyone, we need to get Maya to the night club, *rapidamente*. That is my word of the day. I love this language. Is everyone ready to go? Maya, do you have the address he gave you?"

I nodded like a child following orders. Then I went into my purse to get the paper and held it like a lifeline. Dalley continued like she was organizing a battle plan.

"Josie, do you have Francesco's card? I don't want to take any chances with calling a taxi tonight." Within minutes our transportation was confirmed and Francesco was on his way.

We grabbed our purses and headed out towards the lobby. Before leaving the kitchen Dalley turned and caught eyes with Jade, who was standing near the back of the room. "Come on Jade, everyone's invited," she said looking at me with a smirk and a grimace.

Jade slung her purse over her shoulder and tossed her hair as she walked by us. "Sounds like fun. We should hurry. I would never make a man like *that* wait for *me*."

Confidence

Maya

FRANCESCO ARRIVED AT THE HOTEL within minutes of the call. Josie talked briefly to him in Portuguese. Her memory had clearly loosened up since her arrival in the morning as the conversation was quick and passionate in nature.

"Josie, when did you go from speaking broken to fluent Portuguese?" Dalley teased.

"Oh, about four large glasses ago. Mid-afternoon I remembered that when I was learning to speak Portuguese, I was also drinking copious amounts of wine. I thought I would give it a try and *voila*! Sorry, that's French, but you know what I mean. It just started to flow."

"Where did you learn the language?" Maggie asked.

"Years ago, when I was traveling, I met a man who I was trying to impress."

"You learned how to speak Portuguese to impress a man?" Ellen asked with surprise.

"You bet!" Josie responded with enthusiasm, and then leaned in close. "You should have seen what he did to impress *me*." She laughed, leaving everyone hanging.

"Enough for now. Can we *please* focus?" Dalley said trying to keep everyone on track. "Josie, what did you tell Francesco? He looks like he is ready to throw the car into high gear, if it had one."

"Oh, I just told him we had a love emergency and we were late." She smiled, then put her hand on my shoulder, and whispered in my ear, "I understand Maya; we'll be there in a wink."

The tears started to surface again, but Josie and the others didn't give me a chance to let them fall.

"Maya, do you have the address?" she asked with her hand held out. I was gripping the paper so tightly that when I gave it to her, she had to smooth it out before handing it to Francesco. "We'll be there soon," she said again, appearing to read my face.

It was clear that although Josie could bring a lot of life to a party, she also brought along a lot of heart. When she gave him the piece of paper he nodded as he read it.

"Yes, I know where it is," he said waving his hand. "Ten minutes, maybe six if I hurry."

Francesco sped away from the hotel. The sights and sounds of a summer night in Lisbon were lost on me, as all I could focus on was breathing in and breathing out. By the time we had arrived at the club though, the panicked feeling had downgraded to nervousness.

"Let's go to the front of the line. There must be a VIP entrance or something," Dalley said hauling me out of the limo. Everyone followed behind as we made our way to the front doors. When we arrived, the bouncer looked over our group and Dalley pushed me forward.

"Hello, my name is Maya. Maya Wells?" I said my name like I was asking a question. *Was I really not sure who I was?* "Cristiano said that I should come to the front when I arrived with my friends," I said in a shaky tone.

"Yes, come with me," he said smiling, not fazed by our arrival or my request.

Maggie quietly took my hand and gave it a quick squeeze. "Everything is going to be okay."

The club was dimly lit, with candles flickering on each table. Acoustic guitar music flowed steadily from the stage as people danced closely together on the floor. The place was packed and we stood out like eight dandelions in a field of green grass. With my pendant grasped firmly in my right hand, the buzz in the room moved through me and threads of courage began to return. The passion in the space was inviting and attempted to encompass me in its mystery.

We followed the doorman to a reserved table where everyone in our group took a seat, except me. I couldn't see Cristiano anywhere and little bits of worry trickled in. The song ended and clapping and cheering filled the air. The dance floor cleared and it was only then I could see the stage. I saw the band talking and laughing, getting ready for their next song. The lead guitar player then turned around and there he was, standing in front of the microphone, guitar in hand, getting ready to play. Cristiano was a real live human being. I didn't imagine any of it. He looked over in my direction and we made eye contact. I grabbed the back of a seat to steady myself. He nodded to me and smiled wryly, then talked to the band, and started to play. I couldn't move on my own.

Dalley tugged me by the arm and hauled me into the seat. I was mesmerized by his fingers as they ran up and down the fret board. It reminded me of his gentle touch in Montreal when he wiped the water from my neck. I felt flushed.

The song ended and Cristiano leaned his guitar up against an amp, and then made his way over to our table. He spoke with all the other ladies first. "I am so pleased that you caught the last song of my set," he said nonchalantly.

My heart dropped as I realized he had invited me to hear him play and I'd missed the whole thing.

"I'm finished for the night, but there is still a lot of music to be enjoyed." He made little eye contact with me and my heart fell farther, almost hitting the floor. *What happened? What's wrong?* Emotion surged inside me and I didn't know what to do. I couldn't say anything; my tongue was tied, and covered in negative thoughts.

The music started up again and the dance floor was filled in an instant as salsa took over the room. Josie stood up and grabbed Cristiano's hand. He took it, laughed, and allowed our sixty-four-year-old powerhouse to spin him onto the dance floor. She was able to match every step he took.

"I wish I knew how to salsa," I said quietly. "There's no way I can keep up with him." I sunk into my chair once again filled with nerves, now about the dancing.

"Look at her. That is incredible," Ellen marveled.

Everyone laughed and watched the two of them spin and turn.

"Maybe I could learn," I said loud enough for the group to hear.

"Well you know Josie taught lessons when she was down in South America. I'm sure she would love to teach you, maybe all of us?" Maggie said offering some hope.

"I've never seen this kind of dancing up close," Sachi said with interest.

"Don't leave me out," Dalley jumped into the conversation.

I heard a chair scrape across the floor, but before I knew what was happening, Jade was tapping Josie on the shoulder. My body lurched forward and Dalley grabbed my arm.

She smiled, and then said stiffly, "Maya, that is not going to get you anywhere! Just sit and watch."

"Sit and watch?" I said raising my voice to challenge her. "Watch this? No way!"

I moved again, but that time it was Maggie who stopped me. "Don't you dare," she sputtered, holding up three mom fingers, shaking them in my face. "Confidence, faith, and trust. You may not know him well enough to see if *he* has all those qualities yet, but you have a chance right now to learn if they are part of you."

What could I say? Maggie was right. So I made my body let go and sat not-so-patiently, watching as Jade and Cristiano moved effortlessly around the dance floor. Her hands brought him in closer until their bodies touched. He led her into multiple turns and dips. They looked perfect together. It appeared she was trying to make some kind of point. I only had one question: was *he* listening?

When the song was over, she moved in closer like a spider ready to pounce on her prey. But he pulled away slyly. I sat up immediately, seeing that the story I had been creating was only just that, a story. He nodded politely, thanked her for the dance, and then released her into a spin landing her in the arms of one of his friends. I took a tentative breath waiting to see what would happen next. She looked at her new dance partner, then back at Cristiano, furious with the rejection he had cast upon her. Stomping off the floor, she angled her way through the crowd and back to the table. Then she grabbed her purse and left in a dramatic flurry of French foul language. I was never so excited to hear that much profanity in all my life. When I went to stand, no one held me back. My path to him was clear and it was now just up to me.

He stood on the dance floor and watched me for a few moments. I wanted to move, but I couldn't. It wasn't until the next song began that I was able to break free and take one step forward. He sauntered over, not once breaking his gaze with my heart. The music was slow and magical. Holding out his hands, he offered himself to me, inviting me into his world. I told him I didn't know how, but that didn't matter to him. He held me close and convinced me he could teach me everything I needed to know. I willingly gave myself over to him, and for the remainder of that night there were no negative thoughts, no worries, and no one else but us. The music bound us in touch. There wasn't a moment that passed where I couldn't feel his warmth and the pounding of his heart pulsing through me. It was like breathing new air. He showed me how to follow, how to let him lead, and how to let my body go and find the rhythm in the music. The ladies joined us on the dance floor and Cristiano called on his friends to partner up with each of them, allowing all the dance lessons to begin.

Near the end of the night, he moved in closer, whispering into my ear. "Close your eyes," he requested artfully.

"I can't, there are too many people," I said aware of the crowd around me.

"No there is not. It is just you and me, together. Do you trust me?" he whispered again, irresistibly this time.

"Yes," I said melting into his words.

At that I closed my eyes and imagined us standing in the middle of an empty dance floor. But this wasn't my imagination—it was real. He held my body close and breathed deep into the nape of my neck. I could feel the warmth of his breath increasing my body temperature from the inside. We danced for what felt like a moment and seemed like forever.

When the music stopped, my body kept going. I opened my eyes to see him staring at me, smiling.

"That was the last song for the night, Maya."

Looking at him, I found no words to describe my feelings.

"I know, I feel the same way," he said matching my resistance of not wanting to move.

"I don't want this night to end."

"I have an early flight in the morning and you have things to do tomorrow. It is only six days until we see each other again," he said trying to comfort both of us.

"Goodbye Cristiano," I whispered wanting to make sure his name was the last word left on my lips.

Right then he grabbed me with great force. I could feel every muscle in his chest connecting to mine. It was like nothing I had ever experienced before. I thought he was going to kiss me, really kiss me, and my heart raced and the world stopped. But he didn't. His lips passed over mine, not touching, just breathing hot air into my lungs. He pulled his head back slowly, never breaking his gaze with mine, never releasing my body. He gently moved the hair from my eyes and ran the tip of his finger down the side of my body. I trembled under his touch. There was a single bead of sweat that had rolled from my temple, traveled down my cheek, and rested in the nape of my neck. He caught that single drop of me and placed it on his tongue.

"That taste, it is so familiar," he said with a quizzical look on his face. His embrace tightened and then he was gone, lost in the crowd, and into the night.

When I turned around, all the ladies were speechless. No one said anything about the goodbye until we got back into the limo.

"Did you see that? He was brilliant! The way he ran his finger down her neck?"

"Oh my God! I thought I was going to lose it right there."

"That was nothing! Did you see the way he took a bead of her sweat and tasted it?"

"Okay, that was pretty strange, even for me."

Interrupting the banter, Sachi piped in, "No, not really. It appeared that he was savoring her, embedding the memory, like you do with fine wine or food. Taste creates a muscle memory and he was exercising his new muscle."

We all stared at Sachi while taking in her intriguing philosophy. She looked away, a little embarrassed by the attention.

Petra, a very pragmatic woman, looked at me and said, "Well, I have to tell you, that was one of the best goodbyes I have ever seen. Can I use that in one of my ads when I get home?"

"Sure Petra. Having the most romantic moment of my life splayed on a corn chip ad would be great," I said sarcastically.

"Corn chips? What are you talking about? I'm thinking about a long distance ad or maybe diamonds," she said teasing me.

"Oh, that would be *much* better." I shook my head and laughed, adding, "Definitely a long distance ad!"

We all laughed so hard that our stomachs ached and permanent smiles sat happily on our faces.

Francesco took a longer route back to the hotel and began showing us the beauty of Lisbon. When we finally arrived, I climbed the stairs with Dalley at my side. The rest of the ladies were linked arm and arm behind us. Josie bid us all good night as she slipped off to the kitchen, to keep her date with the chef.

I entered our hotel room and collapsed on the bed after the most extraordinary two days of my life. The last thing I heard was the distant tapping of fingers on a keyboard.

12

The Letter

Cristiano

THE NIGHT AIR WAS WARM and when I stepped out onto the busy street, flashes of the previous twenty-four hours ran like a looped tape in my head. It had all seemed like a dream until I saw her standing there on the edge of the dance floor—waiting for *me*.

"She is real, and today did happen," I exclaimed, grabbing the front of my shirt and lifting it to my face. I held my breath for as long as I could, letting her strangely familiar scent trickle down my throat and fill my empty stomach. "That is real." My body shook.

As I stood frozen in my thoughts a car filled with my friends drove by, the sounds of honking and yelling breaking my loop of images. With resistance, I was snapped back into the present and threw on my well-worn façade.

"Cristiano, you playing next weekend?" Hugo yelled to me from the car.

"No, I've got plans," I said, suggesting that I was going to be *very* busy.

"Too bad for us. Hey where's the girl?" laughed one of my friends.

I retorted sarcastically, "Which one? I sent them both on their way. You know, I have things to do."

"Yah right!!! Losing your touch already? You're getting old Cristiano." My friends sped off, leaving a sour trail of laughter stuck on my palette.

Was that me? Was that who people thought I was?

"I'm not that person, am I?" I asked myself while I marched down the narrow streets, heading back to my apartment. It didn't take me long to find the truth, as the answer scorched my lips waiting for me to say it out loud. "Yes I am—or I have been, but I don't want to be that guy anymore." *It was time to become the man I was supposed to be, who I was raised to be.*

I had blamed the whole world for the pain in my life and in the end there was no one to blame but me. I could have done something to make it better, but I was too afraid. Instead I developed a persona that kept *me* hidden. But when I met *her*, somehow she made me believe I could face my fear, and that change was not only possible but necessary.

My march slowed to a stroll as I allowed myself to imagine a life where I could be happy, where I could trust the reflection I saw in the mirror and the woman standing beside me. When I walked through the front door of my apartment a familiar face greeted me.

"Why hello Cristiano, it has been weeks since I've seen you. Traveling lots? Playing at the club tonight?"

Mrs. Dutra had lived in the apartments since long before I was born. She pointed to my old guitar case in my left hand. "You should buy a new one. That one is falling apart."

She was right, the only thing that held my case together was tape and string, but I couldn't let it go. I'd had that case since I was a boy.

"Good evening, Mrs. Dutra. Yes, the club was busy tonight. I went straight from the airport over there to practice," I answered quickly, hoping to get away from the series of questions that were sure to follow.

"Where were you traveling this time?"

"Oh, I've been going back and forth to Canada, with a few other trips in between. I leave again tomorrow so I better get to bed," I said taking a step towards the stairs.

"You work too hard. You need a holiday, and you need to settle down. Your parents would have wanted that for you."

A long-standing ache rolled through my body when she mentioned my parents. "Thank you, Mrs. Dutra. I hope to someday. Good night."

She called out to me just as my foot hit the first step, "Cristiano, something came for you today. Let me get it."

Impatience prickled in my feet as I waited at the bottom of the stairs.

When she came out she was holding a large yellow envelope in one hand and a neatly wrapped bowl in the other. The bowl held her trademark Saturday night stew; the envelope was a mystery to me.

"Thank you for holding the mail Mrs. Dutra, but you don't have to feed me too!" I exclaimed, pushing the food back halfheartedly.

"Pah. It makes me happy. All my grandchildren are grown. I have no one to cook for but you. You don't want to make me sad do you?" she pouted.

"No, my Avó warned me about making women sad." We both laughed and I hugged her tightly.

Looking into my eyes she saw it. "Something is different."

"Yes, Mrs. Dutra. It is," I said reflectively, thinking about the last few hours of my life and how much everything had changed.

Placing the envelope under my arm, I took the dish in one hand, and my guitar in the other, and headed up the dimly lit staircase.

When I unlocked the door, stale air greeted me. After I opened the windows, the breeze of the night soon cleared the room and left me alone with my thoughts and my package. I looked around at my dull apartment and leaned my case up against my favorite surfboard. It was good to be home. I loved the fact that from the living room I could see the city from one side and catch a glimpse of the ocean on the other.

It had been a long time since I'd visited those beaches. Seeing them reminded me of my mom. She used to live for our beach days. She loved the way the sand felt between her toes, but for me it was all about the waves. There were times when she took me out of school and we would sit on the sand and let the roar of the ocean weave its way into our imaginations. She'd thought our outings were a secret, but my dad knew about the ocean adventures from the beginning. One day I saw him sweeping up the sand we had tracked into the apartment. All he asked me to do was to remind mom to sign me out of school properly next time. Later that night at supper he started a conversation about secrets and stated that everyone should hold a secret or two, just as long as they weren't hurting anyone. So, on our ocean days when we came home windswept and covered in sand, he hugged us both, laughed, and let my mom and me keep our special secret. After they died I stayed away from the water as long as I could, but when I was fourteen I was drawn back to the waves. I used to cut out of school and take the bus down to the ocean. The beach was quieter during the week, with mostly serious surfers. That's when I met Jack. He was a thirty-four-year-old American surfer who had set up shop on the beach offering surf lessons. When we met he only asked me one question. 'Do you wanna surf?'

I took to surfing like it was part of my DNA. I felt freer in the ocean than anywhere on earth. I escaped from school whenever I could, but always made it home in time for supper with Avó.

The scent of Mrs. Dutra's stew gently nudged me back to the present. I grabbed a water from the fridge and settled into my favorite chair by the window. Running my fingers over my name on the envelope, I felt a sense of urgency surge through the familiar handwriting; I broke the seal on the envelope and pulled out the papers.

It was a letter from Avó. I hadn't talked to her for twenty-six long months, but I had kept watch over her through my old friend Puro. She was healthy and well, but I was worried that her heart would break if she knew what kind of life I had been living: few rules, no room for self, no room for God, and no room for anything good. That was until Maya walked into my life.

Smoothing the pages out on my lap I took a breath and then dove in. I smiled as I realized that the entire letter was carefully crafted in English. When I was a child back at the cottage, my parents started teaching both of us how to read and write, but Avó pretended English was too hard to learn. My dad knew she would learn when she was ready, so he left the books neatly stacked on the dining room table. I knew she could understand the language, and speak a little, but write? She always liked to surprise people.

My Dear Cristiano,

You have been dancing in my thoughts for many days now. You have missed me; I can feel it. When I started this letter it was only to tell you I love you, but …

You know I have always believed that every person has a story and at some point, that story needs to be told. Well my boy, it is your time, and as I sat in our field near your tree, it began to flow. What came forth was not only the story you do know, but a few parts you do not. Please read it, and let it fill you with peace. Then maybe you will find the answers that you seek. I love you now and always and will see you next week.

Avó

"How does she do that? How does she know my heart and mind?" I whispered. "Yes, Avó I will see you next week."

I took a bite of supper, and then continued to read her letter. I wasn't sure what to expect, but I trusted Avó and knew that the package had arrived in my hands on *that* day for a reason:

How Cristiano Came to Be

Your mom and dad had tried for many years to have children, but their prayers were never answered, and it appeared that life was not meant to be.

For a long time their sadness became the ground where they planted all their dreams. It was green and healthy but lacked texture and depth. Somehow they moved through their lives, holding hands and loving each other and finding laughter in the simplest things, learning to be happy with what they had. They traveled around the world, collecting who knows what, but always collecting.

One day while shopping in a small market outside of Lisbon, your mother overheard some of the women talking about a young girl who had become pregnant a few villages over. She was curious, so she quietly asked around and found out who the pregnant girl was. The girl's name was Euphemia. She was just sixteen and had become pregnant by a boy of nineteen. They were in love, but keeping the baby was not an acceptable solution for either family.

Your mother found out that both families had decided the baby was to be given away and the teens were no longer allowed to see each other.

That night she went home not filled with quiet sadness anymore but touched with determination. She talked to Michel, your father, about approaching the girl's family to see if they had found someone to take the baby. Your father was nervous about such a conversation.

I am not sure if you remember, but he was a shy man. He trusted your mother though, and knew if this was something she wanted she would not stop until she had you in her arms. In her heart she knew you were already theirs. So your father went about the business of organizing everyone and set up a time for all of the families to meet.

I placed the letter down on the coffee table carefully, then stared out the window. Snapshots of memories I had created of my mom being pregnant with me were replaced by the face of an unknown young woman. *Who was she? Where did she come from? Who was my father? What was he like?* The questions whirled inside of my head. I was neither sad nor mad, I just felt different. I was adopted.

I chewed slowly, thinking about the truth that Avó had decided to share with me. Then with courage I picked up the letter and continued.

When your parents arrived at your birth mother's home, both families were present. Everyone was there but the son, your birth father. The front room was quiet and filled with loving parents, including yours. You must know your mom and dad loved you even before they knew you existed.

As the young lady entered the room, her belly and her quiet smile welcomed your mom. They connected in an instant. Rosa and Euphemia took one another's hands and never let go. They knew this child would always need to be loved in the greatest and most pure way. That afternoon your dad spoke at length with the two families. A decision was made, two handshakes were completed, and your mom and dad were to become your parents in just a few short weeks.

Rosa and Michel's world came to life, waiting for the call. Each day was more perfect than the last and they savored the feelings of anticipation and preparation, and all they would teach you. Bread was baked, quilts were made, and everyday your mom walked in my fields, thankful you were on your way.

Tears streamed down my face as I read the story and could see my mom walking in the fields. I let the tears flow just as she would have wanted. "I miss you so much, Mom. I know you're out there, I can feel you watching over me. I wish you could have told me about the adoption yourself though. I have so many questions."

Curious about the next part of my life, I returned to the letter.

Then the day came. There was rain and thunder and a storm that matched no other, but for your mom and dad, it was perfect. In the middle of the night they received the call that Euphemia had gone into labor. You were ready.

As the lightning flashed around them and rain poured down, their smiles and hearts lit the way in the dark night. On February 27, their son Cristiano was born. You stayed with Euphemia for three days, with your new mom at her side, as she did not want to miss a moment with you. On your third day, it was time for you to say goodbye to the mother who gave birth to you. Your mom left you that night so that Euphemia could spend one last evening with you sleeping in her arms.

Your mom and dad had moved in with me right after they had agreed to adopt you. They owned the apartment in town already but wanted you to be in the country and for you to know me, your Avó, right from the beginning.

We hardly slept that night, running around the house, moving and cleaning things, making it perfect for you. Your father had carved you a crib, finishing it just that night. He was no wood craftsman, but his heart led his hands and the finished product was filled with his love.

The next day we all returned to the hospital, even before the birds started to sing. But there were no birds needed to greet us that day for as we walked down the hall we heard a lullaby being sung ever so gently. The song was coming from Euphemia's room. When we entered we saw a young man holding you in his arms, singing.

'Hello Rosa, Michel, Avó. I would like to introduce you to Marcos, Cristiano's father.' Euphemia said his name with such love. She and I had met a few times at the house before you were born, but we'd spoken little, we hadn't needed to. She was just happy you would have an Avó.

Marcos shone, just like you. He gestured towards your mom with the intention of handing you over, but she shook her head and told him to keep singing for a bit longer. You were awake, eyes wide open, lying peacefully in his arms, listening.

'I shouldn't even be here, our parents will be very angry,' Marcos whispered.

Your mom walked over to you both and gently put her arm on his. 'The only person that matters right now is Cristiano. Tell him that you love him. Then he will always know that the two of you loved him, and each other, and did the best for him. When he is old enough, we will tell him about you. He will know where he came from and know that he was loved deeply by both of you.'

Marcos continued to sing. His voice was like an angel filling the empty halls of the hospital, and each heart in the room. Your mom and dad hoped that someday his music would be yours. I am sad that they never had a chance to hear you sing and play.

Marcos handed you back to Euphemia. She wept as she said goodbye to you for the last time, and your mom wept as you were placed in her arms. Both sets of tears fell over you. You laughed and cried at the same time. I believe your heart was set in place in that moment: great sadness and joy, forever mixed and embedded in who you were.

Our home was small, but when you arrived it grew in ways that seemed impossible. There was more joy and laughter in our little home than I could have imagined. Your parents rarely left your side during your first year, never wanting to miss a moment. They watched you learn to walk and run and stood back with hesitation when you started to climb. At first they wanted to hover, to make sure you were safe, but I encouraged them to give you some room to make mistakes. How else would you learn?

When you were two, your mom and dad started traveling again and working at the university. Your mom was very close to quitting as she found it almost impossible to be away from you, but your parents were a teaching team, and they had to go together. So I looked after you; well we looked after each other. Over the years we played many games. One of your favorites was laughter jars. We spent hours filling jars with laughter, sealing them and putting them in the pantry. When your mom and dad came home they would ask 'So Cristiano, what did you and Avó do while we were away?'

'Oh we climbed trees and filled jars with super smiles and roaring laughter,' you would explain. You made me label all the jars so that we would never forget which one was which.

Your dad asked you one day, 'Cristiano what are you and Avó going to do with all the laughter? You have so much now, maybe it will go bad,' he said teasing you.

Your four-year-old smile disappeared and you put your hand on your dad's shoulder and said, 'Dad, this is magic laughter, it never goes bad. We can use this forever and ever, and someday we may need it.' We all cried happy tears that day.

Those first four years were magical. No one little boy could have received so many different kinds of love from three people, but when you were just about five, your mom and dad recognized that you needed to be closer to a good school and other children your age. The day you left and moved to the apartment in Lisbon, I packed up half of our laughter jars and sent them with you. You cried and cried as we said goodbye.

A flash of memory surged into my thoughts and I remembered Avó adding five of my favorites: three roaring laughter and two super smiles.

I'd never opened them. I looked over at my bookshelf. The only thing that it still held were those five jars. I walked over and grabbed one marked super smiles. While opening it, I started to laugh.

"We must have mislabeled that one Avó," I called out to her, and then returned to the letter.

Life jumped and whirled for you and your family during the school terms, and we did not see each other a lot. But during the summers your parents' travels increased and visits with me became a cornerstone in both our lives.

When you were seven though, everything changed for both of us.

I knew what was going to be written on the following few pages and I thought about skipping them, but I had to read it for Avó and for myself. I needed to face the past, and the pain that went with it. So I continued.

Cristiano, you have spent so many years searching for answers to a sorrow that was never meant to be a question.

It was a warm summer afternoon and you were out in the garden running free and climbing trees when an unfamiliar car pulled up. At first I thought the man had come to pick something up from me, but that was not the case.

My body tensed like I was preparing for a car accident, while memories of that day flooded my mind. Although I had spent my life trying to erase that moment, there it was; there was no running from it anymore.

I remember you sitting in the tree and looking curiously over at the car. I greeted the man in the doorway, then stood and listened to him as he delivered our fate in just a few simple words. 'There has been an accident, I'm sorry but your son and daughter-in-law were killed in a plane crash outside of Cairo.'

I swayed for just a moment, but thankfully the door frame kept me standing.

My body stiffened and I started to feel sick, as the letter took me back to the worst day of my life.

You ran from the garden yelling my name, knowing that something was wrong. But by the time you got to me, the man was gone, and I was frozen and grey. You helped me inside. At first I said nothing, I couldn't, I had no words. The only thing I could do was bake. I still remember your questions.

'Avó, what is it? What did that man want?' you asked, filled with fear. 'Fetch me the millstone and the wheat, I need to teach you how to make my bread.'

'Avó no one knows how to make your special bread,' you responded with rising concern.

'You are the only person I trust enough who I can teach this to,' I said, hardly able to get the words out.

'What about ...?' You attempted to ask. But I interrupted you as I couldn't bear to hear you say his name.

'The only one.' I ended the conversation.

You did what you were told. We spoke little but worked hard into the night, grinding and mixing, kneading the dough and letting it rest. In between when the dough was rising, you lay your head on my lap drifting in and out of restless sleeps. It was early into the morning when we took the last of the loaves out of the stone oven in the summer garden. I held one loaf in my hands and you cried out to me.

'Avó, put that down. You're going to burn yourself!'

But I held it firm, staring at you, looking so deep into your eyes. No laughter jars would help us that day.

The bowl of stew dropped to the floor as I covered my ears trying to block out the sounds of Avó's grief and the uncried tears of my past. Fear struck me in my heart, the pain bringing me to my knees.

I felt a swell building inside and prepared myself for the unstoppable wave. Then it hit. Twenty years of tears gushed from the bottom of my soul and engulfed me. The pain was no less than it had been all those years ago, but for the first time I cried. I cried for my mom and dad and for me. I'd lost a piece of myself when they'd died and thought I could never be whole again. I was wrong.

Soaked to the skin in tears and memories, the wave receded and the sobbing slowed.

What happened next surprised me. I had always thought that if I cried for them, they would disappear, I would disappear, but we didn't. The tears gave me permission to invite them into my memories and in their own way to become part of my future. I ran my fingers across the words that had just changed my life, feeling a sense of resolution that now anything was possible.

You watched me, as I lay on the ground holding the hot loaf of bread to my chest. Then all the pieces came together and your eyes went blank: the strange visit, the bread making, the hours of silence, and the broken me on the ground.

Your parents were dead and you knew it.

I tried to reach out to you, but my hands were frozen in grief. You walked over to the loaves that were cooling on the table and took one in both your hands, and began to walk into the field. It was still dark; I couldn't move. You ended up at your favorite tree, and then climbed. It was two days before you came down.

I never came to get you, but I watched you carefully from the garden. I believed you had to come down on your own or maybe I was being selfish and just needed to be alone. I'm sorry if you needed me and I was not there.

Your mom and dad had been killed in a plane crash, and the visit to my house became permanent. You never went back to your home in Lisbon again, and we began to re-build our world, one loaf of bread at a time.

I carefully placed the unfinished letter on top of the coffee table, stood up and walked over to the shelf of jars. I picked up the now empty super smile one and opened it. "I love you too," I said gently. Then I sealed it up again.

On the outside of the jar I scratched off super smiles and wrote, *Open in Case of Emergency (A Dose of Love and Truth)*.

Maple Seeds from Home

Maya

THE MORNING SUN DANCED ON my sheets as I lay there, eyes wide open. I rolled over and saw Christopher peeking out of my purse, waiting patiently for me. "Yes, that would be a good way to start my day."

Sunday, August 20th

The last two days have felt like a dream, but I know it wasn't. I'm here and he's real. He tasted a bead of my sweat last night. I can honestly say that has never happened to me before. Sachi had a theory that he was embedding a flavor memory into his taste buds or something like that. In short, she thought he was savoring me so he wouldn't forget me. I'm not sure about the savoring part but I do know that my knees almost crumbled on the dance floor when he did it. I can't imagine what I'm going to do when he actually kisses me.

What a night. I think I could fall in love with this man. Ha Ha!! It's crazy, I know, but when he looks at me it's like he's surprised and relieved all at the same time. Right now, I'm somewhere between not sure what's happening and completely understanding it. It's like being offered a gift that you never asked for, and when you open it, it's exactly what you needed; let me rephrase that, what I needed.

When I won this contest, I thought it would be a great way to escape from my life. Maybe it's more than that, maybe it's the path to my life?

JOY! That's what Dad instructed me to find on this trip, and I've found some of that already.

Oh, that is the coolest; I can hear the Cathedral bells ringing. Oh crap!! Breakfast!! Ahhhh I'm late ... again.

Until Later,
Maya

Dalley was still sleeping. "Get up, we're late again. Breakfast is going to be served soon," I nudged her.

She rolled over without opening her eyes. "Don't worry Maya. They'll survive without us," she whispered groggily.

I wasn't going to be late again. Jumping up, I headed for the shower, then paused in Dalley's direction. "Do you want to shower first?" I asked as I saw her starting to stir.

"No, that's okay. I want to hang out here for a bit. Not much of a morning person," she croaked out.

After showering I dressed quickly. "Are you sure you don't want me to wait for you?" I asked, trying to get her going.

"Yes, yes, Maya, contrary to popular belief, breakfast is not everyone's most important meal of the day. I'll be down for a coffee in a little while," she said burying herself under the covers.

Her cranky tone was not going to take anything away from my great morning, so I decided to hurry up and leave her be. "Okay then, see you later."

I left the room bouncing out the door, excited about the evening that was, and the day that was yet to be.

Dalley

"If we are going to be roommates for the next four weeks, that girl has to leave me alone in the mornings. She is quite entertaining though."

I continued to laze around in bed until my curiosity got the better of me. I had stayed up late writing my first article for the paper. It was more like a story though, recounting my adventure of the first couple days of the trip. I wanted to see if Joe, my boss, liked it. That never usually mattered to me, but before I left, he'd told me that the interest in my online articles was waning and that if I couldn't boost readership in my markets, my feature would be scrubbed. So I guess I was trying to impress him.

I looked over at the laptop. I had mail!

To: Dalley

Subject: Mile High Maybe?

I loved it Dalley. All you need to do is a quick edit and add a bit more about the two love birds on the plane and the model. That will really get people reading. Oh, I want you to reformat your writing and turn the piece into a blog. I came up with the name Price's Portugal and have the site already set up for you. You can get started tomorrow and upload the edited blog. Just send me the re-write to review first.

You had me hooked at them joining the mile-high club!

I was furious. How dare he tell me what to do? I was not going to write any more about Maya and Cristiano.

To: Joe

Subject: NOT!!!

Go to hell Joe!! That name is lame and screw your blog. Oh, and let's be clear, my writing, my adventures. I'm not writing a romance novel for you. My readers have always wanted to read my stories.

I pressed 'send' jamming my finger into the keyboard pretending that I was poking Joe in the chest, trying to get my point across. I felt invigorated. I jumped up and ran over to the bathroom putting thoughts of shoes and shopping bags ahead of Joe. After the shower, I heard my phone ping.

The blue cloud only read:

READ YOUR EMAIL NOW!!!

To: Dalley

Subject: Oh Yes you will!

Dalley, you don't have to be so rude. Price's Portugal stays. I like the way it sounds. The blog is non-negotiable and remember you work for me. Like I said, I need a rewrite of the first blog by tonight. I want this posted by your time tomorrow.

Oh if you haven't figured it out, you don't really have a choice. Have fun in Portugal!

Taking a breath, I pushed 'reply'. When I think back now I wonder why I didn't just tell him to shove it, but for some reason, the idea had started to grow on me. As long as it was on my terms and not his, I thought that it might actually work to get me some recognition. I knew that I might have to bend my rules a bit and cross a few lines, but no one would get hurt. It was just a story on a blog.

To: Joe

Subject: So sorry to offend!!

Fine, but honestly Joe, it's a blog. I'm not letting you edit my blog. Send me the link and password. My first entry will be posted by tomorrow morning.

I pushed 'send' and a perverse wave of excitement began to build, like watching a tsunami roll towards me while sitting at a beachside café.

Maya

"Thank you for joining us, Miss Wells. Late night?" The chef called out to me as I buzzed into the dining room.

"I'm so sorry," I squeaked. "Please don't let me interrupt."

He cleared his throat, with a little chuckle drifting in at the end. "As I was saying, this morning's breakfast is made up of a variety of cross-cultural dishes. I thought I would make something different and fun for all of you."

Josie laughed out loud like a schoolgirl, even though he didn't say anything funny. It was obvious that the chef and Josie had connected the night before, as they kept stealing glances, and smiling at one another. It was very sweet.

All of us looked over the tantalizing buffet of foods that had been prepared. I was not sure where to start, but my stomach grumbled and told me I had better get to it. Maggie, Ellen, and Sachi tried a little bit of everything, whereas Petra stuck to fruit and yogurt. Jade was a total sweet tooth, taking every pastry that she could fit onto her plate. And Josie, well, she just picked at the food, preoccupied with other thoughts. I myself was drawn to the chicken dumplings wrapped in some kind of pastry, as I wanted to try savory over sweet. Everything was outstanding. The chef was right—a little bit of something for everyone. As people were taking their last bites, I dropped my napkin on the floor. Leaning over to pick it up, I noticed that Maggie and Ellen were sporting running shoes.

Popping back up and pointing at their shoes, I asked, "Where are you guys off to this morning?"

"Oh, we've already gone and come back. Our internal clocks had us up before 6:00, so we thought we would make the most of a beautiful morning in Lisbon and go for a walk. We met Petra along the way, but she was already coming back from a run. We thought *we* were early risers," Maggie chuckled.

"Ah, don't worry," Petra said in a relaxed tone. "I'll whip you guys into shape. In my regular life, I'm up at 5:00 a.m. every day and finished working out before I go to the office. Yesterday was the first day in six years that I didn't go for a run in the morning. I was going a little squirrelly by the time we got back from the club. I contemplated going running last night, but when I texted my husband, he yelled at me with capital letters, and told me to go to bed."

Everyone laughed, as Petra had a way of making even the simplest story fun to listen to.

"So what are you all doing today?" I asked.

"I don't know about the rest of you, but I'm going to shop," Dalley chimed in with excitement. I turned and she was standing there, coffee in one hand, and a pastry in the other.

Everyone nodded in agreement that a little shopping *was* in order—even Jade looked positive about that suggestion.

The chef noticed that we were finishing up and walked over to the table. "Remember, the limo leaves for Netuno at 4:00 p.m. sharp."

He glanced over at Josie and continued, "I promise to come and visit you at Netuno during your stay. I will be up there in about two weeks to help judge one of the weekly challenges. Let me know if you need anything."

Before we knew it, the morning was half gone and it was time to go shopping. Dalley and I grabbed the first taxi we could find and headed off into the city. The sights and sounds of Lisbon were mesmerizing. Rolling down the taxi window, I began to imagine what life must have been like there many years ago. Then when the taxi stopped abruptly at a light, I bumped my head on the window frame and was brought back. The streets were busier than I thought they would be for a Sunday, but something was different about them. At first, I couldn't figure out what it was, but then it hit me. There was not a pair of jeans or runners to be seen anywhere, and no one was wearing flip flops, or tank tops except for tourists. I felt incredibly underdressed. The women of Lisbon were tastefully clad in fancy shoes and beautiful dresses; and the lack of yoga pants and fleece was staggering. That was when my mission of the day struck me.

"Dalley, I need your help."

"What kind of help? I think you used up your one therapist ticket I keep for emergencies," she teased.

"No, not that kind of help. It's my wardrobe. I'm in desperate need of a few pieces of—something," I groaned.

"Maya, you have come to the right woman. You should see my closets at home."

"Closets?" I stuttered, immediately worried.

"Do you promise to try on anything I pull off the rack?" she asked seriously.

"Well, within reason," I countered.

"No, you need to promise."

I laughed, throwing caution to the wind. "Okay then, I promise— anything," I said, sounding almost confident.

It didn't take Dalley long to find me some of the most beautiful *and* outrageous clothing I had ever seen. We tried on and bought more clothes in one day than I thought possible. My confidence grew as the day progressed. That was, until we stepped through the doors of a little boutique called *Pop!* They had everything for someone else and nothing for me. I took a quick look around, and then stood close to the door, waiting for Dalley; however, she came running up to me with a little black dress and told me I had to try it on. My confidence shrank just looking at it on the hanger.

"Dalley, I don't like clothes like that." Worry coated my words.

"You promised me you would try on everything."

"And I have," I pleaded.

"Yes, so far everything has been lovely and safe."

"Everything?" I rebutted.

"Well, maybe not everything, but at least the things I let you buy. Let's go a little shocking, just a little," she squeaked, rubbing her fingers together.

"Yes, I promised," I said with a relenting tone. "Well this dress is mostly black, at least where there is fabric!"

Dalley cried with laughter. I assumed she thought my modesty was something she could cure. She'd pushed the envelope with the shirt she'd made me wear to the club, but this dress was in a whole different category, like 'Hello, look at me, look at all of me please!'

I went into the changing room and slipped the dress on. Surprisingly, it fit and wasn't too tight. It snugged close to some parts and flowed in others. It was low and for the first time in my life, I was showing cleavage. Taking a breath, I stepped out of the changeroom.

"Well, what do you think?" I asked, closing my eyes, not sure if I wanted her to like it or hang it back up.

"I think that under all that fleece, there's a beautiful woman just waiting to break out. Mind you, a woman who needs a good push up bra and a new pair of boots," she giggled, then got serious. "Well what do *you* think?"

"Hmm … honestly, I think I look great! I've never tried on anything like this before in my life, and it makes me feel beautiful, like I could fit in here with all the women walking down the street." Then I sank when I looked at the price tag.

Dalley caught my reaction. "What's the problem?"

"The price, I can't afford this."

"You can't afford *not* to buy this dress. Think of it as an investment."

I looked again in the mirror and saw a glimpse of an almost fashionable woman. "Well, I'm not sure where I'm going to flaunt this frock, but you're right. I need to have it for so many reasons," I said making my decision.

I returned to the changing room and went to put on my comfy pants and light fleece but decided against it. Instead I dove into one of my new bags and pulled out a great outfit that I'd picked up at one of the other stores.

When I came out, Dalley snickered. "And so, it has begun. Down with stretch pants and fleece," she said in a booming voice.

"Well at least until I get home and the snow starts," I joked. I'd never had a friend like Dalley. My thoughts flashed to Beth, wondering if she would like her. Of course she would, Beth liked everyone.

I walked up to the register and reached into my wallet and reluctantly pulled out my credit card. There was a little sticky note on the front of the card, written by my mom.

Hi Dear, Thought you might use your card at some point. I came into a little cash and put $2873.65 onto your card for fun money. So have fun! Love Mom.

I carefully peeled the note off the card and placed it inside my wallet and smiled, wondering where *this* mom had been hiding for so many years. Then I tried to figure out where she'd gotten the money from. It didn't take me too long to remember that a few days after the non-wedding, she came into my room and quietly removed my wedding dress from the closet while I was lying on my bed. I know there was a no-return policy on the dress, but somehow she must have convinced them to take it back, because that was the exact price we had paid.

"What is it, Maya?" Dalley asked.

"Oh, just my mom. She's my shopping angel today. She left me a little gift."

"You're so lucky. My mom would just as soon strip the money from my wallet as leave me a gift."

I paused reflectively.

We headed back out into the sunshine in search of the perfect footwear for my dress. During our travels we came upon a tiny, very exclusive looking French lingerie shop. I shook my head, but Dalley made me go in. "When was the last time you had a beautiful piece of lingerie?" she asked abruptly.

"Never!"

"Not even for your wedding?" she asked with surprise in her voice.

"Not even for that," I said sheepishly.

"Well, let's get started then!"

She had me try on things that I would never wear. Peek-a-boo bras, things with lace, and others with so much wire I wasn't sure what to do.

Then sailing over the changeroom door came the most luxurious piece of deep purple satin I had ever touched. It was encrusted with little jewels and velvet ties. I was in love. I slipped it on and started doing up the ties with some challenge. She could hear me struggling. Not being able to stand it a minute longer, she bounded into the room and lent me her hands. "Oh my God, look at you. It's gorgeous. You're perfect. Here let me help you with that," she said, leaning in and pulling on the ties.

"Thank you. Far from perfect," I muttered under my breath.

"Are you kidding me—just because you're not a size two doesn't mean that you're not petite, and beautiful and sexy," she said, defending me to myself.

"Oh, I hate that word." I shivered.

"What ... sexy?" Dalley laughed. "No seriously, you are perfect the way you are. You don't have to change anything. You just have to wear the right pieces to help you feel more confident."

"Are you sure you're a journalist?" I paused. "I might take you for a fashion advisor."

"Hmm, could be a new career, but not yet. Maya, you have to buy this and at least three sets of lingerie before you leave here. You have the money. And *that* one is going to look and feel great under your new dress," she said pointing at the satin piece I was wearing.

Looking in the mirror, I did feel striking, although a little awkward with Dalley cheering me on. "Okay, I'll do it."

In the end, I purchased three new matching bra and panty sets along with the bustier and left the peek-a-boo number hanging in the change-room. She picked it up and threw it on my pile.

"Not practical," was all I said.

She laughed and shrugged her shoulders. "Who needs practical? Does Cristiano look like a *practical man* to you?"

I then added it to my purchases for the day.

We stepped out into the sun. "So what's next?" she asked. "Ready to keep going?"

"I think I'm done for the day," I said sighing.

"Oh, that's too bad. Do you mind if I go back to those shoe stores that we missed a few blocks over?"

"No, go right ahead. I'll stop in at the café down the street that we passed. I wanted to do a little writing anyway."

"Sounds great! Wish me good boot luck."

"Dalley, I don't think you need my luck. You make your own luck happen!"

"That is true." She smiled and almost skipped off towards the stores.

"She's such a funny bird, as Aunt Olive would say." I touched my pendant. "Thanks, Aunt Olive," I whispered into the wind.

On my way to the café I crossed the street and looked up at the old buildings. *People have been crossing these streets for hundreds of years*, I thought as my feet touched the cobblestone. I felt so happy to be part of that street's history, even if it was only in a little way. Taking an outdoor seat at the café, I pulled out Christopher and Athena, and then looked at the menu. "Coffee—no, tea. Well, as they say, when in Rome …"

When the waiter returned with my special coffee, he brought me a little snack. I said thank you and smiled, intrigued by the gift. I laughed when I looked down and saw my new cleavage. "Boys," I mused, and then uncapped Athena and started:

> *Sunday, August 20 at the café in Lisbon*
> *The air tastes different here. Right now I am sitting downtown at the coolest coffee shop. Dalley's shopping, but I'm done for the day. Shopping was fun. Mom's gift was such a lovely surprise. I'll have to send her a note.*

I think my favorite part of today though is right now. Buying the clothes was awesome and the lingerie—well, that was an adventure, but sitting here, taking a breath ... it feels like the real gift.

It's been twenty-four hours since we arrived in Portugal and my insides are still buzzing ... Wow what just touched my shoulder? I can't believe it, it's a maple seed. You know, the ones that look like helicopter wings when they float down from the trees. It reminds me of home. Let me take a picture.

The wind has picked up and I am holding your pages down so that they don't blow over. My hair is flying around and I am sure that if Cristiano were here right now, he would try and gently move the hair out of my eyes or leave it, I think he likes it both ways.

Where was I? I'm sitting here and for the first time since arriving, thoughts of home are trickling in. It was inevitable that my brain would find its way back to thinking about the messy life I left behind. How did I let things go that far in my life? Hmm. Maybe that's not actually the question I need to be asking anymore. Maybe the question is, so what do I do now?

I think I'm on the right track. At least I am asking the questions? I have to believe that the answers will come when they are supposed to. I feel like I'm in the right place for good things to happen. I have to trust that. Oh here comes Dalley and she has at least three, no four more bags.

Just finishing my surprisingly lovely cup of coffee and my delicious snack. Here's to new-found cleavage. Ha! Ha!
Maya

"Maya!" Dalley yelled, running up the street. "You should see the boots I found! Shopping always makes me feel better."

"Why, were you upset about something?"

"No, I'm not upset about anything. It's just that finding the right boots, always makes me feel even better than I already do," she stuttered clumsily.

"Oh, I bought you shoes to go with your dress, they are *perfect*. No need to thank me. We are the same size. Oh, we better get back to the hotel. The limo will be there to pick us up in forty-five minutes."

As luck would have it, a taxi zoomed up the street and stopped in front of the café. The two of us jumped in with all our packages, laughing and covered in color, our friendship sealed with receipts.

When we arrived back at the hotel, we rushed up to our room to collect our suitcases. I looked out the window over Lisbon. My heart raced as the next part of my adventure was about to begin.

14

The Road to Somewhere

Maya

WHEN FRANCESCO ARRIVED AT THE hotel with the limo, he frowned intensely at all the additional shopping bags piled on the curb beside each woman in the group. "Hmm, I may have to leave a couple of you behind," he joked half-heartedly.

Dalley feigned weakness, falling onto a bench. "I won't be separated from my new boots," she cried out dramatically.

He shook his head, entertained by her antics, and then began his plans for the most efficient packing job ever. "Well ladies, let's see how we do. To start, please take your most important parcels into the SUV and buckle yourselves in. At least then I can be assured that I haven't left any of you behind. Puro would never forgive me."

It was as if everyone's luggage had given birth to a series of shopping bags, leaving him few options. By the time we were all buckled in, there wasn't much room for us to move as no one wanted to leave their newfound treasures to the trunk or to chance.

Francesco looked into the back seat and shook his head. "Well, we almost made it. But even with my amazing packing skills, I cannot fit the last two sets of luggage in. I have to call a friend to help us out. But do not worry, he will be close behind." He looked happy with his solution.

"Argh! Humph!" was all I heard coming from the other side of the limo.

The sound was like a disgruntled rhino that had missed a meal or something, but it was only Jade craning her head out the window to see if it was *her* luggage that had been left behind.

"Jade," Sachi said gently, "You and I were down early today. I am sure our luggage was packed first."

"Well I hope so, but who knows considering the debacle this trip has been so far!" She spat her words out with an acid tone that leaked all over Sachi's attempt at kindness.

The latest Jade moment was not lost on our group, as we all looked at one another, shocked again by her never-ending rudeness. I had a strange feeling though that when it came to Jade, the worst was yet to come.

Dalley and I quickly realized that we were the last to arrive with our luggage, which possibly meant it was us who could be wearing our Sunday outfits on Monday morning. In the end it was our luggage that sat on the curb as we drove away.

The trip to Netuno was filled with a quiet calm. Some of us slept, while others read. As we drove farther out of town, the simple and elegant land of rural Portugal unfurled in front of us. Along the way we saw old castles and broken-down battlements. I found myself lost in thought, wondering about how many hearts were shattered and left in the dirt of those battlefields.

The hour and a half passed like minutes. It was not until I noticed the landscape change again that I wondered if we were getting close. As I looked out the window, all I could see were rows of grapevines, elegantly espaliered against ancient, weathered posts. Seeing the vines in the late afternoon sun ported me back to my childhood. Before I realized it, my thoughts spilled out like a jar of marbles rolling over the limo floor. "My father had always dreamed of seeing his vines grow into such a magnificent garden," I said reflectively. I could feel the attention in the limo shift to me as all the marbles settled into place. I closed my eyes hoping that when I opened them again, no one would be paying attention. But the silence in the limo was deafening, and my news appeared too interesting for the group to let go of. I could feel the questions coming. It was Jade who spoke first.

"Your family owns a vineyard?" she asked with doubt. My head shot up in response to her disbelieving tone.

"Not anymore," I said abruptly. The pause that followed was long and quiet enough that I knew I had to say something else. "When I was a child my father bought a vineyard in the Okanagan. We had it for about five years before he had to sell." Unsuccessfully, I tried to end the conversation.

"Why did your family sell the vineyard, Maya?" Petra asked with genuine interest.

"It's complicated."

"I understand. Everything in life has its complication," she said, then nodded her head, indicating that she understood. "Tell me, what does a man do after he sells his dream?"

"You go back to being what you were before. He was a lawyer, corporate," I answered flatly.

"Maya, why don't you come back later and do some photos of the vines for your dad? I bet he would love that," Maggie interjected.

"Thank you, I think I will."

When Francesco turned the corner, the final bend in the road offered everyone in the vehicle something more interesting to focus on: Netuno.

The vineyard was nestled into an enchanting valley and the scene from the top of the hill was breathtaking.

"I always love this moment," Francesco said, as he slowed his drive down so that we could take in the full beauty of the scenery. The inn sat at the bottom of the hill, with an olive grove at its back and grapevines growing in every other direction. It looked like a 19th century estate home from the deep south of the United States. It left me both breathless with its splendor and a little curious about how it came to be.

"Oh my," Ellen gasped. "I never imagined. My husband would never take me to a place like this in a million years."

Josie leaned over and patted her lap. "But you're here now, and we are going to make sure that you have a wonderful time," she said giving her a little poke in the ribs.

Random thoughts about friendship, home, and my old life danced through my mind. The last three months, the endless days in the garden, not talking to anyone that I didn't have to—it was like I had been frozen, but somehow everything else kept moving and growing around me. It wasn't just the non-wedding though; it went deeper than that. I'd been stuck for a long time, wading through a life that I didn't choose, and missing out on the life that I had been given. I'm not sure if it was seeing the vineyard, or just having a moment to think, but something touched my heart. The trip, the winery—it was the perfect setting for change. It was time to take responsibility for who I had been and who I wanted to become.

When Francesco rolled to a stop and put the limo in park, I slowly climbed out, expecting nothing, and enjoying everything. The veranda around the inn was furnished with comfy chairs and modern tables, adorned with snacks and bottles of wine just waiting to be tasted. Standing proud and handsome at the foot of the stairs was a gentleman who appeared to be in his early fifties.

"Good evening," he said in a soft, warm voice. "I hope you had a pleasant drive, and that Francesco took good care of you. My name is Puro. I manage the inn and the vineyard here at Netuno and will be caring for you ladies throughout your stay here. If you need anything, it is my job to find it for you. Congratulations on winning this contest. Please take your time settling into your rooms, and then at your leisure come join me for a glass of wine. Bedrooms will be shared, but each person has their own bathroom. Please discuss amongst yourselves who you would like to share a room with, and then let Carmo at the front desk know. Bento will collect your bags and take them to your rooms. Supper will be served at 8:00 tonight and at that time you will meet your hosts, the owners of Netuno Vineyards."

Dalley and I looked at each other, confirming with a head nod that sharing a room together was a good idea. Everyone else went with the same roommates they had been with the night before. I felt a twinge of sadness for Sachi, knowing she'd have to room with Jade, but she remained stoic.

We all signed in at the front desk and headed to our rooms to freshen up. Dalley and I had no luggage, but she had her boots, and I had Christopher and Athena. We were good, at least until tomorrow morning.

When I walked into the room, my mouth dropped open, as every part of it was perfect. The walls were painted an engaging warm grey, with crisp white accents. Fresh delicate flowers were arranged in vases throughout the room, filling the space with the scent of freesia and other flowers that I didn't recognize. My mom would have known; she had a knack for remembering those kinds of things.

The beds were veiled with canopies, creating a sense of luxury and pure beauty. I made my way around the room and headed over to the balcony.

"Wow, this is bigger than my first apartment. I feel like royalty. I'm not sure leaving is going to be an option," I said flirting with a dangerous idea.

The balcony door was open and the sheer curtains were billowing in the warm, early evening wind. Dalley walked past me without even hesitating.

"Isn't this place amazing?"

"Yes, Maya. It's wonderful," she said sarcastically.

"Dalley, give me a break, I've only seen places like this in magazines." I took a breath and stepped out onto the balcony and wrapped myself in the sheers like I used to do with our old heavy curtains back at our vineyard home.

"Maya, what are you doing?" she asked with a hint of judgment.

I paused with embarrassment. "When we were still living at the vineyard, playing pretend was one of my favorite things to do. I would stand on the back porch and open the sliding glass door. Then I'd take the curtains and wrap myself in them, imagining that I was a king ruling over my kingdom of peaches and grapes."

"Don't you mean the queen?" Dalley queried adding a little humor to my serious tale.

"No, I thought that a king would have more power. I believed that the vineyard and the orchards were the one place where I could make all the rules and no one could tell me any different."

Before I knew it, I began to share memories about my orchard days. Dalley leaned against the balcony rail, not saying a word. She was right when she described herself as a good listener. Once I started telling my story, I didn't want to stop.

"My parents bought the vineyard when I was just three. My earliest memories are intertwined with lazy days wandering through the grapevines, and playing hide-and-seek with my dad. In the springtime, we'd run through the orchard while the pink blossoms floated down around us like dreams falling from the sky. I loved those days." My eyes welled as I looked over someone else's kingdom.

She sidled up close to me. "So you've found your way back to the vineyard. What are you going to do now?" she asked with a playful smile.

I sighed as I ran my hands through the sheers again, staring out at the never-ending fields.

"A glass of wine seems like a good place to start. Don't you agree?"

15

Netuno

Maya

DALLEY RAN BACK INTO THE room and claimed her bed by diving through the shimmering fabric that hung from the canopy. I followed her in and placed my purse and a few parcels on the other bed. From my window I had a perfect view of the vineyard and the olive grove. I couldn't ask for anything more.

"What about that glass of wine?" I reminded Dalley as she lay sprawled on her bed.

"Yes, what about that wine?" The two of us freshened up and then made our way downstairs.

Stepping out onto the veranda, Josie and Petra had arrived ahead of us and were already laughing up a storm and entertaining Puro with their stories. Maggie and Ellen were fast on our heels, and somehow Sachi was already sitting down, with five tasting glasses in front of her, ready to start. Dalley and I poured a glass of something red and joined in to listen to one of Josie's travel tales.

Carmo, the young lady who was at the front desk when we arrived, came outside looking distressed.

"Excuse me, Puro. May I speak with you?" she asked with urgency. He stepped over to deal with her concern. "One of the contest winners is very upset. She wants her own room, and I'm not sure what to do?"

"Don't worry, Carmo," he said, patting her shoulder. "This is all part of running the inn. I'll take care of the situation. You go into the kitchen and get some more wine for our guests." He turned to us with a dashing grin. "It appears that duty calls. Please excuse me. Enjoy yourselves and I will be back momentarily. But in the meantime, I think my new friend Sachi has the right idea. I encourage you to join her."

With a wine glass in her hand, Sachi looked up and smiled. Then Josie grabbed the two bottles that she and Petra were drinking from and added them to Sachi's table.

"Well now, this is the way to do it," Josie chuckled.

"So, how many different kinds of wine do we have to taste?" Petra asked.

"Looks like eight all together!" Dalley chirped in, clearly excited about the task ahead of us.

"One for each of us," Ellen added picking up the corkscrew. "Which one is next?"

"It's very important. When you taste so many wines that you must only sip, swirl, and spit," Sachi explained with a serious tone.

"Spit? Are you crazy?" asked Josie. "Sip, swirl, and swallow—that's *my* way of tasting through the evening," she shouted while finishing her first glass.

"Okay then," Sachi smiled. "But you may not make it through all eight bottles."

"Are you kidding me girl? If I can outdrink a Brazilian football team, I know I can make it through a few bottles of wine!" Josie quipped back at her.

"Are you calling us lightweights?" Dalley pretended to posture.

"I don't know. I guess we'll just have to put it to a test."

We all laughed and cheered at the challenge that was now before us.

The tasting was Jade-free except for one brief moment when I saw her come out and take a few pictures with her phone. Other than that, the wine took us straight through to supper. Everyone was happy and relaxed, enjoying our first evening at Netuno. I have to admit though, far more swallowing than spitting went on during our tasting.

When Puro returned to the veranda, he let us know that it was time to come in for supper. "My goodness, is it all gone? Any favorites? Seems that I have a team of wine connoisseurs on my hands," he openly teased.

"That would be one way to describe us," Petra retorted. Then she leaned back into her chair and finished the last of her wine.

"Puro, you were gone for so long. Is everything okay?" I asked.

"Oh yes, I took care of *everything*—nothing for you to worry about." He nodded then raised his glass. "Please make your way over to the dining room. I will meet you there in just a few moments."

I wasn't sure what he meant by *everything,* but I had a feeling that Puro knew how to deal with all types of people. As we walked to the dining room, I overheard Jade complaining to Sachi. It seemed she had been given another room, but it was small *and* had no redeeming view. Sachi politely listened, but she made no effort to invite her back. It was clear from her lack of response that that door of opportunity had closed for Jade.

As Dalley and I walked into the dining room, Puro exclaimed, "Ladies, I'm pleased to see you found your way."

"It wasn't that far, Puro," Maggie laughed, and Puro matched her charming smile with one of his own.

"Rest assured Miss Maggie, if you got lost I would come looking for you myself."

Maggie blushed. A few minutes later, I caught Puro stealing a glance in her direction.

Puro distracted himself with rearranging a place setting when he saw me watching him; then he addressed us all. "I am sorry I could not spend more time with you earlier. It sounded like you were having great fun learning from my friend Sachi."

"Oh yes, it was a fantastic way to start our first day," I laughed, then changed the subject. "Puro, I have a message for you." I paused nervously. "Cristiano asked me to say hello."

"Oh!" His face brightened. "Yes, Miss Maya Wells ... Cristiano called me early this morning before his flight left to let me know you were coming. He didn't say much, just that you were very special to him, and for me to take good care of you until his return. When did you meet?"

Embarrassed by the truth, the moment left me speechless. But Dalley saved the day and explained our forty-eight hour history in almost complete detail. "Imagine what the next four weeks will bring the two of them," she teased.

Puro's full attention turned back to me. "You must have made quite an impression on him. I have not heard from Cristiano for many months and then yesterday he explained he would be coming back this week for a visit. I raise my glass to you for inspiring his return home," he said with gratitude.

With embarrassment still holding me hostage, I smiled and turned away, not sure what to do in the moment. Dalley and Puro laughed and continued with some witty banter as my face returned to a normal shade of pink. My stomach grumbled and for the first time in hours all I could think about was what we were having for supper. Perfectly cued to my silent question, a lean, rugged, and very attractive man bounded through the kitchen doors. Puro laughed and then explained that the man was Gervais, Netuno's head chef.

Gervais greeted us all, and then quickly jumped into a story about cooking with his mother when he was a child. At the same time, a screen came down and images of a little boy cooking at his mother's knee filled the wall. He then went on to share his unique perspective about cooking and building a meal with stories and images, and how with a little guidance and creativity anyone could learn. During his talk, he convinced me I might be able to become a decent cook during my stay there.

"I believe that the food we make can tell the story of our lives, and the flavors you choose can give clues of who you are and what you want to be. Are you salty or sweet? Do you need to throw in a handful of chilies or just one? Or do you sprinkle in a dash of cinnamon?" Maggie, Ellen, and Josie laughed. Then he turned to Sachi, "Or do you keep your cooking skills secret for a lifetime until just the right moment? Let me start with what I know. I know that each of you won a spot to be here. I do not know what you can or cannot do in your kitchens at home, but by the time you leave my kitchen, I hope that my food and your food, my stories and your stories, my photos and your photos, will change all of our lives."

When he finished speaking, I looked around. Sachi was sitting on the edge of her chair listening intently to every word.

He winked at her and then clapped his hands. "No more talk, *mangeons!*!" he yelled. Everyone broke into applause and our table was soon filled with food and drink and everything that a Portuguese banquet could hold. During the meal, beautiful images were projected onto the large screen, exploring how each dish came to be. The food was superb, filled with flavor and color.

As supper began to wind down, Puro stood up from his table and clinked a glass with his spoon.

"May I have your attention? I would like to introduce your hosts and the owners of Netuno Vineyard and Inn, Mateus and Reinaldo Chavis." He said the family name with great pride.

Out from the kitchen strode two men, smiling and laughing, each holding a glass of wine.

"Hello, my name is Mateus and this is my brother, Reinaldo. We want to welcome you to our home. Yes, I say home, as we too live here on the property with our families. This vineyard was owned by our father and before that, our grandfather and great-grandfather. We take great pride in the wine that we make, and the olive groves that we care for and cultivate." Reinaldo continued with passion, "When our father died ten years ago, he made us promise never to sell our land, and that we pass the legacy on to our children. Our great-grandfather tilled this land and planted each vine by hand. I still remember him at ninety-seven taking his hoe every morning and walking out into the fields. He was a man of great strength and integrity and believed that you had to stay ahead of the weeds or they would choke the sweetness out of the grapes."

Mateus took over seamlessly. "Our grandfather spent his life caring for the vines, shaping each one by hand, and then later planting the olive grove. When we were children, we would follow him around the vineyard, hour after hour, watching him taste grapes. He was a man of few words, but his smile always invited us to come closer. He taught us many techniques in pruning and cutting, in watching the temperature, and in harvesting at just the right time. Our father told us stories of when he was a young man working in the fields and how frustrated he was that our grandfather continued to sell the grapes to others. After several years, he finally convinced our grandfather to stop selling and to expand Netuno into a full winery. Until then, they had always made wine for themselves but had never thought about making wine on such a large scale and moving into the commercial market of winemaking.

"Our grandfather was resistant at first, but our father had big plans for Netuno and would not take no for an answer. When he was just eighteen, our father took over production and the expansion plans. He opened up the back fields of our land, started growing new grapes, and tested new wines. His creativity and tenacity were astounding and soon his wine became known throughout our region and farther into Portugal and Spain. He taught my brother and me everything he knew."

Reinaldo finished the story as Mateus had become too emotional to speak. "As he aged and we got ready to take over the vineyard, he made only one additional request, besides our keeping the property in our family. He asked that we be creative, use our imaginations, and invite others into the dream. My brother and I sat down and began to formulate a plan. Our dream was what you see: a retreat, a place where people could come and learn, rest and grow. And now it is time for *you* to join us and become part of the Netuno family and the Netuno dream."

Maggie raised her hand, like she was in school. "Yes, your name please?" Mateus asked.

"I'm Maggie," she giggled.

"Very pleased to meet you, Maggie. How can we help you?"

"First of all thank you for sharing your story. It is an amazing family tale, but I do have one question that has been driving me with curiosity since we arrived. How did you decide upon the design of the inn?"

"Oh yes, we built it in honor of our father who loved America's Old South and the grandeur of the estates. Now it is time for the whole dream to come to life. Our ultimate goal is to turn Netuno into a unique international retreat destination where people can unearth talents and rejuvenate themselves."

The brothers hugged each other and waved to us, then raised their glasses of wine and in unison cheered, "*Viva!*"

16

Excited

Maya

"*VIVA!*" SPILLED FROM OUR LIPS as we raised our glasses and toasted our hosts.

Puro jumped up like a kid at Christmas ready to open his first present and continued, "Over the next four weeks, we would like to invite you to experience all sides of Portugal. Feel free to wander the grounds of Netuno and discover all of the amazing treasures we have to offer. It is hoped that in the midst of your adventures, you will embrace and execute each of the challenges that we give you with heart, creativity, and a little competitive spirit. I have heard talk there might be weekly prizes. You will receive a challenge each Sunday night at dinner, and will be given whatever resources you need to accomplish that challenge during the week. On Friday evenings, we will all come together to share your experiences, your images, and your food."

Gervais joined him and began describing some of the expectations he had as one of the judges. "Images taken and food created hold equal value to me. I want you to take time telling the story of the food you make. We need food to live, and each bite we take has a story. I know that each of you comes to us with different talents. Your time here is not about becoming a chef and creating the fanciest dishes. Instead, it is about how the flavors you create and the images you capture tell the story of your food and your heart. Each person has found their way to my kitchen and to Portugal for a reason. Let's embark upon this journey together and create life-long memories. I will give one-hour cooking lessons Monday through Thursday starting at 7:00 a.m. You are all invited, but it is not required. Remember, cooking with me is not just about food—bring your cameras," he said with a chuckle. "And, in regards to prizes, Puro was correct. This week, we will be giving away two new digital cameras, compliments of your hosts." He looked over to the brothers as they raised their glasses again.

While we finished our dessert, Puro announced our groupings for the first week. "First is Maggie and Maya," he said smiling at us. "Next is Dalley and Jade." Dalley rolled her eyes, and then smirked like she was planning on giving Jade a hard time. "To round things out, we have Sachi and Josie, and then Ellen and Petra. Please note that the groups are randomly drawn, but we will make sure there are no repeats during your stay here."

Dalley turned around, making eye contact with Jade. "Well Jade, looks like we get to spend the first challenge together," she said clapping her hands. Jade appeared less than impressed with her enthusiasm as her lip snarled up and she made that awful wounded rhino sound again.

I shifted my chair so I could ignore her and then turned my attention to Maggie. "I'm so excited that we get to work together!"

She reached across the table, grabbed my hand, and spoke in a sparkly tone, "It's going to be *epic*. My sons would laugh at me if they heard me say that."

Gervais held his glass up waiting for our attention so he could finish his presentation.

"The theme for this week is *Movement*," he said jumping up and down. "You need to portray movement in the image, in the food, in the whole experience."

I stared at the others around the table and hoped I wasn't the only one puzzled by the idea of *Movement* as a theme for making food. Thankfully my bewildered look was matched by almost everyone, except for Sachi. She appeared to be both eager and intrigued by the challenge.

Supper ended and everyone broke into their groups, including Dalley, who attempted to pull Jade off into a corner to get started.

"Maggie, this whole experience feels surreal. I have no clue where to start. Do you have any ideas?" I asked, ready for anything.

She leaned in so that no one else could hear. "All of this is such a pleasant surprise. And yes, I think I might have an idea for this week's challenge."

"Sounds good to me. What's first?" I whispered back happily, thankful for her energy and for making things so easy. She pulled a notebook out of her bag and went straight to work.

"I think that we should rent a car and go out to the countryside tomorrow," she said with an undertone of mischief.

I laughed, not knowing where she was going with the idea, but happy to jump on board. "This sounds very adventurous, filled with movement."

"Yes exactly!"

She then fell into a little story which gave roots to her idea. "Oh, I remember these trips we used to take as a family. My husband was a teacher, so in the summer we were able to get away. On the July long weekend we would pack the boys up, grab a couple of maps, and just go. Each person got to make one destination choice on the map. Then my husband would plan a route so that we could hit every one of the spots. Some summers we would be gone for three weeks, others we wouldn't be back until the September long weekend. It was glorious." There was a wistful tone in her last words. I glanced at her and saw that the memory had taken her back to a very different time in her life. She became very still, then looked over at me after collecting her thoughts. "The boys and I haven't been on one of those trips since their dad died."

Taking a deep breath, she pulled a map of Portugal out of her purse and said to me, "Pick a spot, any spot. We leave tomorrow. Can you drive? I've never been really good at that part."

"Sure," I said, as tears trickled down my cheeks. I went to wipe them away but she stopped me with a few simple words.

"Let them fall. It was a wonderful time in my life." She paused. "Well I had better send an email off to my boys. They knew I was going out to the night club last night and will want to know what happened and if their mother did anything embarrassing that might end up on YouTube. See you tomorrow Maya."

As she walked out of the dining room, I called out to her, "Oh, I'll have Puro rent a car for first thing in the morning."

"Sounds great, but let's get started after cooking class!"

I sat for a little while in the lobby then wandered over to the front desk. "Excuse me, Puro. Could you book a car for Maggie and I to use tomorrow morning? We are going on an adventure into the country-side." I crossed my fingers hoping that he could find us something at such late notice.

"Yes, I'll take care of it." He hesitated, then his brow furrowed and his voice deepened. "But please be careful. The back roads are not well kept and sometimes have big holes." He paused again. "Also, the way

Cristiano was speaking about you earlier, I would be in trouble if I let anything happen to you."

I felt a blush come upon my face, and Puro's worry turned to a smirk.

I pressed my hand to my cheek, remembering the warmth of his fingers on my skin. "Thank you for booking the car. I'm exhausted. When you have a chance can you send a pot of tea to my room please?"

"Of course Miss Wells, right away." A smile formed on his face as I walked away.

Puro

I picked up the phone and dialed over to the kitchen. Gervais answered on the second ring. "Bonjour Gervais. Could you please send a pot of tea to Miss Wells' room?"

"Yes, Puro, that is perfect timing. Bento is putting a cart together right now. I will add the tea to his list." He paused. "It was a lovely evening. You've done a superb job getting this contest set up."

"Thank you, Gervais. But I can only take credit for organizing things from this side. Branca organized all the contest details. She kept it all a secret though, until she handed me the winner's names just a few months ago. After that, Carmo and I had to scramble to get everything ready."

"I thought Branca would have been here tonight. Her absence is interesting."

"Yes, she is in Spain at a gallery opening. She has always been a free spirit, but Reinaldo knew that when he married her years ago. His father warned him, but he was in love. Branca will grace us with her presence only if she chooses. Enough of that though—we have our hands full over the next four weeks."

"Yes, it *should* be quite a month. Puro, do you know anything about the young woman ... Sachi is her name, I believe?"

"No, I don't know anything about her except that she knows a little something about wine tasting, but you should ask her. I think she is still in the dining room. I hear from a few of the ladies that she is quite the chef herself."

"Yes, I got a call from Alfonzo last night and he told me a little about the food that she'd prepared for him. I am very curious to find out more about her."

"Good night, Gervais," I laughed.

I stood by the front desk and made a list of all the things that needed to be done for the week. Then the phone rang. "Hello, Netuno Wineries and Inn. Puro speaking."

"Hello Puro, how are you? It's Cristiano."

"Cristiano, I've heard more from you in the last twenty-four hours than I have in over a year."

"Yes, I know. I'm sorry Puro. I will make sure I come around more. So, how are things?" He tried to sound casual but failed miserably. I knew why he was calling.

"Do you mean, how is Miss Wells?" I asked pausing long enough to make him answer.

"Yes, I mean Miss Wells. I mean Maya." He sounded flustered. "Have you always been this irritating?" he joked.

"Yes, I have. You just haven't been around enough to remember. She is settling in. I have to tell you Cristiano," I said, lowering my voice and using a serious tone. I heard him take in a breath. "I like her. She makes me laugh. Avó will like her too."

"Do you think so?" he asked, with child-like anticipation. "I cannot wait for them to meet. Please don't let Maya know I called. I just wanted to make sure she was alright."

"She is more than alright, she is happy. You should have seen her when I mentioned your name this evening."

"Really? What did she say?"

"Cristiano, trust me when I tell you that she was happy to hear your name. Oh, that reminds me. I need to go. I promised her I would rent a car for her for tomorrow and it is getting late."

"Puro, don't do that. Just let her use my car. It probably needs a spin anyway."

"Are you sure? You don't let anyone drive that car, except me."

"Yes, yes just tell her you found a special car for her. She'll find out on Saturday when I see her that the car is mine."

"Oh, you're coming in on Saturday?" I tried to hide my excitement.

"Actually, I'm arriving on Thursday night, but I have to see Avó. So much has changed in my life and I need to talk to her first."

Just then, a single source of laughter erupted from the top of the stairwell. I looked up. Miss Wells had turned around and was waving to me.

"Yes, Cristiano, I think that there are many changes coming your way."

Maya

Heading up the stairs, my exhaustion lifted briefly, with the thought that Cristiano had been thinking of me too. I had a sudden urge to do something silly, so I started jumping up the stairs. By the time I reached the top, I was laughing so hard that I must have looked ridiculous. It felt good to laugh. I saw Puro look up at me while he was on the phone. I waved goodnight and strolled back to my room.

When I opened the door, I was relieved to see that all of our luggage had arrived. I didn't even have a chance to sit before a knock came from the door. When I opened it, I was greeted by the most gracious smile.

"Hello, Miss Wells?"

"Yes, it's Maya, thank you."

"I have your tea for you."

"Oh, that is wonderful. Thank you so much."

"It is my pleasure," he responded genuinely.

"Your voice, your smile—you remind me of …"

"Yes, my father is Reinaldo." He must have seen the surprise in my eyes that one of the owner's sons was delivering me room service. He handed me my tea. "My father believes if I am to take over the business one day, I must work each job, and earn my way into a position of leadership."

"Your father is both very kind and wise, even if his wisdom has you bringing hot tea to people in the middle of the night," I said apologetically.

"It is not so bad. I get to meet people like you," he responded, again with his contagious smile. "I hope you received your luggage properly."

"Oh yes. It's all here, thank you." He turned to leave. "By the way, what's your name?" I asked.

"Bento."

"Bento, that's curious. What does it mean?"

"It's a Portuguese nickname meaning *blessed,*" he said a bit sheepishly.

"That's lovely," I mused.

"Yes, lovely would be one description. It was my mother's choice."

"Oh, where is your mom? I haven't met her yet."

"She is at an art gallery opening in Spain for a few weeks. I'm not sure if she'll be back before you finish your time here." Disapproval rang through his tone.

"Oh, that's too bad. I would have liked to meet her. It would be incredible to live here full time," I said, taking a breath in.

"Hmm, not everyone feels the same. She doesn't spend much time here at the vineyard anymore."

"Oh, I'm sorry."

"Well, I had better get to my next delivery. Miss Axeline ordered some ice cream and I don't want it to melt."

"Miss Axeline?" I ran through the names I had seen in Dalley's files. "Oh you mean Jade. No, you're right. You don't want to bring *her* a melted dessert."

"No need to elaborate Miss Wells. I heard from Carmo earlier today that she is quite particular about everything."

"Well, that is a polite way of putting it. Thank you for the tea Bento." I closed the door and poured myself a cup, then went out to the balcony with Christopher.

> *August 20th First evening at Netuno.*
>
> *The grapevines are rolling over the hills mile after mile.*
>
> *The evening breeze is gently caressing my skin, and my hot cup of tea is warming me from the inside out.*
>
> *I keep asking myself, 'Can life really change this much in such a short amount of time? Can one person, one destination, one book, and one pen really be the answer? I'm not sure if it would work for anyone else, but I know I am on a new journey marked by all these points and there is no turning back! Why would I?*

Suddenly there was a crash and a bang. Dalley burst through the door and fell over the luggage and lay sprawled out over the suitcases. At first she looked mad, but then she started to laugh.

"Dalley? Are you alright?"

"That little girl is impossible." She shook her head in disbelief. "I have never met anyone like her before in my life and I have met a lot of horrible people." She paused for a moment then continued to tell her story while sitting on the floor. Whatever Jade had done, Dalley was exasperated.

"What happened?"

"After supper I approached her. I thought that we could take a few minutes to discuss the challenge. She wasn't finished yet, so I let her know I would come back and see her in a bit. When I came back she wasn't in the dining room anymore, but in the lobby drinking a martini and reading a magazine. 'Excuse me, Jade,' I said to her politely. 'I see that you're done with your supper. We should get to work.' She took an intentional, long sip of her drink, ate an olive, and then kept reading. Then I persisted with a little more intensity. 'Jade, why don't we sit down and have a drink *together* and talk about the project?' She put her magazine down and looked me straight in the eye.

"'No. I have no desire to have a drink with you and I think that *you* should take care of it on your own,' she said belligerently, not even blinking. Then she picked up her magazine and started to read again. At that point, I took her bait. My voice escalated, I grabbed the magazine out of her hand, threw it on the ground and started to shout. I went from 4 to 10 on the irritation meter. She impressed me with how effectively she was able to get under my skin. The remainder of the conversation went something like this ..."

Dalley stood up and went on to act out the whole scene:

"'No, that's *not* fine, and I will *not* take care of it on my own! So why don't you pull your prissy head out of your French ass and change your attitude. We *are* going to do this together!'"

By then I was laughing and holding my sides as Dalley played both parts so well.

"Then she leaned over and picked up her magazine from the floor, stood up and in a low-toned voice hissed, 'Listen to me, bitch. I have *no* intention of doing any of these ridiculous cooking projects. I'm not here for that and I can do whatever I like. So stay out of my way!'

"I was so mad I could have spit in her drink, but I gathered myself together and moved in close to her. So close that I almost choked on her expensive perfume. Then coolly I whispered into her ear: 'Actually no you can't, not while you're in my group *bitch*. So you can shelve your spoiled brat attitude, and for whatever reason you *think* you're here, you can shove that up your ...' Well at that point Puro ran over. But I did calm down enough to get the last word in, and then set a time for us to meet in the morning."

"I see our luggage has arrived!" she laughed, changing the subject.

"I'm glad to see you're almost feeling normal again. Did you know that your chances for having an aneurysm reduce dramatically with every ten points that you lower your blood pressure?"

"Are you serious?"

"No, I just thought it sounded very practical and kind of funny and it does make sense. Dalley, what do you think Jade meant when she said, *I'm not here for that ...*'"

"I don't know. I wouldn't believe anything that comes out of her mouth. I don't trust her." Dalley stepped out onto the balcony and noticed my tea and open journal. "Oh Maya, I'm sorry, I interrupted."

"It's okay, I'll finish later."

She exhaled, then smiled weakly, grabbed her laptop, and stepped into her bathroom without saying another word.

"Good night, Dalley," was all I had time to say before the door closed and the lock clicked. I stared at the door, curious about the change in her demeanor. But I didn't have much time to think about it as the exhaustion of the day hit me with full force. I took a sip of cold tea, closed Christopher and Athena, and held them close to my chest like I was holding onto my heart. I walked back into the room and made my way over to my canopied bed, undressed, and crawled under the cool sheets. When I turned out my lamp a striking shadow was cast on the wall caused by the light that shone from under Dalley's bathroom door. I shivered, rolled over, and let the fullness of the day wrap itself around me.

17

Maggie, Me, and the Goat

Maya

THE MORNING CAME QUICKLY WITH no dreams to mention, and when my eyes flickered open it only took running my hands over the crisp cotton sheets to realize that Portugal was not a dream. Christopher, Athena, Cristiano, and the vineyard: they were all real. I sprung out of bed, showered, dressed, and headed downstairs to meet Maggie at 8:15.

Before I left, I called out to Dalley, "It's just after 8:00 and you don't want to be late for Jade? Do You?" She groaned, and I think threw something in my direction as I heard a thud on the door just as I closed it.

It was a beautiful day and the lobby was bustling. Maggie was waiting for me, talking with Puro. As I approached them, they were laughing and chatting up a storm.

"Hi Maggie, how was cooking class?"

"Oh Maya, Gervais is like a motivational speaker who uses food instead of words. This morning he gathered up every variety of fruit that he could find, then had us taste-testing with blindfolds, and identifying flavors while he took pictures of us reacting to the scents and textures of the fruit. It was great fun. I'm going to attend every class I can. You have to come tomorrow!"

"Who else was there?"

"Petra, Ellen, and Sachi arrived early, but Josie wandered in just after 7:00 and interrupted Gervais' introduction. He was not pleased with her nonchalant attitude and tore a strip off her. She listened politely, but at the end of his rant, she started to laugh. He couldn't help but crack a smile; you know how catchy her laugh can be. He made it clear though, that in the future if she was not on time, then Do Not Enter." She paused thoughtfully and then continued. "The one person who really surprised me though was Sachi. You should have seen her. She was smiling and chatting, not with us mind you, but with Gervais!!"

"Gervais? Really?"

"Yes, it was the funniest thing. They had this crinkly energy that seemed to surround the two of them during the whole class. It made me laugh."

"Sachi and Gervais?" I repeated trying to imagine them together. "Yes, I know. It's wonderful isn't it?"

"How did it happen? When?" I asked with curiosity.

"Well, I'm not sure, but I think that they were cooking until about 4:00 a.m. Sachi said she went to bed for a few hours before the morning class, but I'm not sure Gervais has even slept," she mused.

"Portugal appears to be giving everyone a little bit of something special so far," I sighed happily.

"Ah yes, there appears to be a whole lot of *something special* being spread around here." She smiled back at me.

"You're so funny, Maggie."

"Yes, I can be sometimes. Now let's get to it." Puro waved me over.

"Miss Wells, your car is ready. I hope it meets all your needs," he said with a smirk and a head shake.

"Please call me Maya. Miss Wells sounds too formal. Puro is the car reliable?"

"Oh, you don't have to worry about that. I test drove it this morning myself and it's running smoothly."

"Thank you! I'll let Cristiano know that you are making all efforts to keep me safe," I said reassuring him.

"Oh *thank you* Maya." He nodded then continued. "I *know* that Cristiano would approve of this car. It's waiting outside. The keys are in the ignition and the gas tank is full," he said proudly.

"Thank you, Puro, I'm so excited. So—which side of the road do I drive on here?" I teased.

Horrified by my comment, he opened his mouth, and only got out, "Maya?"

"I'm just kidding, Puro. We'll be fine. I promise I will come back in one piece and so will the car."

He laughed nervously, "I hope so, for all our sakes."

I turned to Maggie and asked, "Should we eat first? Or should we find something along the way?"

"Oh, I've already taken care of that. Gervais packed us a thermos of hot coffee and a picnic basket. We are ready to go."

She threw on her sunglasses and a wonderful floppy hat and we stepped outside into the sunshine. The only vehicle I could see was some-body's gorgeous little convertible. Looking around further, I realized that there were no other cars. I smiled and knew that Puro must really like me. I had no idea what year, make or model it was, but it looked kind of like the one that James Dean used to drive. It was just awesome. I had never driven a car like that in my life.

"This is fantastic," Maggie squealed. "Much finer and far less practical than the minivan we used to drive for our family treks. It's perfect. I like Puro more and more each day."

I shook my head, blew out my nerves in one breath, and got behind the wheel of the car. I sat still for a moment. The leather on the seats was worn, but not worn out, and the grips on the steering wheel held grooves embedded so deeply that it looked like someone's hands had been molded specifically for that car. You could tell it was well taken care of, loved, and not a typical rental.

Maggie got into her seat and took off her hat. "This is a sunglass-wearing, no-hat, scarf-whistling-in-the-wind kind of car. Get ready to have some fun."

I buckled in and started the engine. It was loud and rhythmic. I never thought I could love a car, but I loved that one. I threw it into gear and for the first time in my life, sped away creating a great plume of dust, which floated up into the clouds. Maggie had her camera out and took a series of pictures as the two of us sped away from the vineyard. It was not until about twenty-five minutes later that I thought we should stop and look at the map. I yelled to Maggie through the whistling wind.

"Sounds great," she yelled over the engine without looking at me, staring into the fields. I kept driving and let her stay in her wind world a little longer, until my stomach commanded that I stop. I slowed down when I saw a grove of trees and pulled over to the side of the road. There wasn't a soul around and the morning was absolutely glorious.

We found our way over to the shade and set up a little blanket and our food. When Maggie opened the basket, the scent of fresh pastries triggered a ravenous response. Biting into a croissant, I was shocked by the warm chocolate sensation that drifted over my tongue and said hello to my heart.

"How could something taste so awe-inspiring? I will never be able to look at pastry the same way. I'm not sure if I'm sold on all the coffee they drink here though, but I'm trying."

She laughed and began eating some fresh fruit. "Maya, it's like you're tasting everything for the first time."

I paused briefly, contemplating her comment. "I guess in many ways I am. I can't explain it, but something has changed inside of me. Since I left home, everything feels different."

She smiled, looking satisfied with my answer. We sat and ate in beautiful silence.

She looked up into the tree and poked me. "Hey Maya, look at that. I think there's a swing up there?" She finished her coffee and started climbing the tree.

"Maggie, what are you doing?" I couldn't believe how quick and fearless she was. *I* hadn't climbed a tree in years.

"I'm going to investigate."

"Are you sure?" I was worried she might fall.

"Oh, Maya!" She was halfway up the tree before I could say anything else. Then she threw down the ropes of an old woven swing. "Heads up!" She made her way back to the ground, but not before I got a great picture of her standing on a tree branch, laughing and jumping.

"It's old and worn, but it'll hold," she claimed with confidence.

"Are you sure?"

"Maya, when did you stop playing? Taking chances?" She looked at me with compassion, then continued. "Sometimes you seem so guarded. And then there are these moments when you just sparkle and shine."

My body tensed briefly. The idea of me being able to sparkle was foreign to me, but I liked it.

"I'm sorry, I shouldn't have said anything. My boys say that I do a little too much armchair therapy sometimes."

She held the swing in her hands and motioned for me to sit down. The tree shook, but the seat held true with no sign of letting go. I started the motion with my legs, moving them back and forth. I could hear my dad's voice; it was like he was standing right next to me. 'Push, pump, push, pump, that's the only way Maya, come on, harder.' I concentrated on the movement and thought only about going higher and feeling the wind. Maggie had pulled out her camera and began taking shot after shot of me. At one point I swung so high that my head brushed the leaves of the tree. I laughed out loud. My legs ached, and it was wonderful.

She yelled, "It's time to jump!"

"I can't. It's too high!!"

"Jump, Maya! You can do it!"

She was right. I needed to jump off that swing and land. I took a breath and left the security of those few woven knots and flew into the wind. I soared and time stopped for a second and then I landed and fell into the grass.

"You did it! Maya, I'm so proud of you!"

I sat up from my not-so-graceful landing. "Yes, I did!"

After the excitement subsided and my heart started to beat again, Maggie and I pored over the photos for our project. My favorite series was when I jumped off the swing. She was able to catch my expression of fear that turned to determination and ended with exhilaration. She got it all!

We decided that Gervais' theme of movement and food had to incorporate a level of playfulness and fun—a picnic. That was the answer. Our Friday meal was going to be a picnic.

Maggie hugged me.

I hugged her back and didn't want to let go.

"Whoa, Maya, what is it?" she asked, clearly concerned about the sudden unbreakable hold I had on her.

I wasn't sure what to say, so I just blurted it out. "You asked me when I had stopped playing."

"Yes, I did." She tugged on my arm letting me know that it was okay to loosen my grip on her, and that she wasn't going anywhere. The two of us made ourselves comfortable under the tree and I began to talk.

"The kind of play you're talking about only existed briefly in my life and even then, it was tinted with grey. I was eight when my world came crashing down around me. We still owned the vineyard and the peach orchard at that time. It was late summer and I was out on one of my roaming adventures looking at the grapes and finding which trees had the best peaches. The scent in the orchard was like breathing in the best dream ever. Later that afternoon, while I was walking on the outer edge of the vineyard, I saw someone pounding a sign into the ground near the road." My heart ached as I told her the story. "I demanded to know what he was doing. He responded very matter-of-factly saying that the family who owned the property was selling the vineyard. He then went on to rebuke me and told me I shouldn't be walking around on their land, and that I should go home. 'I am home,' I answered."

Maggie held me until the wave of memories passed and I was able to continue. "I made my way back through the grapevines. It felt like they were grabbing at me, trying to tie me down. The one place that had been my haven and my best friend had turned on me. I ran faster and faster trying to get back to the house. I stopped running when I smacked into the second For Sale sign, and opened a gash on my forearm, which then covered me in my own blood. My dad ran over, but I pushed him away. He ran to the house and grabbed some towels, but when he came back out, I wanted nothing to do with him. I sat in front of the sign, blood running through my fingers, and on to the grass. He waited patiently for me to look at him and then sat down beside me. He offered me a towel and then quietly insisted that we go to the hospital, but I wasn't moving. So, he took a water bottle out of his bag, cleaned the wound as best as he could, and closed the gaping hole with his fingers, holding it tight for what felt like hours."

My body sagged, exhausted by the memory. "While he held the wound together, I sat still on the grass as he explained why we had to move. I wasn't dumb. I knew my mom was sick. My sister and I could always tell when she was having a really bad week. We called it the dark house during those times. Everyone would stop talking and she stayed in her room. At night I could hear her crying. My dad did everything he could to make her feel better, but it wasn't enough. He told me about how when they'd moved to the property things improved, but that in the last few months all the symptoms had returned and things were worse. Somehow my dad thought he had shielded my sister and me from the truth, from her depression; but in reality, we'd just found ways to cope. Mine was the orchard and the vineyard.

"The bottom line was she needed more help than he could give her." I sighed and looked over at Maggie, whose facial expression led me to believe she knew a thing or two about depression. "So, he sold the property and moved us into town. Oh, I fought him. I rebelled, telling him that I wasn't moving, pleading that we should just send her away. He tried again and again to help me understand, but I was lost and sad and so angry."

Maggie shifted in her spot for the first time during my story. "Maya tell me about your mom. Tell me something good," she said with an engaging smile. I paused thoughtfully. Then I cautiously allowed myself to walk a path that was rarely stepped on in my life.

"Well, my mom wasn't the easiest person to live with; most of the time she was just really sad. There were days though when she tried, I guess. For a little while she put paper hearts into my lunch box, but some of the kids at school saw them and laughed at me, so after that I would just take them out on the bus and throw them away."

"You threw them away?"

"Yes, I was so mad at her I guess, I didn't want anything from her. Some kids didn't even believe I had a mom.

"The holidays were the worst around our place, especially in winter. The snow and cold were hard on her. I didn't like being inside with her. It felt heavy and we always had to be quiet. I spent all my extra hours in the orchard, walking in the snow, and imagining when spring would come." I paused, feeling a whisper of the dark house touch me. Then I continued.

"After we moved, I think my mom got a little better, but life was different for me. I felt like I had lost everything, and I was angry at my mom, and sad at the world. Some days when I really needed her, I would climb into her bed and just lay beside her. She would stroke my hair, not saying a word. Doing that always made me feel a little better." I looked at Maggie wondering if that was an answer at all. "I felt sad for my dad because he wanted to do the right thing for all of us, but I was really mad at him too. Sometimes he would try to hug me, and I would just stand there. He would say, 'One day you will understand. For now though, know that your mom and I love you.'" As I said those words I grabbed my arm and traced the faint outline of the ragged, but now faded scar.

Maggie and I sat still.

"You know Maya, something struck me in your story. You said that your mom would cut out hearts and put them into your lunch. Who made your lunch every day?"

I paused, never thinking of it that way before.

"My mom, I guess? By the time I got up in the morning, it was made, and she was in bed. Maybe she got up early?" I said baffled by the idea.

"Maya, do you have any idea what it must have taken for her to get out of bed, on the days that she could, then make your lunch, cut out hearts, and put them in your bag?"

Her words punched me in the chest. I was winded, but managed to sputter, "I never thought about lunch. I was just mad that she never made me breakfast."

A whirl of pain washed over me as I realized what Maggie was saying. Tears streamed down my face. She touched my arm then squeezed it gently. I closed my eyes and let the breeze of the late morning dry my tears and ready me for the rest of our day, as I let a new truth take hold in my body. "So where to next?" she asked quietly, pulling the map out of her purse. "It's already 11:30 and we need to find some peach trees."

"Peach trees? For what?"

"Well, if we are going to have a picnic, then we need peach pie, don't we?" she asked with a little smile sitting on her lips.

"Do they have peaches in Portugal?"

"I don't know, but we sure are going to find out," she said, sounding like she was on a mission.

We laughed, packed up our food and our new memories and headed east, keeping an eye out for the stray peach trees that we hoped to find along the way.

The landscape changed from grapevines to grass, and amongst the sea of gold were farmers' fields scattered with stray cows and goats roaming the land.

We continued to drive along the bumpy gravel road, passing several more farms, when my eyes suddenly locked on a lonely kid who stood frozen in the middle of the road. Maggie yelled for me to stop. I slammed on the brakes and swerved, barely missing him. He brayed loudly. I got out and tried to shoo him back through the hole in the fence, but he ran from me, frightened.

"Maya, what are you doing?" Maggie yelled as I chased the goat all over the road.

"I don't know. I just need to help him. I need to help him find his family."

Maggie chuckled. "One lost soul looking out for another, hey?"

She got out of the car and began helping me herd the kid closer to the hole. He finally found his way through and started to run. I looked at the old wooden fence and began to climb. Maggie followed me without a word. She was right somehow about the kid and I being the same in some strange way. I needed to make sure he was going to be okay. As we inched towards his herd I saw him jumping and playing and I relaxed. He was safe—home. "Maggie can you record this on video?" I whispered as I stepped closer and closer to the family. She pulled out the camera and started recording me. I was almost close enough to touch them when suddenly they got spooked and were on the move and so were we. Maggie was chasing me while I was chasing the goats. What we didn't realize was that one big goat was chasing all of us.

Maggie turned her head following her own instincts and noticed the mother goat was in full pursuit of us, as we were in pursuit of her family. All I heard from Maggie was "RUN! RUN, MAYA!!! RUN." I turned around and the crazy quest to get a video of me running with the goats turned into a run for our lives away from Mable, which is what we named her after the whole ordeal. I say ordeal, because things didn't end there.

Maggie caught up to me as I jumped around the goat landmines. She yelled as she passed me, "Don't worry about those. Worry about the angry mom that is fast on your heels."

I saw Maggie scrambling up a hill and I was quick to follow. Before we knew it, we were at the top, and Mable was at the bottom. She stared at us for a long time while her young brood stood eating grass and relaxing after all the excitement. We collapsed in a heap after our exhausting run, watching Mable carefully. But it was clear that climbing the hill was too much trouble for her and eventually she turned around and walked back into the field, taking her kids with her.

"Wow that was just crazy! I can't believe how fast you can run!" I exclaimed.

"What? You mean for someone my age?"

"Well yes, kind of," I said with embarrassment.

She laughed out loud and then took a thoughtful pause. "I'm forty-eight. After my husband died, I started running. I thought it would help me feel better. I guess it helped in a few different ways." We both laughed.

"Maggie, can you tell me about him?" I asked tentatively.

"Sure. James was joyful," she responded with a beautiful smile. "He brought life into my world every day. Similar to you, I grew up in a home where one parent always made things challenging. When I met James, it was easy. When we went on our first date, it was as if I could breathe for the first time—really breathe. He wasn't complicated and only asked one thing of me." She paused momentarily.

"What was that?"

"Truth! That was a hard road for me coming from my world, as I had to keep a lot of secrets. During my time with him, I learned something new every day, and I believe that he gave the best of himself to me and our boys." She sighed, and then looked out over the rolling hills. "When he died, my breath was cut short. I stopped breathing from my core and literally could only take short little breaths, just to get through each moment. Then a friend told me I had to come with her one day. She took me to a running shop. I wasn't sure what she was doing, but before I knew it, she had me dressed and signed up for a running clinic. I was too tired and sad to refuse. My boys thought that it would be good for me, as it had been six months since their dad's death, and I had barely left the house.

"The first class was excruciating! It felt like I was fighting every move. My lungs screamed at me. I wanted to hold onto the pain, hold on to the short little puffs of air that I was only letting myself have. But the running made me breathe. At the end of the first run, I vomited all over the street. That was the first and the last time that happened. After that day, I took it more seriously. I ran everywhere. I started to breathe again—without James. Since then, I just kept running."

I sat quietly, waiting for the story to continue, but it didn't. She stood up and shook the dirt off her shorts and gently noted that we had better find our car and get out of the afternoon heat. She surveyed the fields, trying to figure out which way we should go. Then she spotted a vehicle lumbering through the grass.

"Oh look, a hay truck. I'm sure he won't mind giving us a ride," she said with a smirk. And with that she dashed off down the hill, running after the truck.

The driver turned his head when he heard us yelling. He didn't slow down but motioned for us to speed up and jump on. Maggie caught up and jumped on the back easily. She had her camera out and was taking pictures of me as I struggled to catch up.

"Maya, you can do it! Run!"

I laughed out loud and almost choked, but put all of my effort into catching that truck. My legs burned, but I was not going to give up. When I was only an arm's reach away, the last push was almost easy. I was not sure where the energy came from, but I could feel the surge break through my muscles. I caught the truck and jumped on to the flat bed! I had never felt so proud of myself in all my life.

The driver took us back to the road and we found the convertible about a mile away. Getting into the car, we shared our last bottle of water. As we drove back to the inn, neither of us spoke, as it had already been a day filled with words. When we arrived, we looked at each other and hugged. "I have to tell you, today was one of my best map adventures ever. See you in the morning, Maya," she said sounding tired.

"Maggie, it's still early. You want to meet for supper later?" I asked keenly.

"No, I think I'll have supper in my room tonight." She smiled gently at me. "We can go over the rest of the pictures and the menu tomorrow." She got out of the car and took a deep purposeful breath, then walked through the front doors.

18

Writing it Out

Maya

I SAT IN THE CONVERTIBLE for almost an hour, looking out over the vineyard, thinking about the day and all of the things that had come clear to me. A sudden urge came over me and I knew I had to write. Before getting out of the car, I ran my hand over the dashboard and understood why so many men fall in love with their cars. Then I grabbed the keys and my things and raced up the stairs onto the veranda.

I wandered around, testing out chairs before I found the right place to sit and settle in. Before I knew it, Puro was standing beside me with a cup of tea.

"I thought you might like this," he said with a quiet voice.

"You're amazing," I responded with appreciation.

"Oh, it's in my nature to find ways to make people happy," he answered joyfully.

"Well thank you, Puro. I like your nature."

"How did the car drive today?" he asked curiously.

"It was heavenly." I handed him the keys. "I don't think I've ever been in a rental car like that. Where did you get it from?"

"Oh, I have my sources," he said with a mysterious grin. "No more questions. Drink your tea while it's hot. See you at supper, Maya." He smiled and then turned to leave.

"Oh, Puro?" I called to him before he could vanish through the doors. "Maggie wants to have supper in her room tonight. Can you arrange that?"

Puro's regularly joyful face flashed a moment of worry. "I will take care of it myself." He left immediately.

I took a sip of tea and relaxed into the chair, then opened Christopher and began.

August 21st

Dear Friend,

Wonderful, simply wonderful. Today was my first full day at the vineyard. Maggie and I went on an adventure looking for movement, but we found so much more.

We found truth, and joy and laughter. I learned so much about myself and my life. I can hardly believe that it happened.

Athena you are looking extra sparkly today. Whenever I see you, you take me to this place of calm and inspiration. The other day when I thought I lost you at the airport, I tried to be rational, that you were only a pen, but the truth was I was screaming inside.

Then there he was, standing with you in his hands. Cristiano saved you.

Okay, refocus Maya!

Wow, hearing Maggie talk about James today and the world that they'd created together was monumental.

I know I did the right thing in not marrying Steven. He never created a feeling of joy or adventure for me. I want someone who can give me that opportunity. That chance to be something more than I thought I could be. To push me and pull me if needed—well give me a strong nudge at least.

Oh, the other thing that happened today was some stuff I figured out about my mom; but I will have to save that. Supper is in a couple hours and we are all meeting for drinks beforehand.

I can't wait to tell Dalley about the goats.

Maya

I took my last sip of tea and slipped Christopher and Athena back into my purse. As I walked slowly into the lobby, I passed by the front desk and noticed some stationery. I grabbed a few sheets and an envelope and tucked them away for later. Puro was filing some papers and noticed me at the desk.

"So how was the tea?" he asked smiling and looking pleased with himself.

"Oh, it was very noisy today!" I exclaimed.

"Noisy? What do you mean?"

"Oh, that's something that my mom used to say when I would bring her a perfect cup of tea," I answered, giving myself permission to remember some of the beautiful memories I did share with her.

Puro smiled. "I see you took some stationery. The mail gets picked up in the morning."

"Thank you, Puro. I get a feeling that I'm going to be saying that a lot to you over the next four weeks."

⁂

The room was quiet when I arrived. Dalley was nowhere to be seen.

After cleaning up, I had some time and thought that I might seize the moment and write a letter to my mom.

Dear Mom,

It's been just three days since I arrived in Portugal. Everything is different.

I don't mean just here, but inside of me. It feels like I can see, and almost breathe for the first time. I'm not sure where to start, but I guess the best place is with—I Love You.

Today was kind of crazy, as I drove over the speed limit in a beautiful convertible, jumped off a rope swing, went flying in the air, ate chocolate croissants under a tree, and was chased up a hill by a goat. (I'll tell you about the goat and the hay truck later.)

Outside of all those adventures, I had a chance to really think about some things today.

For the first time in my life, I thought about you and all you have been through ... and Mom, I'm sorry. I'm so sorry for not being able to love you the way you deserved. I'm sorry for being mad at you for so many years. I wrapped myself in a blanket of sadness and blamed it on you.

After we moved, I figured that was just the way life would be. I held on to your sadness even when you were trying to let it go. I didn't even notice when you were getting better. I blamed you for taking away my peach trees and my grapevines. I blamed you for making me not fun and not happy. What I failed to see was at some point, the only person that I could blame for my unhappy life was me.

I never understood fully why we had to move when I was eight. The only thing I knew was that you were sick. Dad tried to explain about your sad feelings, and that some days they were like weights that held your body hostage. Clearly I must have freaked out a bit, so after that, all he said was we were moving closer to the doctors so they could help you feel better.

I remember there were days when you would be in bed, and would try to smile for me, and drink my tea, trying to find small ways to include me in your life, but I accepted little of it. And then there were other days when I would try to lay beside you and it would be like you weren't even there.

I wish there was some way you could have told me, explained your depression to me, explained that what was happening was not my fault.

I know now it wasn't, but for a long time there was a part inside of me that felt like it was. I had so many feelings I kept inside for so long and in the end, it started making me sick too.

Well Mom, they're out now, all of them. It's crazy, I feel like a walking kaleidoscope. I think you would laugh if you saw me. I'm happy and working on being peaceful.

I've met a boy, well a man, but he makes me feel young again, like I can push the refresh button and just start over here.

His name is Cristiano, but I'll tell you more about him later. We have our first—well, second date this weekend.

Back to my letter about us. Mom, for years I think I stretched your sadness around me, not just like a blanket, but like a thin protective cloak. I think it was the one way I could feel close to you. I hope this doesn't make you sad, that's not why I'm writing this. I am writing this letter to thank you. To thank you for all the little things you were able to do for me. To thank you for the little cut-out hearts you put into my lunch box. To thank you for getting up to make my lunch when you could. And to thank you for the ugly teapot that led me on this beautiful journey.

I understand now. My life is different. Something has changed inside of me, and I am finally becoming the Maya I was always supposed to be. I'm not sure how everything is going to turn out, but I'm not afraid anymore.

I know this sounds a little mixed up and I'm not sure when you'll get this, but know that I love you and that my heart is happy.

Send my love to Dad, let him know the joy is real and it is wonderful.

Love Maya

I sat for some time with the letter held close to my chest. I reread it, wanting to make sure that it said everything I needed it to say. The tears that flowed and splashed on the lovely parchment assured me that the letter reflected a true snapshot of my newly awakened self. I folded it carefully and slipped it into the envelope. On my way down to the dining room, I stopped at the front desk and handed the completed letter to Puro.

Before-supper drinks, became our opportunity to tell our tales of the day. As I told the story about being chased by the goat, I could hardly contain myself. Everyone laughed so hard that Puro had to come over and ask us to keep it down. That only made us laugh louder. He gave up after the second try and just brought us another bottle of wine.

"Puro," Josie chided, "come join us."

"Thank you, but I have supper plans," he said, nodding his head and excusing himself politely.

The six of us continued on throughout supper causing a great ruckus, but no one really seemed to mind. As everyone moved on to after-supper drinks, I could feel the multiple glasses of wine taking hold of me, so I stood up to say goodnight. "Well my friends, I am done for the day. I can see that you are well taken care of and have a few more bottles to test, but …" I lost my balance, fell and hit my head on the table, going down with a clunk and for a moment, everyone froze. I jumped up as quickly as I'd gone down, rubbing my head, and exclaimed "… and I thought it was the goats that were going to get me today!" Everyone erupted with laughter. I waved good night and could still hear the laughing as I made my way up the stairs. I had one more thing I needed to do that night and the balcony was the perfect place.

> *August 21th later*
>
> *Supper was fun tonight. I hope that Maggie is doing okay. It was such a busy day, but as I sit here on the balcony and let the night sky surround me, my thoughts keep drifting to Cristiano. It has only been two days since we said goodbye, but my heart aches just to hear his voice or to catch a glimpse of him. His touch, his smile—hey, he hasn't kissed me yet??!! Well not on the lips anyway. Maybe this weekend. I'm nervous and excited all at the same time …*

*Oh Dalley just came in. My head is spin-
ning. Gotta go.*
M.

"What a great night," Dalley called out. "Hey how's the writing going? My timing is terrible, I just keep interrupting."

"No interruption, no problem, and yes, it is awesome to write again every day. I forgot how much journaling meant to me. It really is the one place I can write down all my silly and serious thoughts without having to filter anything. It's so freeing. I could never do it your way," I blurted, the wine taking hold. "I could never imagine having to write something that *everyone* reads."

"Yes, it does have its challenges."

"I know you have so many rules to follow, but I get to say whatever I like." I patted Christopher on the cover. "I heard you on your computer the last few nights. Are you working on a project for the paper?"

"Yes, I am. You have very good hearing. It's a special interest piece about Portugal," she responded nonchalantly.

"Oh, I'd loved to read it when you're done." My words slurred. "Sorry, Dalley, I had too much to drink and my head hurts."

"No, no problem, I'll send you a copy when I'm back in the States. I hope you feel better." She began walking towards the bathroom.

"Would you like to join me out here and enjoy the night air?" I asked trying to clear my head of the fog I was in.

She smiled, welcoming the invitation. "That would be great."

We shared many stories that evening, talking about the misadventures in our lives. She told me about a time when she visited Paris and someone had told her that if she drank from the River Seine she would dream about the man she was going to marry.

"So did it work?" I asked jokingly.

"No, all I got out of that deal was a parasite that made me too sick for words." She held her stomach and pretended to vomit.

We laughed, and then things went silent between us and the mood changed. "Can I tell you something?" I asked her hesitantly, not sure if she was really interested in listening to more of my drama.

"You can tell me anything Maya." She leaned in and put her arm around me.

I went on to explain how much my life had changed since I'd gotten on that airplane in Vancouver. We talked about my mom's depression and I told her about the letter. She broke the mood with a laugh. "Well I guess you don't have to worry about the rules anymore. You are now officially a rule-breaking, heart-making, speed-demon, goat-chasing, sparkly-pen kind of woman."

"I guess I am!"

"Goodnight, Maya." She stood up then left me alone on the balcony with my thoughts and my new life. I got up, leaned over the edge, and yelled, "Rule-breaking, heart-making, speed-demon, goat-chasing, spark-ly-pen kind of woman: Yes I am!"

19

Intentions

Maya

THE NEXT MORNING I WOKE earlier than I'd wanted. My head was aching and I couldn't determine whether it was the wine or the fall. I had a bump on my forehead the size of an egg, so I decided to use the fall as my excuse. I dressed quickly, grabbed Christopher and Athena, and headed downstairs.

The lobby was quiet. The only person I saw was Puro, puttering behind the front desk.

"Morning Puro. Do you ever sleep?" I teased.

"Good morning Maya and yes, I just start with the birds every day. It keeps me young. What has *you* up so early this morning? Do you need some ice for that?" he asked pointing towards my head.

"No, thank you. And to answer your question, I figured I should attend at least one of Gervais' classes this week. Oh, could you please have someone bring me a cup of tea outside? I thought I would get some fresh air before the class and do some writing."

"Absolutely! Oh! You might find it a bit *chilly* on the veranda this morning," he commented emphasizing the chilly part.

"Thank you, Puro."

As I walked onto the veranda, the sun was already over the hills and shining onto the vineyard. It was going to be a beautiful day.

I looked around for somewhere to sit and saw Jade a few chairs down.

I thought about going back in, but decided I wasn't going to let her run me off. I wondered briefly why she was up so early and thought maybe there was hope for her if she liked the morning. I approached her cautiously, but with a welcoming smile.

"Good morning, Jade," I said trying to be genuine.

"Is it? I hadn't noticed," she retorted with sarcasm.

"Oh, I thought you might have come out to enjoy the fresh air and the morning sun." I realized quickly that my olive branch was being batted out of the way.

She looked at me like I had grown two heads.

"No, what gave you that idea?" she snapped back at me. "I just needed some air. The room they put me in is uninhabitable." Her beautiful face morphed into a deep ugly scowl.

Before she had a chance to say anything else, I asked her the question I'd been curious about. "Jade, why are you here? It's obvious that you don't want to be. Clearly you hate cooking. You didn't bring a camera except for the one on your phone, and honestly, you don't strike me as someone who would even enter a contest like this. It makes no sense."

She paused for a moment, then twisted her head towards me. She looked ghoulish. Then she responded in an acid-filled tone: "Maya, it is Maya, right? Why I am here or not here is none of your business. Just stay out of my way and keep your low-end, loud-mouth friends away from me."

I stood frozen, taking in the bitterness and sarcasm that punctuated her comment.

Although things had been very confusing and challenging in my own life, I was grateful that my world had not turned me into anything like her. She made it impossible to maintain any thoughts of hope for her. It appeared though that she saw my lack of response as weakness and laughed openly at me. I'm not sure what shifted, but the next set of words came tumbling from my lips.

"Do you know why a man like Cristiano chose *me* over *you?*"

She stared, eyebrow raised, like I was entertaining her. "Actually, it makes no sense to me at all, except maybe … bad taste, temporary blindness?"

I broke into a small smile and found an acceptable degree of calm. "Did you actually just say that?" I countered confidently. My smile grew as I dug into the moment. "There is a simple answer Jade, but you wouldn't understand. The bottom line is you need to grow up and find some manners. You're like a barrel of toxic waste; no wonder they put you in the basement."

I stood my ground and tried to stare her down, but I feared my pounding heart was so loud that it might give me away.

I turned around and walked briskly off the veranda and back into the lobby. Puro saw me, my face red, and my nose slightly flared. "You're right, it is *too chilly* out there; *icy* to be exact. I'll wait until later." I clenched my fists holding them tight to my body.

He smiled. "I'll have them bring your tea to your room and when I see Cristiano, I'll let him know he should be careful not to make you angry. In Portuguese they would call you *"assustador."*

"What does that mean?"

Puro held his finger to his forehead trying to come up with the right word then he grinned. "Scary," he explained while his smile grew.

I burst into laughter as no one had ever described me as *scary* before. "No, no I'll have it here in the lobby, thank you. And please, if you can hold off on telling this story to him, I would appreciate it." I turned to walk away, but had one last question for him. "Puro? You've met a lot of people in your line of work. How does that happen?" I pointed in her direction.

He paused and answered thoughtfully. "Well, you're right. I have met many people in my life, but few so angry. More than likely she has suffered great disappointments all her life. But even when someone is so sad and mad, kindness must always find a way."

"Puro, I don't think that she *can* be kind."

"I'm not really talking about her now," he responded, nodding in my direction.

"Oh!" I paused, understanding what he meant. "I'll have that tea now."

It was not long before I had my tea in one hand, Christopher in the other and about thirty minutes to myself.

Tuesday August 22nd

Okay, so how many awkward moments can one person have in the morning before 7:00 a.m.? Well at least two for sure. Ha! Ha! I guess all I can do is laugh at myself for even thinking that the girl had something else living inside her. But I'm proud I stood up to her.

Darn it, I didn't get to tell her why I think Cristiano chose me over her. Actually, I would have had to make that one up, as I'm not sure myself.

It's been three days and I miss him terribly. I want to see him, to know if our brief encounter was real, or just one of those moments people talk about for the rest of their lives. Real, I keep hoping for real ...

Jade

"Amateur!!" I yelled, but not loud enough for her to hear. "Too bad. I'd like to do that one over again. That toxic waste comment had potential."

I continued to sit and think about the brief encounter that I'd just had with Maya. It was fun! I loved making people mad and I was very good at it. I had learned from a young age I could manipulate almost every situation and get whatever I wanted if I kept them off their guard.

The feeling of victory was short lived as one question bled over into my thoughts. *Why **did** he choose her over me? Clearly, I am more beautiful and better dressed and I have more money than she does.* But I couldn't come up with an answer. Her words started to bother me, 'Simple? I wouldn't understand?' "Oh my God, get me out of this place." I screamed quietly to myself. I pulled out my phone and texted my father.

I've done what you asked, this place is perfect Axel. Now get me the hell out of here.

I didn't have to wait too long for him to get back to me.

Stop calling me Axel. I'm your father. I will send a car and driver on Monday morning and have the plane ready for you at the airport.

When was the last time you acted like a dad? Monday morning? Not fast enough. Send it by Friday.

Point taken about the dad thing. Can't send the plane until Monday. I'm busy this week. Oh remember, play nice with all the housewives, Ha Ha!! Seriously, don't do anything stupid like last time. You're right, Axel is much better.

I cringed at the thought of being stuck there for the whole week. Then I picked up my phone again.

You owe me! I'm going shopping in Lisbon with your personal expense card.

Not sure how you got hold of my expense card, but that is one of the things I love about you Jade; you're such a great thief.

Thief? Really? In the end it's all going to be mine anyway.

Do I have to start checking my food?

No, not yet, I still need you. Maybe when I take over 51% of your company though?

I'm glad to see you're planning for the future—but don't ever think you're going to take my company from me while I'm still alive.

I sat and contemplated my final response, as I knew he wasn't kidding. He never joked about his business. He would crush me before he'd let me take anything from him. I needed to play that moment very carefully.

Off to shop Dad. I'll bring you back a souvenir. Love Jade

I turned my phone off before he could text me back. I was furious he had mentioned the trip from last year. Axel was brutal. My whole life I'd watched him figure out ways to screw other people and destroy their lives in the process, and he expected anyone that worked for him to do the same—that included me.

Looking back at the open door to the inn, I could hear Maya's words: 'You're a barrel of toxic waste.' I thought about the comment for a moment and then smiled. "Good then, you can choke on my noxious fumes."

20

Reflections

Maya

AFTER MY RUN-IN WITH JADE, it took a little while for me to settle down and Gervais' cooking class was just the thing I needed. I had so much fun that I decided to attend classes for the rest of the week.

Over the next few days I forced myself to set aside thoughts of Cristiano. It wasn't easy, but my new friends helped distract me with copious amounts of food, wine, and a week of sharing stories about our lives.

Maggie and I set time aside to work on our presentation and build an electronic scrapbook. We decided that within our picnic theme we would feature fresh peach pie and the perfect sandwich.

Puro once again was a life saver as we were in hot pursuit of a few key items that had to be retrieved on Friday morning in order for our pies and sandwiches to be the freshest they could be. He called an old friend who lived two hours away and asked him about an old peach tree he had growing in his backyard. As luck would have it, the peaches were ripe and ready for picking. His friend was so excited about helping that he offered to pick the peaches on Friday morning himself and drive them down. I told Puro we could drive up on Thursday evening but he insisted, noting that he and his friend hadn't seen each other for years and were looking forward to having lunch and a glass of wine together. He also reminded us that we needed to go into Évora early in the morning to get all the other fresh ingredients.

"Maya," Puro cast his eyes down and paused briefly, "I have hired a driver for you and Maggie on Friday morning."

"No, that's okay, we can drive ourselves. It would give me an excuse to sit behind the wheel of that convertible again," I reflected with anticipation.

"Um, I'm so sorry Maya. The car will be in the shop," he responded hesitantly, like he wasn't sure.

"Oh," I answered feeling deflated. "I hope I didn't break anything?"

"No, no, no, it's fine. Just a tune up, that's all," he said scrambling for his words.

"You have to do tune-ups here on your rental cars?"

༶

Maggie and I met up in the lobby before we joined the group for supper on Thursday night.

"Maya, I think we have everything ready," she noted. "Let's just go over the presentation for tomorrow and then we can relax."

"Maggie, I am relaxed. Having you in my life right now is like having someone take over my brain." We both laughed.

"It's been a pleasure, but after tomorrow, you have to take back full possession. You have a date to get ready for," she teased.

"Don't remind me. I haven't been on a real date in years."

"Oh Maya, how many years could it be? Two? Three? Try twenty-five years for me? You'll be fine. Just remember to be yourself and breathe." We both looked over and noticed Puro. It appeared that he had been listening to us. Embarrassed that he had been caught, he quickly made himself busy, and then disappeared.

"You're right! No need to think about that now. What time should we get started in the morning?" I said, changing the subject.

"I need you down here at 8:00 a.m.," she said rebuking me in her best mom voice before I had even done anything wrong.

"Not a problem. I'm not going to do anything crazy tonight, I promise," I said, giving her my best intention. "We have some time before supper. Let's go see what Gervais has in store for this evening. I bet he and Sachi have created something spectacular to eat. They sure have been spending a lot of extra time together."

Maggie and I went over to the kitchen, but Gervais wouldn't let us in. He said it was too busy so we popped over to the dining room and joined our group. I sat as far away from Jade as possible.

Once we were all there, Josie grabbed the closest wine glass and said, "I want to make a toast." Everyone paused, captured by her commanding tone. "I want to thank the brothers and all of their amazing staff at the vineyard who have created this unique opportunity. I truly believe that if we are the experiment, then so far so good. Bravo!" She raised her glass to Puro, who had just entered the room, and to all of the staff saying, "*Obrigada do fundo do meu coração.*" We all laughed, not exactly sure what she had said. We later found out that she had thanked them with all of her heart. Puro nodded his head and accepted the toast. A few minutes later, I saw him slip out.

We started our meal with a daily plate of olives, cheese, and breads, and then for supper had a choice of either pecan crusted lamb or *farinheira*, a traditional Portuguese smoked sausage. I thought about the sausage, but the lamb called out to me. And then there was the wine. I was captured by a bottle of something called green wine. The liquid took hold of my palette and stayed close to me for the rest of the night. I had never tasted anything like it. It was crisp and sparkling, not like champagne, but fresh like stepping out of the door early in the summer morning. Every sip was like a celebration for my taste buds and it was paired perfectly to Gervais' food.

As I finished off the first bottle of *Vinho verde*, thoughts of Cristiano danced across my mind, but after hearing the second cork pop, an evening of memory making took over.

Puro

Laughter flowed from the dining room like an electrical current. My guests were having a wonderful evening and so was I. I had received a call from Cristiano that he had landed and was heading straight over to the inn. The time had passed so quickly with all the festivities in the dining room that when I heard the crunching of gravel under a set of tires, it took me by surprise. Then the car door slammed and there he was, casually strolling through the front door, like it had only been a few weeks since his last visit.

I always loved seeing him. His heart was pure and he came from a good family. He had gotten a little lost, but I always knew he would find his way back and there he was, looking like a new man.

"Cristiano, it has been too long. You look good, happy." In the past, he was never able to show me how he felt, but that day something was different. He embraced me with great enthusiasm.

"I am good. You are right though, it has been too long. You have gotten gray in the last two years. Carmo must have finally told you about Bento," Cristiano said smirking.

I laughed back, "You knew about Bento?" I chastised him jokingly. "Between you and Carmo, I am surprised that I have any hair left."

"Thank you, Puro. You have always been there for me, even when I didn't think I needed you." He hugged me again. He had been a complicated young man, but I'd never given up on him. I couldn't. He had lost so much when he was a young boy. We both knew what an empty heart felt like. Unfortunately, he'd never allowed his to heal.

I had been friends with Cristiano's father, Michel, when we were both children. His parents were always so generous to my impoverished family, sharing everything they could, always making sure we had bread on the table. And then later as adults, Michel and Rosa had been there to help me in many ways when my dear Fiona died and I was left to raise my little Carmo on my own. They had always wanted children themselves, but it never happened for them. After Carmo and I had settled and gotten our feet back on the ground, we all went back to our lives, and I did not hear from them. A few years later I heard that they'd had a child, a son. When I heard about their tragic accident, it was a horrible shock. I was deeply saddened by their death, as they were two of the kindest people I had ever known, and I knew that the heart of any child of theirs would suffer greatly without them.

A year or so after the accident, I decided to take a different route on my usual Sunday morning walk. I passed by the old vineyard chapel, and was drawn by a sweet, prayerful hymn being played on a guitar. To my pleasant surprise, I found Michel's mother and a little boy playing the guitar. She smiled, knowing who I was instantly. She nodded her head, but Cristiano only peered up briefly, hiding under his long bangs. I told him I had known his parents and I would be happy to help him in any way I could, as I was now managing all of Netuno. It felt natural to welcome them both into our family.

Cristiano became like part of the furniture at the vineyard when he was young. Not the indoor kind, but like the old wooden bench carved out of a tree trunk. As an adolescent though, he stopped wandering the vineyard and rarely came to the chapel with his Avó. When he was fourteen, she wanted him to do some work on the weekends, so I gave him a job pruning and picking grapes and olives. He was not pleased but would never disobey her. So, he begrudgingly came to work and kept to himself most of the time.

"Excuse me, Puro."

Cristiano nudged me and broke the tight embrace and the trail of memories I had been walking down momentarily.

"How did my car drive this week?" he asked with a slightly anxious tone.

"It drove perfectly, no complaints from the driver," I teased. "I'm guessing that you have another reason for coming here straight from the airport, besides seeing me of course, and picking up the car?" Cristiano's eyes darted down and in that moment, I saw the child I had met so many years ago, bangs still hanging in his eyes. But the difference now was that his eyes sparkled and his heart was no longer empty.

"Cristiano, do you want me to let her know you are here?" I asked, starting to make my way towards the dining room.

"No, that's alright," he claimed, but his face deceived him. "I just came to get the car. I promised Avó I would see her tonight and I don't want to be late. I haven't been the best to her these past few years. Is she well?"

"Your Avó?"

"No, Maya," he exclaimed, sounding exasperated.

"Yes, she is well." I smiled. Then I put my hand on his shoulder. "I think she and her friends are having quite the time tonight. Follow me." I guided him towards the dining room.

He followed and peeked in. His eyes were drawn to her instantly. She was all he could see. He watched her as she laughed and smiled.

"Could that be possible?" he asked me.

"What's that Cristiano?"

"I think I just fell in love with her again," he said simply.

"Come, let's get you home or Avó will have both our heads," I chuckled as I directed him away from the dining room. "The keys are in your car. Now go!"

Maya

"Dalley, did you see that?"

"See what?" she responded without looking.

"There was someone at the door." I rushed over, not knowing who or what I saw, but feeling drawn to find out.

"Is there something I can do for you Maya?" Puro asked casually, meeting me at the door.

"No, I just had this funny feeling. Was someone just standing here?" I asked trying not to sound too strange or intoxicated.

"Yes, but no one you know. A gentleman just came to pick up the car and he heard you and your friends laughing," he answered stumbling over his words.

I ran to the front door and saw my convertible speed off down the dirt road. "Isn't it a little unusual to have someone picking the car up at night?"

He just smiled. "Maya, I am sure you have noticed, we Portuguese do everything on our own timeline. Don't worry about such things."

"I'm not worrying, I just feel kind of strange inside," I tried to explain.

"Could it be the second bottle of *vinho verde* you are working on?" he teased.

"Maybe." I shrugged, then let Puro guide me back to the party.

Dalley, Josie, Petra, and I closed the house down, managing to finish another bottle of wine, and a small bottle of port. As Dalley and I made our way back to the room, we hung on to each other, convinced we were sign posts keeping each other standing. We stumbled through the door and Dalley crashed onto her bed fully clothed, but oddly I wasn't sleepy. I felt alive. I knew I needed to have a candle bath and to write! I picked up the phone and called down to the front desk.

"I knew it. You never sleep, do you Puro," I yelled into the receiver.

"Maya, what can I do for you?" he asked patiently.

"Do you have any candles your staff could send up?" I whispered loudly.

"Maya it's late. Maybe you should get some rest."

"No, Puro, I love you, you're the best, but I need those candles. It's a writing emergency," I tried to explain.

"Okay Maya, I'll come up myself," he said giving in to my request.

"You're the best, best. Thank you, thank you," I sang into the phone. He arrived shortly with the candles. I danced around him like a school girl.

"Where do you want them? I will light them for you. I'm not sure giving you matches right now is such a good idea."

"Yes, I think you are right. In the bathroom please," I answered with a sigh and a slur.

When he was done he came out smiling. "Be careful Maya, see you in the morning."

"Bye, Puro." I pulled my spinning brain together for a second. "Thank you for everything." Closing the door, I headed over to the most beautiful bathroom in the world.

I slipped my clothes off piece by piece, sat on the edge of the tub, and then moved the lit candles closer to me. The essential oil that Dalley and

I had picked up at the lingerie store last weekend called out to me. The scent of lemongrass and geranium soon filled the bathroom, as the heat of the water activated the oils. The name on the bottle was Revelation, and it did not disappoint. I carefully found my way into the deep steaming tub under the glow of a few shimmering lights.

I opened Christopher, leaned back into the ever-warming porcelain, took Athena out, and began.

Thursday late, wait it's early Friday.

I can hardly keep things straight, too much verdho verte.

Where do I begin ...? The hot water flowing over my body is like being wrapped in a piece of shantung silk, a sensual touch beyond anything you could imagine.

The last six days have been both wonderful and challenging. Cristiano, cooking, the letter to my Mom, Jade, all the moments rolling every which way through my soul.

I'm glad I sent the letter to my mom, but I know I still have lots of work to do when I get home.

Jordan was right—I was acting selfishly and wrapping it all up in a pretty selfless bow.

I guess it has taken me an almost wedding, an airport encounter, getting chased by a goat, and a candle-lit bath in Portugal to even start figuring it out. I am so sorry to everyone that I have hurt along the way.

It is amazing to be able to sit back and see what my anger and sadness has done to me over the years, but even more so how ready I am to let it go and move forward.

Wow!! I feel like I can take a breath ... My head is spinning, but I can breathe. Maybe that's the point. I've been pushing the sadness and the anger down for so long, and letting it grow and steal my breath.

Maybe finding a new way to breathe is not so much for me about finding love like Maggie, but finding joy. If I can find the joy, maybe all different kinds of love will follow. Yes, I believe that's possible.

I sure am happy that no one will ever read this. One journal reading by Cristiano was quite enough.

Oh the bath is getting too hot. I have to get out. Until tomorrow. One more thought:

Only one more sleep until I see him. Hey I had a funny feeling tonight. It must have been the wine, but he felt close. Maybe he's flying back right now, thinking about me thinking about him. Oh Maya, stop being so goofy.

Goodnight to all the joy that is yet to be.

M.

Stepping out of the deep soaker tub, I stood in front of the mirror in the dimly lit shadows. As the candlelight reflected off my body, I looked at myself for the first time, really looked. I started with my face. I felt the heat in my cheeks and smiled at the pink hue that I could barely see. Then I began to trace the water droplets down my arms. I took a slow breath and allowed my hand to gently brush against the delicate skin. I turned and in the reflection of the mirror saw my lower back glistening like a jeweled crown. Quietly, I began to speak, "*I* am beautiful. I *am* beautiful, I am *beautiful.*"

It took a few minutes for that thought to sink in. I stared at myself, smiled, and knew that my world would never be the same again. I knew I was ready for anything.

I knelt down onto the floor by the tub and blew out each candle until there was only one left. I looked around the room and was surprised by how much light was cast by a single source.

"One light can make a difference," I whispered.

I opened my journal again and jotted down my final thoughts of the evening. Then I blew out the last candle and sat naked on the bathroom floor.

21

I am Beautiful

Maya

THE NEXT SOUND I HEARD was a startling knock on the door. "Maya are you in there? Are you okay?"

"Unh yah? I think so," I answered groggily as I peeled my skin off the cold bathroom tile. "Oh crap, too much wine, mixed with the hot bath last night. I passed out on the floor. What time is it?"

"It's 9:00 a.m. Everyone has already eaten breakfast and Maggie's waiting for you. Your car is here to take you into Évora."

"Dalley, can you please phone Maggie and let her know I'll be down in ten minutes," I pleaded.

"Will do Maya. You sure liked that green wine. Do you remember much?"

I wrapped a towel around myself and opened the door. "I'm not quite sure what I remember yet." I held my head like it was ready to fall off.

"Yah, me too. I remember dancing on the tables, and lots of great food and wine."

"Yes, I have vague recollections of the dancing and the drinking, and then Puro brought me candles. He was incredibly sweet. I am so embarrassed. I'll be out in a few." The bathroom door closed with a thud and my towel dropped to the floor. I found myself standing in front of the mirror again, this time in the light of a perfect morning. I stared at the body that I had embraced the night before. I was still beautiful. I laughed, then jumped into the shower. Whatever fog I should have been feeling lifted under the refreshing water. I knew something important had happened to me that night, and it was just the beginning.

When I finished in the shower, I ran out and saw Dalley lying on her bed. "Do you have everything ready for tonight?"

"Oh yeah, Jade and I have everything under control," she laughed. "Not sure it is camera-winning worthy, but at least I won't let her embarrass me tonight. You had better hurry up. Maggie and the car are waiting. Hey, can I borrow your toothpaste?"

"Yeah sure," I yelled, as I ran out of the room.

Dalley

I walked into the bathroom to grab the toothpaste and stubbed my toe on something. I looked down to investigate and noticed Maya's journal was on the floor waterlogged and looking a little worse for wear. "Oh, Maya! What were you thinking?" I looked over and saw Athena, the mighty pen, sitting on the edge of the tub. I started to laugh. I wasn't sure if I should leave the journal on the floor or try to dry it off. I decided to take it back to my bathroom, as I had one of those cool air buttons on my hairdryer. As I opened it, I remembered the first day on the plane and all the tears and trauma that went along with her almost losing this thing. So I figured she wouldn't have any objections to me drying it off.

I worked on each page, hoping the water had not damaged anything, when suddenly I caught a glimpse of an entry with my name in it. I ignored it at first and continued with the drying but was drawn back to reading it. After that it was like my name was highlighted along with Cristiano's and Jade's, and my curiosity got the better of me. I knew I shouldn't have read the entries, but somehow I just couldn't stop. I was drawn into her writing, the honesty and raw emotion: she was so real.

The last entry was barely legible. It was as if it was written in someone else's hand, which made me even more determined to decipher it. I managed to make it through, even that last paragraph when the lettering seemed to shrink and fade away.

> *Just a few lines, that's all I can write before my eyes fail.*
>
> *With the last candle glowing and the breeze of the early morning slipping in through the open window, I want to thank you. Thank you for letting me see myself in the mirror; for letting me feel each curve of my body; and discover who I really am. I am beautiful. See you tomorrow my new old friend.*
>
> *M.*

Pausing for a moment, I could feel a thought formulating and I tried to stop it, but as I ran my fingers over the spine, my resistance melted. I walked over to my computer, sat down, and opened her journal to page one.

Phrases, quotes, and poetry flung themselves at me. Her words became mine. When I was done, I hit publish immediately, not giving myself a chance to think twice, then tossed the journal onto Maya's bathroom counter, and ran out the door.

22

Who's the Sous Chef?

Maya

MAKING MY WAY DOWN THE hall, my mind split into two directions: one path bringing me to the realization I had forgotten my purse, and the other that I had no time to go back to the room. Giving in to the logic of time, I broke into a run and flew down the stairs trying to find a few lost seconds. Maggie was standing at the front desk looking relaxed, laughing, and talking to Puro. I jumped the last stair like a teenager late for school and ran over to her, out of breath.

"Maggie, I'm so sorry for being late."

She laughed, waved goodbye to Puro, and grabbed my hand. "The driver is waiting."

"Maggie," I said quietly as we walked out to the car, "next time, please remind me not to have so much fun."

"Now why would I do that?" she said laughing again. "It was a memorable evening wasn't it? I only stayed until about midnight though; after that my coach was ready to turn into a pumpkin." She smiled and then changed the subject. "The peaches arrived. They're in the kitchen waiting for us. They are beyond perfection: their shape, color, scent. They are stupendous! I couldn't have asked for anything more. Our pies are going to be unforgettable."

"Oh, can I go smell them, please?" I pleaded like a child.

"No, not right now," she said firmly. "We have to go into Évora to get our sandwich supplies and then scoot back here to bake our pies."

"Maggie, I forgot to tell you one thing. I've never baked a pie in my life. I don't know the first thing about pastry or even how to prep the peaches." "Oh Maya, it's not rocket science," she teased. "It's just a little simple food chemistry."

"Chemistry? Are you kidding me? Home Ec. and Chemistry were my two worst subjects in school." I shuddered with historical images of gingerbread men on fire and chemistry exams that made me cry.

"Maya, you're not in high school anymore. I'll teach you. It just takes a little time, patience, and love; not even love for the baking, but just love for something in your life. That way when people bite into your food they'll say, 'Oh what is that flavor? I can't quite put my finger on it, but it tastes amazing.' It works every time. Trust me."

"I do. I'm just not sure I trust myself, but lead the way. I forgot my purse upstairs. Should I grab it?"

"No, I have everything we need."

We climbed into the car and headed off on our food mission to Évora. We knew exactly what we needed, and the driver made it easy.

When we arrived back at Netuno, the lobby was filled with the most inviting scent. Even if I was blind, I would have found my way to the kitchen with the fresh peaches guiding me all the way.

Maggie looked at her watch appearing distracted. "What is it? Are we running late?"

"No, it's not that. I was just thinking about my boys."

"Have you had a chance to talk to them lately?"

"Yes, I called them yesterday. It was early in the morning back home, but they were up and getting ready for school. They're doing great; having a blast without their mother hovering over them. CJ has a little cold, but he said he was fine and was going into school to check on his schedule. My sister is keeping an eye on them." She paused briefly then added, "They are my whole heart. They keep telling me I have to start preparing for when they go away to university next year, and I keep pretending it will never happen. It's a perfect mismatch of plans." She smiled and shook her head, laughing a little at herself. "When I won this contest, I wasn't going to accept, but the boys insisted. So here I am, having one of the best times of my life. Thank you for being part of that."

I dropped my bags and hugged her tightly.

When we entered the kitchen, it was almost noon. Everyone was at their stations, doing something interesting. Even Dalley and Jade were hard at work. I'm not sure how Dalley had convinced Jade to do anything, but I was sure I didn't want to know.

Gervais cleared his throat. "Excuse me. Now that our last team has arrived, and everyone is prepping their dishes for tonight, I want to remind you of some of our guidelines. Remember you are asked to present two specific dishes. The theme this week was movement. All food and images need to be on the table by 8:00 p.m. Don't forget that the winners will receive gifts of new digital cameras. But remember, this is not about winning. It is about telling your story through food and images. I will be here all day helping with anything you need."

Everyone went back to work. I ran my tongue over my teeth and remembered I had not brushed them before heading out that morning.

"Yuck," I said out loud.

"Yuck?" Maggie asked.

"Maggie, can I go freshen up? I forgot to brush my teeth this morning. I'll be back in fifteen minutes."

"Not a minute longer. We need all the time we can get for the pies."

"I promise," I yelled as I scooted out the door. I ran up to my room in record time, bounded into the bathroom, grabbed my toothbrush and knocked Christopher onto the floor. "Sorry friend." I bent down to pick him up as he opened to last night's journal entry. "What a crazy night! It was awesome though," I said scanning my words. "Shantung silk? Where did that come from?"

I brushed my teeth quickly and noticed I had a few minutes remaining on my stopwatch, so I grabbed Athena and threw myself onto the bed.

> *August 25th 12:30p.m. Friday*
>
> *Oh I just looked over last night's entry and it was quite the night. I can hardly make out some of what I wrote. I'm sure glad that you're okay. I know that I got you pretty wet when I was in the tub. But you seemed to have dried out quickly.*
>
> *This morning was so much fun in the market with Maggie. She's like the mom I always thought I wanted. But I guess each of us is given what we are supposed to have.*
>
> *Maybe, Maggie was just saved for me until now.*
>
> *The peaches came in for our pies today. I wish I could have picked them myself. Someday I will have a peach tree in my own yard. Someday I'll have the whole life that I want ... but for now I'll just settle for the pies.*
>
> *Maya*

23

Peach Pie

Maya

"ARE YOU READY MAYA?" MAGGIE asked like a coach waiting to start a training lesson.

"You bet, as fresh as a daisy," I said, pulling out an old phrase of Grandma Stella's.

Josie turned and laughed, "Daisy fresh? That's funny."

She had been one of the final four who closed things down with me the night before and she too, along with Petra and Dalley, was looking a little worse for wear.

"I need a beer! That should do the trick," she exclaimed.

Sachi raised an eyebrow, then reached down under her station and pulled out a bottle of sake and poured Josie a small cup.

"I love this girl," Josie chirped, then drank down the sake in one shot.

"Excuse me, Maya. The pies—focus." Maggie poked.

"Sorry, you now have my full attention. I am ready to make the best pie that anyone has ever eaten."

I followed Maggie's every move. It was like shadowing a dancer. We started with the slow measure of the flour into the cold bowl, spooning and sifting quietly as we worked.

"Why don't we just use a cup and dump it in? It would be much faster that way," I whispered.

"Why? Are you in a rush?" she rebutted my query, like a tennis volley.

"No, but …?"

"No buts, Maya. No short cuts, just time and love. Think of something or someone that you love while you are prepping the pastry with me. And no talking!"

It surprised me how easy the task was to accomplish. Images of Cristiano were all I could see.

Maggie's sharp tongue that forbade me to talk during the making of the pastry caught several people's attention. Then she took a lump of something out of the fridge and gave half to me and kept the other half for herself.

"What is that?"

She started to laugh. "Lard," she responded with a smirk.

"LARD? Who uses lard anymore?"

"I do," she answered with emphasis. "My grandmother always told me, 'If you're going to make a pie, do it right, and lard is the only answer.'"

Then we both started to laugh.

"Honestly Maya, we have lots of work to do. Are you always this distracted in the kitchen?"

I looked around and saw several people peering over at us from behind their own stations.

"What is it now?"

"Um, I think we have an audience," I answered in a low voice. Maggie took a quick look around and saw that I was right.

"Well friends, if you've got the time, I've got enough flour and lard." She searched the room for Gervais, who was also watching her with curiosity.

"If all goes well, you may have enough pies for your entire supper menu." She smirked at Gervais. "Roll up your sleeves and get started everyone, but you have to follow my rules, and no talking while making the pastry and no drinking anything," she said, looking directly at Josie.

"Also, just a friendly reminder that the peaches belong to Maya and I, so you all will have to find your own fruit." She peered over at Gervais who raised a finger indicating that he'd received her point. He then ran off into the large fridge returning with just about every fruit known to man.

"*Oui, oui j'ai des fruit,*" he exclaimed with excitement.

"*Merci* Gervais. Grab a bowl and a spoon and let's get to it everyone." Time slipped away as she worked with each person, sifting, measuring, cutting and rolling, all in hushed tones. She even had Josie quiet for a moment or two.

By the time we had finished, everyone had made at least one pie, and they were all ready to go into the oven. Maggie was right. I didn't even need to taste my pie to know that it was going to be the most delicious and heart-fulfilling food I had ever made. My pie didn't look as perfect as Maggie's but it was a pie—a real peach pie—and I had made it all by myself. In that moment it felt like I had accomplished the impossible.

Our group had once again fallen into an afternoon of spontaneous memory making and surprisingly quiet laughter. I swear, even Jade looked like she'd almost had a good time. But that was short lived, as her sour face returned when Dalley made her go back to preparing for the evening's competition.

Maggie and I prepped our sandwiches and spent the remainder of our afternoon making sure that all the pies were perfectly baked. Just after the last of the pies came out of the oven, Puro came in to talk to Maggie and asked her how things were going. A few minutes later, I saw him scooting out of the kitchen with a slice of pie, hidden under a napkin, and a content smile resting on his lips. I laughed at their little bit of secrecy and loved what it added to the day.

As our precious pastry cooled, I snuck away to review the scrapbook that Maggie and I had prepared earlier in the week and quickly added a few shots of Maggie's pie-making extravaganza.

Dinner went off without a hitch and the presentation was a great success. Maggie and I could hardly contain ourselves as we recounted the story about the goats chasing us up the hill, and the two of us running after the hay truck in the field. She shared memories about the picnic under the tree and wove a tale of truth about the day, without revealing my epiphany about my childhood, and my relationship with my mother.

Our picnic brought back many fond memories, both recent and past for everyone. And Maggie received a special gift of a beautifully hand-crafted ceramic pie plate from Gervais, thanking her for her afternoon of pie making. In the end, Sachi and Josie won the new cameras. Sachi had been so taken with Josie's salsa dancing at the nightclub and all her stories that she decided to build their food menu based on Josie's past experiences. She re-invented two of Josie's favorite Portuguese dishes: *Pato com Damascos e Arroz* (Duck with apricots and rice), and *Salame de chocolate* (chocolate salami that disappeared before I could even get a slice). While the brothers sampled the food, Josie presented the history of Salsa dancing, giving a few lessons along the way. Later in the evening, she and Reinaldo took over the dance floor. It was spectacular.

After the prizes were given out and everyone had finished eating supper, Gervais came up to speak. "I have to tell you that this afternoon my kitchen sang with heart and much flour. Each one of you left your stations to join together in the effort of learning. You laughed and rolled and chopped and baked. It was beautiful. Thank you, Maggie. I will always remember your theory on lard! And now, pie for everyone!"

Facing the Bread

Cristiano

AFTER RELUCTANTLY LEAVING THE INN, the drive over to Avó's cottage was short, but allowed me the time to take in the rolling hills and the scent of the dirt and the grapes growing all around me. It was as if the vines were welcoming me home. They were not angry about my absence, just thankful I had come back. I turned down the road to the cottage. The light was still on. She was up and waiting for me. When I walked through the door, she sat at the kitchen table with her right hand placed on a sack of grain. I smiled at her, knowing what the sack meant, and that together we would be baking well into the early morning.

We slept on and off between the risings of the dough and several times I tried to talk to her, but she only placed her strong, firm finger on my lips and nodded her head like she knew what I was going to say. After we finished baking, we sat in the garden and watched the sunrise, eating our bread and holding hands.

The rest of the day was spent grinding grain for the two large orders that she had agreed to make. I found it strange that she had said yes to the orders as she had stopped taking large ones years ago, but I knew better than to ask any questions. She always had a reason for everything. We worked side by side, speaking little, but saying so much. She was joyful and I was thankful. Early in the afternoon after we finished grinding the grain, we went for a walk through the fields.

"Cristiano, tell me what's on your mind. I can sense peace and joy all around you with a whisper of hesitation." She spoke gently to me, placing her hand on my chest.

"I feel something in my heart that is so real, but I am afraid that if I say it out loud it will become just a dream."

"Say it and it will be," she said simply.

I paused, gathering my thoughts together. "I have fallen in love."

"I know." Her eyes sparkled with joy.

"You know?"

"Yes, I knew before you did." Another smile crossed her face.

I gripped her hand more tightly and shook my head. I had forgotten how very talented she was in so many ways, besides her bread making. After we pulled the last set of buns out of the oven, we made our way to our rooms to rest as we had many loaves to finish baking the next day.

As I lay in my old bed, the thought of Avó's letter laying open on my coffee table back at the apartment tapped me on the shoulder. I had made no mention of it to Avó when I'd arrived, but I had questions about the adoption, my birth parents and why no one had told me sooner. I wasn't sure how or what I felt, but at least I felt something other than sadness and anger. The reconnection to my other emotions was odd at first. It had been so long. It was like stretching a muscle that had been in knots for years. But the ache felt good—the slow twist, the bend and hold of the emotional stretch. It was going to take time, but I would get strong again. I would be able to love, the way it was supposed to be. I wiped my eyes with the palm of my hand, and knew that both Maya and the truth of the adoption came into my life at the same time for a reason.

I slept soundly for the first time in many years, allowing love and truth to let my heart rest.

When my eyes opened, the sun had taken hold of my room. I looked around, took a deep purposeful breath, and let the warmth of home spread over me. My small smile turned into a great grin as I couldn't believe that my life could change so much in just one week, but it had.

I dressed quickly and headed out to the garden. All of the loaf pans were sitting on the table, cleaned and ready for use. Sometimes I wondered if she ever slept. I lit the fire in the outdoor oven, enjoying the invitation of warmth and watched the flames dance gleefully, fed by the kindling. As I turned from the fire, a glint of silver caught my eye. Something familiar leaned up against the bench, like an old friend I had not seen for years. It was the guitar from church, the first one from the cupboard when I was a child. Within seconds music filled the garden as the old hymns I used to play for Avó came flooding back into my fingers. It wasn't long before her voice joined in with my music. She sat with me while I played, then began mixing and prepping the dough. I could feel the rhythm of the loaves being kneaded through the old wooden table. After the second rising, we placed the bread into the oven with hope and excitement that each loaf would turn out the way it was supposed to. Avó didn't believe in perfection. She felt that accepting imperfection was a gift given to all of us.

As we sat and waited for the last of the bread to bake, I looked at all the loaves we had already completed and wondered aloud, "How are you delivering the bread today?"

"Oh, didn't I tell you, my dear?" she smiled. "I need you to do the deliveries for me early this evening."

I froze. "Avó, I have plans tonight. I'm meeting Maya."

"Cristiano, that is fine. She will help you. I am sure you have chosen a girl who would love to help you deliver a few loaves of bread for me?" She chuckled, knowing I would never say no to her.

"Oh, of course. We would be happy to help you," I said sighing and resigning myself to a change in my plans. "Where do we have to go?"

"First, I need you to go the Black Castle Tavern outside of Évora and drop off the small order of buns we baked last night. It is for a wedding."

"And then?" I asked trying to be patient.

"Ah yes, I need for you to go to the Medieval Festival in Silves. Dionisio is working the gate and will let you in when you arrive. Maybe you can stay and enjoy the festival."

"Avó, we can't attend unless we have costumes," I said trying to get out of the second delivery.

"Then you are in luck. Rondo in Évora said you could drop by the store and pick up anything you need."

"So you've taken care of everything?" I asked suspiciously.

"What? What are you saying Cristiano? Get back to work. We still have eight dozen egg tarts to make today."

I shook my head, knowing that my date had just taken a new and curious direction at the hands of a woman who somehow *always* got what she wanted.

25

Tasting a Future

Maya

SATURDAY ARRIVED, AND WITH A gentle nudge from the morning light shining through the window I opened my eyes. I took a breath and could hardly believe I had made it through the last seven days. I rolled over and saw Athena shimmering in the sunlight and heard her calling out to me.

August 26th

Tiny writing. That's what I feel like today.

I love when each letter falls perfectly on the page, when my hand, pen and heart all come together to say hello to the paper.

You know, that is why the right pen and paper are so important. They find a connection to the heart that I've just never been able to make to the computer.

Right now I am wrapped in a fine cotton sheet, taking in the morning air and filling up my lungs with a fresh new breath. What a gift to just lie here and see the sun rise and say good morning.

Has it really only been seven days? I can't believe it.

Every day has been filled with new and old, laughter and curiosity, excitement and adrenaline, but no fear. I really did leave my fear behind at the airport in Vancouver. I wonder though, was it that I left my fear behind, or that I finally faced it? Either way, I am here now living a life that I didn't even know I wanted.

My thoughts keep drifting over to Cristiano, like he is part of my consciousness now. I have held off for days trying not to get distracted, but now I can let thoughts of him take over. I get to see him tonight.

I had better get up as I have a lazy day planned of walking in the vineyard, and thinking about Cristiano, and I don't want to miss a minute of it.

Everyone else is heading off to Lisbon for the day. It should be lovely and quiet around here.

Bye for now,

Maya

"Dalley, are you up?" I whispered, hoping she was.

"Yes, Maya, between your pen scratching, the sun blasting in, and the singing of that crazy bird outside our window, I had no choice."

"Oh Dalley, we always have a choice. Isn't that what you said last week?" A dash of sarcasm fell out of my mouth. "Are you going into Lisbon today?"

"I was planning on it, why?"

"Oh, I was just thinking I might need some help picking out an outfit for my date tonight. I have no idea what I should wear." It was true. Although it felt like everything in my life had changed over the last seven days, my fashion sense was surely not part of that picture, yet.

"Yes, I think I can manage to add that to my calendar." She sounded almost excited about the invitation. "Did you want to hang out together for the day?" she asked.

"No, thank you. I have something planned. But if you could be back for around 3:00 that would be great. Cristiano is coming to get me at 4:30," I said, smiling.

"That should give us enough time—barely," she joked.

"Am I that far gone?"

"No, I'm just teasing but I do want you to look perfect for tonight."

I was still lazing about in bed when she emerged from the bathroom and began packing up her computer. "You don't have to work today, do you?" I asked feeling disappointed for her.

"Yes, Maya, some of us still need to make a living. Not all of us have paid holidays." Her tone was playful, yet I could tell she was still trying to make a point. She was right though. I was very lucky to have paid holidays, benefits, and a steady income. But I would have given it all up just to stay as happy as I was right then.

"Don't work too hard and make sure you get some good shopping in." The look on her face softened and then she broke into a big smile.

"Nothing could keep me from my quest of finding more shoes. See you later Maya. Have a good day. Don't think too much about Cristiano, it could be dangerous for your smile quota," she teased.

"I think shopping with you would be far more dangerous!"

"What are you talking about? You still have money on your pre-loaded credit card. No danger there."

"Dalley, get out of here and leave me to my imagination. Good luck with the writing and the shoe hunt."

"Have a good day," she yelled back.

"No worries. This is already the best day ever and I haven't even gotten out of bed." I rolled over and indulged in my cotton luxury. I could never go back to my poly/cotton sheets. I was ruined forever.

When the door closed, the energy in the room shifted from we to me. I lay waiting for something to happen, and it did. Thoughts of Cristiano slipped over my skin warming me like a beautiful embrace.

A date? It sounds so silly, but my heart is fluttering and I can hardly believe it. Did I really say yes to going out with a man that I met on a plane just seven days ago? Yes ... and do I have any second thoughts? Not one. He's coming by at 4:30 to pick me up and I have no idea where we are going or what we are doing and it doesn't matter, as long as we're together.

I lingered a little longer and let my thoughts of his warm smile and mischievous eyes embed themselves in my skin.

Sitting up, I realized that I had the rest of the day to ponder and wander, and if I didn't get started I could waste it away in this beautiful bed, getting lost in images of my future. Not such a bad option, but taking a page out of Dalley's book, I hustled out of bed and decided to start the next part of my day with a quiet walk through the grounds and then over into the olive grove.

As I wandered down the stairs, Puro was sitting behind the front desk. He looked so peaceful.

"Hey Puro, what are you doing?"

"Just thinking."

"About anyone in particular?" I inquired, trying to be subtle but failing miserably.

"Oh, Maya, I'll leave that young love piece to the likes of you and Cristiano." He winked, successfully changing the subject and causing me to blush. "Oh yes, I have known that boy for many years, and I have never seen him like this."

"You saw him?" I asked with excitement, my head darting around.

"No, I mean when I talked to him ... before," he sounded befuddled with my question. "If I am right, there will be a few broken hearts strewn around the globe when they find out he is taken."

I wasn't sure what to say so I opted for nothing, smiled, and then scooted out the door. I could hear Puro laughing as he sent me running out into the fields.

The walk through the vineyard was brilliant. I smelled the sweetness of the grapes coming into their own, and the olive grove was fascinating. The trees were pruned so that you could pick the olives just by raising your arm ever so slightly. It was like being a giant in a forest and seeing all the treetops. I tugged at one of the green olives, never having eaten one raw from the tree before, and popped it in my mouth. Not sure what to expect, I allowed my senses to embrace the new experience. I was stunned by the bitterness of the flesh yet held it in my mouth just long enough to feel the texture and experience it fully. It reminded me of unripened bananas, woody and odd; but it made a lasting impression. I couldn't help but wonder how they made olives taste so good.

I laughed at my olive adventure, making a mental note that I had to tell Beth this story on the next postcard. Over the course of the week, I had kept up with my promise to write postcards for her grade one class. So far I had one from the Kelowna Airport, Vancouver, Montreal, Lisbon, Évora, and several from the inn. They were all written and ready to go. I wished Beth had been with me right then. That would have been perfect. On my journey back to the inn, the heat of the morning made me sweat and my already very flat hair lay limp, falling into my eyes. Puro was on the veranda sweeping and whistling.

"Excuse me Puro, could you see if the there is room in the spa for me to have my hair done today?"

"I was just down there and all the ladies are looking for something to do. I'll give them a call and let them know you are on your way."

"Sounds good. Also, could you please send down a pot of boiled water, a teapot, and an empty cup?" I asked, hoping I didn't sound too demanding. I raced upstairs to my room and pulled out my tea ball and the Cream Earl Grey that I'd bought from the Granville Island Tea Company in Vancouver. I knew that this was the perfect time to share a cup of special tea with my Beth, even if she was a million miles away.

When I arrived at the spa, three lovely ladies greeted me with smiles and an eagerness to please. They showed me the water and the teapot and watched me carefully as I scooped the precious tea leaves into the ball. I always loved the fragrance of that tea. It was like the beginning of an enchanted tale. The ladies came closer, drawn in by the scent and I knew then that I might be able to open a few more palettes to the wonder of a good cup of tea.

It had been months since I'd been at a spa. Actually, the last time was the day Beth and I were at the kitchen store and entered the contest. I released myself into the care of three friendly and very enthusiastic women, and without a word of English they went to work. I sipped my tea and enjoyed the calm of the moment, and over the next three hours I let them take over. There was only one moment when I saw them mixing up a color and noticed that it was red. I shook my hand telling them no. They grabbed the color chart and motioned for me to choose. My eye was drawn to the most engaging and fun blond sample, and without hesitation my finger landed on L645. All the ladies squealed and the colorist started over.

While sitting under the dryer, letting my new streaks of color take hold, I pulled out Christopher and began to write.

Later in the day ...

At the spa ... I went for a walk earlier around the vineyard. It was beautiful. The grapes looked almost ready to pick, but I know that they need a few more weeks. I remember with our vines back home, the grapes were never ready until after I went back to school in September.

I'm sad that I won't be here for that. Puro told me they still harvest the grapes by hand. Maybe I could stay a little longer and help them pick.

Anyway, right now I am sitting in the spa. I decided to get my hair done. Well I didn't really decide, they just started and I let them, but I did choose my own color— blonde AHHH! I can't believe it. I feel it changing as I am writing this right now.

At one point they were trying to translate, explaining that they wanted to add "viva" life to my hair. I just nodded my head and said yes to it all.

I've had my longish hair forever and it feels like it has been weighing me down. It's time to let go of that too. Oh! The dryer just turned off, time to rinse and cut AHHH! This is good. Moving to the next chair. Will fill you in later ...

M.

When the color was ready, the stylist began to cut. Large chunks fell to the ground and everyone cheered and laughed, as the event became like a team sport. They would not let me look in the mirror until they were finished. I have to admit, I did have a twinge of regret as the last of my length fell to the floor knowing I could no longer hide behind my hair.

Glory, the woman in charge, looked at me and smiled. "You have a date tonight? No?" she asked with excitement.

"Yes, his name is Cristiano."

"Cristiano!" She broke into laughter and looked over at the other ladies.

"Yes, Cristiano. Do you know him?"

"Oh, yes, we've known him since he was a boy," she commented carefully. "He was a good boy." She paused again. "He is a good boy. I have bad English." The other ladies smiled and nodded, appearing to hold back their comments.

I tried not to think about Cristiano and his past, but there was so much I didn't know about him, that we didn't know about each other. How was this going to work? What did Maggie say? 'Faith, and trust.' She was right, we had to start somewhere, and we all have a past. So, I cast my doubts onto the floor and got ready to see the new me.

In the end, they made me close my eyes before they turned me around. At first, I didn't want to look, but when I did what I saw in the mirror was a woman ready for anything.

They'd helped me find the best Maya that had been hidden under all the mousy brown hair. Who knew I was supposed to be a blond? It was fun and exciting, layered and sleek, with just enough side bangs to hold a cute little clip. I loved it.

Then I heard a yell from the other side of the spa.

"Oh my God, Maya, you look DAZZLING!" Dalley screamed, running across the room and dropping all of her bags. The ladies in the shop clapped their hands and laughed when they saw how excited Dalley was to see the new me.

"This changes everything! Now I have to come up with a whole new outfit," she sighed sarcastically.

"I'm sure we can find something. Actually, I think I may have a few ideas myself," I blurted out with a surge of confidence.

"Hmm, I'm leaning towards the dress you bought when we were in Lisbon."

"That's too fancy. I'm not wearing that for our first real date."

"First of all, this is Portugal. You are not wearing jeans and a t-shirt—he surely won't be. And technically this is your second, almost third date, between the airport in Montreal and the nightclub in Lisbon," she said smugly. She clearly had been keeping better track of my life than me.

"Let's take this upstairs. You only have about forty minutes to get ready!"

"What are you talking about?" I screeched.

"It's 3:50 Maya. He's going to be here in about half an hour."

I jumped out of the chair, and tripped over Dalley's bags, stumbling all the way down the hall. "Thank you so much!" I yelled and waved to the ladies. "I love it!"

Dalley laughed and called out to me as I ran up the stairs two at a time. "Maya? Do you trust me?"

I stopped short and turned, letting her know I took her question and her tone seriously. "Yes, but I trust me too. Let's do this together." Dalley smiled. Then we ran.

26

The Date

Maya

With specific instructions not to get my new hair wet, I entered my bathroom, slipped off my light and intriguing day, and then turned on the tap. The water felt soft. The pressure was low, but the temperature made up for it as the heat trickled over my body, washing away any nerves that were starting to emerge. Water had always been my healer since I was a child, and this afternoon it did not disappoint.

I stepped out of the shower and looked in the mirror. My face, my body, everything seemed different. I traced the outline of my shoulder down to my fingertips. "Yes, I like this me!"

A hard repetitive knock came on the door reminding me I was on a timeline.

"Maya, you've exceeded your shower time. Let's go. I've placed a set of your new lingerie on the bathroom counter. Put it on and get out here. No time to be shy." Dalley's instructions were clear and exactly what I needed, for without them I might not have been able to stay on track, and I was determined not to make Cristiano wait.

As instructed, I slipped into the satin and was one step closer. I felt confident and excited. I wasn't sure though if the feeling was coming from me or the lingerie.

While I showered, Dalley had pulled out every relevant item of clothing we owned. Everything was strewn around like a clothing tornado had just touched down. Intermixed with all the clothes were the multitudes of chocolate bars I had packed for the trip, but to date had had no reason to eat.

"Maya, what's up with all the chocolate?" she asked cautiously.

"It's complicated. A story for another day," I said not wanting to expand. "If you see anything you like, help yourself. I don't think I need them anymore." I then stared at the fashion hodgepodge that lay on the bed and whispered, "Let's get started."

I wanted to wear something simple, so I grabbed a light summer dress from the pile. But Dalley disagreed and thought I should go dramatic. After a few failed attempts at my choices, she pulled out the black dress that we'd bought in Lisbon.

"Just try it on," she pleaded, as I shook my head. "If it doesn't feel right, then we can choose something else."

I knew she was lying and once I had the dress on, she would never let me change. With cautious optimism, I slipped the dress over my head, and slowly turned around.

Dalley was right. The dress felt like a second skin. There was no other choice. She and I looked into the full-length mirror. Without a word, she reached into her pocket and took out a little container of lip gloss, opened it, and dabbed the edge. She smiled gently, then brushed my lips with the shiny rose color.

"Perfect," she said with quiet satisfaction. I smiled, not knowing what to say, but answered with a simple thank you. I took a deep breath and grabbed my purse just as she slipped the lip gloss into the side pocket.

I left the room feeling beautiful and—dare I say—stunning. As Dalley and I walked down the stairs, I felt an ease come over me when I saw Puro standing there. It was like having my dad in the room with me.

Dalley cleared her voice garnering everyone's attention, then in a commanding tone announced, "I would like to introduce you to the new and improved Miss Maya Wells."

There was an intake of breath in the room that could be felt instantly. I waited for everyone to exhale, including myself, before I took my next step. Josie was the first to run over when I got to the bottom of the stairs. "I love the hair, Maya! How fun is that?" The rest of the girls came crowding around, making comments and laughing.

Maggie hugged me and whispered, "You look spectacular. I can't wait to hear all about the date tomorrow."

Petra and Sachi came over, admiring the dress, and Jade, well the only thing she commented on was my pendant.

"Is it real?" she asked, her tone insinuating there was no way that it could be.

Ellen piped in with a quiet but assertive voice saying, "If you knew anything about precious stones you wouldn't have to ask."

Puro stepped towards me with a broad smile and a contagious excitement. Then he pointed to his watch, letting me know that it was after 4:30. "Excuse me, Maya, but someone is waiting for you." He then motioned in the direction of the front desk.

My heart began to race as I looked over and saw him standing there.

I must not have hidden it well as Puro leaned in and whispered in my ear, "Maya, you're not the only one. You should have seen him when he arrived."

Puro and Maggie exchanged a glance and smiled ever so slightly at each other, but the subtlety of the moment was not lost on me. The thought was fleeting though, for when I looked again, my world had shifted. Cristiano was leaning casually up against the counter, his dark hair slightly messy, like it had been caught in the wind—his face gentle and beautiful. His eyes sparkled as he watched me from across the room. Then a mischievous smile popped up on his lips. As he walked towards me, he offered his hand and with a silky tone, simply asked, "Shall we go?"

My words were lost and all I could do was nod. He took my hand and held it tightly. It felt like home.

We walked out of the inn and there parked before me was my convertible—well, the convertible, his convertible? I shook my head and smiled. "Yours I assume? You are so bad!"

"Bad? Why?" he asked wryly.

"Bad—because you got Puro involved in your little scheme."

"He was willing to play along. I just wanted to know you were safe while you were out on your adventure this week."

As we walked to the car, I heard a quiet voice behind me. "Maya?" It was Dalley. Cristiano waved her to come closer as he stood holding the car door open for me.

"You look radiant tonight, so happy," she said with what sounded like a mixture of admiration and longing.

"I am. I'm happy to be me right now." Then my thoughts wavered a little and I took a step towards her whispering in her ear, "I've never felt like this before. I'm worried it will just—vanish."

"Have fun tonight. Start exploring the person that you want to be and remember, no matter what happens, always hang on to the Maya you've discovered here in Portugal: man or no man." She winked playfully and gave me a peck on the cheek.

I touched her arm and we both paused letting our friendship grow beyond words. As she walked back towards the veranda, I watched her for a moment, her usual sprightly step was replaced with a slow thoughtful pace. My thoughts were soon interrupted by the hand that landed on my shoulder. I breathed in quickly and turned around. I was taken again by his smile and a face that could keep no secrets. He leaned in brushing his cool lips across my warm forehead revealing his true intentions.

"I didn't know it was possible to miss someone as much as I've missed you."

His words were filled with more truth and beauty than I had ever heard. I wasn't sure I could move, but his hand shifted from my shoulder to the small of my naked back and guided me into the car. In an instant, he slid into the seat beside me and moved in so close I could feel his every breath. There was a scent coming off him that was enveloping. He smelled delicious and familiar, but I couldn't place it so I stopped trying, breathed it in, and embedded his scent into my memory.

"Maya?"

I bit down on the side of my lip and then stammered, "You smell so good you took my breath away." A smile opened on my lips and the two of us broke into laughter. "I think I've smelled it before, but I can't place it."

He brushed his fingers along my chin, over my bare shoulder, and then took my hand and kissed it ever so gently.

"Could this really be happening?" I asked him with the hope that there was only one answer.

"Yes." He smiled, then started the car, and threw it into gear.

A little way down the road he began to chat. "Maya, you asked me earlier about a scent. What do I smell like?" He asked nervously.

"Oh it's silly," I whispered shyly, hoping to change the subject.

"No, tell me, please." He placed his hand on my thigh. The moment he touched me; a surge ran through my body.

I took in a small breath. "It is warm, full, and rich." he raised his eyebrows to my words.

"No ... rich as in creamy and inviting. Oh, this sounds so silly!"

He broke into my sentence, saving me from any further embarrassment. "No, not silly. It just sounds like you've missed me too."

We turned a corner and the wind changed direction. "There it is again. It smells like ..." At the same moment we both exclaimed, "Fresh bread!" "Yes," I answered with resolved exasperation. "That's it exactly. New cologne?"

"No, Maya." He slipped his warm hand off my leg and back onto the steering wheel. "That scent is because of my Avó, my grandmother. I think I mentioned her before. The Medieval Festival is tonight in Silves and she has been baking for the event—well we have been baking for the event for the past two days."

"You've been here for two days already?"

"Yes, I came in on Thursday night. I had a few things to take care of before I could see you." He sounded worried that I might not understand.

"Oh, don't look so worried! I'm just relieved that I'm not going crazy. You were at the inn on Thursday evening, weren't you?"

"Yes," he said shyly. "I only stayed for a minute. You were having such a good time, I didn't want to interrupt."

"I knew it! Puro sidetracked me. I knew no one would be picking up a car in the middle of the night to take it to a repair shop. You came to pick up your car!"

"Yes, it was me." His eyes gleamed.

"Tell me more about her bread." I leaned in closer to him. "I am very intrigued." He placed his hand back on my thigh again only a little higher up.

"You keep stealing my breath—when are you going to stop?"

"Never," he declared. "Now, back to the bread." His eyes twinkled as he told the story like it was a children's tale. "No one can escape from the lure of my Avó's bread. She is known everywhere in the region for the magic of her loaves. People say that to share a loaf of her bread will protect new found love, or solve an impossible challenge in someone's life." He paused, looking briefly at me. "I'm not sure about the truth to these stories. I just know I have been delivering them since I was a child and I've watched many people come and go, waiting for their special loaf from my Avó. I hope you don't mind, but we have to drop two orders off before we can start our evening." He pointed to the back of the car gesturing that all the bread was in the trunk.

"Do you see your Avó often?"

He paused, looking like he wanted to tell more fairy tales. "No, I have not been a very good grandson in the past few years, but I want to be better." His voice lightened. "I am lucky though, she always has my room waiting for me and knows when I am coming home."

"I hope one day to meet this magical woman." I tried to imagine what she might look like. "I have a few very special women in my life too," I said reaching up to my pendant.

We looked at each other and smiled, not needing to say anything more about the women in our lives.

"So where to first?"

"A small tavern on the outskirts of Évora and then we will go to the Medieval Festival in Silves."

"That sounds like fun. Are we going to stay for the festival? I'm up for anything."

"Really? Then we need to make one stop before we drop off the bread." He smirked and then sped up. "Just so you are prepared, these people take their festivals very seriously. If that is our plan, then we are a little underdressed for our evening," he noted cryptically.

"Underdressed?" I laughed out loud thinking about the clothing whirlwind I had left behind at the inn.

He looked over at me with a crooked smile. "Well maybe underdressed is not quite the right word, but wrong century might be more appropriate," he winked.

"Dalley is going to kill me if I change."

"Oh, I doubt that. I think by the time I am finished with you, she will be a little envious."

"Tell me more!"

"Well, the festival takes place down in Silves, about two hours away, but I have a short cut we can take."

"What are we going to do when we get there?"

"It's a festival! We are going to eat and have fun. You don't want me to spoil all the surprises do you?"

"Nooo," I stretched the answer out. "But it feels like there is something else you are not telling me. Wrong century? We have to get dressed up, don't we?"

"Yes," he said quietly, shoulders raised, appearing nervous about what might happen next.

"Sounds like fun," I said simply, opening myself up to the possibilities.

His smile brightened. "It is one of my favorite festivals of the year."

The drive to Évora was quick. When we arrived in the city, he made several sharp turns, and then stopped. He had brought me to a dimly lit shop. The front curtains were drawn, and it looked like it was closed. I went to open the car door, but Cristiano shook his head, and asked me to wait for him. He ran around the car and opened my door, helping me out with an open hand. I sighed knowing that his actions of old-school chivalry further embedded him into my heart. We had not even had our first real kiss and I was already taken. As we walked through the door, the scent of history consumed my senses. The armor and artifacts hanging on the walls, and the vases and goblets placed ever so carefully on the shelves, suggested that the store owner collected for the love of the past.

"Amazing, isn't it?" Cristiano's admiration could be seen in the way he touched one of the goblets. "I used to come here when I was a child." His eyes closed briefly. I couldn't tell if it was pain or pleasure that showed on his face. He opened his eyes and then smiled broadly. "Wait until you see this." He pushed through a set of heavy damask curtains and behind the fabric was a wall of color, texture, and imagination. He had brought me to a costume shop. He smiled and brushed by me closely. "I was told we could stop by and pick up anything we needed," he said, answering the question that sat on my lips.

"It's all so beautiful, but where do we start?" I asked, overwhelmed by the vast racks of costumes.

"We can become anyone we like this evening: a nobleman, a knight, a princess, or an Arabian dancer ..."

"Arabian dancer?" I was confused.

"Maya, our history here in Portugal is long and colorful. I look forward to teaching you more. Come over here. I think one of these dresses would look beautiful on you. Or if you want, you could dress as a belly dancer?" he gently teased.

"No belly dancer for me, thank you very much. I will take a simple gown to match whatever you're going to wear." We waded through racks of costumes laughing and enjoying each other. It was wonderful. Then we split up and began searching on our own. With luck, I found the most beautiful gown. It was something a true princess would have worn six hundred years ago. I slipped behind another rack of gowns and undressed, chuckling as I looked at my new lingerie. Then I stepped into the shimmering gown but couldn't reach the fasteners at the back. Knowing I only had one choice, I mustered up my courage and called out: "Cristiano, could you please help me with my gown?"

"I'll be there in a minute." I heard a clatter of hangers and waited for him patiently. Then a knight rounded the corner, his chain mail glimmering ever so slightly in the light. He walked over and gently touched Aunt Olive's pendant.

"This is beautiful. Is it from someone special?" he asked warily. The realization that we had only met days ago and knew little of each other's pasts twinkled in the moment.

Smiling with my eyes I answered, "Yes." He paused but I quickly added, "My Aunt Olive gave it to me a few months ago. She told me it was a tear of bravery."

"Bravery?"

"Yes, but that is a story for another day." I straightened my shoulders. "Now, how about these buttons?" My words were his invitation to come closer. His fingers answered my request. They were warm, yet a small shiver moved through my body as he touched my spine. He started at the small of my back, one button at a time. I felt a soft pressure on my skin—a kiss.

A kiss for each button, each move he made. It set my nerve endings on fire. I froze for a moment and he stopped, neither of us saying a word until my body softened again. No one had ever touched me like that before. I could feel it within every nerve. With the last button he turned me around, and I thought for sure he was going to kiss me. But with the chivalry of a true knight, he took my shaking hand, and without a word, he led me out into our evening of promises.

Silves

Maya

As a noble knight and a fair maiden, we stepped into the street ready for an evening of adventure. His armor glistened in the late afternoon sun, and he gallantly jumped ahead of me and lay his cloak down on the ground. He held out his gloved hand and I lay my arm on his. I half expected to find a fine steed waiting for us, but was just as pleased to have him help me into his sports car. The scent of fresh baking whirled around us as we prepared to complete our Bread Quest.

"The tavern isn't too far from here," Cristiano said excitedly. "We'll drop the bread for the wedding and then be on our way to the festival."

"A wedding?"

"Yes, Avó and I made the buns and egg tarts." He smiled and sighed as he looked over at me. "I never told you how beautiful you looked earlier tonight. You took my breath away when I saw you at the inn." His words were like a new blanket wrapped tightly around me. He believed I was beautiful and I believed him.

The engine accelerated and the streets whizzed by. I felt a sense of anticipation in our space. There was an excitement, an electricity I could almost taste. Then suddenly, he made a hard turn and we stopped. With the engine still running, he leaned over and pressed his lips to mine. The funny thing was, it didn't feel like our first kiss. We both pulled back and started to laugh. It was like he felt it too. Answers and questions all at the same time, that's what we kept offering each other.

He laughed again, then hopped out of the car and grabbed a basket from the trunk, dashing into the small, music-filled tavern.

My head and my heart swam as I could feel the warmth of his kiss still sparking on my lips. I ran my fingers around the edge of my mouth sealing the moment into my skin. When the tavern door opened, I could hear his laugh mixed in with the love and joy that flowed freely from the wedding festivities. Then he bounded towards me and jumped into the car, revved the idling engine, and we were off.

My heart raced as the wind caressed my skin and sent the scarves of my gown billowing behind me.

"Are you okay? You look a little flushed."

I nodded. "I'm more than okay. Just curious about how all this could be possible?" I moved my hands, drawing an invisible line that connected the two of us.

"I don't know, but let's not try to figure it out tonight. We have all the time in the world." His finger traced around my pendant sending a tidal wave of energy through my body. "Bravery," was all he said with a smile.

He drove so fast it felt like we were flying.

⸙

Within the hour, we arrived at the gates of the festival. Cristiano spoke quickly to the guard and the two of them exchanged some friendly banter. The guard smiled at me like he knew something I didn't, then he waved us through.

"Do you know him?"

"Yes, he is one of Puro's nephews, Dionisio."

"Dionisio? The Greek god of wine?"

"Yes, Puro's sister was a great believer that her children should all be named after the Greek gods. She raised quite a ruckus in Puro's family by not choosing a Catholic name for her eldest son."

"So they're Catholic?"

"Yes, Maya, almost everyone here is."

I looked at him with a question stuck on my tongue. "Are you?"

"That is a difficult question to answer." He pondered for a few moments and then responded very slowly, "I was—I am—I do not think you can ever stop being Catholic. It's just the way it is."

"I understand." It appeared a new dimension had been added to our relationship.

"You do?"

"Yes, I *do.*" I nodded to support my words. He smiled.

I thought for a moment, about my almost wedding, and the quiet argument I'd had with my parents about not getting married in the church. It was the only thing I had really stood up for in regards to the wedding plans. Steven had thought I'd made the choice out of respect for him, but the truth was I just couldn't say 'I do' in front of God—with him. Cristiano placed his hand on mine. "I think you're right. It is just part of who we are."

He looked at me and then squeezed my hand.

He parked the car, dashed around to my door, and ushered me over to a beautifully lit bench and motioned for me to sit. He walked back to the car, opened his trunk, and called out to a set of fellows who quickly ran over. They took the bread from him and continued to laugh as they walked back to the vendor stalls. Cristiano yelled to one young man who put the basket down and looked through the loaves of bread. A second later, a loaf of bread wrapped in simple brown paper flew through the air and Cristiano caught it in mid-flight. He waved and yelled, "*Obrigado*," as the young man disappeared into a wall of color and sound.

I sat quietly on the bench taking in the world around me.

"Avó baked this one special for us tonight. She told me not to forget it." He then broke open the paper and roughly tore two pieces from the loaf.

"So what did you say this bread could do?" I smirked, just wanting to hear him say it again.

"They say that eating the bread will protect new-found love among other things."

As I bit into the bread, that first day in Lisbon rushed into my thoughts. "I've tasted this bread before." Somehow it was different, and yet the same.

"I'm not sure how that is possible. Avó is very particular about when and who she bakes for." His face was filled with questions. "Tell me more about where you purchased your loaf?"

"I was in a market outside of Lisbon on that first day. A woman placed it in my arms and then disappeared when I tried to pay her."

"What did she look like?"

"Honestly, I can't remember. She handed me the loaf of bread, wrapped in a simple cloth. I bent down to put it into my bag and when I stood up, she was gone. The interaction was just seconds long. I'm sorry."

"No reason to be sorry. Do you still have the cloth?"

"Yes, I have it in my room."

"I'd like to take a look at it later. Tell me more about the bread."

"It was special. Actually, it was amazing. I've never eaten anything like it. I almost finished the entire loaf myself. I felt so indulgent, but I couldn't stop. The chef at the hotel asked me about it too, after I'd given him a little piece." I paused. "Was it *hers*?"

Cristiano smiled. "I don't know, but she has always had a way of being in the right place at the right time." As curious as I was, he shrugged his shoulders and moved in closer, pushing all thoughts of his Avó from my mind. We sat quietly and ate one morsel of bread at a time, watching each other carefully. I felt calm, peaceful. When we finished, he dusted the crumbs from my dress, then held them in the palm of his hand. He pressed his finger into his palm, and then brushed his lips with the last of the loaf. I leaned in gently and satisfied my appetite.

Before I had time to think, he grabbed my hand and we were off.

❧

We stopped at a small kiosk and Cristiano gave over a few euros. In exchange, the costume-laden young maiden batted her lashes and handed him a sack of coins. He smiled at her and she giggled. Walking down the path, my arm rested gently on his as we kept our eyes open for special treasures. As the night's festivities began to unfurl, the crowd became dense and loud, but he held me close, creating a buffer from the carnival chaos that revealed itself. The rest of the night was filled with more mystery, excitement, food, and joy than I have ever experienced in my life.

We took up in a little make-shift café and danced into the wee hours of the morning. My feet ached, but in a good way, like they had just been on the best journey ever. He cradled my body into his chest as we watched a group of people run past the café, arm and arm, singing songs of friendship. He tightened his embrace, and then motioned for me to look over to the horizon. It must have been close to 5:00 a.m., as the sun was getting ready to make an appearance. He took my hand and we made our way through the now quiet medieval village. As we neared the car, I slowed my steps and tugged at his shirt, not wanting the night to end. He took my unsubtle cue and led me towards the bench where we'd shared our loaf of bread earlier in the evening. "Happy?" he asked as we sat watching the colors of the horizon change.

"Yes." He wrapped his arms around me. Suddenly, I pushed my lips against his. The passion was instantaneous and the possibilities of our future were all thrown into one single kiss.

He picked me up from the bench and I found myself backed up against a large ancient tree, thankful for its existence as my knees had buckled. It was the only thing that kept me standing, besides his embrace. I could have handed myself over to him right then and there, but he stopped.

"Maya …" he whispered in my ear so quietly I could hardly hear him. "It's time to go."

"Really? We have to go right now?" I asked pushing him.

"Yes, right now would be a good time."

"I know you're right, but …" I realized that I didn't need to say anything. He understood.

"This is different. We need to do this the right way." He smiled and then let out a slow breath releasing the passion ever so tenderly into the early morning air.

I knew what he meant. He kissed me one more time and then walked me back to the car. There was some satisfaction in knowing that we could have—but didn't.

We were both exhausted and elated. The journey back to Netuno felt like minutes as the cool morning air rushed over me. A brief thought bounced off my mind that I had only three weeks left in Portugal, but before it took hold, I handed it over to the wind, determined that nothing was going to change my mood.

When he dropped me off at the inn, he took my left hand, turned it over, and gently kissed my palm. Then he slipped a small cell phone into my purse.

"I'll text you during the week to touch base and let you know where I am. I'll be back late Friday and I will come to get you for breakfast on Saturday morning." His voice was filled with anticipation for our next meeting.

"Cristiano, are you able to get a few hours of sleep before you fly out today?"

"Yes, I will. Do not worry." He walked me to the front steps and slowly unwove our fingers.

"I will see you in less than a week. I promise. Have fun, but not as much fun as last week," he teased. He looked down at his watch and for the first time in hours, reality insisted that he answer. "I had better go."

I waved goodbye as the car sped off, and I watched him disappear into the morning sun. Still in costume, I lifted my dress, kicked off my shoes, and bounced up the stairs, my feet not touching the ground.

28

Crushed Grapes

Maya

MY JOYFUL EVENING CAME TO a crashing halt as I stepped through the door and was hit by a dramatic wall of sadness. The tension in the space tasted dark and irreversible. My new family of women were gathered around Maggie, attempting to protect her from an invisible intruder. Her eyes were puffy and her breaths came from an unnatural place. I could feel my chest tighten, knowing there was only one thing that could tear her apart like that. I made my way over to the group, but Dalley pulled me aside before I was able to speak with her. The tone that she spoke in was all I needed for confirmation. "There is a situation back home. One of the twins is sick," she whispered.

"Yes, I know. CJ wasn't feeling well the other day. Maggie thought it might be a cold or a flu bug."

"Maya, it's more than the flu. He's really sick. He's contracted bacterial meningitis."

My body reacted more quickly than my mind and before I knew it, tears began to form. "He can't be *that* sick, someone would have called sooner—right?" The words fell from my lips and landed flat on the floor.

"Maggie is flying back home this afternoon, but the doctors have told her there is a good chance that she will not make it in time."

"What the hell do they know?" Ripples of defiance flooded through me. "Kids pull through things every day. He's not going to die." My voice cracked as I said the last word.

Dalley pulled me closer, then shook me hard. "There is a good chance she will *not* make it in time." Her words were sharp and painful. "Don't make this more difficult on her with false hope. You weren't here when she got the call. Puro had to chase after her as she fled the inn and ran out into the vineyard. He caught her, but he had to wrestle her to the ground. The guttural screams that came from her woke most of the guests in the inn. She is still now, but I think it's because she's in shock."

Her scolding tone brought the reality of the moment into focus. While I had been engaged in a night of enchantment, Maggie was living the worst nightmare of her life.

The welling tears had found their way out of my ducts, streaking my cheeks while following a well-traveled route down my face. I wiped them off as that moment was not about me, then made my way over to Maggie.

She smiled weakly and whispered with a rasped voice, "Did you have a nice time last night, Maya? Oh, what a beautiful dress." Tears glistened in her eyes as she tried to bring a little piece of normalcy to the moment, but there was nothing normal about what had happened to her. She had already been through so much, and I feared that she would never find her way out of the grief if her son died too.

My knees hit the floor hard, as I slumped down in front of her. I wasn't sure what to say or how to feel. She stroked my hair and briefly we were all held by the silent tears that fell around our circle.

Footsteps could be heard coming down the stairs and when I looked up I saw Josie and Puro carrying her bags, exhaustion and worry embedded into their eyes.

I got up from the floor and slowly walked over to Puro, hardly able to lift my feet. "Who is taking Maggie to the airport?"

"I am," he said firmly. "I've booked her into First Class. She will have everything she needs," he assured me stoically.

Josie heard me talking to Puro and rushed over to join us. "I spoke with her sister Gretchen back home, and she will be at the airport in Vancouver to pick her up." The twinkle that I usually saw in Josie's eyes was replaced with desperate concern.

"Josie, is there anything else that we can do for her?" I asked grasping at straws, trying to make some sense out of all that had happened.

"No. I think we have done everything we can. I am worried though, as she is barely holding things together and am concerned about the long flight back. I wonder if she should be sedated." Josie's concern was echoed by Puro's deep sigh. She then went into her purse, pulled out a little pill box, and handed it to Puro. "Here, give her one of these before she gets on the flight."

"What airline is she flying?" I asked as I formulated an idea. "Portugal Air?"

"Yes," Josie answered. "It will be the reverse route to what we took to get here."

"Give me a second," I said rushing over to my purse, "I need to make a call."

"Maya, we have to go. The limo will be here any minute," Puro noted with insistence.

"No, just wait. Let me make one phone call." I pulled out the phone Cristiano had given me and dialed the only number programmed into the contacts. The phone rang once, then again. I held my breath and on the third ring, he answered.

"Maya?" his voice was filled with playful curiosity. My pause was long enough that the space between us quickly turned to concern. "What's the matter?" Alarm now filled his words.

I wanted to break down into raging tears, but there was no time for that. I mustered up my calm and tried to explain, "Cristiano something terrible has happened."

"I'm turning around!"

"NO!" I yelled back at him.

"Are you okay? What's going on?" His words flipped instantly from alarm to panic.

"Yes, I'm safe. But one of my friends is not. Maggie has to fly home today. She found out this morning that one of her boys has meningitis. He is very sick and could die within the next twelve hours. Puro is taking her to the airport right now. She is flying out on your carrier, but I'm not sure which flight. She'll be landing in Vancouver where her sister will pick her up and take her straight to the hospital." I paused briefly to catch my breath and then continued. "Cristiano, are you working that flight today?"

His voice shifted again this time from panic to professional. "Yes, there is only one flight going out to Vancouver, but we do have a layover in Montreal. I will go straight to the airport right now and make sure that some special accommodations will be made for her. I will stay with her throughout the flight. When she arrives in Vancouver, I will walk her through customs and get her to her sister as fast as I can. I will do everything to make sure she makes it to the hospital in time." It felt like he wanted to say something else, but there was no time.

"Thank you, Cristiano. Call me as soon as you arrive in Vancouver. I had better go. The limo is here for Maggie and Puro." I ran back over to Puro and caught them as they walked out the door.

"Puro, I just got off the phone with Cristiano. He is working the flight that she is taking today. He will make sure that she has everything she needs and that he'll be with her during the whole trip."

"Thank you, Maya. I know he will take good care of her."

Maggie sagged in his arms like a rag doll, torn at the seams. "Don't you dare give up Maggie." She looked up, her eyes connected with mine and I could feel her heart breaking. The next sentence tumbled from my lips, "I'll pray for you every day."

Puro rushed her into the limo and they sped off into the tragic morning sunshine.

The doorway was filled with empty and defeated souls. Turning around, we made our way back into the lobby, lost and not sure what to do next. I noticed Jade standing off to the corner with a strange smile on her face, looking like she had something to say.

"Jade, what is it?" I asked icily. "Do you have something useful to offer?"

She fixed her gaze at me and her smile grew. "Well maybe a little more than a lame party dress and a promise for prayers. Not to mention, who leaves their children alone for a month without even a nanny to watch over them?" Sarcasm and loathing oozed from her lips.

I snapped like a brittle twig and the minutes that followed were like a scene from a movie, a monologue written just for me; but it was no movie.

"Who the hell are you to judge anyone? Who are you to have an opinion about anything?" I screamed. My body shook with each sentence. "I have never in all my life met anyone so strikingly beautiful and horribly ugly all at the same time. It doesn't take but one word out of your mouth for people to figure out that the only thing that your body creates is toxic venom. I had always believed there was good in everyone, but after meeting you, I know I was wrong. You take pleasure in other people's pain. It is your only joy. You like to make people sad because deep down you are the saddest, most pathetic person I have ever met. The vile path that you walk pushes people so far away from you that you will never know the kind of love Maggie had with her husband, or the bond she has with her children. The joy and kindness that woman has is lost to you forever. You will always live in darkness and fear, and God help you because at this point in your life, he is the only help that you are ever going to get."

I could feel every nerve in my body, and almost hear the blood rushing through to my heart. I felt exhilarated and frightened at the same time. The tears started making their way to the surface and I knew I had to finish quickly. "And you know what, I don't care. Go to hell Jade. You're already halfway there."

Jade froze.

I grabbed the train of my dress, turned, and stormed out the doors. The paths of the vineyard opened up, offering me their protection. I walked slowly at first, trying to be strong, but then made a hard right turn in the olive grove and broke into a full sprint. I ran until my lungs hurt and my veils became tangled in the low-hanging branches of an olive tree. My body shook, like I had just expelled some kind of evil that had been cast upon me, and I wanted to vomit, but I kept going.

As I ventured farther into the grove, the olive trees gave way to a small forest and the sounds of nature became muted. My shoulders fell and I wandered aimlessly. Tripping over roots and landing on the ground, I scraped my hands and tore my beautiful gown. Ready to give up, I sat down on the forest floor. It was then that I looked up and saw a path. I followed it and soon found myself in front of a small stone chapel, then took a step towards the wooden door and tentatively pushed it open.

The chapel was empty, but warm and inviting. The space was filled with olive wood pews and icons on the walls. I walked over to the candle holder at the front of the chapel and struck a single wooden match. Every memory from the last twenty-four hours flashed through my mind and unlocked more tears. I wasn't afraid. I wanted to remember everything. I knew that all of it had changed me: the joy of finding Cristiano, Maggie's pain, and the vanquishing of Jade.

When the tears finally stopped, I settled into the pew. The wood was so soft, and I could feel myself surrounded by decades of prayers, sadness, and hope. It was not until the warmth of the mid-afternoon sun had heated up the chapel that I started to feel tired and knew it was time to go. When I stood up to leave, my feet ached and I sat back down. It was only then I realized that they were scratched and bleeding.

I heard a scuffle of feet and turned to see an old woman enter the chapel. She passed by my pew without a word. I watched her carefully as she replaced a few burnt candles while singing quietly to herself. She turned and smiled, then sat down next to me and took my hand. She sang for a long time, emanating a peaceful story through her songs. When she finished, she touched my forehead with a kiss. Her lips were rough but filled with love. "*Obrigado*," I whispered to her. Taking a breath, I stepped outside into the sun and made my way back to the inn one careful step at a time, as my feet were no longer impenetrable and protected by the adrenaline.

The lobby was strangely quiet when I arrived, so I climbed the stairs and went back to my room. Dalley sat on the bed working on her computer.

"Hi Maya, I'm glad you're back. I was just about ready to send out a search party." She smiled cautiously.

"Yeah, thanks," was all I could muster.

"Why don't we get you changed and cleaned up? We're all going to meet for a bite to eat in the dining room in a little while."

"Yes. Thank you." She undressed me and wrapped me in a towel, never asking me any questions. "Maya, your feet!" she exclaimed with concern. I looked down and saw that they were worse than I thought. She walked me over to the bathroom and ran some warm water into the tub. I sat on the edge as she cleaned them, neither of us saying a word.

When I emerged from the bathroom, I saw the remainders of my magical night sitting in a pile on the floor. It felt wrong to dump all of that happiness into a heap. So with great effort, I picked up the gown and laid it carefully on my bed, giving the memory the respect it deserved.

I wasn't ready to see everyone, so I told Dalley that I was going down to the veranda to do some writing. She nodded her head and left me to do what I needed. As I crossed the lobby floor, I saw myself yelling at Jade earlier in the day. I couldn't believe that had been me.

I settled into one of the large chairs on the veranda.

August 27th Sunday Afternoon

So what just happened? In the past 24 hours I have had the most amazing experience of my life, witnessed a level of fear and sadness so deep that it shook me to my bones, went off like a crazy person in front of everyone, then ended up wandering through a vineyard, wearing a medieval gown in the middle of Portugal.

During my wander, I discovered a small chapel on the vineyard grounds. No one was there but me and God for most of the morning. I spent my time just sitting and thinking about all that has been happening in my life. Not just today or the last three months, but all those lost years.

It feels like I have been walking in a fog. Who was that girl? It sure wasn't me. I will never be her again. I have had a taste of who I can be. A person with power and purpose, with beauty and passion. My dad always said that when I was little I had a spirit just aching to get out.

He was right. Well it's out now and it's not going back.

I met a lady at the chapel today. She said nothing, but sang a hymn and kissed my forehead. It was comforting; it was like she knew me.

Dalley popped her head around the door and broke my solitude with her kindness. "I thought you might need this." She walked towards me with a cup of tea in her hand. "Lunch is on the table."

Write more later,
Maya

I put Athena down and gathered my things. Dalley waited for me at the open door and together we walked to the dining room, ready to meet all of our friends.

Our hosts Reinaldo and Mateus joined us for lunch, wanting to share their concern for Maggie and her son. When Carmo entered the dining room, we collectively held our breath until she was close enough to share the most up to date piece of news.

"My father called." I could hear the relief in her voice. "He met up with Cristiano when they arrived at the airport. Cristiano was able to pull some strings, which allowed my father to stay with Maggie at the gate until she boarded. He's on his way back to Netuno right now."

Reinaldo nodded. "Thank you for the update Carmo, and for looking after the front desk while your father was helping Maggie. Let us know if we can do anything to help him when he returns."

With sadness in their eyes, the brothers then turned to us and Mateus began to speak. "I know that today has brought great worry to all of you, as it has to us. Although it has only been a short time that you have been here, it feels like we are family. My brother and I would like to know if you want a day off before starting the new challenge."

No one knew quite how to respond. That was until Josie piped in, "No. We do not want a day off. Maggie would not want us sitting around worrying. She would want us to get started on the next project right away." No one opposed her idea, not even Jade who sat brooding in the corner.

"Well then," Mateus said, looking a little relieved. "Let me assign the new groups. Although Puro is not back yet, I think it best to do this now and not wait for supper. That way everyone can take time for themselves this evening."

Gervais came out from the kitchen with no grand entrance, just a humble spirit as he helped place the last of the food on the table for lunch. He looked at Sachi, and she smiled back at him as he placed a plate in front of her.

"Please enjoy your meal as best as you can." We could see that he too was touched by the tragic parting of our friend.

Mateus placed slips of paper on the table in front of us. Nothing felt right without Maggie there. Ellen cleared her throat then asked, "Does anyone mind?" She picked up the papers and then began reading them out loud. "First we have Petra and Dalley."

"This should be interesting," Petra exclaimed. "You are aware, Dalley, that my husband does all the cooking in my house?"

"That's perfect." Dalley joked. "We can fly him over to cook for the two of us on Friday night then."

Mateus chuckled. "No cheating, ladies, if you want to win the spectacular prize at the end of the week."

Everyone's ears perked up at the mention of a prize. Ellen continued, "Next on the list are Sachi and Maya." I felt pleased that Sachi and I were going to work together as her quiet spirit was just what I needed.

"And lastly Josie, Jade and myself," Ellen revealed.

At first, no one said anything about the groups, but within moments the awkward tension in the space appeared to motivate Petra.

"Mateus? Reinaldo? What is our theme this week? And what great prize are you offering?"

Mateus sighed. "Let me call Gervais out to explain. He does a much better job than either of us talking about this kind of thing."

Sachi jumped up from the table. "I'll let him know that you want him," she said making a quick exit towards the kitchen.

Within minutes Gervais joined us, "Your goal is to tell a story using food, image, and emotion. Three dishes, three images, one story, any format. Be creative. The winners are going to receive a weekend getaway to a spa in the Azores. They will leave on the Friday night after supper and be back for week three, early Monday morning."

Ellen literally jumped at the idea of winning the contest, but then sighed heavily as she stole a glance towards Jade. I felt bad for her and hoped that Josie would be able to keep Jade under control.

We finished lunch and a wave of fatigue hit me hard. I could hardly keep my eyes open. Sachi smiled from across the table saying sweetly, "I'm looking forward to working with you Maya, but you look exhausted. Why don't you go lay down?"

Sachi didn't need to convince me. "Yes, that sounds like a good idea. I think I'll just have supper in my room tonight. Can we get started in the morning?"

"Yes. Should we meet for breakfast after the cooking class?"

"Sure, that would be great." As I stepped away, something struck me. I didn't want to be alone for the whole night. I turned around. "Actually Sachi, do you want to meet in a few hours after supper? Maybe we can go for a walk on the grounds with our cameras."

Sachi lit up. "Yes, I would really like that. I'll meet you down here around 8:00."

⌒๛

I entered the room and collapsed on the bed, closing my eyes for what I thought was a moment. When I woke it was around 7:00 and there was a sandwich and a hot pot of tea on my side table with a note.

Maya, just a little something to help keep your energy up. Dalley

I sat on the edge of the bed and ate my sandwich slowly, then poured my tea into the cup. I thought a hot bath might do me good, so with a little effort I shook off my early evening rest and made my way over to the bathroom. As the tub filled with water, I went back into the room and picked up Christopher, but Athena was nowhere to be found. I pushed her absence away and allowed my mind to wander to thoughts of Cristiano. I was sure he was somewhere over the Atlantic and wanted to reach out so he would get my text as soon as he landed.

Thank you for helping with Maggie today. How is she doing? Everyone here is beside themselves. Let me know as soon as you land. I can't believe this is happening.

I settled into the tub and the phone pinged.

Good tailwinds. Flight just landed in Montreal. I am with Maggie right now. She is calm and very quiet. I am doing everything I can. I transferred us to a flight that will arrive two hours sooner in Vancouver. I texted her sister to let her know of the change. No news yet. I'll let you know when we arrive. Miss you.

Jade

I walked onto the veranda, stared out over the vineyard, and glared as the sun dipped down behind the hills. "Only one more night. God, I hate this place." A cool gust of wind then suddenly picked up and cut straight through me. As I passed by one of the lounge chairs, I noticed something sparkly. I stopped and started to laugh—Maya's stupid, blue, gaudy pen.

I slipped it into my purse and felt happy for the first time since I'd boarded that plane in Montreal.

29

A Hint of Haiku

Maya

AFTER MY BATH, MY HEART felt cleaner and calmer. I had just enough time to make an entry in Christopher before Sachi and I were supposed to meet. I searched my purse for Athena, but she was nowhere to be found.

A wave of panic began to form. Thinking hard, I backtracked my steps through where I had been.

"Where is she? Where did I leave her?" I wracked my brain. "Where was I? Outside? Yes. I was writing outside, Dalley came with the tea, I put my pen down, that's it! I put Athena down on the lounge chair outside."

I ran down the stairs and stopped short when I saw Puro at the front desk. His ashen face transported me back to the reality of what had happened earlier in the day.

"Hi Puro," I said quietly as he worked. "Cristiano texted me from Montreal. They just arrived a little while ago."

"Thank you, Maya. He texted me too. CJ has slipped into a coma. He said that Maggie's managing, but he is very worried about her—I wish I was with her."

"I'm sure she wishes you were there too."

He smiled warm-heartedly at me. "I knew when I met Maggie that there was something special about her—her walk, her voice. I wasn't sure, but it was just something wonderful, simple. On that first day when she got up early in the morning and went for a run, I watched her as she stood in the early morning light trying to figure out which way to go. She turned around and asked me which way to the steepest hill. I laughed a little and sent her through the east part of the vineyard that overlooks our lake. It is hard to get to the top, but well worth it. When she came back, she thanked me and we shared a cup of coffee. Then on Monday evening, when I brought her supper, she invited me in, and we talked and talked into the early morning hours, then later in the week she smuggled me pie." He chuckled quietly to himself. His smile soon faded, replaced by a few forming tears.

Seeing the need to change the subject, I asked, "Puro, I left something outside earlier on one of the chairs. Has anyone turned in a sparkly blue pen?"

"No, have you looked outside yet?"

I shook my head then walked out onto the veranda, cautiously optimistic that I would see Athena sparkling in the evening sun. I made my way over to where I had been sitting—my heart sank—the chair was empty.

Breathing deeply, I decided that there would be no more tears that day and reached into my purse for a regular pen. Puro walked out on to the veranda.

"Any luck?"

"No, I think she's gone for good this time." He looked at me quizzically. "This time?"

I shrugged my shoulders with resigned sadness.

"Cheer up, Maya," he laughed revealing a piece of pie from behind his back.

"Is that Maggie's peach pie?"

"Yes. She baked a fresh one for me last night before she got the call. I thought this might make you feel better."

I smiled, taking the pie and settled into a seat. He was right—the pie did help—a little.

August 27th

This doesn't feel right without Athena, but what am I supposed to do?

Breathe. Imagine I am sitting in the gazebo at home, rain falling. The cool breeze knocking at my back. No- stop. I do not want to imagine myself in that life. I want to be living this life. Let's start again.

Breathe. Imagine I'm sitting under a tree and the warm summer air is blowing Christopher's pages around. Cristiano is lying beside me and holds the paper down with one finger. Without a word, he takes his other hand and begins to trace circles on my arm, his fingers moving ever so slowly, my skin tingling under his touch. He moves in quietly, slipping the pen out of my hand and closing Christopher. His eyes meeting mine, our lips finding each other, each kiss like it was the first.

All that with a ballpoint pen. Athena would be proud.

This pie really is amazing. Maggie was right. It is all about the love. I can feel her with me. Maggie wherever you are, we love you. I know I said no more tears today, but here they come again. Time to close up for the evening.

Going for a walk with Sachi.

Maya

I heard footsteps approaching and tried to wipe my tears away.

"Hi Maya, more tears?" Dalley asked with a sigh following her comment. Then she looked down at what I was writing with and continued, this time with a little less sarcasm. "A regular pen? Where's Athena?"

"It's been a horrible day, Dalley. Don't you cry when you're sad?"

"No, I don't. I gave it up years ago. It never seemed to get me anywhere." She shrugged her shoulders. "So, where's Athena?" she asked again with keen interest.

My voice cracked and I held back the last few tears that were just waiting to fall. "Gone! I left her out here this afternoon and when I came back, she was gone. I guess she wasn't meant to be mine."

Dalley shook her head and appeared ready to refute the point but took a different approach. "Well, she didn't get up and walk away on her own."

"Dalley," I said, needing to change the topic. "I'm meeting Sachi down here for a walk. Can you take my journal upstairs? I've already lost Athena today. If anything happened to Christopher, I think that would be the end of me." Placing him carefully in my purse, I handed it over to her.

"No problem, Maya, I wouldn't want that to happen. I'm not sure I would be able to deal with all those tears again anyway. I'm heading there right now."

Dalley

I ran up the stairs, my heart hammering against my ribs. I couldn't figure out if it was nerves or excitement. It had been several days since I'd read her last entry and I needed to get the blog posting done as soon as possible. I locked the door and pulled the journal out. I just couldn't refer to it as Christopher; it was a little too weird for me.

I logged onto my blog and began to copy her words. When I read the last entry, I was entranced by the love and frustration, and the passion and sadness that filled the page. She had written enough material over the weekend to back log three blog entries for me. All I needed to do was add a few details that were not in the journal about Maggie's son's illness and the stinging monologue that Maya gave in the lobby. I didn't know she had it in her.

After I finished, I carefully placed the journal back into her purse, put it on her bed and then walked straight over to her dresser, which was filled with chocolate from home. She had given me permission to take whatever I wanted. My fingers wrapped around as many bars as I could hold. Then I sat on the floor and carnivorously ate my way through the pile, not tasting a single piece!

Maya

Savoring my last bite I sighed, hoping that someday my pie would make Cristiano smile like Maggie's did for Puro.

Sachi wandered onto the veranda, camera in hand. I was thankful for the distraction and made a conscious effort to change gears completely, at least for a little while. "The new camera looks amazing. Is it hard to use?"

"No, not so bad. Gervais gave me a crash course over supper tonight. I think I figured it out."

"I noticed you and he have been spending a lot of extra time together."

"Yes, I have not met anyone like him before. When he eats my food, he understands me without having to ask any questions. He makes things easy for me," she said reflectively.

"I'm happy for you, Sachi. It's not common to meet someone who you are able to share your gift with." She smiled shyly and looked out in the vineyard. "Which way would you like to go? You choose."

"Let's see where this path takes us," she said, pointing to one that led up a hill.

As we walked, I tried to think about ideas for the project, but my mind was blank. "Sachi, what kind of story do you think we should tell this week?"

"I'm not sure yet, but it will come to us." She walked ahead of me then stopped to photograph the simplest things: a leaf, a twisted old vine. Everything she saw appeared to capture her interest.

We meandered through the winding paths surrounded by beautiful vine stocks on either side of us. It was like the people who planted them so many years ago knew the vines needed to follow the landscape of the earth to grow their best fruit. Back home, the vines were planted in straight rows, very organized, maximizing space, and increasing yield. But at Netuno, it was as if the grapes told the growers what they needed, and their people listened. We continued until we were surrounded in every direction and the grapes were almost singing to us, making their own music as we enjoyed their scent and color.

"You asked me about the story. I have always found that food has a lot to say, if we stop and listen."

Momentary silence lay between the two of us. I was intrigued by the mystery of her words, and when she started again I listened with even more intensity. "Sachi, you talk like a chef, but you're an engineer," I said trying to put the pieces together.

"Maya, it's not as impressive as it sounds, and in the end there is a big difference for me between what I do and who I am. I had to become an engineer. But my heart has always been about creating food."

She paused and lay on the ground under a series of vines, photographing the last light of the evening bouncing off a bunch of grapes. "When I was a young girl we had to come to America, as I had a rare blood disorder. They had the money and the U.S. had the medical technology. It took a few years, but I was eventually cured. My father wanted to go back to Japan, but my mother said no. She thought it was best for me if we stayed. As I grew older my father spent most of his time in Japan, and my mother spent at least half of the year at our summer house five hours from where our home was. They became preoccupied with their own lives and too busy for me. I spent most of my time with the kitchen staff and I started cooking and learning about food. I soon realized that when I cooked, people could see me.

"When I was getting ready to graduate from high school, I decided I wanted to become a chef. However, before I had the chance to tell my father, he told me I had been accepted into an engineering program at a university of his choice, and that I would start that September. I said nothing. He told me what I had to do and I did it. It was my duty. I kept cooking on the side. Then when I graduated two years ago, my father got me a job with an engineering company owned by a family friend, and since then, every day I build buildings, and on the weekends, I build food. I know it is a funny way to look at it, but for me, a well-thought-out recipe is like a well-designed blueprint for a building." She paused mid-thought and moved farther under the vines so that I could only see her feet but I could still hear the clicking of her camera. I sat in the dirt and continued to listen to her story, taking a few of my own shots, trying to see what she saw. Then she continued.

"A few months ago, I was at my favorite kitchen store and saw the contest entry. I knew one way or another that I had to come. When I found out I'd won, I went to see my boss and told him I was taking five weeks holiday and leaving for Portugal in two months. He said little, as I had never taken holidays since I had started at his company. I gave him the dates and walked out of the office. Over the next few days, I received several notes from my father telling me he did not approve of such a long holiday. For the first time in my life, I did not do what he asked of me.

When I left my apartment to go to the airport, I locked up and paid for four months rent in advance. I was following my dream, and no one was going to stop me."

"Four months?" I asked, looking perplexed.

"Yes, the pull to come here was so strong I was not sure that five weeks was going to be enough." She sat up, looking at me and waving the camera with excitement. "I got it!"

"The picture you were looking for?"

"No—well, yes the right picture, but what I'm talking about is our story. I just want to run something by you."

"How do you do that?"

"Do what?"

"You were telling me your life story, taking photos under a grape vine, and figuring out our project?"

"Oh, that is how I work best," she responded smiling shyly.

"What's your idea?"

"It's about Maggie." She paused looking for my reaction. My eyes widened as I wasn't sure what she meant. "Let me explain more. I am thinking about her journey—from coming here to going home, the happiness, the sadness and all that was in between—the sweet and sour of her life. I just have to cook on it." She jumped up and grabbed her things. "I'm going back to the inn. Let's meet in the morning."

She waved and ran back down the hill. I sat still in the dirt. When I felt the first drops of rain fall on my head, I looked up, not sure where the clouds had come from. They were neither dark nor ominous, just filled with purposeful water. I let the rain fall as I finished watching the sun set. There were so many colors in the sky and so much movement; it was beautiful and peaceful. As the rain burst slowed, my mind had become clear, and my heart was ready to face whatever tomorrow had to bring.

I ran back through the musical vines, jumping in every puddle I could find. My mom would have been so proud of me!

⁓

I arrived in the room dripping and exhausted. Dalley looked up from her computer and started to laugh.

"What?" I asked, not realizing that the last set of puddle jumping had left me with a spray of mud that landed in my hair and across my face.

"Looks like you and Sachi used your time well," she said sarcastically, then went back to typing.

"Actually, we did," I said satisfied. "She had the most fascinating story and after everything that has happened today, it was good to think about something else for a little while a least." I paused noticing I had lost her attention and she was back working on her computer. "Hey Dalley! Sorry to interrupt."

"No sorry needed, just sending some emails." She snapped the screen down. "So, what was so fascinating about our dear Sachi?"

"Her world is amazing, and she is full of surprises."

"Really, what kind of surprises?"

I told Dalley about Sachi's childhood and how she found her way to Portugal.

When I finished telling the story, my eyelids started to feel heavy, but I wanted to tell Christopher one more thing. I saw my purse on my bed and pulled him out then opened him up and started to read my last entry. My head hit the pillow before the lid was off the ballpoint pen.

30

Happy Day, Sad Day

Maya

WHEN I OPENED MY EYES, the room was filled with the pre-dawn light
of Monday morning. I checked my phone to see if there had been any
news. Nothing. Still wearing the muddy clothes from the night before, I
peeled them off and slipped into my favorite comfy sweats. I soon realized
that more sleep was not an option and decided to see if I could catch the
morning sunrise. Heading out into the quiet, darkened hallway I made
my way to the lobby and saw Bento sitting at the front desk.

"Good morning, Bento. What time is it?" I asked. "Where's Puro?"

"Oh! It's just after five, but he'll be here in a couple of hours. My dad
sent him home last night to have a rest. Is there anything I can get you?"

"Yes, thank you. Just a pot of black tea. I'm going to watch the sunrise
this morning."

Bento reached down behind the counter and held up a beautiful
handmade quilt. "Sunrises are very popular around here. I'll bring your
tea out when it's ready."

I walked onto the dimly lit veranda, seeking out one of the big comfy
seats, but then noticed an old rocking chair pushed into a corner. It was

clearly not a favorite with many guests, but I was drawn to it. I pulled it out from the wall, sat down, and enjoyed the smooth, worn wood under my fingers and the creak it made when I settled in and began to rock. The motion offered my body the comfort I needed. I curled up in the quilt and closed my eyes, tasting the morning dew on my lips. Questions trickled into my mind about Maggie and her son, but the only answer that came to me was knowing that it was a new day and I had to be prepared for anything.

When I opened my eyes, the sky was still indigo, but minute by minute it began to shift and change hues. I caught Bento placing my tea on a table in one stealth motion and when I looked up from the pot, the horizon had changed again and a series of oranges and pinks started to shine from behind the hills in the east. I knew it would only be a matter of minutes until the sun broke over the hill's crest, and the day would start. I poured my tea into the cup and took my first sip. My body relaxed into the rocking chair and took in the silence and the growing light. Although I knew it was coming, the sun startled me with its brilliance when it finally appeared.

My morning light was interrupted by a town car that pulled up to the inn. I figured it must have been early morning guests arriving for their stay, but no—as loudly as she had arrived in my world, she actually left with little fanfare. With purse in hand, Jade walked down the stairs and got into the car. The driver collected her luggage, slammed the trunk shut, and quickly got back into the vehicle. I could hear Jade yelling at him just before the door closed. He started the car and peeled away. I didn't move. I just turned, closed my eyes, and let the dust settle.

When I looked again the car was gone. I took another sip of tea and from behind my rocking chair, I heard the scuffling of feet.

"Good morning, Maya," Petra said smiling. She was dressed and ready for the day.

"Petra it's … really early."

"Yes, I know, mornings are my favorite time of the day."

"And you're dressed and ready to go?"

"No, not ready to go, just dressed. I just like to get up early." She paused. "What are you drinking there?"

"Tea. Hot, black, perfectly steeped tea," I answered reveling in the great taste.

Petra laughed. "Boy, you Canadians sure take your tea seriously." When she sat down, I motioned to pour her a cup, but she shook her head. "No thank you. My tastes fall in the coffee bean direction." She continued with her story recollection, "A few years back, I was on a cruise and ran into some Canadians who were complaining about the 'horrible tea' on the ship." She mimicked the passengers wonderfully, which caused me to laugh out loud.

"Yes, that would be about right. Mind you, not everyone in Canada drinks tea, but those who do generally take it very seriously. I have to admit, I'm one of those serious tea drinkers. I brought a bag of my favorite teas just in case they didn't have anything here that I liked. I like to match the moments with the right cup of tea."

"Now, that's why I get up early every morning," she said. I looked at her trying to figure out what she was talking about. "Oh don't mind me. I'm always working, looking for that next impact ad. What I mean is: can I use the phrase? 'Match the Moments?' I think it would be great for a coffee ad."

There was a brief pause and then both Petra and I laughed again. "Glad to hear you are not jumping ship like Jade." I said with sarcasm. "Yes, I saw that little scoundrel taking off this morning. She was giving

Bento a hard time. He couldn't get his pen to work, so he asked her if she had one on her. While she cursed him out she went into her purse and pulled out this awesome pen, it was all sparkly and stuff."

"Sparkly? Are you kidding me?" Fury took over my peaceful morning. I could feel my face contorting and the anger I felt inside caused me to start seeing spots. I put my teacup down and pressed my hands hard up against my face trying to make the spots go away.

"Yes, really sparkly and blue. Maya—what's wrong?"

I inhaled quickly and held my body rigid. "I wish I had the ability to cast curses on people. She would be my first."

"Curses? Yes, they would be very useful. Anything I need to know about?" Petra smirked.

"Ah, she took something of mine, something very important."

"I'm sorry, Maya. I've seen girls like her before. She will fade and burn out very quickly, but clearly not before she does a little more damage. But no, back to what you asked, I'm not jumping ship. I'm having too much fun, except for yesterday mind you. The whole thing was awful, well almost the whole day. I have to tell you, your rant with Jade was outstanding. I'm not surprised she took a little revenge on you. I loved that last moment when you picked up the train of your dress and walked out of the inn. Oh, I wanted a video clip of it."

I wasn't sure if I should be pleased or embarrassed. "Thank you for the compliment?" I replied, throwing a question mark at the end, not sure how to take her comment.

Petra changed the subject easily which was great for me as I did not want to think about Athena, Jade, or yesterday.

"Anyway, this is standard fare for me," she blurted. I get up around 4:30 every morning, get dressed, and go for a walk around the city. My husband thinks I'm crazy, but I love this time of the day." She paused, drifting somewhere else. "I'd lived in New York my whole life, and then one day about seven years ago I woke up early, really early. I had an important meeting that week and had yet to come up with one decent idea for the client. So I got dressed and headed outside, hoping to clear my mind. It was still dark when I stepped on to the sidewalk. There was something different about the city at that time in the morning, something mysterious. I had never felt it before.

"It was a secret world. I walked and walked, meeting different types of people who said good morning and asked me how I was doing. This was a strange thing, as I had lived in the city my whole life and never had anyone stop to ask me how I was." She paused. "Or maybe I just never walked slowly enough to let them. At any rate, I found myself at a bakery, a newspaper stand and a coffee kiosk, saying hello back to everyone. I woke early the next day and headed out on the same route. The newspaper man smiled and nodded, the bakery girl asked me my name, and when I stopped for coffee, the vendor Gino gave me a cup for free. I took that feeling and translated it into one of the most successful ad campaigns of my career. My life changed in several ways that year. For the first time, I really started to care about who other people were, and I started to live it every day. My work changed and success followed me. My husband and I started our own agency. It was risky, but it was the only way I could live this new freedom I was feeling."

I stared at Petra with admiration and saw how happy and satisfied she was with her world. For her, all it took was an early morning waking, a kind hello, and a free cup of coffee. I started rocking again. "Portugal has changed everything for me, just like Gino and the bakery girl did for you. My life will never be the same again; I never want to go back."

She looked intrigued. "Back to the life you were living or back home?" "Neither, basically they're the same. There's not a lot for me to go back to, but everything to stay for," I paused. "Mind you, when it comes to my parents, they might have a different opinion, or maybe not. I honestly don't know."

Petra laughed a little but asked no more questions. We sat for a moment, enjoying the breeze, me with my tea and her with a coffee that Bento had discretely brought out a few minutes earlier.

"This is good."

"The coffee?"

"Yes, the coffee is good. But I'm talking about Jade leaving."

"In what other way besides the obvious?" I asked, smiling.

"Now we have even numbers again." We both chuckled and then sat quietly enjoying the remainder of the sunrise.

August 28—Breakfast—Monday

Just sitting here outside, eating breakfast in the sunshine. She's gone. She left. Jade packed her bags and left. She said nothing to anyone. Should I feel bad? No, I don't think so. I hope Athena springs a leak all over her expensive purse. Actually I don't because she would throw her away. Change subject, before I cry.

I'll keep writing but it's just not the same without her. Curse you Jade. Well, that might be a little dramatic.

I am looking forward to my day with Sachi. It will help distract me. I'd better get my things together—we are meeting in a little bit.

Oh, this morning with Petra on the veranda was great. What an interesting woman. I love the fact that even after seven years she still gets up every morning at 4:30 to remind herself that all you need to solve a problem is to look at things from a different perspective. So simple, but true.

Hey, with everything that happened yesterday, I never told you about my date with Cristiano on Saturday. It sounds so petty to be talking about the date with all the horrible things that Maggie must be facing right now.

Let's do that later okay?

Haven't heard from him yet. I know that they must have landed several hours ago. Can't think about it right now. He will text me when he can.

Maya

After breakfast, Sachi and I met up. I decided the best way to keep distracted was just to listen and follow her plans for the day. We spent the first hour looking at the photos each of us had taken the night before.

"Wow, Sachi your images are amazing," I said wishing I had that kind of talent.

She responded kindly. "Maya, your photos are unique in their own way. Don't underestimate yourself and what you are capable of accomplishing."

"You might be right, but looking at these photos it's hard to believe we were in the same vineyard last night. We captured everything so differently. You should add photographer to your resume along with engineer and chef."

We were both quiet for a moment and then she dove back in. "Last night I went to the kitchen to work things out, keeping the idea of sweet and sour on the edge of my thoughts. As I experimented with a recipe that Gervais had left on the counter, it came to me. The recipe was simple in its ingredients, but complex in its execution. All I could think about was Maggie and how she was very much the same—simple yet complex. Then it came to me: Haiku. I think the food story should be based on a Haiku about Maggie."

Sachi was very serious, but I didn't understand what she was talking about. I knew that Haiku was a form of Japanese poetry, but I was at a loss for how a piece of poetry could help us to complete our task. Sachi read the confusion on my face and launched into the next part of the explanation. "Maggie had a simple authenticity about her—a sweetness. She experienced true love and lived it with a courageous spirit. She had been married twenty-six years and lost the love of her life, and yet she managed to hold hope in her heart even after her husband's death."

I held my breath waiting for her to continue.

"When Maggie got the call about her son, the information hit her like a rock slamming into a pane of reinforced glass. The hit was solid and caused her to scream in agony, but—she—did not shatter. The process was longer and far more painful. After the initial strike, the large cracks were easy to see, but if you looked closely enough there were thousands of tiny fractures. They multiplied by the minute, her strength waning with each additional fissure. As the pressure increased, the cracks traveled along any major fault lines they could find. She held things together long enough to deal with a little reality, but no matter how hard she tried to mask it, hope was slipping away from her by the second. Then it happened. The cracks were everywhere and her window was lost. The pain in her eyes was haunting.

"It was during her first week with us; you more than anyone experienced her true sweetness. Spending time with her was like being in a spring garden. But when she received the call, the garden blackened, leaving a sour smell around her." Sachi waited a moment. "As the minutes pressed on and we waited for the limo to arrive, Puro was able to calm her, but her pain and fear lay just under the surface. With each moment, she became more fragile. She was pleased when you arrived, but she gave you the last of herself when she ran her fingers through your hair. Then she gave up and let Puro take her in his arms, no longer able to hold her pain by herself."

I sat mesmerized, taking in Sachi's view of Maggie's world.

She changed the subject quickly giving me no time to transition. "So, do you write poetry too? I see you writing in your journal a lot. I have many thoughts but can never put them down on paper like that."

I shook my head trying to keep up with her stream of consciousness.

"Yes, I have written poetry, but nothing since high school."

"You can write the poem then. I want you to keep in mind the theme of sweet and sour. I will get started on the recipes."

"I'll try my best, but I'm not making any promises," I said laughing nervously. "Find a peaceful place to write, then let the words come."

⁓

"Sweet and sour? How am I going to make this work? I can't even remember how to write a Haiku!" I said with frustration.

I went back to the room and asked Dalley if she could lend me her computer. She was hesitant at first, but then offered to help me find what I was looking for. We found several examples and I felt like I was ready to give it a try. The balcony looked like a good place to start. When that didn't work, I moved over to the bathroom floor, then migrated over to the bed, but still nothing came. Exasperated, I thought about what Sachi had said regarding a peaceful place. The only thought that came to me was the chapel. I left the inn and walked out into the vineyard, hoping I could retrace my steps and find it again.

After searching the grounds for what felt like an hour, the path to the chapel appeared. I stepped back into the sacred space and lit every candle

I could find, naming all the people I loved. I had never felt at home in church, but that place felt like it was made for me. Enjoying the flickering candles, I pulled out a sharp pencil and a fresh sheet of paper, hoping my Haiku would stop being so stubborn and show itself already.

Open heart finds love
Sweet love ends in sour bites
Sour tastes the joy

I really didn't know if it was any good, but it was from my heart and showed the best of what I had to offer. I did not see my chapel friend that day, but I had a feeling I would see her again soon.

∽⌇∾

On my way back to the inn, I heard my phone ping. I stopped.

We arrived in Vancouver several hours ago. Call me when you get this.

"Maya!" he answered on the first ring. Something was wrong.

"Cristiano?" His silence answered my unasked question. "CJ?"

"He's dead. Maya. CJ is dead." Weighted silence filled the miles between us. "Maya are you still there?"

"Yes, I'm here." My brain started to spin. "I thought he had more time."

"So did we. When we stopped in Montreal, Maggie talked to her sister. She said CJ was in a coma, but he was stable. Maggie missed him by an hour. I'm so sorry Maya. I tried everything to get her there in time, but I couldn't do it."

"Oh, Cristiano, it's not your fault."

"It was a terrible scene. Maggie's brother-in-law came to pick her up at the airport. When she saw him, she knew right away. Maggie crumpled like a paper doll, but I managed to grab her before she hit the ground.

I held her shaking body until the paramedics got there. The ambulance rushed her to the hospital and I followed them with her bags. When I arrived, she had been sedated. Her sister Gretchen, told me that a couple hours after we texted, CJ's heart stopped. They were able to bring him back but he remained in the coma. Tim sat with him, joking, telling stories, doing whatever he could to keep CJ's heart beating. When it stopped again, the doctors worked on him for over forty minutes, but he was gone.

"She said Tim wouldn't give up though, and that after the doctors had called CJ's time of death, he jumped up and started his own compressions, pounding his brother's chest, and yelling at him to breathe. There was no stopping him. She said the scene was so painful that even the doctors didn't know what to do. It wasn't until Gretchen's husband came over and lay his hands gently on Tim's that he stopped and let his brother go. She said then that he started to yell about getting all the tubes out of CJ before his mother arrived. That she couldn't see him like that, like the way their father died."

Although Cristiano and I were thousands of miles apart, our hearts wept together. I think it was in that moment that I knew. I knew I felt something for him that was different. He was different.

"Gretchen thanked me for trying to get Maggie there in time. I felt so alone, it was like … As I made my way out of the emergency room, I saw Tim, curled up, sitting on the floor, rocking back and forth, his uncle trying to console him. His eyes were vacant and he looked so lost. I knew there was nothing I could do to help him, nothing anyone could do."

There was silence, then a sigh. His tears had slowed and his voice began to come together once again. "You just have to learn how to live with that kind of pain. Maya, there's so much about me you need to know before we go any farther. I'm coming home."

"Home?"

"I need to see you. I need to see my Avó. I have some emergency time available and will be back tomorrow night."

I didn't know what to say. My emotions felt like an eddy in a fast-flowing river. I was heartbroken by the news of CJ's death, yet drawn to the fact that this tragedy was going to bring Cristiano back to me in less than a day.

"I'll be here," I said, hoping to sound strong.

"Maya, could you please let Puro know about CJ first? He and Maggie care deeply about one another and I know he will want to try and reach out to her as soon as possible. I will see you soon. I love you, Maya."

The phone clicked before I could say anything else.

I started to run. It took me a few hundred meters before my mind caught up to my legs. I traveled back through the woods and then let the vines guide me the rest of the way. When I broke through into the grove I was still running at a frantic pace.

Josie saw me first, then Ellen, and Petra. By the time I arrived at the stairs, I was breathless and from the look on their faces, they had figured out why.

"Where is Puro?" I cried, panting and stricken.

Petra ran inside and within an instant Puro followed her back out.

"Maya what is it?" Desperation filled the air.

I took a couple of deep breaths and steadied myself against the railing, trying to think of the *right* words, but found none. There was only the truth: "CJ is dead."

"She made it in time?"

I said nothing. Then he stood and tapped the nape of his neck with his fingers. His voice intensified. "She got a chance to say goodbye, right?"

I shook my head as the words were lodged in my throat. When they were finally freed, they came out only as a whisper. "No, Puro, she didn't."

His face went blank. He said nothing but walked down the stairs and headed into the hills.

I turned to go after him, but Carmo held my arm. "No Maya, let him go."

31

What's up Dalley?

Maya

THE MORNING AFTER THE NEWS, we all gathered for breakfast and sat quietly, unable to find any words right for the moment; that was, except for Sachi. "Good morning." Sachi interrupted the silence that surrounded the table. "Over the past few days, we have been struck with tragedy and it seems almost impossible to know what to do, but as Josie said on Sunday, Maggie would want us to continue. I believe Josie was correct and we need to find a way to keep going through this difficult time." Her speech was steady and strong, and it offered enough safety to awaken several conversations.

Sachi touched my arm unexpectedly. "Maya, I know yesterday was difficult, but did you get the poem written?"

"Yes," I answered with reluctance.

"Do you have it with you?"

I reached into my purse and handed it to her. She opened the paper then whispered, "I think you should read it—right now."

"No, I really don't want to," I whispered back.

Then she turned to face everyone. "Excuse me. The story Maya and I decided to tell for our project this week is about Maggie. I asked Maya to write a poem and I think she should read it."

Hesitantly, I took the sheet of paper back. My heart pounded with discomfort and I could hear a ringing in my ears. I was never good at public speaking.

"It's really short, kind of a Haiku, but it's missing a couple of syllables."

"Excellent!" Josie exclaimed. "I can't stand those long drawn out poems anyways. A full Haiku is just over the top," she chuckled, trying to help me feel more comfortable.

"I don't have a title for it yet," I said almost apologetically.

As I looked at the poem, I ran my fingers over the words and a feeling of calm came over me. The table went quiet and the words just came.

Open heart finds love
Sweet love ends in sour bites
Sour tastes the joy

I quickly tucked the paper away. "I'm still trying to figure out exactly what it means."

"Thank you, Maya. That was beautiful. I think though, that each one of us needs to find our own meaning for it." Sachi's thoughtful words made me pause.

The table was silent at first, then Ellen spoke. "Thank you. It's good to know she will be remembered this week in some way. In my culture, death needs to be surrounded by community. Although we cannot be there for Maggie physically there are other ways we can help."

Ellen's words created an opportunity for everyone to share their minds and their hearts. We learned that Josie had lost a child when she was just eighteen, and when Petra was fourteen, her best friend had taken her own life. Ellen shared stories of the smudges she attended on the reserve with her father, and Dalley chose not to say a word but wrung her hands like they ached from the inside out. I told everyone the story about Maggie's husband's illness and his death, and how running had saved her life. After another round of tears, we found ourselves cried out and strangely feeling a little brighter, or at least less sad. Ellen had a moment of inspiration about the project and took a quiet Josie by the hand, heading off to Lisbon for the day.

Petra looked over at Dalley, who by then was preoccupied with her phone. "Dalley, let's go to my room and see if we can pound out an idea."

Dalley looked up, oblivious to Petra's question. "Pardon me? What?"

"I said, let's go to my room. I'll have coffee sent up and we can pull some ideas together."

"Yeah, sure that sounds great," Dalley said, looking back down.

Petra shook her head, stood up and made her way around the table and then grabbed the phone out of Dalley's hands. "What are you doing that's so interesting?"

Dalley yanked the phone back from Petra, blurting out defensively, "It's nothing, just a bunch of numbers that my editor sent me."

Petra threw her hands in the air, let out a sigh, and then left the dining room. I stared at Dalley and wondered why she was acting so strangely. "Dalley, what's up with you? Petra was just trying to get on top of the project."

She smiled weakly and rubbed her fingers across her forehead, like she was trying to push away a headache. "Sorry Maya. I've had a few other things on my mind. I'll head up and apologize to her right now." She threw her phone into her bag and then scurried out the door.

Sachi and I were the only ones left in the dining room. We sat beside each other and said nothing for a few moments. Then she broke the silence. "Maya, I loved your poem. It was perfect. I don't want you to change anything. I think we can build a menu around it quite easily. Come to the kitchen and do some test cooking with me today. We don't need to talk. All we need to do is cook."

She stood up and gave me a little bow with her head, then silently disappeared into the kitchen. I followed her, feeling slightly nervous about spending the day in her domain. When I pushed through the doors, she held out an apron and told me to go wash my hands. I knew from there on out, she was completely in charge.

As I helped Sachi get things started, I could see how comfortable she was in the kitchen, in *that* kitchen. Her shoulders were relaxed and her face was so serene, she looked like a different person. She cooked like she was conducting an orchestra. I wasn't sure where I fit in, so most of the time I just watched and listened. Several times I caught Gervais watching her too. I couldn't tell if it was envy or admiration. Twice she sent me on an adventure to the market in Évora to find some special ingredients.

During my second trip when I walked through the market, I was taken by the beauty and spirit of the Portuguese people. They were kind, generous, and filled with life. It felt like I was home, and it was a home where I really belonged.

When I got back from Évora, it was late in the afternoon and Petra was downstairs, pacing back and forth.

"Petra what's wrong?"

"Dalley is distracted. Even when she was with me, she was somewhere else. She couldn't decide on anything. I thought for sure a newspaper girl and an ad executive would be able to come up with a great story, but she gave me nothing. Something is really wrong!"

"Maybe it's the stuff about CJ. She didn't say a word while everyone else was sharing. Maybe it brought up some really bad memories."

Petra appeared to contemplate my answer then responded carefully. "No, my instincts tell me it is definitely something else. Honestly though, I can't worry about it anymore. She's a big girl. I've asked her if there was anything wrong and she said she was fine. So I'm going to pretend everything's okay. I haven't been on a holiday in four years Maya, and as bad as it may sound, I can't spend any more time worrying about Dalley."

She then changed her tone along with her body language. "I had an idea though about the project and what we could do. I know you and Sachi are going to wipe the floor with us, but at least I'll try—we'll try. Earlier in the day when a young bellman came upstairs to deliver us coffee, he was very friendly, and told us about his family and how they were making a big meal later in the evening. His excitement started me thinking about the idea of 'the family meal' and the stories that people often share during that special time. I asked him a few more questions about his family and with great surprise, he invited us for supper. I know I'm going, but I'm not sure Dalley was even paying attention. She can do whatever she wants, but I think we should build our project around the family meal."

"That sounds like so much fun. Don't worry about Dalley. She'll come around. You can trust her."

With a clank and a rattle Josie and Ellen jumped into the lobby. They were laughing and looked like they had spent the better part of the day shopping. Their mood was a welcome reprieve from all the tears and stress of the previous two days.

"What have the two of you been up to?" Petra inquired, trying to peek into one of the bags.

Josie tugged the bag back. "No peeking! Ellen made me sign a non-disclosure statement!" Then she looked at Ellen and pleaded for permission to share their idea.

"Go ahead and tell them," Ellen said giving in easily.

"We're creating a celebration," Josie said with a little twinkle in her eye. "Ellen was sharing thoughts about her past and explaining how they used to have potlatches to bring people in the community together for weddings or funerals. And she explained how the planning of the event was just as important as the actual celebration. We decided we're going to tell the story of how a good celebration comes together. Ellen said she may even do some drumming. Maggie would have loved it."

"I can't wait to see what kind of food the two of you come up with for the event." Petra exclaimed.

"Oh, the party food has been all taken care of," Josie whispered to us. "We went to visit Alfonso, our chef from the hotel in Lisbon. He's going to give us a little hand with the menu."

"That's cheating," Petra responded with feigned indignation.

"Well, not technically," Ellen said. "He's going to help us organize parts of the food, and then we'll put it all together on the night of the event."

"I don't know, Ellen. It sounds like cheating to me," I said laughing along with Petra.

The four of us sat in the lobby, enjoying the stories that were already developing within each of our projects. Then Sachi poked her head out of the kitchen.

"Maya, where have you been?" she sounded concerned, as I had been gone for a long time.

"Sorry Sachi, I got distracted. I did make it there and back though." I lifted the bags up and showed her that I had gotten my job done. "But I got caught up with the girls when I came through the door."

"Yes, I heard the laughing. What's so funny?" she asked, wearing a little smile of her own.

Josie answered, "Nothing in particular. I guess we were all in need of a little laughter this afternoon." She put her bags down, walked over to Sachi, and threw her arms around her. Everyone stopped laughing, not knowing how Sachi would respond. At the same time Dalley walked into the lobby.

"Don't stop laughing on my account," Dalley said as sarcasm bit into her tone. I wasn't sure if she was joking or not, so I reached into Ellen's bag and pulled out a noise maker and blew it as loud as I could. The sound broke the odd tension and Dalley smiled and pulled a bottle of wine out of her own bag.

"I can do better than that," she commented looking at me. "A peace offering," she said handing the bottle to Petra.

The offering seemed to work, as Petra ordered up six glasses. The bottle was opened and we toasted our dear friend Maggie.

As the day's planning came to a close and the laughter of the afternoon ended, we all sat, not sure what to do next. There was an emptiness that would not be solved by drinking more wine.

Thoughts of Cristiano filled the empty spaces in my mind. I couldn't get the sound of his voice out of my head, his desperate need to get home, to get back to me. He told me he loved me.

"Are you okay, Maya?" Petra asked.

"Yes, I think so. I just had the oddest feeling."

"Are you dizzy? Did you drink too much?"

"No, it's not like that, it's like …" I heard the engine just outside the open door and my heart slammed against my rib cage. I could feel him even before I saw him.

"Cristiano," Petra said without missing a beat.

I smiled and blushed. I touched my pendant, stood up, and waited for him. "Maya?!" He called my name.

"Yes!" was all I needed to say.

His pace quickened as he crossed the room and intention filled each step. There was no stopping him. Our two bodies crushed together. His lips met mine, sealing a love that had barely just begun.

"I need you to come with me right now." His voice was filled with vulnerability and pain.

Instinct took over. I wrapped my arms around him, cloaking him in the protection he sought. Then I kissed him back, forgetting about everything and everyone that surrounded us.

32

Avó's Letter

Maya

He pulled back from me, then gently kissed my forehead and without saying a word guided me out to the car.

Our drive was filled with silence. Not the uncomfortable kind, but the type that allows a person to see and hear and smell everything that's around them. Cristiano didn't speed that night but took his time. He continued to steal glances of me as he drove, several times wiping tears from his face that snuck out from beneath his sunglasses. It wasn't until I saw the outskirts of Lisbon on the horizon that we began to speak.

"Are you going to be okay?"

He smiled a little and grabbed my hand. "I am now. Thank you for knowing just what I needed. You're perfect."

I laughed, "Perfect? I've been called many things, but perfect has never been one of them."

"Well, perfect for me."

"That is something I could get used to."

He smiled and took my hand, his thumb slowly, rhythmically rubbing the inside of my palm. He shifted in his seat and changed the tone of our conversation to something a little lighter. "That was quite a kiss."

I smirked back at him. "That was quite an entrance."

"I'm not sure what came over me, but I just—needed you in my arms. I'm sorry if it was too much."

"No, it wasn't too much. It was inspired. You followed your heart, and I got a chance to be in a scene from my own romance movie."

"Romance movie? Is there any adventure in the next scene?" he teased.

"Oh, I heard there might be some drama and maybe a few tears." I stroked his cheek, knowing that at some point we would have to talk more about what had happened in Vancouver.

"Well, there may be a little drama coming, but I guarantee a happy ending." I squeezed his hand, allowing myself to believe.

As we turned down a little side street, I realized I had no idea where he was taking me. My hair whipped around in every direction. He stroked my leg and then ran his hand through my bangs, pushing them back from my eyes.

"Do you miss it?" he asked.

"Miss what?" I smiled, not sure what he was referring to.

"Your long hair?"

I paused. "No, I don't miss anything about it. I don't miss anything about the old me."

"The old you? Would I have liked her?"

"I'm not sure. I think I was in there *somewhere*, just hidden under a lot of layers."

"Well then, I'm pleased *you* decided to let your new self find her way into the open."

"I'm not sure I had a choice around it. She started to break free a few months ago, and when she met you, she refused to go back into the box, and well—here I am."

We eventually made one last turn and parked outside of a little apartment that must have been built back in the late 1940s. His faced changed as he looked at me with concern. "It's not very fancy. I'm sorry," he said apologetically.

"Sorry for what? I take it this is your apartment?" He nodded.

"Actually, I think it's quaint. I did have a question though: What are we doing here?"

His face changed again, only this time he looked mortified. "With everything going on, you don't think I brought you to my place to …"

"No, not really, but I am a little curious with the sweeping me off my feet thing and driving to your apartment. You could see where I might have a question or two?"

"I haven't explained myself very well have I? That's *not* why I brought you here," he said, struggling to find the right words.

"Just take a breath. We're in no hurry."

He took the breath I offered and tried again. "This place is very special to me and I needed to spend some time alone with you, considering everything that has happened. So much real life has been tossed into our laps in the last week and I think it's important for us to slow down."

"That's more than fair," I said, brushing a dark curl away from his face and lifting his chin so our eyes could meet. His body relaxed and we both smiled at one another. After opening my car door, he took my hand and we walked into the little entryway of his building. Our laughter filled the hallway as he guided me towards the stairs. Before we took our first step, a door opened behind us. Cristiano and I turned, and an elderly woman stood in the hall, arms across her chest.

"Mrs. Dutra! Good evening," he said with a little surprise.

"Good evening," she replied while staring first at me, then at Cristiano. He quickly dropped his hand from my back and held it close to his side.

"Mrs. Dutra, I would like you to meet Miss Maya Wells," he said slowly.

She looked sternly at first, but her cheeks softened as she stared into Cristiano's eyes.

"Why Miss Wells, it seems that you are the answer to the question I was looking for last weekend." She smiled cautiously then stared and without a word told me how important Cristiano was to her.

"Cristiano, you're back sooner than usual. Is everything okay?" she asked focusing on him.

"Thank you, Mrs. Dutra. Everything is fine. I just had a few personal matters to attend to."

"Well I am pleased to hear that. You know I would do anything for you if you ever needed it." She began fussing with the buttons on her sweater, then continued. "Enjoy your visit in Lisbon, Miss Wells."

"Thank you, Mrs. Dutra."

She turned and slowly walked back to her apartment. When the door was closed, he laughed quietly, and shook his head. We then made our way up the narrow staircase.

"That went well," he said, letting out a deep sigh of relief.

"Who is she?"

"She's like my gatekeeper. I have known her since I was a child." He paused. "This was my parents' apartment when I was little. When I started flying, I needed a place to stay that was closer to the airport, and Avó reminded me that I still owned the apartment here. Mrs. Dutra took care of it for many years after my parents died, and then took a keen interest in me once I started living here again."

We walked up the darkened stairwell, Cristiano's hand resting firmly on the small of my back. At the top of the stairs he guided me to the apartment at the end of the hall. He unlocked the door and we stepped into a space that felt like it had been stopped in time.

"Well, what do you think?" he asked with a little wrinkle on his forehead.

"I think it's perfect, right down to the sunny yellow paint," I said with a smile.

"That was my mom's favorite color. She painted the walls herself." He gave me a peck on the cheek and then sat me down on his couch. "Wait here!" he said emphatically, putting his hand up like a traffic cop.

"Where are you going?"

"I just realized it has been several days since I showered and …" He grimaced. "I need to get cleaned up."

I smiled and waved him towards the bathroom. "Take your time."

He turned back, took my face in his hands, and kissed me. My body leaned in, responding without hesitation. There was no audience this time. I wasn't sure I could stop, or that I wanted to.

He pulled away and smiled broadly, then laughed and walked back to the bathroom. When he closed the door the latch must not have caught, as a minute later, the door opened slightly and I could hear the shower running.

No one had ever kissed me like that before. My memory flashed to my first kiss with Steven. It was anything but passionate and actually a little messy. I shook my head to knock that thought free and then walked over to the open door. Through the small space I caught a glimpse of him behind the translucent shower curtain. My face flushed and I side-stepped back to the couch thinking about Montreal and how he'd toweled the water droplets off my back. Goosebumps ran over my body, as I remembered his first touch on my skin.

I tried to distract myself and flipped through a magazine that lay on the coffee table. Under another magazine I saw an envelope with the corner of a letter peeking out of the top. I picked up the envelope. My curiosity got the better of me and I slipped the letter out. My only intention was to find out who it was from. But as I read I fell into a story, his story.

My Dear Cristiano,

You have been dancing in my thoughts for many days now. You have missed me; I can feel it. When I started this letter it was only to tell you I love you, but …

I read all about Cristiano's world, told by his Avó; about his mom and Euphemia and how determined Rosa was to adopt Cristiano and make him her son. The tale continued with the heart-wrenching day when his birth father held him in his arms and sang to him before he had to say goodbye. Then there were the laughter jars, his parents' death, and the night of bread making.

It wasn't until I felt his breath on my neck that I realized he had been watching me read his story.

"I'm sorry Cristiano. I shouldn't have," I said with embarrassment.

"All's fair in reading things we shouldn't. I read your journal and you read my letter. I guess we are even," he said smirking. "But seriously, I *want* you to know everything. This is one of the reasons I brought you here. Before we move forward, I *need* you to know more about my life and where I came from. Please, can you read the rest out loud to me? That's where I stopped the other day."

We sat close to one another. His bare chest was warm and inviting, and his wet hair dripped on to the letter leaving a little stain of himself to mix with the ink.

"Do you need anything?" he asked smiling.

"No, I have everything I need right here." I touched his face gently with my fingertips and then fell back into his arms and the story. My voice wavered at first, then he gave me a comforting hug, and I began to find a rhythm.

Cristiano it's important that you hear the next part of your story, as sometimes I think you need to be reminded of who we both were and are.

When you were a child, some people thought of me as a special woman, different. I looked at the world upside down and backwards. It was beautiful. I saw you for who you really were and walked with you through a world of confusion, pain, growth, rebellion, and escape.

But through it all our love for one another never wavered. I knew when you were going to get into trouble, when to stop you, and when to let you be. I thought I was everything that you needed.

I was a prayerful woman, and encouraged you to join me at church every week, but never forced you to attend. All I ever did was ask for you to walk with me to the church steps.

Many people in the village thought I was too lenient, that I should have made you go in, but I always wanted you to have a choice. I would kiss your cheek and wave to you as you crossed the street and climbed a tree. Every Sunday after service, I came out and would ask 'So how is God today?' You would look down from the tree and answer, 'Oh He has been very busy.' Then you would climb down and share stories of all that you thought about while I was in church.

One day, one of the parishioners saw you in the tree. They told you to come down, and so you did. They grabbed you by the arm and dragged you into church. There was such a ruckus that the priest stopped the service. I came over, shouted one sharp phrase at the man who held your arm, and you and I walked out of the church.

"Cristiano, do you remember any of that?" I asked.

"Only flashes. I remember being in the tree and then Avó tearing a strip off the old man for even touching me." He smiled, then paused thoughtfully.

I took your hand and we walked together down the road. From that day forward, I made sure Sundays were a little different. We no longer went to regular church, but got up early and walked to a little chapel in a nearby vineyard.

"The vineyard chapel? At Netuno?" Surprise sprung up in my tone.

"Do you know it?"

"Yes, I found it the other day, or it found me."

"Hmm, it has a funny way of doing that." He laughed, then held me closer and nudged me to keep reading.

There was no priest, but the doors were always open. It only took two weeks before you entered and sat in the back pew. You watched me light the candles and listened to my songs. It was a happy and safe place for us. One Sunday, while I was singing and praying, you started to investigate and went through a few cupboards in the back and found an old ratty case that held a guitar. Running your hands over the beautiful wooden neck you gently tapped your fingers onto the strings. The guitar was old and out of tune, but just what you needed. You listened to me sing and carefully twisted the tuning pegs until you thought it sounded right. For months on end you came into church and played, creating new melodies each time your fingers touched the strings and I believe that guitar saved your life.

A year later, your playing improved and so did your heart. The sadness and dark hole that you felt after your parents' death had started to heal.

When you were ten, we were walking home from the chapel one Sunday and you looked at me, paused, and asked, 'So how is God today?' I smiled and began telling you about everything I'd seen that day.

That was the beginning of a new part of our world. From that day forward, you and I were bound together, not just as a family, but as spirits who truly understood each other.

We never had to worry about money, as your father was a very good planner and made sure we were taken care of financially. That was a good thing, as it allowed me to continue my life as a special baker. I stopped selling bread to put food on the table and focused only on my special bread making.

People traveled from very faraway places for a loaf of my bread. Some days, they would wait for hours outside under the trees, and then when the baking was done for the day, I would place the loaves on the outdoor table letting the scent of hope fill the air. I would go out and sit and chat with the strangers as they waited. Then I would choose who belonged with each loaf. There were some days when people would leave empty handed and would have to come back again another day. I just let them know that they weren't quite ready for my bread—yet. There were disappointments some days, but always understanding and acceptance, and every day you sat quietly and watched as I did my work.

One afternoon, when a few people were waiting under the tree, you noticed one man standing back from the rest. He had been coming every day for two weeks, but had never asked for anything. Your twelve-year-old curiosity got the better of you and you went over to speak with him. I heard you while I was taking loaves out of the garden oven, saying, 'Excuse me sir, I noticed that you have been coming to our garden for almost two weeks and have yet to ask for anything from my Avó. Is there something I can help you with?'

He shook his head, and looked down at the ground, almost embarrassed. Then he responded, 'I have heard great stories about the power of your Avó's bread and how a loaf can change a person's life and set them on the path to attain what they want most in the world.'

You looked at him with slight awe and then asked, 'Is that why you have come? To find your path?'

'Yes, that is why all of us come. Your Avó has been gifted with grace and insight, and for many years, through her baking, she's offered people that gift. But she only gives it to those who she feels are ready. I am not ready yet, but I am trying. I have been sitting near your home for many days, listening to the grinding mill, hearing the kneading of the bread, and the quiet time of the rising. The first time I smelled the bread baking in the garden oven, I felt drawn and knew that there was more for me to discover, so I came every day to learn.'

You looked at the man with intensity and said, 'I think that my Avó would like to meet you today.'

You guided him to the garden and his loaf was waiting for him. Do you remember what I said to him?

I turned and looked up at Cristiano. The serenity in his face led me to believe that yes indeed he remembered all of it. His gentle smile answered Avó's question.

I spoke briefly to the man telling him, 'You have found your path and taught my grandson something beautiful today. Thank you. Go out and share your gift of patience and teaching.'

We learned a lot that day about each other, and for a long while, you baked with me. It was a wonderful time. But, as you grew, my old ways and mysterious loaves became overshadowed by adolescence and an outside world that didn't have any room for mystery or hope. At school everyone knew who I was and that your parents had died many years before. People did not always understand and at times were very cruel. You defended me and our life to everyone else, yet your hand-stitched musical heart began to unravel again. By the time you were in high school, that dark hole in your heart had returned.

I paused again when I felt something wet on my hand. Cristiano's tears fell freely and splashed down on both myself and the letter.

You stopped baking, stopped going to church, kept playing your guitar, and started to surf.

I turned my head towards him intrigued by the thought. "You surfed? Do you still?" I asked, imagining him on the waves.

He smiled at me and nodded towards the surfboards that were leaning up against the wall. I shook my head and added, "Yes, those are hard to miss, if you are not distracted by other things—like letters and showers."

"You should try it sometime." Then he gave me a squeeze. "It helps to clear your head." He paused. "I didn't know she knew about the surfing."

Smiling, I nestled deeper into his chest. "It sounds like she knows almost everything."

Once in a while you would play your guitar for me after a long day of baking. One night I stopped you before you went to bed, telling you that God and I would always be there for you. Although I didn't make you go to church, I did make you go and work with Puro. He was good for you, but even he couldn't offer you all of what you needed, especially that Christmas before graduation when you left us.

You did come home eventually, but after graduation you didn't want to stay. You were lost in a hole and I could not follow you there. It had taken me a long time to find my own way out after your parents died. So I just waited until you could come back.

One day you called to tell me that you had started school to become a flight attendant. You asked for nothing from me. I reminded you of the old apartment your parents owned in Lisbon. At least I knew you would be safe when you were not in the skies.

Cristiano cleared his throat, took the letter from my hand, and folded it up gently. He stood up from the couch and walked over to the window. I followed behind him and placed my hand on his arm.

"I think it best if I read the rest of it later," he said staring out the window.

I stood with him and we watched and listened to the sights and sounds of Lisbon for almost an hour, both of us caught up in our own thoughts. His letter played out in my mind like a story book—everything from his adoption to the mysterious loaves of bread. I pondered on what kind of life we could have together and whether going back to Peachland was even possible. I knew I needed to be part of his life and I wanted to be the next chapter in his story.

More Truth

Maya

HE PLACED HIS ARMS AROUND my waist and squeezed me tightly.

"So where do we go from here? More stories, more truth?" he asked, as he cast his gaze out into the night and then guided me back to the couch to sit down with him.

"How about a little bit of both. Tell me more about the flying. Why did you choose to become a flight attendant?"

He chuckled to himself. "It was the little boy in me at first. I simply wanted to be near my parents and I thought that flying would help me feel closer to them. But things got mixed up for me really quickly. I was very good at my job and everyone seemed to love the smiling, happy Portuguese flight attendant that I had become. They made it easy to pretend. In a few short years, I was able to pick and choose any flight that I wanted. I traveled almost everywhere and left a string of broken hearts to prove it." He paused briefly. "The truth right? That's what you asked for."

I reminded myself that both of us were adults, and our histories did not have to define us and who we could become together. I nodded for him to continue.

"By the time I met you, I had almost morphed into someone I didn't recognize."

I knew exactly what he was talking about. We were the same in our hearts. We were pretending to be someone we weren't and searching for answers to questions we hadn't even asked ourselves yet.

"I knew if I were to go home at any point during that part of my life, I would not have been offered a loaf of bread from my Avó's table. My world was empty with no path. Something had to change, and so I started looking for signs, for something meaningful to happen—then in walked a spilled cup of tea, a lost journal, and a very sparkly pen."

Taking in a quick breath, I realized that all of those pieces added up to … me. I was the spilt cup of tea that had changed his life. My hand drifted over to his cheek. I understood what he was telling me; that somehow Maya Wells had created his paradigm shift, that I was his sign. My heart winced when he mentioned Athena. He sensed my shift in mood. "What's the matter?"

"Oh, it's nothing really. Well yes it is, but with everything else that has happened, I forgot to tell you, Athena is gone!"

"What do you mean she's gone? Did you lose her? Leave her in an airport perhaps?" He smiled trying to add a little humor to my sadness. "I'm sure she's buried somewhere in that flashy Paris purse of yours."

"I wish my purse was the answer, but it's more complicated than that. Jade stole her—well at least found her and then kept her, but she knew Athena was mine."

"Why would Jade keep your pen?"

"Where do I start?" I thought back. "I guess the first encounter occurred at the airport in Montreal. I stepped in front of her to block her view of you right after our first date."

He smiled. "Really? You didn't want her to see me?"

"No, I didn't. I'm not sure what came over me, as I'd never done anything like that before, but from that moment forward I was marked— it was worth it though." I smirked as I thought of how bold I'd felt that afternoon. "Then later that evening at the night club when you shuffled her off to your friend so that you could dance with me, I anticipated that the next four weeks might hold a few challenges. I didn't know it at the time, but I was preparing for a great part in my own drama with her."

"That night with you at the club was incredible," he reflected pensively. "I never even gave her a second thought. She's not my type. I only agreed to dance with her to be polite. Everything had already been decided for me, from the moment we met." His words were so honest I couldn't help but blush a little. "Was she really that bad?"

I cringed. "Earlier in the week I did try to talk with her, but she was so horrible and mean. After that, I told her to leave me alone and that I didn't want to have anything to do with her. She just laughed at me."

"Maya, the truth is people like that are usually born into ugly families. Their hearts are black and they are never taught how to love or feel joy. They feed off of other people's pain and vulnerabilities and are always looking for a way to improve their position and find leverage over someone, anyway they can."

"Interesting thought. It makes sense and it could explain a little of what happened on Sunday after you dropped me off." I had his full attention. "So it went something like this: You said goodbye and I walked in the lobby. I went from having the most amazing evening of my life to being hit with a sorrow that was so deep and tragic I could hardly hold myself together, or so I thought. That's when it happened."

"What happened? What did you do?" he asked looking a little afraid.

"Well, after Maggie and Puro left for the airport, our group remained in the lobby, not sure where to go or what to do. I saw a smile break across

Jade's face. She tried to cover it up but was unsuccessful. Her smile turned dead as I walked over to her, dressed in my medieval evening wear. I took the bait and I asked her what she was smiling about. She shook her head like she was laughing at a joke. When I challenged her, she started going on about Maggie not being a good parent and that somehow she was responsible for her son's illness. She went on to make a few more disturbing personal comments about me, and then I felt something pop inside.

"I wasn't sure if the pop meant that something was broken or slipped back into place. All I knew was that it felt right and there was no stopping me. I was white hot with anger."

I paused, suddenly feeling self-conscious with the attention he was paying to me. It was like he was studying me. I slowed my words, owning each one of them. "I've never felt that kind of power before."

Cristiano leaned into my space and my heart raced. "So what happened? Did you punch her?"

"No," I laughed. "Although I felt like I wanted to. I used my words like iron fists, and at the end of my very loud tirade she stood frozen, along with everyone else in the lobby. The smile on her face had been wiped clean. I think I gave her the equivalent of a good right hook. Then I picked up the train of my dress and ran out the front doors of the inn. Petra said it was a brilliant scene and she hopes to use it in a commercial one day. I had never done anything like that before! It was freeing and dramatic and a little frightening all at the same time.

"Adrenaline raced through my veins as I ran between the vines. I became confused and a little disorientated and eventually slowed down and started to wander. My thoughts focused on Maggie and the hell that lay in front of her. I was thankful that you were with her, but I wanted you with me, too. I just wanted to be sitting on the bench at the festival under the twinkly lights and pretend like none of it had happened. During my wander, I tripped and tore my dress, and fell to the forest floor. When I looked up, I found myself on the edge of a little path, well-worn and loved. The path led me over logs and up a little hill where there was a clearing."

He opened his mouth like he could have finished my story.

"I had sought out someplace peaceful and without knowing why was led to …"

He broke into my sentence and blurted out, "The chapel! That's when you found the chapel."

"Yes, so I sat and prayed for a lot of things that day. I wasn't sure if God would even listen as it had been so long since we'd really talked."

"And did he?"

"He not only was listening but started to answer questions I hadn't even asked."

Cristiano smiled. "Yes. He's good that way, helping us find things we weren't even looking for, or had given up on finding. I think God has a much greater sense of humor than we give him credit for.

"I'm curious—how do you know Jade took Athena?"

"Long story short, Petra saw Jade with it in the morning when she left, but Petra didn't know it was mine at the time."

"Jade left?" he sounded intrigued.

"Yes! Thank goodness."

"I'm pleased you do not have to deal with her anymore. I'm sorry about Athena. I would do anything to get her back for you if I could." His earnest words reminded me once again of the kind heart that lived inside of him.

"Thank you, but sometimes we just have to let go of special things that come into our lives. Besides, maybe Athena did her job already and it was time for her to move on. She did help bring us together, didn't she?" I said with a big smile.

Cristiano grabbed me, then studied my face farther. The kisses that followed started at the nape of my neck and ended on my lips.

The two of us sat back on the couch and took a breath from the last forty-eight hours of tears, laughter, tragedy, and new beginnings.

"Is there anything we can do for Maggie from here?" I asked, wishing there was some magic solution to my question.

"No, not right now. I have spoken with Puro and he'll let us know if there is anything we can do. I fear the worst is yet to come," he said clenching his teeth, fighting back his own memories.

Cristiano grabbed the edge of the couch and began. "When Maggie collapsed in my arms at the airport her grief hit me like a weighted vest. I couldn't move. I was transported back to my Avó's garden on the day when I found out about my parents' death. It was horrible. It was like living it all over again. After getting things settled with Gretchen at the hospital, I knew I needed to come home."

"Am I part of your home now?"

He took my face in his hands and stared deeply into my eyes. "Maya, I love you. You are my home, wherever you are."

We had only known each other for days and he was declaring his love for me before I even knew what his favorite food was. 'I love you' did not come as easy for me. The feeling was there, but the words danced on my tongue. My moment had not come yet.

"Do you want me to finish reading the letter?" I asked, not sure what to say.

"No, thank you. I think I'll read the last part later. I can't have her reveal all my secrets to you in one night. There needs to be some mystery, right?"

"No mystery needed," I laughed. "I just need to find out things like your favorite food and color."

He placed his finger on his chin, pretending to give it a great amount of thought. Then he answered, "Avó's bread and green. My turn."

"You want to know my favorite food?"

"No, that's too easy. I'm going to make you work a little harder than that. Tell me about the diamond? What did you do that was so brave?"

I straightened up and decided to hand my world to him as he had given his to me.

"I was born in Peachland, British Columbia and yes we do have peaches there—lots of them. My family used to own a small vineyard and a peach orchard." His eyes widened, but he kept silent.

"When I was eight, my dad sold the property because my mom was sick and she needed to be closer to her doctors."

"What was she sick with? Cancer?"

"No, sometimes though, I think that would have been easier." I cast my eyes down, embarrassed by my comment. He pressed himself closer to me. "Actually, she was clinically depressed." I tried to hide behind a small smile on my face, but it didn't work. He took my hand. "She had been sick for most of my life and although technically I had a mom, most of the time she was not the kind I wanted or needed, but she did her best. It's taken me a long time to finally see that. It's only been in the last few years that we have seen the biggest change in her. When her old psychiatrist retired, they changed her meds and she started counseling. My dad kept telling me things were better, but I didn't want to believe him. It was easier to blame all of my unhappy feelings on the life I didn't have growing up, rather than take responsibility for the choices I was making as an adult. I was sad pretty much all the time, but I hid it well. My sister was one of the only people who was honest with me about her thoughts when everything happened."

"You have a sister? What happened?"

"Yes, her name is Jordan. She's generally angry and irritated and has been that way since she was a child. I have to warn you though, she probably won't like you just because I *do*, and in addition to that she's extra mad at me right now because of something I did."

Cristiano stroked my hand and adjusted his body preparing himself for my next truth.

"Don't worry. I promised I would tell you everything," I said, reassuring him. Taking a deep breath, I dove in. "I was a good student in high school, never missed a day, had a few friends, but only one good one: Beth. She, on the other hand, will love you. I went to university, got a job at a sprinkler company, and got engaged." I peeked over at him.

"Engaged? How long ago?" He asked with an uncomfortable laugh.

"Do you really want to know about this?" I closed my eyes, hoping we could skip over that part.

"I think I should, don't you?" he asked, tilting his head to the side.

"About four months ago I was supposed to get married. The night before the wedding, I marched into my parents' bedroom and told them I couldn't marry him. Within a few hours, everything was cancelled. They never asked me why. It was only after I stopped the wedding that I found out they'd been worried about me, for a long time." I said the last part with my eyes closed again.

"I'm sorry you were so sad and didn't feel like you could tell anyone. I know all about that kind of loneliness. What was his name?"

"Steven." I opened my eyes watching his reaction carefully.

"Did he love you?"

"Yes."

"Did you ever really love him?"

"No, I didn't, but I love you." When I said it, all hesitation was gone. "Cristiano I love you."

He responded with a smile. Then laced our fingers together like that first day when we ran through the airport.

"No more questions?" I asked.

"Well, maybe just one. The diamond?" he said, pointing to my shimmering pendant.

I sighed. "Yes, my eccentric Aunt Olive gave it to me on my non-wedding day to congratulate me on not getting married. She actually referred to the pendant as a tear of bravery."

"I think I would like to meet this aunt of yours," he said with a hint of appreciation.

"Yes, she has been the source of many family conversations, but in the end, I think she is quite sane. She just plays the role of the crazy aunt very well to keep people off her trail."

"Smart woman."

"Yes, I would say so. I know she would love you, too."

He stood up from the couch and headed over to the kitchen. "You want something to eat? I think I have some crackers here in the cupboard."

I got up and helped him forage through his barren cupboards. "You don't spend very much time here, do you?" I said, as I stared into the almost-empty fridge.

"It's funny. Some days I love it here and other days I can't stand it. It's hard being in this place without them. Even after so many years, there are days when I turn around and think I can smell her perfume, or hear my father reading out loud to her at night." He closed his eyes.

"Your dad used to read to her?"

"Yes, she loved the way he would use different voices for each character. They loved each other so much."

As he started talking about them, tears welled in my eyes. He looked at me lovingly and wiped one that had slipped out.

"Over the years there were times when I missed them so much that I ached to be with them. I just wanted to get lost. When I was a child, I climbed trees and played the guitar, and then when I was a teen, as you know, I started to surf. I'll have to introduce you to Jack. He's the one who taught me. He still lives on the beach and teaches surfing."

"What about the Christmas before graduation?"

"I ran. I just needed to be away, to be someone else for a while. I spent most of my days on the beach with Jack. He let me be anyone I wanted. Eventually though I went back to be with Avó and to say goodbye properly. After graduation I left. As I got older, I ran faster and farther, flying around the world, hoping to find something to fill the empty space that I felt inside."

"And you found it?"

"Yes, but only recently," he said while holding me tightly and stroking my hair.

"When was the last time you really ate?" I asked, changing the subject. There was a sudden knock on the door and Cristiano laughed.

"Who could that be?" I wondered.

"I always suspected that woman could hear through the vents or had psychic powers. Can you see what she wants? I had better throw a shirt on, as she is very old fashioned."

I walked over to the door and opened it, not sure how Cristiano knew it was going to be her. "Hi, Mrs. Dutra. What can I do for you? Cristiano is in the bathroom."

"Well dear, it is getting close to supper, and I didn't see the two of you going out. I know Cristiano has been working very hard and has had no time to get groceries. I thought you could do with a meal."

She stood in the doorway with oven mitts, holding a steaming dish of what looked like some sort of Portuguese stew. The scent was so inviting that I could have eaten a spoonful from the pot right then and there.

Cristiano dashed boldly out of the bathroom, wearing a crisp white t-shirt that fit his body perfectly. I breathed in deeply as he wrapped his arms around my waist, showing Mrs. Dutra how I fit into his life without having to say a word.

"Why yes, Mrs. Dutra. We were just talking about supper and that I have nothing in my cupboards. Thank you. We really appreciate your kindness." He grabbed a tea towel and took the freshly orchestrated meal from her and placed it on the stove. Then he went back and kissed her on both cheeks, and started closing the door little by little, discouraging any further conversation. She hesitated, and then he gave her a nod. "Good night, Mrs. Dutra. We had better eat, as I have to get Miss Wells back to Netuno tonight and it's a long drive. I will give Avó your best when I see her later."

She smiled with a look of satisfaction on her face, then turned and walked away without another word.

"What was all that about?" I asked, laughing at the extended explanation that he'd given her.

"Oh, I have never brought anyone home to the apartment before, not even my friends, so I think she was a little nervous that you might be staying the night." He smirked and motioned for me to sit at the kitchen table.

34

Yesterday and Today

Maya

I WATCHED HIM PULL TWO old soup bowls from the cupboard and carefully place our food in each of them. He paused, momentarily lost in thought, then placed the food on the table and sat down to join me. There was hesitation in the way he held his spoon and took his first bite, like something was holding him back. He put his spoon down and touched my hand.

"Cristiano, are you okay?"

"Yes, I just didn't realize how difficult this was going to be." He smiled faintly at me.

"Difficult? In what way? How can I help?"

"You already have, more than you know. But this ..." he waved his hands around the table. "It's been twenty years since I've had a meal at this table. I always sit and eat on the couch." He traced the pattern on the bowl with his index finger. "I feel thankful to be sitting here with you, but it's just hard.

"I was seven and Mom and Dad were leaving on their trip that day. My dad had decided to make waffles, something he wasn't very good at, but he knew I loved them. Mom and I laughed as we tried to figure out which ones we should eat, and which ones we should send to the waffle graveyard." His eyes glistened. "They talked about their trip and promised to get me something really cool from Cairo. They were both professors at the university and traveled all over the world searching out special collectibles and art for galleries. Every summer they would drop me at my Avó's for several weeks and go on their own adventure, bringing gifts and stories back from faraway places. They'd told me that morning it was their last summer traveling alone, and that the following year, I would be old enough to go with them. I was so excited. Then I tried to convince them to take me with them to Cairo. They changed the subject to the future and dreams of the following summer by pulling out the globe."

I gasped slightly, remembering my time in the peach tree with my own imagination.

He watched my reaction carefully, then continued with his story. "I spun the world around and looked for the best place to start our adventure—Paris, that's where I wanted to start. My mom brushed the hair out of my eyes and told me how proud she was of me, and how much she and Dad loved me. I packed my bag and headed off to Avó's and, well, you know the rest of the story. Mrs. Dutra had tidied up the apartment, but all of my parents' possessions were left in place, just waiting for my return."

He placed his finger on a chip in his bowl and rubbed it gently. "My dad offered to buy my mom a new set of plates for Christmas the year before they died, but she refused to get rid of these. She said they came from her mother's kitchen and eating off them was like having supper with her."

"I think they're beautiful." I touched the tiny flowers on the edge of my dish. "I wish I could have met your mom." I imagined being seated with her at the table, the two of us loving her son, each in our own way.

"Yes, I wish you could have met her, too. I miss her. I miss both of them." His face wrinkled as if he were trying to solve a problem. "It's strange for me to imagine I have another mother and father out there."

I wasn't sure what to say, so I opted for nothing.

We finished our meal in quiet and let the new memories of the moment take hold in the table, the bowls, and even the little blue flowers.

"Are you all done?" I asked, then moved the dishes to the sink.

"Thank you," he said simply.

I took great care making sure all of his precious childhood memories were washed, dried, and carefully put away until our next meal.

స్

He locked the apartment door and we headed down to the car. I settled into my seat and let the warm night air and fantastical thoughts of our future swirl around me during our peaceful drive back to Netuno.

When we arrived, I wasn't ready for the night to end, but Cristiano looked tired.

"Today was very special. Thank you." He smiled and touched my cheek.

"Yes, it was one of our best," I mused.

"One of our best?"

"Yes, I'm still waiting for the best. You promised me a happy ending, remember?"

"How could I forget?" He leaned over and kissed me goodnight, making my body quiver, then pulled back and smiled again, took his finger and traced my face with his silken touch.

"If we keep going like this, I'm not going to be able to let you leave tonight," I said, with exasperation in my voice.

"If we keep going like this, I won't want you to," he smiled, with mischief in his eyes.

"So tell me then, why are we waiting?" I asked bluntly.

"It's just too soon. One day when we make love everything in our lives will change and I want the two of us to be ready for that. Besides, we have all the time in the world, right?"

"You better walk me to the door now, before I change both our minds," I said, trying to slow my heart rate.

He came around, watching me intently, and then shook his head.

"What is it now?" I asked.

"You! You surprise me."

"What do you mean?"

"Just when I think I have you figured out, you say or do something that makes me love you even more. I never knew falling in love could be like this," he sighed. "I've never had a reason to *want* to come back before, and now I do."

"Avó doesn't count as motivation?" I teased.

"Oh, that's different. She has a way of being with me all the time. You'll know what I mean when you meet her. She just—stays with you."

"What have you told her about me?" I asked nervously.

"Everything I know. I'll have to give her some updates from this evening. She will find the almost marriage very interesting."

"Do you have to tell her about that?" I asked, wincing a little.

"Well, it's better I do. She always has a way of finding things out. It was very annoying growing up. I should have known better about the surfing secret and that she had known all the time. You know, these last few years I never stayed away from her because I didn't want her in my life. I stayed away because I wasn't ready to be part of hers. She helps people live a more authentic life, and I wasn't ready for that."

"When do I get to meet her?"

"Not this weekend, as I have something special planned for us, but I will ask her about next Saturday."

"You have something planned for the weekend? Sounds interesting. If Sachi and I win the challenge this week, we could also have a free weekend in the Azores to choose from."

"Sounds lovely. I surfed there a few years ago. The waves were amazing. It's always good to have choices though," he said mysteriously.

As he walked me to the front door, his gaze penetrated deep within me and his final kiss of the night sent one last roll of electricity surging through my body.

"Are you free tomorrow afternoon?" he asked, appearing to search for a solid yes. "Dress casual and wear your sandals."

I was intrigued about the outing, but still found myself dizzy from his electric touch and was only able to give a nod to assure him I was free.

"Until tomorrow," he whispered in my ear, then sauntered back to his car. I watched him speed down the road until he was out of sight and the dust had settled.

I heard a shuffle of feet and turned to find Dalley standing close behind me, looking awkward like she had been caught doing something wrong.

"Hi Maya, did you have a good time? I have to give the guy credit—his entrance and exit strategies are quite impressive, but I'm curious what he's like the rest of the time," she quipped, raising her eyebrows and letting out a laugh.

"Even better!" I replied.

"Even better? Tell me how could anything be better than that entrance he made today? Or the poem he wrote you on the plane last week when the two of you first met?"

"The poem. I had forgotten all about that. Yes Dalley, he really is quite remarkable. His touch, his stories, his lips. Hands down he's the best kisser I've ever had in my life, and every time he touches me, I feel like I'm going to melt or fall over, I'm not sure which." I paused again thinking into the future. "I wonder if it will still feel like that in twenty years?"

"Twenty years? What? Do you have a china pattern picked out already?"

"No, no china pattern for me—ever!"

"To answer your question then, maybe for some, but not too many. I think I've only met one couple in my lifetime who was like that. I had a friend in high school, whose parents were madly in love. My friend said it drove her crazy how they were always holding hands and kissing, but I think a part of her loved it. So many of our friends' parents were divorced, it was kind of cool to see love survive and thrive. She would often sleep over at my place on Saturday nights because she said they were too noisy. It was gross at the time, but when I think about it now, isn't that what we all want, to be in our mid-50s, with the person we love, having crazy sex on the kitchen table?"

"Kitchen table?"

"Sure, why not?"

Happiness filled our space, like a good friend joining us for a drink. She smiled, and then put her arm around me. "Do you realize you only have two weeks left here? What are you going to do?"

A wave of panic rushed through me. My body language must have said a lot more than I thought, as she apologized very quickly.

"I'm sorry, Maya. I didn't mean to upset you."

"I can't think about it right now. The idea of leaving him or Netuno isn't something I can even wrap my head around yet!"

"Okay then, tell me something wonderful. Tell me about the date on Saturday or about what you did tonight." She paused then smiled broadly. "Just one more thing before you start. A few of us placed a friendly wager on why he needed you to come with him tonight." She raised her eyebrows, and then poked me in the ribs with her elbow. "Please don't disappoint me, I have money riding on this."

"Dalley, that's awful."

"Maybe, but I need to know who won." She stood with fingers crossed, holding her breath. "So, is his everything else even better than his kissing?"

I blushed, not knowing quite how to answer that question, but decided on the truth. "I don't know—yet."

"You don't know? Or you won't tell me?"

"No, I REALLY don't know."

"Oh!! Damn it. Petra wins the whole thing. Josie, Ellen, and I were certain that he was going to whisk you off your feet."

"He did, but not in that way. Not that we weren't moving in that direction. We could have, but he wants to wait. We want to wait."

"What do you mean wait? Nobody waits anymore."

"We just want to do this the right way."

"And what is the right way, Maya?"

"I don't know and neither does he. But we do know when the time comes it will be the most incredible experience of our lives, and until then—we wait." I flung myself back into the chair and fanned myself pretending like I needed to cool down.

"Sounds like something worth waiting for," she commented thoughtfully.

"Yes, I think so."

"Tell me then, what did you do during your last two dates?"

"Saturday night was magical, every spine-tingling moment, from delivering the bread to watching the sunrise."

"Can you be a little more descriptive? I need more."

"Maybe a little. After he picked me up, he told me his grandmother needed help with two bread deliveries—she's a baker. Before we could even do that, he asked if I wanted to attend the medieval festival in Silves, and that we would have to wear costumes."

"Ah, that explains the gown you were wearing on Sunday morning."

"Yes, and the time in the costume shop was mind-blowing." I blushed as I thought about him kissing my back and doing up my dress, button by button.

"Are you kidding me? That's all you're going to give me about what happened in the shop?"

"I get to keep a few secrets, don't I?"

"I guess so, but I think that one needs to be shared."

"Not likely. Do you want to hear the rest?"

She sighed, resigned with my minimal disclosure. "Keep going!"

"After the costume shop, we drove madly into the country and delivered bread to a wedding at a pub, and then we delivered more loaves to the festival, staying for the evening." I stopped.

"Is that it? Is that all you're going to give me?"

"I thought you were more of the short and sweet type."

"Maybe I was, but you two have converted me. Now I prefer long and detailed."

"Well, at the medieval festival we danced, held hands, kissed, and talked about life and food. Then we sat under twinkly lights in one another's arms until the sun started to come up."

"That's less information than you would give me on a postcard," she said with disappointment.

"Ah, but on a postcard it's the quality of what you write, not the quantity that is important."

"Are you going to make me fill in all the blanks?"

"Um, pretty much. I'll tell you though, the evening was like nothing I have ever experienced before. When we kissed that night, and his lips touched mine, it felt like he had just figured out the last number on the combination to my safe. All the locking mechanisms whirled and moved, and by the time he was done, I was open, completely and utterly open." I closed my eyes, realizing I'd revealed a little more than I'd wanted. Dalley took my hand and squeezed it gently.

"It's okay," she said sensing my hesitation. "You can trust me."

I smiled and relaxed my shoulders. "Tonight was different, though. Tonight we talked and kissed and cried and talked some more. I found out he was born to teen lovers. Then he was adopted at three days old, but at seven his adoptive parents died in a plane accident before they had told him."

"Maya, that's terrible."

"Yes, it is."

"He was raised by his grandmother, his Avó, and spent most of his teenage years picking grapes for Puro and surfing."

"Surfing? Wow that's quite a tale, almost hard to believe. But that's just the journalist in me."

"Are you always so skeptical?" I asked, feeling a little sorry for her.

"It's taken years of practice."

"After we talked about his life, he wanted to know more about mine, so I told him about Steven and the non-wedding, and my mom and her depression, and my life selling sprinkler systems. Not as dramatic as his story, but tragic in my own way."

"What did he say when you told him about Steven and the wedding?"

"He paused and then carefully chose his words. He simply asked me if I ever really loved him. I told him 'no' and then, it happened. The words just landed on my lips and slipped out: 'I love you,'" I said. "That was pretty much it with lots of other little stories in between."

"You told him you loved him?" Shock was all I could hear in her voice.

"Yes, I did."

"How do you know? It has only been ten days if I am counting correctly."

"Actually eleven. But that doesn't matter. I just know in my heart he is the one I am supposed to be with. There is no question for me."

I started to feel my body fade and knew it was time to get some rest.

"Hey Dalley, I'm going back to the room. Are you coming?"

"No, I'm going to stay down here a little while longer."

"Thanks for listening tonight. It felt good to say it out loud to someone else. This falling in love business is very exciting, but exhausting." We both chuckled and I left Dalley sitting on the veranda, looking contemplative.

Dalley

I pulled my phone out and texted Joe.

I'm done with this blog piece. It's getting too complicated for me. People could get hurt. I'll send you a little snip to finish the story, but that's it.

I sat back and closed my eyes and let the cool breeze of the evening clear my heart of the guilt that had been creeping in and weighing me down. It was only moments later that my phone chimed.

I mean this in the nicest way, but you're done when I say you're done. You knew what you were getting into after you won the contest and presented the idea to me about writing while you were there for the paper. You used our resources to get all the background material on your friends and we have a contract in place. It was just providence the people you ended up with had so many great stories to tell. The love story, the bitchy French model, and the death of the teenager? What more could I ask for? The readers are eating it up, they can't get enough. The hits on your site have tripled in the last few days and they want more details, a lot more. I have wedding proposals coming in for the guy and the girl, and someone has just offered to pay for the kid's funeral. Dalley you don't have a choice. Just blog it and post it. I promise I'll never tell.

Screw You Joe! I'm quitting when I get back. I hate this job.

Yes Dalley, I know but you are very good at it and getting better and better. Now get me my blog.

I pulled out my computer and logged directly onto the site, and then started to read through the comments that people had been making about my story.

He was right, people loved it. But what was not to love? My fickle conscience was engulfed by a rush of adrenaline and I pounded out Maya's next set of stories into the keyboard: the kiss, the declarations of love, and everything in between.

Maya

August 28th Tuesday evening.
Just said good night to Dalley and climbed into bed.
I love these sheets. This cotton is so soft and cool.
I told him that I loved him tonight. There's no going back. I love him and I don't need to ask anyone. Mom was right, if you have to ask then he's not the right one.

About tonight. It was an incredible evening of touch and truth and eventual restraint. Yes, I say restraint, for as much as we wanted to be with each other, it wasn't the right time yet. We both just want to start fresh. I know we can't erase the other people that we have been with, but it does feel like we have a choice to do this a different way.

I used to laugh when I was a teenager about waiting until I got married. What an old-fashioned idea I thought. Maybe it just took being with the wrong man and then meeting the right one to change my mind. I don't know, but I do know that I want to spend my life with him, and for that I'll wait.

My eyes are falling and my heart is full. Until tomorrow.

Maya

35

Walk and Talk

Maya

WHEN I WOKE, THE SUN was up, but not fully lighting the sky, and I felt that an early morning walk might be a good way to start the day. I dressed quietly not wanting to disturb Dalley, then placed Christopher in my pack and headed downstairs.

Puro was at the front desk pushing papers and looking distracted. "Good morning Puro, how are you doing today?" I asked hesitantly.

"That is a difficult question. My heart and mind are heavy and somewhere else."

"With Maggie," I guessed.

"Yes, with Maggie. She has been Skyping me every day. She doesn't feel like she can talk to too many people there." His voice was filled with sadness.

"Hey would you like to go for a walk up to the lake you told me about? I don't know how to get there and I really want to see it."

Puro thought about it for a moment. "Sure, I'll call Carmo to watch the front and I'll get a thermos of coffee from Gervais. Don't fight me on the coffee part. Trust me when I tell you how good it will taste when we reach the crest of the hill and look out over the valley."

I had a few minutes to spare while I waited for Puro and began to look at the photographs that were mounted down one of the halls. Gervais' work was striking. His ability to capture food in its raw form and then tell a story was truly amazing. One particular photo captured me immediately. It was of a child swinging upside-down in a tree with an apple in his hand, trying to hand it to someone. I reached out to the photo like he was offering me the fruit.

"I know, it's one of my favorites too," Puro said coming up from behind. "Maggie and I spent several hours in conversation talking about all of Gervais' art. She said she liked the apple image and that it reminded her of you. But her favorite was over here."

I walked with him into a little hallway and looked up on the wall to find a large photo of a rugged pair of hands kneading dough on an old wooden table. You could see every wrinkle in her skin and the smooth texture of the dough. It was like she offered up a part of herself to make that single loaf of bread.

"Yes, I can understand why Maggie loved it so much. Let's walk."

Puro and I headed out in the opposite direction of the vineyards. The ground was a little rocky at first, but soon a well-worn path began to show itself. I could feel a sheen break out on my forehead as the grade became steeper and my breath a little shallower. Neither of us spoke as we continued to climb. Within about thirty minutes, we arrived at the crest of the hill and onto a small ridge. I walked to the edge not sure what to expect, but as I peeked over, I gasped. I was home.

"Is it that surprising that we have lakes here?" he asked, now laughing.

"It's not so much the lake. It's that somehow I feel whole standing here." I stared out over the valley, the water, the vineyard, and even the castle in the distance. Puro waited to speak, allowing me a few minutes to take it all in.

He then began quietly. "Yes, it is quite grand isn't it? Maggie loved the view from here, too. Would you like some coffee?" He poured a cup for both of us and handed one to me.

"How could I say no?" I bantered with him.

We sat down on the rocks and I sipped my black liquid, letting its warmth prepare me to hear his heart.

"She doesn't feel like anyone understands. She's confused and often repeats herself. The other day she made me walk over to the bread image, photograph it, and send it to her. She said the image helped keep her calm. She told me about the night she signed herself out of the hospital, and when she said goodbye to CJ. The doctors didn't want her to see him at first, but she insisted. She told them she was prepared to make a large scene if they did not comply." Puro took a long drink of coffee, like he was swallowing reinforcements to continue. "Then she described in detail what it was like when she saw him." He stopped. I sensed he was worried that the next part of the story might upset me, but with a hand on his arm I encouraged him to continue.

"She walked into the room and saw him lying there, explaining that when she saw him her fear and panic disappeared. She described each detail down to the color of the paint on the walls. They had placed a sheet over his body so she carefully folded it down, just far enough to reveal his face. She said she saw a little smile on his lips and his eyes were closed and his cheeks were cool. She put her head on his chest, and listened to the silence of his heart. She sat for an hour and told him all about the adventures of her first week in Portugal, and made sure he didn't miss a thing. At the end, she told me she tucked him in like she had when he was a child.

She said he always liked it when the sheets were pulled tight around him. It helped him feel safe. She kissed his blue-tinged lips and said goodbye."

Puro took one more sip of his coffee and threw the rest into the grass. "We'd better get back." He paused. "Oh, the funeral is on Friday."

No more words were needed, as the last image of a mother saying a final goodbye to her son hung heavy around us.

༽◌༼

Puro reinvented himself with each step as we walked back to the inn. It was as if he needed to share her story so that he did not have to hold it alone. Sachi was in the lobby talking to Carmo when we arrived. The two ladies stopped and looked at each other. Then Carmo motioned to Puro and Sachi motioned to me.

"Maya, why don't you come to the kitchen and help me with some menu prep for Friday?" Then she turned back to Carmo and added, "Thank you for the lovely chat. I appreciate your thoughts."

The kitchen was quiet when we entered. We sat down on a couple of stools and Sachi started to make a list of everything that needed to be done. The dishes looked complicated, but I trusted Sachi and her culinary skills. As she talked about the menu and the balance of sweet and sour, I was having trouble understanding the sweetness part and how it related to Maggie. I found myself distracted and thinking about the poem I had written for her. Sweet Love Ends in Sour Bites. Then it struck me: Dessert. We needed dessert to show a different kind of sweetness.

"Sachi, I think we are missing something."

"Really? What?" she responded, genuinely surprised.

"Well, I was thinking we should make some sort of dessert."

"Hmm ... that is very interesting. I hadn't thought about it. Do you have an idea?"

"What if you designed a cake—and then we set edible photo images of the people and things that Maggie loves or has loved, right into the icing?" I held my breath.

"Sweet and Sour," Sachi buzzed. I could almost see her thoughts whirl around us. "Maya, you get me ten edible images for Friday and I'll take care of the rest. I want this to be a surprise though!"

"I'll have them to you before noon tomorrow," I promised. I had no idea where to start, but I knew if it could be done, Puro would be the one to help make it happen.

Sachi jumped into action and shooed me out of the kitchen. "I need to bake and you need to find the images."

I spent the next couple hours poring over pictures, trying to find the ones that could tell Maggie's story. I included the image of the bread maker's hands and added a candid photo of Puro working at the front desk. After finding all of the right pictures, I quietly approached Puro.

"Excuse me Puro, do you have a minute?"

"For you Maya, I have as many minutes as you need."

I told him about our plan to bake the cake and that we needed to find a bakery that could create edible images and have them delivered by Friday. After just a few calls he found a bakery in Lisbon that could help us. We downloaded the shots onto his computer and sent them off.

"Thank you Puro, you're a life saver." He smiled at me and nodded his head.

I grabbed a little lunch and decided to head over to the chapel before Cristiano arrived. Walking the path to the chapel now felt natural, like it was part of me. It had only been days since I'd found it, but it felt like it was already part of my history too. When I arrived, the candles had already been changed and newly lit. I stepped outside into the sunshine and saw my friend walking in the distance. She stopped, looked back at me, and waved like she knew I was going to be there. I watched her walk off until she disappeared from my sight.

Stepping back into the chapel, I found a pew at the front where the sunlight was shining in through one of the beautiful stain glass windows, casting colors on the olive wood. I sat bathed in those colors and enjoyed the warmth and love that surrounded me, then pulled Christopher out and wrote a brief note, but not for me.

> *Dear God,*
>
> *Thank you. I'm not sure many people do that anymore. Me included, but how could I not, being in a place like this? I'm not sure I've ever let myself get this close to you. It feels kind of strange. I remember seeing people at church when I was little who would be there before we arrived and still be praying after we left. It made no sense to me. I just wanted to get out of there. But I think I get it now, or at least I'm open to trying. I'm not sure where things are going to go with you, but I do know I feel different now and somehow you are part of that. So, thank you!*
>
> *Maya*
>
> *PS. I'm the girl in the peach tree who used to yell at you. Sorry about that.*

As I sat for a few moments longer, I remembered the story Puro had told me that morning about Maggie. My heart ached for her. I dropped my money into the candle box and went on to light three candles. One was for Maggie, one for CJ, and one for—my candle lady. The walk home was quiet.

When I returned, Petra, Dalley, Josie, and Ellen were sitting on the veranda, sharing a bottle of wine.

"So what's the meeting about ladies?" I gestured to the open bottle.

Josie piped in. "A planning meeting with a little extra help today." She pointed to the wine.

"Planning what?" I asked.

"We are trying to coordinate the order of the presentations," Ellen explained. "When do you want to go?"

"I'll talk to Sachi, but somewhere near the end I think."

"You do that Maya," Dalley blurted out sloppily.

"Dalley?" Her sarcasm was biting. I looked to Petra for answers.

"Oh, don't mind her. She's been doing some extra planning with the bottle this afternoon." She leaned in and went on to explain. "Puro told us about the funeral taking place on Friday. It got a little messy for a bit. Ellen and Josie cried and Dalley just drank."

My heart filled with compassion for her. "I didn't think Dalley would be so affected by CJ's death."

"I know, she has been acting very strangely," Petra remarked with a hint of irritation.

I clumsily changed the subject. "Anyways—so how did things go last night?"

Petra smiled. "Our family dinner worked out great. We are going back tonight to practice making a few dishes."

"Yes, it was so much fun," Dalley slurred. "We became like part of the family, didn't we Petra?"

"Yes, it was quite a night," she said shaking her head. She then changed the subject. "What are you up to for the rest of the day? Would you like to join us?"

"No, thank you. I have plans with Cristiano. I'm off on a mystery adventure with him today. Oh and by the way, no more bets ladies, please!" Laughter erupted from the table of four.

"Hey, that's right, all of you need to pay up. Thanks for being such a good girl, Maya," Petra yelled as I walked back into the inn.

I entered my room and began the task of getting dressed for my adventure. It didn't take long for all of my clothes to be strewn on the bed, again.

In the end, I decided on my most comfortable pair of old khaki shorts and a fresh white t-shirt.

As I walked down the staircase, a series of new photographs hung on the wall—Shots of Sachi and Gervais picking olives in the grove. They were magical. As I took my next step, one spell was broken and another cast by *his* laughter. I felt like I was floating—but in reality I was falling. I fell all the way to the bottom of the stairs landing in a messy pile of embarrassment. By the time Cristiano ran over, I was already trying to get up, but I was so humiliated that I buried my face into my hands. I just wanted to disappear. He whisked me up in his arms and lowered me gently to the couch, yelling to Puro to call 112.

I was slightly confused, but quickly figured out that his 112 was my 911. "NO!!" I screamed, horrified about the direction the moment had taken. "I'm not hurt. Hang up Puro, please!"

Cristiano's hands shook when he took my pulse and *his* breath was shallow. My four friends stood in the door with wine in hand, only laughing once they realized I was not really hurt.

"Cristiano I'm fine, except for maybe my ego," I whispered.

"Did you trip on something?"

"No, I got *distracted*."

"By what?" His voice boomed, still clueless, and pushing the point.

Was he serious? Was he going to make me say it out loud? "By you," I finally responded in exasperation.

"So you're saying *I* made you fall down a flight of stairs?" he smirked.

"Yes, that is exactly what I'm saying."

"Seriously—are you okay? I can take you to Emergency if you need." His voice was now a little less stressed and his hands had steadied.

"No, what I need is to stop almost having a heart attack every time I see you."

He smiled, pleased with himself. "Well I hope your heart never stops beating fast when you see me."

"That's IT!!!" Petra yelled across the room, laughing and shaking her head. "I can't stand it anymore! Are you guys for real? I need another drink. This one is on you Maya. Come on ladies. Let's get back to our meeting."

Cristiano held my hand as he helped me stand.

"Are you okay? Really?" he asked again. I watched his face, as concern took precedent over all the smiles and smirks in the moment.

"Yes, I think I landed on my tailbone. It's a little sore, but I'll survive." "Maybe we should stay and enjoy an evening here," he offered as a solution.

"No, you said someone is expecting us, so let's go."

"Puro, we'll talk more about the trip later. Thanks a lot. See you on Friday night," he winked.

"Friday night?" I was a little shocked.

"Puro invited me to the presentation."

"He beat me to it. I was going to ask you this afternoon."

"I know, I know, that's what they all say." He paused then put his arm around me and we walked out to the car.

As we passed by the ladies, Josie whispered loudly, "My money's on *no more waiting*, it's way more fun."

"What is she talking about Maya?" he asked as he opened my door. "Oh, I'll fill you in later. I'm sure you'll enjoy the running bet they apparently have on us," I explained simply.

"Hey, Cristiano, when are we going to *salsa* together again? I miss you," Josie exclaimed.

"Friday night is a possibility, but I'm not sure I can keep up with you though."

"Oh, I've seen some of your moves before. But I hear you are pretty good at *everything*. I'm sure you'll manage!" she teased.

He laughed, climbed into the car, and then looked to me for answers.

"I know nothing. Just remember they have been drinking since noon." He started the engine and we sped off to the west, following the afternoon sun. While driving, it looked like he was going to ask me something several times, but kept stalling. Finally he couldn't hold it any longer.

"What did she mean that I am good at *everything*?"

"Do you really want to know?"

"Is it funny?" he smiled.

"Yes, it is."

"Then tell me."

"Yesterday when you came to get me, they made a bet that we were going to have sex."

"Really?" he smiled broadly. "What did you tell them?"

"I told them the truth—that we have decided to wait."

"Did they believe you?"

"I think when it comes to us, they won't believe anything we tell them."

"Good, then let's leave them guessing. They don't really need to know anything more about the two of us do they?"

"I guess not." My mind flashed to what I had revealed to Dalley the night before. I realized that maybe some of what I told her wasn't my truth to tell. I decided from that moment forward, Christopher was the *only* place for the truths about Cristiano and me.

I changed the subject and asked, "So where are you taking me today in my finest shorts and sandals?"

"It's a surprise. We should be there in about an hour. Just sit back and relax." The engine roared and the landscape whirred by us at top speed. Driving with him had become second nature to me. I no longer worried about the speedometer and realized that speed limits in Portugal didn't mean the same thing as back home in B.C. He smiled as he saw my body relax into the well-worn seats and took my hand, holding it tightly until the outlines of a city started to pop out of the distance.

"Please tell me, where are we going today?"

"Oh I have a special treat for you. Close your eyes."

"Right now?"

"Yes, I don't want you to guess where we are going until we get there."

"What makes you think that I am that good at guessing?"

He shrugged his shoulders. "I'm not taking any chances."

I closed my eyes and played along with the game. Soon we slowed down and I heard more regular traffic sounds. The car stopped, but was still idling. I figured we must be at a light. I opened one eye and was shocked to see the most brilliant yellow building. All of the buildings in the town were colorful. It was one of the most joyful places I had ever seen.

"Wow, this place is beautiful. Where are we?"

"Close your eyes, you're cheating."

"Just tell me the name of the city and I will close my eyes."

"Promise?" he asked with insistence.

I agreed with a single nod.

"We are in Setubal. Now close your eyes."

"And what are we doing in Setubal?"

"You are very bad at this game. Shh. Just listen to the sounds."

I stopped talking and started listening. I could hear cars, people on the street, vendors yelling. I took in a big breath and smelled something familiar. Soon the sounds of the city decreased and left me concentrating on what remained. I smiled as my senses welcomed the feel of the wind, the taste of the salty air, and the roar of the breaking surf. I wanted to open my eyes, but I didn't. I wanted to show him I could keep a promise.

36

Crashing Waves

Maya

HE OPENED MY DOOR AND OFFERED ME HIS HAND.

"Do you trust me?"

I nodded, afraid to say anything that might ruin the perfection of that moment.

"Follow me," he said quietly in my ear.

The gravel under my feet soon gave way to grains of sand that found its way between my toes. I almost spoke, but decided I wanted to play his game out to the end.

We walked for just a few more minutes. He told me when to duck, when to speed up, and when to slow down. Finally, he turned me towards the sound of the waves and told me to open my eyes. Even if I had wanted to say something there were no words. The beach we were on was breathtaking.

"Your beach?" I asked smiling.

"Well not exactly mine. There's someone here I want you to meet."

He walked slowly over to a series of huts that were huddled against the rocks. Then he tapped on one of the make-shift doors.

"Yo, who's there?" A man with a Texan drawl bellowed from inside.

With his best southern accent Cristiano quipped back, "I heard if I came to Portugal, Jack was the man to teach me to surf. Are you him?"

"Yah," the guy yelled through the door. "Who sent you?"

"It was some Portuguese dude. Tall, dark hair, really good looking. Said he'd been surfing with you since he was a kid. He *said* he could out surf you any day, but he was too busy to teach me." Cristiano tried to contain his laughter, but eventually gave up.

The door broke open and out ran a middle-aged man, with blond hair down to his shoulders. I almost laughed, as he looked like a character out of a 1960s surfer movie.

"Cristiano!!" He hugged Cristiano, and then threw him down to the sand. They wrestled for a few moments, finishing their hellos.

"You almost had me for a second with that southern twang! You've been practicing." Jack stared up at me from the ground and nodded his head, then looked over at Cristiano, and back to me. "So who do we have here?" He offered out his sun-weathered and muscular hand.

"Hi, I'm Maya." I reached down, but instead of the expected handshake he grabbed me and pulled me down to the sand with the two of them. I was so shocked all I could do was laugh.

"Sorry there Maya, you okay? I just figured you needed a proper welcome. You must be the real thing if he brought you here. I didn't want you to feel left out. You know I've never met any of Cristiano's *friends*."

"Jack, that's enough."

"What, you don't want me to tell her all your secrets from the past? I know *everything*."

"Jack, there's nothing you can tell her she doesn't know about me already. Actually, she may know a few things you don't."

"Well now that takes the wind out of my sails. I don't like secrets."
Jack looked at me with a squinted eye and his face curled up on one side
like an old sailor. "Let's talk and share stories," he laughed heartily. "Well
then, I guess we're all family now."

We stood up, brushed ourselves off, and found a little patch of shade
outside the hut. Jack went in and brought out a few drinks.

"It's nothing fancy, but what's mine is yours," he said gesturing
towards his huts. "So what brings the two of you out to Setubal today?"
He looked over at Cristiano. "I thought you had abandoned me for all
of those other surf destinations." He pretended that Cristiano had hurt
his feelings.

"Are you kidding, Jack? My heart and home are always here with you
and these waves. It's been months since I was on the water. I could feel
the waves calling to me and thought I might be able to get a lesson in for
Maya today too. That is if you are free?"

"I'm always free for family. You bring me any bread?" Cristiano
opened his knapsack and pulled out two loaves. "I've never met her, but I
could kiss that woman! She makes the best bread in Portugal."

Jack ripped a hunk off and started to chew slowly, savoring every bite.
I could see how much he appreciated the gift.

"Can I borrow a suit, Jack? Mine is back at the apartment."

Jack nodded at Cristiano between bites and pointed towards his hut.
"Help yourself."

"Hey I was wondering if you still had my old board kicking around."

"That board is part of the family, too. I'd never get rid of that thing.
It was old even before you started using it. I'll grab it in a second."

Cristiano smiled, excited about the idea of going surfing, and ran off
to get ready. When he was out of ear shot, Jack looked over at me.

"So, did you really want to learn how to surf today?" he asked, observing the mounting fear that grew in my eyes as I watched the three meter waves crash down in front of me.

"Well …" I started. "I know it's something he loves, and I would like to learn one day soon, but the waves seem a little big today for a beginner."

Jack laughed. "Don't worry, Maya. We'll get you started on the sand. No need to even get you in the water today, unless you want to."

"I appreciate that, Jack. Thank you," I said breathing a sigh of relief. "We do need to get you into some proper beach wear though. You don't look very comfortable. There are a few suits in the other hut you can try on."

A whole new level of panic mounted deep within me as I turned and walked towards the hut, and it had nothing to do with facing the waves. There were two things I had historically hated doing in life: trying on lingerie and trying on bathing suits. But I knew there was no way out of that situation. I was scared to death about putting on a bikini, so I grabbed onto my pendant, mustered some courage, and reminded myself that I was beautiful, *all of me*. When I walked into the hut, I looked through the piles of bathing suits and was horrified to discover that all I could find were bikini bottoms.

"No tops!!" I yelped. *Topless beaches. Oh my god. What am I going to do?* I started planning an escape route, but reality flanked me on all sides. I regrouped my thoughts and searched through another pile again. I finally found my answer: a short sleeve rash guard with matching bikini bottoms. Not that it really covered my bottom very much.

I tiptoed out of the hut, not sure about very much in that moment.

"We thought you got lost in there. Who were you talking to?" Jack said with a smile on his face. "Nice choice. You North American women are so modest." He looked me up and down.

Cristiano could no longer contain himself and laughed so hard that he doubled over and fell into the sand. Obviously my yelp was a little louder than I had thought. He stopped laughing, got up, and kissed me freely like it was part of the conversation. There was something different about him: a freedom? I wasn't sure.

"You would look fantastic no matter what you decided to wear, or didn't." He and Jack started to laugh again, and I curled up my nose and pursed my lips at the two of them. He kissed my forehead and smoothed out the wrinkles.

"We are just teasing! Have fun with Jack."

Cristiano laughed and gave me one more peck on the cheek, then grabbed his board and ran straight into the ocean, crashing through the waves like he owned them. He disappeared for a few seconds and I held my breath. My hands prickled as I waited for him to emerge from under the wave. Seconds seemed like minutes, but then he popped up like a cork and paddled farther out. I could see the muscles rippling in his arms as he fought hard against the water and pulled himself farther and farther away from the shore.

"Are you done? You can breathe now. He's fine. He's just working on catching the next wave that's coming in. He's always been bold with the way he rides these waves. I never worry about him." Jack paused. "You ready to get started?"

"In a second, I want to watch him."

"Fair enough. I've been watching him surf since he was fourteen, and I still never get tired of it."

Just as Jack finished talking, Cristiano caught a wave that could have been as tall as a three-story building. I gasped as I saw him riding the water and navigating all that power.

"Yes, I know. He puts the rest of us old surfers to shame. Now let's get started before you see him fall. If that happens, I'll never get your lesson in." I spent the next hour standing on my board trying to find my balance, my center of gravity. Every time I thought I had it, I would look out into the ocean and either see Cristiano and fall, or *not* see him and fall. Jack noticed my level of distraction and said laughingly, "Maya, I think it might be a good time to take a break and grab a drink."

"Yes, hopefully that is something I can do without falling," I said, laughing at myself.

Quiet filled the air for a few moments as Jack studied my face, then he piped up saying, "You may want to come back to finish your lesson one day when Cristiano is *not* in the water."

Jack became quiet again and stared at me.

"So, he never brought anyone else around to the beach for you to meet?"

"No, not anyone. There were always plenty of girls on the beach, trying to talk to him, but he didn't have time for any of them. Pretty soon he developed a reputation for being a snob and the girls just left him alone. They thought something was wrong with him." He paused, then asked, "How much do you know about him?"

"I think almost everything."

The tone of his question made the hairs on the back of my neck stand up. Then without any warning, he launched into a conversation that would complicate my new-found love.

"I knew his dad you know."

"His adopted dad?"

"You know he was adopted?" he said with shock.

"Yes, I do," I responded holding my cards closely.

"And Cristiano, he knows too?"

"Yes, Avó told him last week." My level of personal discomfort continued to grow.

"This changes things," he said simply. Then he stared out into the ocean while Cristiano rode another amazing wave. "You asked me if I knew his adopted dad. No. He died before I met Cristiano. I meant his *real* dad."

My jaw dropped as I tried to process what he was saying. I heard him, but I could hardly believe it. "Jack, what are you talking about?" I tried to wrap my brain around what he had just told me.

"Family secrets, Maya. That's what I'm talking about, and I've been holding this one for a long time. Cristiano and I are like family, but I figure since he has you now it's your turn to hold this information." He paused, and then added. "It's good he knows about the adoption, but he doesn't need to know about his bio-dad too." He leaned back and exhaled like he was releasing bad air. "Secrets are bad for my health."

My body froze at first. I had not asked for the secret, but Jack was obviously tired of holding it. After his deep exhale, he studied my frozen state and waited for me to make the next move.

The words finally came. "How did you meet Cristiano's dad?"

Jack then told his story without hesitation. "Oh, he was here long before I was. He grew up on these beaches. Marcos was one of the best young surfers on the coast. He used to carve his own boards. That's how we met. When I arrived in Portugal, I found my way to this little beach. There was no one here but a young man carving a board in the morning sun. He didn't talk much, but boy could he surf. He went home every day and I just stayed on the beach. We became friends, and for a few years we surfed together all the time. Then one day he came to the beach looking like someone had ripped his heart out. He simply told me that he and Euphemia had to break up and that he had to move. It didn't sound or look like it was his choice. He left his surfboards and asked me to take care of them for him. I assumed he would be back one day, but he never came."

Jack paused and rubbed the board he was sitting on, then continued. "But I held his boards in my hut and kept them ready just in case. I heard later from another surfer that his parents made him go to school. It wasn't until fifteen years later that I talked to him again."

"So how does Cristiano fit into this whole thing?" My irritation rose quickly.

"Relax Maya, just let me explain. Cristiano found *me* when he was fourteen—and broken." I grimaced, imagining his body and mind in so much pain. "The trauma from the death of his parents had resurfaced and it had taken over most of his teenage thoughts. I told him from the beginning I wouldn't ask him any questions, but that he could tell me anything when he was ready. Over the years he did. Little by little he told me everything about his life that *he knew*." He searched my face with his weathered eyes, looking to see if I had picked up his not so subtle clue. "You okay?"

"I'm not sure. It depends on what you tell me next."

"When Cristiano took to the waves, he was a natural. He rode them like they were old friends. Within a year, he turned fifteen and I noticed that things started to change for him. His face grew softer and he looked content. Honest to God Maya, there was something about his smile and the way he surfed. It was driving me crazy. It wasn't until one day when I saw him waxing his board that it hit me … Marcos. He looked just like, Marcos.

"Once I made that connection, the resemblance became even more striking. So, I went on a mission to track down my old friend. When I finally found and called him, I told him about a kid who had been surfing with me and using *his* favorite board with great success. I didn't tell him though that the kid looked just like him, only that he was the best young surfer I had seen since *he* had ridden the waves with me fifteen years earlier.

"He came down that same day, no questions asked. When he arrived, the swells were high, and Cristiano was surfing like a pro. Marcos looked out at the water, then over to me.

"'Long time no see Jack. You're looking good for an old man.'

"I laughed at him, as he too had aged. He was then thirty-three years old, but he still had that look that made all the ladies swoon, just like when he was nineteen. He looked out to the ocean again.

"'That young surfer of yours must be something else to get you to call me. Euphemia wasn't pleased that I took off in the middle of the day to drive down here, but how could I refuse my old friend Jack, and the lure that some kid was using my board?' He showed a keen interest in finding out more about the surfer.

"'Oh, so you did marry her! I thought you had to break up with her when you were kids?' I asked him, fishing for more information."

I was riveted as Jack recounted Marco's visit from all those years ago.

"What happened next?" I asked, almost afraid of the answer.

"Oh, he confirmed everything that I suspected and a little bit more.

It was then I started getting a bad feeling. But it was too late, Jack had no intention of stopping and launched back into his story.

"'Yeah we did get married,' Marcos said, smiling. 'I loved that woman from the first time I saw her at sixteen, but I was stupid and got her pregnant. She had the baby, but they made us give him away. Our parents forbade us to see one another. But we stayed in touch without them knowing. After a year or so, we ran away and started our life together up north, leaving behind all the memories from here.' He sighed, then wiped his eyes. 'We have a family now … a girl—five—and a boy, six. Hey you have any more of my boards kicking around? I think my kids would love it if I brought one home.'

"'I have a few,' I told him. 'But your first board, it's out there.' I pointed out to the water just as Cristiano had caught a great wave.

"'That's my board.' He swallowed hard.

"'Yes he's been using it for the last year,' I said to him, not sure if he had started to put the pieces together yet.

"'Boy that kid sure can surf.' He took a step closer to the water.

"'Yes, like I said, he reminds me a lot of you.' That's when I think it hit him.

"'Where's he from Jack? How old is he?' A sense of unrest grew in his tone.

"'Near where you used to live, Marcos. He's fifteen.'

"His brow furrowed, 'What's his name?'

"I paused, and for the first time was not sure if I had done the right thing. 'Cristiano,' I said quietly. Whatever doubt that either of us may have had disappeared in that moment and we both knew. Marcos was Cristiano's biological father. He threw his hands up to his face and let out a guttural cry. I wasn't sure if he was happy or sad, but he staggered and fell to the sand, shaking his head in disbelief. He sat for a long while, not taking his eyes off of his boy. He told me the heart-breaking story of the day they'd had to say goodbye, but that they knew he went to a good family who would love him. Euphemia had met his Avó and said that she was very special. Tears streamed down his face as he watched his first son conquer wave after wave.

"'How did he find you?' he asked me.

"'Just life I guess.'

"'Does he know that he is adopted?'

"'No,' was all that I decided to tell him.

"'Is he safe? Happy?' he asked like any parent would.

"'Safe yes, his family loves him very much.' Which was true. Happy, well as much as any fifteen-year-old boy can be, but he loves to surf.'"

I looked over at Jack, only able to squeak out one question. "You didn't tell Marcos that Cristiano's parents were dead?"

"Nope, not my story to tell. That kid had enough on his plate, and was just starting to find something he loved to do. I wasn't going to ruin that or Marcos and Euphemia's life. I saw the look on Marcos' face. He would have taken Cristiano home that day if he knew his parents had died. There would have been no stopping him. Imagine what that would have done to both Cristiano and Avó. Next thing I knew, Marcos got up, shook my hand, and told me he would be in touch. He said he wasn't going to tell Euphemia, as he knew bringing up the past would tear her apart.

"Before Marcos left he took one last step towards the ocean, 'That's my boy,' he said with pride."

My heart cracked and the tears flowed.

"Oh, Maya, he'll be fine. Look, he's got you now."

"Well what happened after that?"

"Marcos came down from time to time to watch Cristiano surf, but he never hung around long enough to talk to him. There were a few times I thought he was going to stay, but he didn't. Cristiano saw him from the water once or twice and asked about him. I just told him he was an old friend."

I wasn't sure what to say or do with the piece of Cristiano's life that I held in my hands, but I knew I wasn't going to keep it a secret, I couldn't. Looking out into the ocean I saw the love of my life riding a wave back to the shore. Then I looked at Jack. He shrugged, no longer worried about anything as he finally cast off a burden he'd held for many years. I hadn't made my mind up about him yet, but who was I to judge? Jack did it to protect Cristiano, and I would tell Cristiano for the same reason—but not that day.

I Promise

Maya

August 29th – Wednesday night

It's late. He dropped me off a few hours ago. That was the longest drive of my life! I forgot how much energy it takes to pretend. I'm exhausted but I can't sleep. I can't believe this ... Any of it. Why didn't I just tell him on the car ride home?

If I stay curled up in a ball long enough would the sad and scared feelings go away? No, I've tried that before, it only makes things worse.

I'm so scared. Scared for him, scared for me. If you had arms right now, I'd ask you for a hug. I need you! I want Athena back! Screw Jade!!

I need the new me that I saw glimmers of last week. Oh, that's great Maya, start crying now. How's that going to help? My head feels heavy; like if I move it too fast everything will start spinning.

Breathe deep Maya, what would Aunt Olive say? 'Time to put on your big girl underpants and do the right thing.' Okay that's really funny, as serious as all of this is, she can still make me laugh a million miles away.

The question is, what is the right thing? I guess I'll have to work that out tomorrow, my eyes are falling now, and I can hardly hold the pen.

Thanks for the hug Christopher.

Maya

When I woke the next morning, I grabbed Christopher, who lay on the pillow beside me, and looked for my pen. It was nowhere to be found. So I reached over to the side table and frantically searched through my purse for something to write with. Much to my relief, I found a little pencil and sharpener in one of the inside pockets. If I couldn't have Athena, a pencil would have to do. I placed the pencil in the sharpener and turned it ever so slowly, listening to the blade shave off any old wood that was not right for the task at hand. I could smell the shavings and smiled, remembering all those days in high school when I would sit in my exams and sharpen my pencil endlessly while trying to figure out the next answer.

I pulled the pencil out of the sharpener, and micro pieces of wood shavings and lead littered my sheets. Then I started to construct the most important answer of my life.

Thursday Morning

Yes this pencil will do just fine.

I made it through and now the hard work begins.

I am hoping that I'll find the answers between the lead and the pages. The question is, where do I find the courage? In Aunt Olive's pendant? My prayers? Maybe a little bit of both.

How do you hold a piece of someone's heart in your hand—a piece they didn't even know was missing—and give it back to them? What can you say that will make sense?

Honestly, I know what I have to say, but it's the how that I need to figure out. I could just sit him down and tell him straight out, or write him a letter like Avó did about the adoption. Maybe I'll just go with that, and then read it to him when the time is right.

Dear Cristiano,
The other day I found out some things about you. My heart has been aching with how and when to tell you.

"No that's not right. Again."

Cristiano, I never knew my heart was allowed to feel this way. Meeting you has given me a chance I thought I never deserved. I'm scared. What would you do if I told you I knew something important that could change your life?

"Wrong!! Maya!!! Just relax and remember this man loves you. Take three. Pretend he is right here sitting beside you, stroking your palm and staring deep into your eyes."

Dear Cristiano,
Hold my hand. I promise to always be truthful with you and to love you like no one has ever loved you before; to walk with you into the darkness, knowing we will always find light. To bring you joy and laughter when you least expect it and to humble myself when I have hurt you and ask for your forgiveness. I'm not perfect,

but with you in my life I strive to be a better me and for that reason alone I could love no one but you ... but before we can move forward you need to know something.

A few days ago when you took me to meet Jack, he told me a story. He told me about when the two of you first met, and how broken and lost you were, and how with time you finally found a way to start healing and smile again. I know that smile. It's the one that captured my heart on the day we met.

As he shared your story, he told me more information than I knew what to do with. He talked about your birth father, Marcos, and how he had met him long before you were born, how they used to surf together, and that your father used to carve his own boards, right on your tiny beach. The board you used the other day was your father's favorite.

As you know, Marcos and Euphemia were forced apart after you were born, but they secretly kept in touch and then later ran away and moved up north to get married. They started a family and had a boy and a girl. You have a brother and a sister.

It wasn't until well after a year that you were friends with Jack that he started making some connections and speculations about Marcos being your bio-dad. One day Jack called him and asked him to come and see you surf. Jack just needed to know.

At first Marcos didn't know it was you. He thought Jack just wanted him to see some young new surfer, but it didn't take long for him to figure it out. Jack told him you were happy and that you had a family who loved you. He didn't tell him that your parents had died. He *didn't want to wreck things for you and Avó. So Marcos turned and walked away and chose not to tell Euphemia, as he knew that it would almost kill her to know where you were. Over the next few years he came down to watch you surf and checked in with Jack to make sure you were okay.*

I should have told you at supper that evening. I should have told you when we were driving home, but you were just so happy, and excited about the surfing and having me meet Jack, I didn't want to ruin it.

So there it is. Outside of that I have no secrets and my heart is your heart.

Love Maya

Well I just reread it and cried again. But these tears are different than last nights. These ones have intention.

I am going to have a good day. But it will be even better tomorrow night when I read this to him.

Until then, put one foot in front of another.

I closed Christopher and slipped him under my pillow, keeping my heart in a safe place. After I'd made the decision to tell Cristiano, it allowed me to clear my mind and focus on what I needed to get done for the presentation. I would tell him tomorrow night, and then we would figure out together how this information was going to shade or tint our lives.

I got out of bed and walked over to the bathroom. I stepped into the shower and turned the water to hot. When I came out, Dalley was sitting on the balcony, pouring a cup of tea with one ready for me.

"Wow, I thought I might have to send someone in to rescue you. Thank goodness we're not paying for the water bill around here," she said with a chuckle. "You were sleeping last night when I got in from my family cooking lesson with Petra. How was your adventure with Cristiano yesterday?"

I paused, wanting to edit my thoughts before any unchecked worry came spilling out. "Tea? That's just what I need!"

"You like it extra hot with a little milk, no sugar, right?" she said, quite pleased with herself.

"Yes, that's right." Before I sat, I took my first sip and let the tea gently roll through my body, giving me a positive nudge. It wasn't quite a noisy cup of tea, but loud enough for me to sit down and answer her question. "We had a wonderful time. Cristiano took me surfing and introduced me to his old friend Jack. He is this funny American who immigrated to Portugal many years ago and lives on the beach teaching surfing. He tried to teach me, but I had a hard time staying on the board. I didn't even get into the water. The swells were too big, so I left the wave breaking to Cristiano." I paused. "He was incredible."

"Was there any doubt?"

"No, not really."

"What else did you do?"

"Oh, not too much. We just went for supper and had a quiet drive home. Setubal is a beautiful little city on the sea. I think you would really like it," I answered simply. "After he dropped me off, I went straight to bed." I sighed deeply and slouched back into the chair, trying to enjoy the tea and the warmth of the morning sun.

Before closing my eyes, I glanced over at Dalley and noticed she was ready to ask another question. I shut my lids tight and the two of us sat in silence for a long time.

"Thanks for thinking of me." I looked at Dalley, then pointed to the tea. "I'd better head down to the kitchen and see if I can help Sachi." As I was getting up, Dalley remained in her chair, looking at the beautiful view.

It was then I realized I hadn't even asked her how she was doing. How selfish could I be? I knew she had not been herself lately, and I was being anything but a good friend. "Hey Dalley, how are you? Is everything okay with Petra? Things seemed a little tense a few days ago. You haven't quite been yourself."

"Have any of us really?" she asked turning to me. "With Maggie leaving, her son dying, and my roommate falling madly in love, it's been a very intense week." She paused for a second. "But in regards to Petra, we worked everything out. Actually, we had a blast last night. I'll tell you about it later. You better get downstairs. I don't think I would want Sachi mad at me. She's quiet, but I've noticed she can be very particular about things."

"See you soon." I picked up my purse and headed towards the door. Dalley was right—everything had been a little awkward that week for all of us. I was already lost in thought when she called out to me before the door closed.

"Hey Maya, are you coming back to the room this morning?"

"No, I don't think so. Not unless I decide to go for a walk. Why?"

"Oh! Petra and I may be working on some last-minute secret plans for tomorrow night. I wouldn't want you to walk in on us and ruin our surprise."

"No problem. If I need to come to the room I'll knock before I enter," I laughed lightly.

Dalley

I placed my almost untouched cup of tea down on the tray and shook my head. "Give me a good strong cup of coffee any day of the week." I only had one thing on my mind. I needed to get my next blog entry done, and since Maya was less than chatty about her date, I had to find Christopher to get the answers I wanted. I walked over to the door and locked it. At first, I looked casually through Maya's drawers, then a surge of impatience crept through my body. "Where the hell did she put him?" I pulled the duvet down and threw the pillows to the floor. With the last pillow tossed, I exposed Christopher from his little hiding space. I speculated something really big must have happened on their date as she was tight lipped and looked like she didn't want to talk. I felt driven to get through the next entry as I was certain it would reveal something valuable I could use.

I was certain it had to do with her *let's wait* policy, and imagined they had given in, and she was too embarrassed to tell me.

As I opened the journal, a small slip of paper fluttered to the ground. On it I found the love poem that Cristiano had written to her on the first day they met. I read the poem carefully, and then reminded myself that there was no longer room for sentiment in this situation. It could only get me into more trouble. I tucked the note away, as I had already used it, and then turned to the last few entries hoping my assumption would be confirmed. But what I found was so much more. I swallowed hard and began to work my way through Maya's thoughts.

❧

The hole in my stomach filled with acid as I delved deeper into her words. Steadying my hand, I gripped my camera and methodically took pictures of all the entries. When I snapped my last shot, I hastily threw Christopher back onto the bed, my fingers burning after looking so deeply into Maya's heart!

38

Calling Home

Maya

SACHI AND GERVAIS WERE WORKING on opposite sides of the kitchen when I arrived. Neither was talking and there was an obvious chill in the air.

"Sachi?"

She looked up to see me and smiled weakly.

"Hi Maya, how are you?"

"I'm alright. Just recovering from my time at the ocean yesterday. Cristiano, took me to Setubal. It is a lovely fishing village, very quaint. Maybe we can go one day?" I asked then looked over at Gervais, "Maybe we could all go together?"

"Thank you, Maya, but I'm very busy. I have a kitchen to run *all* by myself," he said shortly then walked out of the room.

"Sachi, what's going on with you two? What did he mean *all* by himself?"

"Simply, he wants me to quit my job in Chicago and cook with him full time. He has asked me to stay on with him here at the inn. He has all the details worked out with the brothers and they are offering me a full-time position. They anticipate things are going to get busier here and they'll need someone who can work well with Gervais. They even pulled some strings with Immigration and got a working permit approved."

"He did all this without speaking to you first?"

"Well not really. One night about a week ago, I was dreaming out loud about staying here. He took that as a sign," she said quietly.

"Oh, Sachi as unexpected as it is, it's just what you always wanted!" Her face dropped. "Isn't it? Isn't that why you came here? Why you stood up to your father? You wanted to do something you love?"

"Yes," she smiled. "But what he's offering is a little more complicated than taking an extended holiday. I can't just quit my job." She paused, picked up a wooden spoon, and rhythmically began folding ingredients into a very large bowl.

"If I were to do this, it would be seen as me turning my back on my family duty. I would lose my father and he would be shamed in his circle of friends. If they were to find out that there was even *more* involved in this decision than the cooking … well, like I said—it's complicated."

"Sachi, this is the 21st century! People don't act like that anymore. You can do anything and be with anyone you like. I'm the best example of that. I walked away from a future that was not meant to be. It wasn't easy and there were a lot of people angry at me, and a few who I'm sure will never forgive me, but there were also a few who knew I did the right thing. They loved me for having the courage to stand up for myself. We'll help you; all of us."

"Maya, I come from a different world than you. I may have grown up in America, but my home, and my family, are very traditional."

She stopped for a moment then continued mixing the batter. "Maya, I think I've worked out the recipe and the design for the dessert. I made this lemon-lime cake once for a party and it was very popular. I went through my book last night and found it tucked away between an apple strudel and peach muffin recipe. I baked into the night, coming up with a few variations, and found one that I think will work for us. It tastes better if left overnight, so I am baking it today and it will be ready for icing and images tomorrow. There really isn't a lot left to do. Why don't you take today off?"

"No that's okay. I can help you bake!" I said laughing a little. She looked up and shook her head. It was clear she wanted to be left alone. "Well, I'll check in later and see if you need anything."

Before I even left she was elbow deep in cake batter again, falling back into her safe world of mixing bowls and egg whites. As I walked out of the kitchen and into the lobby, all I could think about was how complicated life was for everyone. My thoughts then drifted over to Cristiano and my letter. I knew if I was going to get through these next two days that I'd have to make a plan of distraction. So, I grabbed a pen off the front desk and started writing on my hand:

Stay calm, find something to do, laugh a little.

I stared at the simple phrases now scribed on my palm and decided it did not have to be any more complex than what I had written.

Thoughts came and went as I tried to figure out what I could do to keep occupied for the day. I wandered back to the front desk and saw they had a new display of postcards. There was a beautiful one of the sun setting on the vineyard with the inn in the background. I immediately thought of Beth and the travel corner she had intended to build for her first graders. I flipped it over and started to write.

Dear Beth, Just another perfect evening in Portugal. Wish you were here. I miss you so much.
Love Maya

It had been exactly two weeks since I'd seen Beth. It was the longest we had gone without talking since we'd met. I longed to hear her voice and catch up with her.

The thought of the two of us sitting in the garden, drinking tea and wrapped in our quilts, filled my heart and gave me some well-needed peace. Beth would know what to do. She always had a way of figuring things out.

"I need to talk to her right now!" I said louder than I had intended. Carmo looked up from the front desk, startled by the volume of my comment.

"Can I help you, Maya?" she asked.

"Yes, Carmo, that would be great."

"What can I do for you?"

"I need to call home."

"Is everything okay?" she asked with concern.

"Yes, I just wanted to speak to a friend of mine, but I can't use the phone in my room because Dalley is up there working on her project."

"Um no, I saw her come down a little while ago. She is having breakfast in the dining room."

"Oh, she must have changed her mind. Maybe she decided to meet Petra over breakfast," I said more to myself than to her.

"Maya, just a reminder, we are eight hours ahead of your hometown."

"Yes, that should be fine, she's my *best* friend." I began counting back the hours on my fingers.

"Two in the morning," Carmo said smiling. "I keep a few calling cards back here. Just a reminder though, it beeps ten seconds before the call disconnects."

"Thank you Carmo, I really appreciate it."

She handed me the card and I headed upstairs. The thought of talking to Beth was so exciting. I entered the room and kicked off my sandals. "Ow, that hurts!" I yelped. I sat down on the corner of the bed, lifted my foot, and pulled out a small pencil shaving that had poked into my toe. "I must have dropped some shavings when I was writing this morning." I flopped back onto my messy bed and reached for Christopher. At first stretch I couldn't feel him. My heart raced. Then I rolled over and landed on him. I thought I had left him under my pillow, but I wasn't going to question my crazy world. My pulse rate returned to normal, and I was ready to talk to Beth.

After punching in the long string of international numbers, I finally got to Beth's, which was embedded in my fingertips. The phone rang once, then twice.

"Hello," a groggy, but polite voice answered.

"Hi Beth, it's Maya."

Beth's tone of voice changed. "Maya is everything alright? Are you okay?" She was now awake and on full alert.

"I'm sorry to wake you Beth. I just missed you so much and wanted to hear your voice. You are my best friend and I love you—and to answer your question, yes everything here is—amazing."

"Well," she said hesitantly. "Amazing? There are only two reasons I can think of that my *used-to-be* practical friend would ever call me in the middle of the night: either you are in trouble, or in love? Or maybe a mixture of the two. You're not pregnant, are you?"

I started to laugh, "Oh Beth, there's no chance of that. But you are right—there is no fooling you."

"No, you tried that once in grade six and it didn't go very well, did it? So, spill it!"

I took a breath knowing I had to be as honest as I could. "Beth, I would say a mixture of the two would be most accurate."

There was silence. "Really? You're in love? *Really in love?* I'm going to ask you one question: Is this like summer camp when I fell in love with Gary Moon?"

"No, this is nothing like summer camp or Gary Moon." I chuckled deeply as I remembered that very creepy summer when we almost had to send Beth into hiding. "I've never felt more alive and ready to start my real life. He fills my heart up just thinking about him, and every time he enters a room, I almost faint."

"So, what's his name? And what's the problem?" she asked throwing on her counsellor hat.

"His name is Cristiano, but I can't go into the problem right now. It's too complicated."

"He's not married, is he? My situation two years ago was enough for both of us."

"No Beth. He's not married. Has never been married and has no children. You know I should wake you up in the middle of the night more often—you are very funny. The bottom line is I found out something important about his past that he knows nothing about."

"Maya, some information should be left alone. But in the end, follow your instincts, and if you do need to tell him, do it sooner than later."

"You're right, Beth, you're always right," I exclaimed happily.

"Which side of right am I on today?" she asked, injecting a little more humor into our conversation.

"The sooner rather than later side. I know what I have to do. How did I get so lucky to have a friend like you?" I laughed.

"Is there anything else? I do have to work tomorrow. Oh, by the way, thank you for the postcards, the kids are going to love them."

"Hey, I have some time off today. What do you think I should do?"

"Be a tourist. You never know when you'll be back there again. So have fun, go shopping, and spend part of the day at a spa. Problem solved. Is that all?"

"I'm sorry for waking you. I just needed to hear your voice."

"Maya, I love that you called. I just wish I was there with you and that I could meet your mystery man."

"You're going to love him. I'll call you again in a few days. Oh, when you get up, go over to my parents. I left a package for you by the front door."

"Is it what I think it is?" she asked with excitement.

"Yes, Beth. You don't think I would forget about you and our first day of school tea date, do you?"

"Well I have to admit, I was getting prepared to do my first day by myself. The tea won't replace you, but it will help me feel like you are close. Hey by the way, when do I get to meet Cristiano? I'm curious to meet the man who has stolen your heart. When is he coming to visit?"

"Beth." I stopped breathing for a moment. "I don't think I'm coming home." There was a beep on the phone. "I love you. You are my best friend. Believe me when I tell you that I'm good. Thank you. I'm going to …"

39

A Day Off

Maya

I DIALED THE FRONT DESK. "Carmo, it's Maya. Can you book me into the spa for a pedicure later this afternoon, around 4:00?"

"No problem. I'll take care of it right away. Did you manage to speak with your friend?"

"Yes, we were able to talk for a few minutes. I feel much better. Thank you."

"Did you tell her about Cristiano?"

"Yes, she wants to meet him and if she had her way, she would be in Portugal right now."

"You know Maya, Cristiano is like a different person since he met you. I saw him the other day when he picked you up for your date and he looked so happy—almost peaceful. My father told me he thinks you're very good for him. I'm pleased for the two of you."

"Carmo, is there something else?"

"Oh, it's just that he's been through a lot. Please take good care of him. His heart is—*frágil?* How would I say it? Easy to break."

"I understand." The weight of the secret grew as she shared her thoughts. "Could you please book a car for me?" I asked, changing the subject.

"I want to go in to Évora today."

"No problem."

"Please let the driver know I'll be down soon. I just have to change my shoes."

"Oh, no hurry. It will take a little time for him to get here. By the way, please excuse me, but if you are changing ..." she sounded embarrassed. "Évora is like a little Lisbon so you might want to dress up a bit, just to fit in I mean."

I laughed as Carmo was obviously trying to be kind after seeing me in my morning fleece.

"Thank you, Carmo. I appreciate the suggestion. Back home when we go shopping, most people just throw on a pair of yoga pants, but I'll make an effort to change into something more appropriate. The only problem is, I'm not very good at putting things together like that. Dalley has been helping me out since I got here, but she is nowhere to be found."

"Do you need help picking out something to wear? It would be no trouble at all," she said with enthusiasm.

"That would be great."

"I'll see you upstairs in a bit," she said, ending the call with almost a squeal. When she arrived at the room, she was all business—clothing business that is. She asked me to lay out some of my favorite outfits, then went into the closet and the drawers. She paused at the new lingerie. "Very nice, I like these," she said approvingly.

Within minutes she pulled together an outfit that I never would have imagined. I took the clothes and timidly entered the bathroom to change as my new me had not quite developed into a completely free spirit—yet. When I came out, she looked at me strangely.

"What? Do I look funny?"

"Oh no, you look great. You are just missing a few things." She took the scarf she was wearing and draped it around me like I was a movie star. "There, that should do it. You just need lipstick, mascara, and some boots. You have a pair of boots, don't you?"

"No, I don't. Do I need some?"

"Do you need a pair of boots? We all need a pair of boots."

"Well, I know Dalley bought a new pair in Lisbon last week and I think we are the same size. Maybe I can borrow them. I'm sure she wouldn't mind."

"Oh, just one more thing." She ran into the bathroom and grabbed some hair gel. Then she went on to shape my very new hair to match my outfit. "Perfect. Oh, I have to get back to the front desk. Your car should be downstairs any minute. I've arranged for you to be picked up at 3:00 and your spa appointment is at 4:00. I took the liberty of booking in a massage and a few other treats for you too."

She left before I even had a chance to thank her. I went straight to Dalley's closet and pulled out the beautiful boot box. Opening it, I felt a flash of guilt, but as soon as I slipped the boots on and zipped them up, the soft leather hugged my calves and all of my guilt melted away. I looked great.

As I made my way down the stairs, I carefully held the railing and arrived in the lobby without incident. Carmo was back at the front desk helping someone else, but when she saw me, she pointed over to the door where Francesco was waiting.

"Miss Maya? Is that you?" He looked and sounded shocked.

"Yes, it's me alright," I laughed, realizing that he hadn't seen me since the day I arrived.

"Portugal has done well for you, you look different. *Belíssimo.*"

"Thank you." As we walked to the car, I caught a reflection of myself in a window. He was right. I was beautiful and Portugal had done well for me. I was determined to have a good time in Évora and not let any doubt creep in about how to deal with Cristiano. I knew what I had to do.

⚬↬⚬

The ride to Évora was very informative. I sat with Francesco and he gave me the full tour of every battlement, castle, and monastery along the way. When we arrived, he offered to take me on a tour of the city, but I wanted to explore it myself. I was confident that my multiple visits into Évora had prepared me enough to go out on my own. We smiled and parted.

Évora was splendid. I'd been on such a mission the other day that I hadn't really noticed anything. As my senses consumed the sights and sounds around me, I remembered Francesco mentioning I should visit the Temple of Diana. That sounded perfect. I made my way on foot, wandering through the ancient streets following a city road map that he had given me.

When I arrived at the temple, it was more than I could have imagined. I had no idea there was such a Roman influence on the architectural history in Portugal. Francesco had mentioned the temple had been built in the second century, so I found it hard to believe it was open for anyone to just wander through at their own leisure. When I touched the stone, I could almost feel two thousand years of history flowing through the cool, solid rock. I plunked myself down and leaned up against the column, realizing very quickly that I, Maya Wells, was sitting on the stairs of the Temple of Diana in Évora, Portugal.

I sat for almost an hour and people-watched, letting random thoughts fill my mind. Tourists stopped and snapped quick shots and locals passed without even casting a glance. It bothered me that such magnificence had become commonplace in the eyes of so many, but it didn't surprise me. My eyes had been closed to so many things until just recently.

I looked down at Dalley's boots and my feet called out, telling me I had to find a pair of my own.

During my adventure, I stopped along the way and enjoyed every shop, museum, and eatery. I walked slowly, never feeling rushed, and even noticed the small flowers that grew between the cracks in the cobblestone. I found enough trinkets for each student in Beth's class to receive a little piece of Portugal, and eventually bought a pair of boots that all my fashion consultants would have been proud of.

The salesgirl placed Dalley's boots in the empty box and I walked out feeling content and headed back to the meeting place, laden down with gifts. It had been a lovely day of creative thoughts, wandering, and *trying on* the new me.

༄

Carmo ran over to help me with my bags when I walked through the front door. "Did you find a pair of boots?" she asked, holding her breath.

"Yes." I held my leg out for her to see, hoping she would love them as much as I did. Her gasp gave me the exact answer I was looking for and then we laughed.

"They are *deliciosos!*"

"Carmo, are you still working the front desk? Where's Puro?" Worry seeped into my tone.

"He's been Skyping with Maggie for most of the afternoon. Most of her relatives have arrived and she's not sure how she's going to get through the funeral tomorrow. My dad wishes he could be there for her, but it's complicated and unrealistic for him to show up on her doorstep after only having known each other for a week." She dropped her shoulders and sighed. "So until after the funeral, I'm in charge. Oh, you better head down to the spa. Your lady friends have taken over and are keeping our girls very busy this afternoon."

When I walked into the spa, I could almost taste the energy: sweet and luxurious, like the chocolates I used to eat before arriving in Portugal.

"Hi Maya, it's about time," Josie yelled. "We got started early— couldn't wait for you." She lowered her voice. "Thanks for the invite. It's a good change of pace. Yesterday after we heard from Puro about the funeral, it was a little hard to work on the party plans, but I think Ellen and I have worked something out that we know Maggie would have loved if she was here. Ellen and I have pulled out all the party stops."

"Sounds like fun! You're right, Maggie would have loved this."

Dalley broke into our conversation. "Where did you get those boots? They are spectacular." She paused. "I'll *have* to borrow them sometime." I grimaced at the thought. "Yes, I know," she responded to my reaction with irritation. "Can you please put mine *back* when you are done?"

A sudden image of Dalley's empty boot box lying on the floor in our room flashed through my mind. "Dalley, I'm really sorry, I thought you wouldn't …"

"Mind?" She laughed and then looked me up and down. "Nice outfit, it works—kind of." She slammed her head back down onto the massage table without another word.

40

Cake Chaos

Maya

WHEN I WAS FINISHED IN the spa, I went back to our room and carefully wiped Dalley's boots off, then laid them in the box and placed them back in her closet. I thought about her and the odd conversation that had occurred in the spa and contemplated that maybe I didn't know her as well as I thought I did. After finishing, I went downstairs and joined everyone on the veranda.

The conversation was quiet and subdued throughout the evening as the topic of Maggie spun in the air like storm clouds being painfully stretched across the sky.

My appetite was minimal that night and I foolishly drank another glass of wine on an almost empty stomach. When I woke in the morning, my head felt heavy, but it was presentation day and there was no time for excuses. I headed directly down to the kitchen to see Sachi as I knew she would be, hard at work. When I entered I heard her and Gervais in the back room, laughing. Just as I was going to knock on the door, he slipped out and closed it firmly.

"*Bonjour Maya*," he said with a twinkle in his eyes. "*Bonjour Gervais. Çava?*" I asked instinctively.

"*Tu parles français Maya!*" he responded with delight.

"*Oui un peu. J'allais à une école d'immersion français.*"

"I love when people surprise me. Oh, and thank you for speaking with Sachi. She has not changed her mind yet about my offer, but she has stopped saying no," he said with a laugh. "I now have two weeks to convince her that staying here with me will be the best thing for her. I know in the deepest part of my heart that she has to be here, with me, cooking and creating. It is her chance at happiness. You know, some of us only get one, maybe two if we are lucky. I believe we all must take them as they are offered, or they can just …" He snapped his fingers. "*Disparu.*"

He was right. We all have to take the chances that are presented to us or we could miss our own opportunity.

"How are Sachi's dishes coming along? Did she finish baking and shaping the cake?"

"You know Maya, she really is magnificent. She bakes like an engineer following her blueprints. The cake is amazing. I have never tasted anything like it. If I am not careful, they'll put her in charge of my kitchen when I'm not looking," he said with a chuckle. "Oh, Sachi was wondering if you have the images."

"No, I don't think they have arrived yet. Can I go in to see her?"

He frowned a bit. "Yes, but just for a second. She is icing *le gâteau* right now. It is best though that you do not say a word."

I laughed to myself. He acted like she was walking on a tight rope or something and that she might fall off if I made any sudden movements. But I did as he requested and when we slipped back behind the door, I stared at her, and then at the cake, and understood why there was no room for words. The cake was not finished yet, but it was magnificent in its design. Sachi had balanced one part of the cake against another. I couldn't believe how it appeared to be free standing. I gasped in awe.

"I know," Gervais whispered in my ear.

I backtracked my steps and returned to the main kitchen. There wasn't anything else I could do until Sachi finished, so I headed off towards the dining room. There was a large sign on the door letting guests know that breakfast was being served on the veranda and that there would be a picnic lunch later in the olive grove. The only reason given was that the room was being prepared for the evening's festivities.

I wasn't sure how Josie and Ellen had convinced Gervais to close down his dining room, but I imagined their plan must have been quite spectacular. I peeked in and saw all the tables pushed back to the walls and Josie and a few of the staff were hanging from ladders, with strings and strings of lights. I couldn't help but smile watching Josie. She really was a picture of joy. Ellen saw me peeking through the door and rushed over to shoo me out.

"No, Maya, it's not ready yet. We've been down here since sunrise. We have hours of work left to do, but we're having a blast. Tonight should be memorable! Oh, Josie asked if Cristiano could bring his guitar." Before I even had a chance to answer, she jumped back into the room and closed the door which left me with only one choice: to have a leisurely breakfast on the veranda.

I put together a cup of tea and a piece of toast and went to sit down with Petra, who had already finished her breakfast and was drinking her coffee.

"Light breakfast this morning, Maya?" she asked looking up from her book. "Yes, my stomach is off today, but a little tea and toast should settle things down."

"I hope you are feeling better soon. Tonight should be quite an adventure with all of our presentations," she said with a giggle and grin.

"Sounds like you and Dalley have things under control then?"

"Well I guess you could say that. I think we have everything we need and *should* be able to pull it together in time."

"You're not finished with your plans? I thought that the two of you met yesterday?"

"No, Dalley suggested we meet today and just wing it. I'm not worried anymore. I guess though we had better start on all the food prep."

I was confused, but I didn't want to ask any more questions.

We sat quietly and sipped our drinks, and then Petra started talking with a serious tone. "Is there any other news about Maggie? I've been thinking a lot about her. I hope she's doing okay. Maybe we could do something nice for her today. Perhaps send her flowers or something from all of us?"

"That's a great idea."

"Consider it done. I'll email my secretary back home and she'll take care of everything. Where can I get her address?"

"Carmo has all the information that you need. She is working the front desk for most of the day."

"Excellent. Now all I have to do is track down Dalley and start our food prep. At least the PowerPoint from the family dinner the other night is complete. Nothing really special, but it's done."

"No surprises?" I was really confused considering what Dalley had told me before.

"No, we are leaving all the drama to the rest of you." She laughed, poking me in the ribs.

"I think I've had my fair share of drama over the last two weeks." We both smirked and then looked out into the vineyard.

"Hey, any idea when Dalley will be coming down?" she asked.

"When I left the room, she was having a shower, but she usually goes onto the computer before coming down in the morning. She's been writing an article for her editor about Portugal."

"She didn't mention it to me. She's worse than I am. I guess work is always with some of us." She shrugged. "Have you talked to anyone back home lately?"

"Yeah, actually I have. I had a great chat with my best friend yesterday. I woke her up in the middle of the night. She thought I was a little crazy, but I managed to convince her that I was doing great."

"Convince her? Why would she need convincing?"

"Oh, you know with all of this stuff going on with Maggie, it's been difficult. Have you called home?"

"Yes, I called my husband the other evening while he was at work. He was so surprised to hear from me again that he almost dropped the phone. For all the years we have been together and all the business trips I've taken, I've never called him twice while I was away. I didn't go into the details about Maggie, but he knew that something had me rattled. Honestly, the whole thing has affected me more than I thought it would. Strangely, it made me start thinking about having children. I never thought I wanted any, but somehow something has changed."

"Did you tell your husband?"

"No," she started to laugh. "He definitely would have jumped on a plane thinking that something was *really* wrong. Children have never been part of our plans, but I always got the feeling he could bend in that direction if *I* changed my mind. Something to think about when I get home, that's for sure." She paused and a contented smile flashed across her face.

"Well you'll have to call me when you're pushing that stroller at the crack of dawn, with coffee in hand, and searching out new ideas." I laughed, then paused and took a more serious tone. "I would love to keep in touch when this is all over," I said, hoping she felt the same way.

She placed her hand on mine briefly. "You'll love New York." She winked. "You come visit me anytime."

At that moment Dalley bounded out onto the veranda filled with renewed energy. "Hi you two, what's new?"

"Hi partner. Good to see you're filled with happy shopping energy. Grab some coffee and let's go." Petra jumped up. "Hey Dalley, I heard you're writing an article about Portugal. I would love to read it when it's done."

Dalley turned her head, and then stared angrily at me with tight lips. She shifted into a big smile before Petra saw her, but it was clear I had upset her. "Absolutely, Petra," she said enthusiastically. "I'll send it over to you when we get back stateside. Let's go shopping; we have lots to do today." She grabbed two chocolate croissants, put her coffee in a travel mug, and then headed out with Petra to get supplies.

I paused briefly, trying to figure out what had just happened with Dalley, but realized I had no answers. I needed to get on with my day and call Cristiano about bringing his guitar.

⁂

He picked up on the first ring. "Hello Maya, is everything okay?"

"Yes, Cristiano. Everything is fine. Are you *always* going to worry about me this much?"

"I'm not sure. Let me try it out for a few more years and then I'll let you know," he teased. "Seriously though, how are things going with the presentation? Do you have everything you need?"

"It's been a whirlwind around here with everyone getting ready for tonight. Also, CJ's funeral will be just finishing by the time we get started. I hope that Puro is going to be okay."

"I know, I am worried about him, too. I have been leaving him messages, but he hasn't gotten back to me."

"Oh, I wouldn't worry about that right now. Carmo mentioned that he has been Skyping with Maggie trying to help her stay calm. They have been connected for hours! It would be good for him if he decided to join us tonight."

"Do you need any help? I'm almost finished here at Avó's. I've been doing repair work around the property for her, but I can finish up and head over."

"As much as I would love that, I still have things to do and I don't want you to leave until your work is done. But I do have a little favor to ask of you."

"Anything!"

"Josie asked if you could bring your guitar tonight."

"Do *you* want me to play?"

"Yes, but only if you want to. I wouldn't want you to feel obligated or anything."

"I'll ask you again. Do *you* want me to play tonight?"

I thought about the first time I'd seen him play at the club and how his music found its way into every part of my being. "Yes!" I said, jumping at the thought. He laughed at my enthusiasm.

"Let me make a few calls and I'll see if my friends can come too. If they can, be prepared to feed them, and to give them a bed for the night."

"Oh Cristiano, you are incredible. How can I thank you?"

"I have a few ideas," he said with innuendo, but we both knew that he was only kidding.

"I'll see what Carmo can do about the rooms."

"See you tonight. Love you," he whispered, then hung up. I stood with the phone to my ear for another minute, letting his last words trickle through me and fill me with all the nourishment I had been lacking since I had seen him last.

I was so excited that I almost *skipped* over to the front desk to ask Carmo about Cristiano's request. In a wink she had the two rooms booked for the other musicians and had called the kitchen to let Gervais know that we might need some extra food for Cristiano and his friends.

"Oh, Maya, something came for you just a few minutes ago. It was couriered in from Lisbon. It looks important."

"Excellent, it's on time," I said with a little yelp.

"Can I have a peek?" she said pretending to open the package.

"Nope, it's a surprise for tonight! But I know you'll love it." I yelled as I ran towards the kitchen, then stopped and added, "THANK YOU, CARMO! You're the best, but don't tell your dad I said that."

As I walked through the doors, Gervais' kitchen staff bustled around their stations in preparation for the evening's activities and Sachi almost jumped when she saw the envelope. We carefully opened the package to look at the photos. As I pulled them out, the first image I saw was not one that *I* had downloaded to the bakery. It was a picture of Maggie and her boys holding hands. They were laughing. You could feel their love. Puro must have had Maggie send it over and added it to the order. They were so handsome, identical, and now there was only one.

Sachi flipped through the rest of the images, then smiled and put them back in the envelope.

"They're perfect."

Sachi put me to work cutting and chopping as she ran back and forth between preparing the cake and the food. She wouldn't let me see the cake again, as she wanted it to be a surprise for me, too.

Dalley and Petra soon joined the kitchen fun and popped open several bottles of wine, which they happily shared with Gervais' young line chefs.

By late afternoon, all my prep work was completed and Sachi had disappeared into the back room with the cake, leaving me about three hours before the festivities were to begin.

Before I left, I snuck a quick peek into the dining room. The space had been transformed using a million twinkly lights. It was spectacular, but before my eyes could adjust to the lighting Ellen barked my name and I closed the door.

Everyone had something to do except me. I wandered into the lobby and saw Carmo rubbing her hand against her forehead.

"Hi Carmo. Is everything alright?"

"No, there's been a few mistakes with several bookings and I cannot manage the front desk and solve the problems at the same time, and my dad is busy with Maggie and everyone else is working on the event for tonight."

"Well, I'm free."

"No, no I cannot ask you to help."

"Don't consider it help. Let's call it training. I've been thinking about staying here in Portugal—maybe I can get a job working here."

"Are you serious?"

"Yes, about all of it."

"I'm not sure how I can thank you. All you have to do is smile and nod. I'll be in the back room if you need help with anything."

⁊꙰

And so my afternoon at the front desk began. My first in-house call came from someone who started talking to me in Portuguese. I recognized only one word, pão. I took a chance and forwarded the call to the kitchen. I never heard back from them.

The phone rang again, "Hello Netuno Wineries, Maya speaking."

"Maya? What are you doing answering the phone?" It was Cristiano.

"Carmo needed a hand and I was free."

"Oh. You are so amazing. But I didn't call just to tell you that. Can you let Josie and Carmo know that we are good to go. I heard back from the guys and the whole band is coming."

"The whole band? That's fantastic! Are you finished at Avó's?"

"Yes, I'll be there shortly. See you soon."

It wasn't long before Ellen and Josie popped out of the dining room and saw me standing behind the desk.

"What are you doing, Maya?" Josie ran over.

"I had a few hours to spare and wanted to learn a new skill." I leaned over the desk and whispered in her ear. "Puro is online with Maggie trying to help her stay calm and Carmo had a few fires she needed to put out."

"Well, you're doing a fine job. Keep up the good work." Josie teased.

"Oh, I have good news. I just got a call from Cristiano and we are all set, the whole band is coming to play for tonight."

Josie jumped for joy and ran back to Ellen, who did the same.

The rest of my time behind the desk was uneventful, and when Carmo came out from the back room she looked like a new person.

"Maya, I don't know how to thank you."

"Did you get all the booking problems solved?"

"Yes, everything is good. You should go and get ready."

"Oh, Cristiano called. The whole band will be coming tonight."

"I'm glad I booked them two rooms then. *Obrigado* Maya, off you go. Make sure you wear the new boots."

⁓

When I arrived in the kitchen, Sachi was in tears. She sat in a chair near the room that held her cake and Gervais was shouting orders at his tipsy staff, while struggling to help Sachi calm down.

"*Mon Dieu!* Thank goodness you are here," he said with exasperation. "What's going on? What's the matter with Sachi?"

"Her dishes are a disaster and the cake is falling over! She says she cannot serve anything tonight!"

I ran over to her, imagining that somehow, I had wrecked the food.

"Sachi, what happened? It can't be that bad, can it?"

"Maya, it's a catastrophe. The dishes taste terrible—all of them."

"All of them?" I asked feeling guilty, like I must have done something wrong!

"Yes, they have a very strange taste. I'm not sure what it is, but we can't serve them."

"I'm so sorry."

"Oh, it's not your fault. It's mine. I've been distracted all week."

"Okay, so the food is out. What's wrong with the cake?"

"It's falling," she said sounding defeated. "It doesn't matter anymore."

"Of course it matters. Show me the cake." She and I walked into the back room and there it was. A very amazing, image clad, almost leaning tower of Pisa. I took in a quick breath and held it, fearful that Sachi's masterpiece would come crashing down if I even breathed.

"I don't know how to fix it," she cried. "I should, but I don't. One part of the cake started sliding off the second pillar about an hour ago. I didn't notice it at first, but now it's too late. The cream cheese is melting and if it moves any farther it will fall completely and the edible images will be ruined."

I was surprised at Sachi's level of panic; it was clear she had reached her breaking point and needed help. "Come with me, I know just what to do," I said, making things up as I went along. I took her hand and we backed slowly out of the kitchen and then ran through the lobby. Cristiano was leaning against the desk, talking to Puro. I blew him a kiss but kept running as Sachi was my priority.

"We need a branch, about this big," I said holding my arms stretched out. Sachi and I ran to the olive grove and searched the ground looking for the perfect branch.

Sachi held one up. "That's it. That's the one! I can shape it when we get inside," I exclaimed.

While on our way back, her tears dried and were replaced by a fiery determination. I passed Cristiano again, but this time I stopped and kissed him full on. "See you in a bit!" I shouted as we ran back to the kitchen. He just smiled and shook his head.

We flew through the doors and I yelled to Gervais to grab me a large block of cheese. He responded to my emergency request and returned with a beautiful wheel of Mozzarella.

Sachi and I entered the cake room to find two young line chefs looking terrified while literally holding the fate of our cake in their hands. Sachi took over holding the cake while I carefully cleaned and shaped the branch. When it was ready, I plunged the branch into the cheese and pushed it close to the cake. We held our breath. The moment it made contact, we both let out a deep sigh. Inch by inch the cake slowly moved back into place and soon it looked just the way it was supposed to—a sweet and sour engineering feat, with a little help from nature.

"I'm not sure how I can thank you for saving the cake," she said with great relief.

"We're a team, Sachi." I smiled. "You know, the cake is all we need. It tells the whole truth about Maggie."

Sachi walked back into the kitchen and threw away all her spoiled food.

"Yes, you are right. The cake is the story," she replied with unwavering resolve.

Gervais put his hand on Sachi's shoulder then looked into his trash bins and shrugged. "There's always risk in creating something new. Sometimes we succeed, sometimes we fail." He chuckled a bit and gave her a squeeze.

"Sachi, it's close to 8:00. I'll meet you in the dining room in a few minutes," I said, almost sparkling. I was proud of myself. It was a strange and wonderful feeling. For the first time *everything* felt like it was going to be okay. When I entered the lobby, the space was filled with people talking and laughing. Puro was at the desk dealing with a guest, but was able to nod and wave me over.

"Cristiano's in the dining room. Somehow news got out in the last few hours that he and his friends were playing. We are completely booked. I heard that you helped Carmo this afternoon while I was with Maggie. Thank you so much Maya."

⁂

I opened the door to the dining room to find the space elegantly lit with twinkly lights and silver stars hanging from curled ribbons that were attached to a ceiling of golden balloons. It was like walking through a sea of stars. I had never seen anything like it.

Cristiano was on the little stage and motioned for me to come over and sit down. As he started to play any nerves that had been bristling under my skin disappeared.

⌘

The night was crafted like a beautiful piece of origami, every step executed perfectly. Ellen and Josie had outdone themselves creating an evening of magic and hope.

By the time the band finished their second piece, the appetizers were laid out on the tables. Things for Josie and Ellen went off without a hitch. Their party was exquisite and became everything they had hoped for. It was more than just a party, it was a gathering of hearts and souls, a true celebration.

Dalley and Petra's part of the evening did not go as smoothly though. The dishes they'd created were not edible, but Gervais, Mateus, and Reinaldo enjoyed their wine as the two ladies told their stories and showed their images of being invited into a Portuguese family.

For supper everyone feasted on Gervais' fine food and listened to the festive music, consuming it like it was another dish laid out onto the table.

After we ate, Sachi nodded to me. It was time. I took a breath and walked to the front of the room and stepped onto the stage.

"Excuse me," I said timidly at first. I glanced over to Cristiano and he handed me the microphone. The room became quiet as I began to speak, and Cristiano translated for me.

"On Sunday, our dear friend Maggie had to return to Canada due to a family emergency. Her teenage son was very sick. She didn't make it back in time and he died just before her arrival. A few hours ago she went through the impossible task of having to bury him." I paused as a stillness covered the room. I waved to Sachi and she and Gervais wheeled the cake into the dining room. It glowed like the brightest star in our sky and twinkled with magical lights. Somehow Sachi, *the engineer,* had rigged a battery pack into the cake! It was simply … fantastical. Suddenly I understood *why* the cake had started to fall over! I looked at Sachi and she humbly cast her eyes toward the ground.

A collective silence could be heard as the cake stopped in front of me. It was like nothing I had ever seen before. Cristiano squeezed my hand reminding me that I needed to continue. "This cake tells Maggie's story through a series of images, and *yes* they are edible. I have never met anyone with such true kindness and authenticity. Maggie is a woman of great strength and integrity, and in her lifetime she has had to face tremendous adversity, but she has done it with courage and love. I wrote this poem for Maggie and her son:

> *Open heart finds love,*
> *Sweet love ends in sour bites*
> *Sour tastes the joy*

"I welcome you to view the cake in all its beauty."

With those final words Cristiano kissed me gently and walked me back to my seat. The cake was soon cut, and the sadness became joy as people ate each morsel and invited Maggie's story into their own lives.

When dessert was just about finished, the brothers made a quick announcement, anxious to reveal who had won the trip to the Azores. I held my breath. Sachi had already told me that if we won, I could take Cristiano. I had planned to tell him everything about Jack and his family that night. No more waiting, no more secrets.

Mateus stepped up to the mic. My heart almost stopped. "We want to thank these two ladies for honoring the heart of Netuno family values in such a unique and colorful way—Josie and Ellen!" My heart dropped, until the ladies jumped on stage like they had just won a million dollars.

In response, Cristiano prompted the band to play. The salsa rhythm soon shifted the room from joy to passion. Josie was quick to take the lead as she grabbed Cristiano's hand and spun him onto the dance floor. Within moments Alfonso, the chef from Lisbon, stepped in effortlessly, allowing Cristiano to make his way over to our table where I sat with a pout on my lips. He saw the disappointment in my face and smiled, then lifted my chin with his finger.

"Did you forget that I have a surprise for you?" he asked coyly.

"Yes, I did," I said with a sulky tone, not quite ready to give up the Azores, but curiosity got the better of me. "What did you want to show me?"

He reached into his pocket and pulled out a box. Opening it, he held up a bracelet. On it danced a series of charms: Big Ben, Pisa, the Statue of Liberty, and many others. It was beautiful.

"It was my mother's." He unclasped the bracelet and placed it on my wrist. "My father gave it to her when they first met. He bought her a travel charm from each city that they visited together."

I stood mesmerized by the shape of each charm and the way the silver sang to me when it moved.

Carmo slid into our intimate space, almost undetected, and handed Cristiano a travel bag—my travel bag. "Everything is ready," she whispered. "Have a wonderful time."

He smiled and nodded to her. I looked to him for answers. His eyes sparkled with mischief. "I promised you an adventure, didn't I?"

41

What's in a Charm?

Maya

SHIMMERING STARS BRUSHED MY SHOULDERS as he led me out of the dining room. When we stepped out into the night air, I caught the sweet scent of the grapes ripening on the vines. Without a word, he led me to his car and we were off.

My curiosity grew around our final destination. "Cristiano, do I need my passport?"

"Don't worry. We've taken care of everything. Dalley knew where your passport was and Carmo packed your bag. Whatever they missed, I'll buy for you when we get there."

"You'll just buy whatever I need?"

He smirked while listening to the skepticism in my voice. "So, a passport? Any other clues?"

"Maybe just one." He smiled. "We are flying somewhere in Europe for the weekend."

"That narrows it down." My mind started to buzz with excitement as I could only imagine where we might land.

"Maya, what are you thinking about?"

I paused. "The possibilities."

He smiled again, and then revved the engine. "If we don't hurry though, we'll be stuck for the weekend at my place in Lisbon."

"That wouldn't be so bad, would it?" I laughed.

"No, except that Mrs. Dutra would end up being our chaperone, and I don't feel like having a chaperone this weekend. Do you?" He stepped on the gas pedal without another word.

When we pulled up to the departure terminal of Portugal Air, a valet opened my door. Cristiano threw him his keys and grabbed our bags. Then we ran.

Security was easy. They waved us through and motioned for us to hurry.

It was at that moment that he asked me to close my eyes. "You want me to do this again, right now?"

"Yes! You told me you trusted me! Do you?"

I grabbed his hand tightly, closed my eyes, and let him lead.

When he told me to stop, I was out of breath, but could feel my heart beating in my ears. He asked me for my passport.

"Can I open my eyes?"

"Yes, but only to look in your purse."

I found it with ease. Then I closed my eyes again, following his instructions. "Would you like a cup of tea while we wait?" he asked politely.

I burst into laughter. "You're joking, right? Waiting at the gate? Drinking tea? You're almost funny," I said, shaking my head, reaching out for his face.

"Almost?" he chuckled. "Hold my hand. I just got the nod that they are ready for us to board."

"Don't you think they'll find it odd that I'm walking on board with my eyes closed?"

"Oh, I guess you're right. You can open them now. Just keep your head down for a few seconds, then we will move over to headphones to avoid any last-minute announcements about our destination."

As we walked up the ramp, I opened one eye first, then the other. Cristiano was staring at me.

"Are you okay?"

I blinked a few times smiling, "Just getting used to the light again."

Cristiano greeted the attendants as we walked on to the plane and his colleagues smiled back at him. Settling into our seats, he placed his headphones over my ears and soon the sound of classical music filtered through my thoughts. It was not long though before a wave of exhaustion engulfed me and I drifted off to sleep wrapped in the protection of his arms.

When the plane began to descend, I started to stir. The charms on my wrist sang and reminded me that we were on our first real adventure together. I peeked out the window but could only see a few lights showing on the ground.

"Can you tell me yet?" I asked bubbling with excitement.

"I want you to figure it out. I added an extra charm while you were sleeping. It will be the only clue you need."

I ran my fingers over each charm trying to remember which one I hadn't seen, "Was the Colosseum on the bracelet before?"

He was silent, so I kept going. The last charm I touched was like the missing piece of a puzzle, the Eiffel Tower.

"Paris! You've brought me to Paris," I squealed with delight. I took his face in my hands and stared deeply into his eyes, then kissed him with such intensity that the rest of the world disappeared. He pulled back and smiled.

"Paris was the right choice then?"

❧

A car and driver were waiting for us at the airport, and it was not long before Paris's grand landscape began to reveal itself. The driver asked where he could drop us, and Cristiano looked to me for answers.

"I don't know where to go," I said looking to him for guidance.

"Actually Maya, I've never been any farther than the airport myself."

"I don't understand. I assumed you had been to Paris many times."

"You assumed wrong. My first trip to Paris was supposed to have been with my parents. It just never felt right coming here. That was, until now."

We held hands in silence and watched together as all the sights and sounds of the city came to life before our eyes.

When I looked out my window again it was there, in all its glory, my charm in real life: the Eiffel Tower. I had never seen anything like it.

"*Arrête, s'il te plaît,*" I yelled out. Cristiano looked out the window and knew exactly what I wanted. The driver stopped immediately, and we climbed out. I noticed that Cristiano handed him a slip of paper. Then the car sped off and we were left standing in the middle of Paris.

We stood and watched the lights of the tower as people passed us by. We became the couple in those magazines holding one another, caught up in their own world of love, romance, and joy. We were the couple that people longed to be. But soon biology won out over romance, as I realized I had not been to the bathroom since we'd left Netuno.

"Can we find a place to stop for a bite to eat?" I asked with a little urgency. "Oh, there's a nice spot," he said pointing to a café across the street. We ran over and were seated outside. I slipped away while he began to look at the menu. On my return, there were three young waitresses laughing and flirting with him until he saw me. The girls followed his gaze and quickly disappeared as I made my way back to the table. I sat down and kissed him, breathing in his warmth and allowing it to fill every chasm of my being.

"Interesting, I never marked you as being the jealous type," he joked.

"Oh, I'm not jealous, I just felt like kissing you. We are in Paris, are we not?"

He laughed, then took me in his arms and put on an even greater show. "Yes, we are in Paris Miss Wells, and I just wanted to say, I love you."

I wove my fingers through his hair and pulled his body close to mine. "I love you," I whispered back to him.

After we finished eating, we wandered down the path beside the River Seine. It was around 2:00 a.m. when we found ourselves crossing a little bridge into the courtyard of a small park. The lights were dim, but I could see someone sitting on a bench dressed as a harlequin. He had a guitar in his hand and sat as still as a statue, his case propped open at his feet. Cristiano threw in a few euros and he began to play. The romantic music of 1939 bounced off the stones as "A Nightingale Sang in Berkeley Square" rung out around us. We danced until the last note stopped ringing and the harlequin became frozen in time once again.

It was almost 4:00 a.m. by the time we arrived at the hotel lobby. We checked in and the concierge handed us the key to our room. It was only then that I started to wonder how it was all going to work. We only had one room. *Had he changed his mind?* A little bead of sweat rolled down my temple.

We made our way up to the room and our bags were waiting for us. He looked at me and then walked over and opened the bedroom door. Inside were two double beds. I laughed and so did he.

"You can have the bed by the window." He smiled. "You didn't think I could be swayed that easily did you?"

I went into the bathroom, too flustered to respond. As I rummaged through my bag, it became clear that I had one little problem—Carmo and Dalley had packed all my new lingerie, but no pajamas.

"Excuse me, Cristiano …" I called out to him through the closed door. "Do you have an extra t-shirt I can wear? My friends appear to have forgotten my PJs." I opened the door and stuck out my arm, collecting my soon-to-be sleepwear. When I felt the cotton in my hand, I closed the door, and threw his shirt over my head. With courage, I stepped out of the bathroom and scooted over to the bed, the bottom of the shirt barely covering me. He had turned the sheets down, which made it easy to launch myself in without pausing. He laughed as he made his way into the bathroom. A few minutes later, he came out shirtless, and ready for bed.

"Well, they did pack you something pretty, but I think I prefer the t-shirt." He winked and I threw the covers over my head. Sitting down on the edge of my bed he pulled the sheet back. "Are you ready?"

"For what?" I asked, my heart rate increasing ever so slightly.

"To get some sleep?" he chuckled, kissed me gently on the lips then closed the curtain, plunging us into darkness.

After a long minute of silence, he asked me one last question, "Are you happy?"

"Yes, for the first time in my life, yes I am," I whispered.

"Goodnight Maya."

"Goodnight Cristiano."

⚬⚬⚬

When I woke the room was still dark, but I could see the light of the day poking its way through the weave in the curtains. Pulling it back soon engulfed the room in the morning light. I wrapped myself in a blanket and crept over to his bed, then lay down beside him. Rolling over, he opened one eye.

"Good morning. I promise I haven't broken any rules, yet."

He smiled and blinked, then began to trace my face with his finger. His touch was so gentle it felt like a whisper on my skin. Smiling, I rolled off the bed, dropped the blanket and scuttled into the bathroom.

"That's not fair," he yelled as I closed the door. "Today we buy you some real pajamas."

We dressed and made our way to the lobby. "So, what's on our agenda today?" he asked.

"Mmm, where do you want to go?"

"No, Maya, it's not that easy. You choose today. I'll choose tomorrow." As I ran through the possibilities, I remembered a trip Beth and I had taken to Vegas. We'd stayed at a hotel that had just opened an art gallery. It was the first time I had ever seen real fine art pieces, and it was extraordinary. "The Louvre. I want to go to the Louvre, but I'm not sure how we are going to get in. I've heard that you have to stand in line for hours just to get tickets."

"Nothing is impossible, Maya," he said as his stomach growled.

"How about breakfast before your first miracle of the day?"

"Yes, that sounds like a good idea." He chuckled and then pulled out his phone as we walked across the street to the boulangerie.

"Who are you texting?"

"It's a secret."

"A secret?" I smiled.

Then came a flash of memory and my own not-so-little secret smashed into my beautiful morning. My heart sank as I remembered that I had planned to tell him about his bio-parents and Jack the night before. I knew I had to make a decision right then.

"Maya? What's wrong?" he asked picking up on my unsubtle reaction.

I lied. I hid my feelings. I made the selfish decision to wait and then jumped into a weekend of love and memory making instead.

"Oh, it's silly. I was just thinking about having to go back to Netuno."

"Hmm, I want you to forget about everything but us for the next forty-eight hours. Can you do that?" he asked earnestly.

Nodding my head, I let go of everything—but him.

I picked up two café au lait, cheese, and a loaf of bread while he finished his mystery text. Then I flagged down a taxi and we jumped in.

"*Excusez-moi s'il vous plaît. Pourriez-vous nous rendre au Louvre?*" he asked the driver.

"*Oui monsieur.*"

"Tell me Maya, why do you want to start at the Louvre?" he asked.

"A few years back, I had a chance to see a series of paintings at a gallery in Vegas of all places. Being so close to the canvases made me feel like I was part of something bigger than myself. The colors and the layers of paint—I felt like they understood me." I closed my eyes, embarrassed by the memory that fell from my lips.

He kissed me again and again, letting me know that every memory we shared counted.

When we arrived at the Louvre, Cristiano took my hand and led me to the front door past the line-ups of people. He spoke briefly to the girl taking tickets, then showed her a message on his phone and she let us in. A young man in a red coat then guided us through a set of double-gilded doors into a private gallery, then left us alone. Soon afterwards another door opened, and a very well-dressed older man approached us with a large smile on his face.

"Cristiano!" he called out and ran over to embrace him. "I have not seen you since you were a small child when I came to visit your parents in Lisbon."

"Yes Pierre, I remember. You brought me a lamp."

"Not just any lamp, but a shadow lamp I had made for you."

"That's right, when you turned the lamp on, it projected a shadow of a biplane flying in the clouds onto the wall. I loved that lamp. My parents spoke of you often, and of all the fun you had together."

Pierre paused when Cristiano mentioned his parents and I could see the sadness on both their faces.

"Your parents meant a great deal to me. I'm not sure if you knew, but they sometimes picked up special pieces for me or the museum during their travels. Is Avó still baking her bread?" Pierre asked, changing the subject.

"Yes," Cristiano exhaled, letting the wave of memory pass. "Actually, I was just repairing her outdoor oven the other day. People keep coming so she keeps baking. Thank you, Pierre, for getting back to me so quickly today."

"Cristiano, you are family. It is my pleasure. And as luck would have it, you came on the perfect day. I have something very special for you to see. Last year I negotiated with the Musée d'Orsay to house part of the Van Gogh series for the month of August. There are just a few days left before I have to say goodbye to them again, but I have asked that the gallery be closed today for *cleaning* over lunch, just for the two of you!"

After Pierre left, we stood in the quiet room and Cristiano took my shaking hand. I faced him and pulled him close.

"Private gallery? Van Gogh? Kiss me!"

"Now?"

"Yes, now!"

He started gently, but I wanted more. I needed more. I pulled myself into him tightly. His body tensed at first, but he gave in as I fit like a key placed into a perfectly matched lock. I pushed him down onto a purple velvet couch and he gave in with only a little resistance. My need to have him outweighed everything else. But as he turned me over, my foot caught onto an exhibit sign and it was only a matter of seconds before a series of clanks and crashes filled the air. By the time we looked up, Pierre was standing at the door, with a smile, and a nod.

We both sat up quickly—me with my face in my hands and Cristiano laughing uncontrollably. Pierre shook his head.

"*Oui*, that sofa has been my downfall many times." We waved and Pierre left the two of us to gather ourselves together.

"Maya, what got into you?"

"Well, you didn't seem to mind?"

"I would have been crazy to say no. But really?"

"Let's just say, you inspired me."

"Well let's see what else can inspire you today that won't get us arrested."

I took his unsubtle cue, sealed my lips, and dove into the museum. He never let go of me as we walked through a world of sculpture, canvas, and paint. When it was time to eat, the young man in the red coat found us and led us to the small gallery. Van Gogh's life and heart hung on every wall. We sat in silence, allowing the colors of the sunflowers and the stars of the night to blanket that moment in time. I never knew love could feel like that, love for him, and for myself.

The end of the day came too soon, and as we made our way out onto the grounds I smiled happily, taking in the manicured lawns and perfectly shaped shrubs.

"*Excusez-moi*, Cristiano?" An out of breath voice called from behind. We turned to find Pierre pink-cheeked and breathing hard.

"Oh, Pierre. Are you alright?"

"*Oui, Oui*. I did not want you to leave without us saying *au revoir*."

"We tried to find you, but you were in a meeting," Cristiano explained.

"Oh yes, too many meetings."

"Thank you, Pierre, it was a beautiful day." Cristiano motioned to shake Pierre's hand but Pierre spontaneously stepped forward and gave him a hug. "If there is ever anything you need, please let me know. I miss your parents very much."

"Yes, I do too," he responded simply.

An awkward silence hung between the two of them like Pierre wanted to say something else but did not, so I interrupted. "Thank you, it has been one of the most memorable days of my life—in many ways." We all laughed.

"*Non, Merci …?*"

"Oh, Pierre, Maya, my apologies," Cristiano gushed looking back and forth between the two of us. "Pierre La Nou, I would like to introduce you to Miss Maya Wells." He paused and looked at me. "She is *my* Rosa."

"Yes, I guessed that." He nodded subtly.

"We had better go. We have plans for the evening," Cristiano said looking at me. Pierre stepped over and kissed me on both cheeks and held my hands in his. "Welcome to Paris, Mlle. Wells. I extend my offer to you also. If there is ever anything that I can do to help you, please do not hesitate to contact me." He slipped his card into my hand.

"*Merci,*" was all I could say in the moment, as I was still stunned. 'His Rosa'—I was *the love of his life*.

When we arrived back at the hotel, Cristiano told me to head up to the room and that he would be up in just a few minutes.

On entering, I walked over to the window and looked out over Paris. It was everything that I had dreamed of as a child. All the stories were true, and now I was part of its history too.

I wandered over to my bag and pulled out a simple summer dress that would have to do for the evening. But before I could get changed, I heard the shower calling out to me.

Thoughts of the day lingered in my body as the silken water cascaded over my shoulders, I imagined the two of us abandoning our resolve, and *not* going anywhere that evening. Then my imagination was interrupted by a knock on the door.

"Maya, are you just about done in there. Leave some hot water for me will you?"

"You could come join me and we could conserve."

He opened the door a crack, letting in a cool breeze, "Tempting, but no! You almost lured me in once today. I am not going to fall for that again. Hurry up, I have something for you!" He said, shutting the door firmly.

I turned the water off immediately and stepped out of the shower, wrapping myself in a towel, intrigued by his enthusiasm. I walked out of the bathroom still dripping.

"You are not making things easy for me you know," he said with his hands up in the air.

"Yes, I know," I bantered, shrugging my shoulders. "But you can do it." He shook his head at me, walked over, and then seized me in his arms. He held me close kissing away each droplet of water. The balance of passion and patience in the space was excruciating as our bodies were driving us to continue.

"You're right, I can do it." Then he simply stopped and walked straight into the bathroom. I started to laugh as I heard the shower, knowing that hot water was the last thing he needed.

I stood and waited for my heart rate to return to normal. Then he shouted, "Look on the bed." I turned around to see three beautiful dresses laid out. "They should all fit."

Each dress did fit perfectly, but told a different story. The last dress that I tried on though was the story that I wanted to tell that evening. It was a deep maroon, like the shade of an aged port wine. The fabric hugged me in the front, yet plunged deeply, revealing the small of my back. I felt vulnerable, but knew it was the right choice. I decided to take the risk.

Cristiano came up from behind, his gentle fingers tracing my spine, running over every vertebra. "You look stunning." I turned around as he held up the bracelet, clasping it on to my trembling wrist. "It is yours now—only the history is my mother's. You can wear it as you want."

"Thank you. It's perfect."

We left the room hand in hand and walked down to the lobby. Heads turned.

"So where are you taking me?"

"To the top of the world."

"Do I have to close my eyes?'

"No, I want you to see every step that we take together from now on." He led me out to a waiting taxi and we sped off into the busy Paris traffic. The sights and sounds of the city were not lost on me, but Cristiano could not take his eyes off my pendant.

"Bravery. Your aunt was right. It must have taken a lot of courage."

I felt a surge of strength as he talked about me walking away from that life. "I think it took more courage for me to wear this dress tonight," I smirked.

"Then you should receive another commendation for your bravery. He pulled out a little box and opened it. The shimmering lights of Paris disappeared as a set of diamond earrings were revealed. I was speechless. He moved in and carefully slipped the diamonds into my naked ears.

෴

The rest of the evening played out like a fairy tale. He took me to the Eiffel Tower and for a few brief moments we got to sit on top of the world. I never knew that love could be like that. It was clean and messy all at the same time. I'm not sure I even tasted the food on my plate. But I remember the dessert. We shared a chocolate mousse that slipped past my lips and over my tongue. Chocolate was redefined; it had new meaning, and it was love.

✒

"Goodnight my love," he breathed out to me as he drifted to sleep in his own bed. I lay quietly listening to his chest rise and fall. There was a peace in the rhythm of his breath. I crawled out of my bed and lay my hand on his heart.

"I promise to always love you," I whispered.

✒

I woke just after sunrise. When I opened my eyes, he was staring at me. He had been watching me sleep.

"What are you doing?" I asked with great curiosity.

"Just thinking about today."

"Really? Because the crease in your forehead and the little smile lines around your eyes are telling me something different."

"Do you really think you know me that well?" he gently teased.

"I know everything I need to know," I said as a guilty breath cut me short. Sunday was his and that was all that mattered. "So what do *you* want to do today?" I asked light heartedly, inviting myself back into my own storybook.

"Hmm, I feel like shopping—for you."

"Cristiano, I don't need anything."

"Ah then, that's when it gets fun."

He wouldn't take *no* for an answer. So I finally gave in and off we went. Our fairytale continued as we strolled hand-in-hand down the

Champs-Élysées. Stopping and shopping, loving and being loved. It felt like Paris had fallen in love with us too. But some fairytales don't end perfectly, and with one ringtone ours was over.

"What is it?" I asked as he hung up the phone.

"Oh, I have some sad news. There is an extra flight scheduled to go to New York, and I have to work it. I need to go. I'm so sorry. He made a few quick calls and everything was set for me to return to Netuno. Unfortunately, the magic was over and all that remained was my secret. Regret began to seep out, and I wasn't sure how long I could hold it together.

⁓

The attendants at my gate waved for me to hurry. He dropped his bags and took me in his arms. His lips were on mine before I even had a chance to say anything. When I kissed him back a sense of urgency broke through, and so did a few stray tears.

"Maya?" He pulled back feeling the shift.

"I just miss you already," I choked out. "Do you really have to go?"

"You know I do. I would not leave you unless I absolutely had to. I'll see you early Saturday morning," he said reassuringly. Taking the palm of my hand, he kissed it gently, and then placed it on his heart, allowing me to not only hear the words he offered, but to live them in my body. "I love you Maya Wells."

42

The Candle Lady

Maya

As THE PLANE TAXIED DOWN the runway, Paris went dark for me. My body ached with contradiction. I just wanted to feel joyful, but the prickling of my skin indicated that I had no choice but to deal with the truth in my life, *his truth*. I needed to write—to find the words to calm my heart. Instinctively, I reached into my purse for Christopher. His absence left me startled at first, until I remembered that he was tucked safely under my pillow back at the inn.

I pushed the flight attendant signal and a young lady came over immediately.

"Miss Wells, how can I help you?"

"Do you have any blank paper I could use?" I was unable to hide the urgency.

"Oh, just give me a few minutes and I will find something for you," she said very graciously.

"Thank you so much."

"No problem, I'll be right back. Is there anything else that I can get you?"

The first word that formed on my lips was Cristiano, but I kept that to myself. "You wouldn't happen to have any café au lait or something like that would you?"

"We have everything you need."

"Thank you." I anticipated a taste that would allow me to hold onto a piece of Paris for just a little bit longer. When I moved my hand, my charm bracelet felt heavy on my wrist. I took it off and carefully placed it back in its box, deciding that I would not put it back on until I told him everything. The attendant came back with my coffee and some lovely paper that had clearly been torn out of someone else's special book. She nodded her head and then gave me the privacy that I needed.

Sunday Night

No Christopher, No Athena, No Cristiano. I feel lost.

On the plane, far away from home. Where's home? Home is where he is now. Tears are filling my heart and mind, I wish Athena was here. I could use some of her wisdom, but she's probably sitting at the bottom of Jade's expensive purse or worse, Jade's using her. That idea actually makes me feel sick.

I love him. I love him with all my heart.

Guilt is starting to seep in—guilt with dashes of regret. Should I have found a way to tell him this weekend? I had several opportunities but opted not to and went with enjoying the moment, and we did, every single-one.

What a cop-out Maya. Okay only six more days until I see him. I'll tell him everything. It'll work out, it has to.

I can't even write about Paris right now. My wrist feels empty. I'm missing that piece of him, but I will not wear it again until I have made things right.

Sad and tired Maya

PS I need a bath and a cup of tea, the coffee just tastes bitter without him.

⁓

The plane landed and Francesco was waiting for me. I smiled knowing Cristiano must have called him.

"Miss Maya, are you alright?"

"Yes, thank you, I'm just tired and need some sleep. I think I'll rest in the back if you don't mind."

"There's a blanket in the console if you like."

"That would be nice. Thank you."

When Francesco tapped me on the shoulder, I awoke startled and disorientated. It felt good to be back at Netuno. "Thank you, Francesco. I'm sure I will see you soon," I said weakly.

"Take care, Miss Maya."

The lobby was quiet and I slipped up the stairs, not wanting to be noticed by a soul. The room was dark, and I peeled off my clothes and climbed into bed.

"Maya?" she whispered in the dark.

"Hi Dalley. I'm really tired. Can we talk in the morning?"

"Sure, I was just wondering how your trip went?"

"Let's talk in the morning," I repeated. Before letting go completely, I plunged my hand under my pillow and grabbed Christopher like he was a lifeline that could keep me safe. I slept solid until the morning light began to creep through the curtains, my fingers still tightly wound around his spine. I got dressed and crept quietly out of the room, not wanting to wake Dalley.

I walked down to the lobby and saw the familiar sight of Puro behind the desk.

"Morning Puro. It is good to see you at work again."

"Good morning, Maya. I see you made it back from Paris safe and sound. It was unfortunate that Cristiano was called in to work. I hope the two of you had a lovely time."

"Yes, thank you. Did you know this was Cristiano's first visit to Paris?"

"Yes, he mentioned that to me on Friday night, before you left."

"It was the most incredible weekend of my life," I reflected.

"I have always loved Paris. Which part was your favorite?"

"Oh, the Louvre, and the Eiffel Tower, dancing in the park at 2:00 a.m. and—café au lait. Oh! The diamond earrings too."

He started to laugh. "What can I do for you?"

"Are Josie and Ellen back from the Azores?"

"No, not yet. They should arrive in the next few hours. You missed quite a party on Friday after you left. The festivities kept going until the morning. Maggie even made a quick Skype appearance at one point. I was checking in on her several hours after the funeral, and while we were chatting a number of guests ran through the lobby. She asked how the party was going, so I went into a little more detail, just to keep her mind off things. She smiled, you know that smile where she says everything, but with no words?"

"I think she reserves that smile for you, Puro."

Puro changed the subject. "I see you're becoming quite the early riser; not as early as Petra mind you."

"Is she out on the veranda?" I asked.

"No, I think she's wandering around, talking to my staff," he said with amusement.

"I'm sorry I didn't make it back in time last night for this week's assignment. So what do they have in store for us?"

"Well, they've decided to do something different. You are all on your own this week. No partners, just one story, and one dish telling a tale of your experience of Portugal."

"Sounds interesting." I felt both intrigued and a little unnerved by the idea that I would be cooking by myself.

Puro's attention drifted away from our conversation.

"Excuse me, Puro, I'm so sorry. So much happened on Friday, I never asked about Maggie and how the funeral went."

"Thank you, Maya. She managed—mostly. There was an incident at the graveside, but she said she would tell me about that when I see her."

"When you see her? Is she coming back?"

"No, but I have some good news. Cristiano booked a flight for me to go to Vancouver when the contest is over. She *would* prefer to be here, away from all of it, but she cannot leave Tim."

"When did Cristiano book your flight?"

"Oh he took care of it before you left for Paris. He would go to the ends of the earth to help the people he loves and trusts."

The weight of my secret became so heavy I could hardly stand.

"Maya—Maggie will be okay. I'll make sure of it." He tried to reassure me, but he had no idea the sadness that showed on my face did not stem from my worry about Maggie, but from my shame. The shame I felt for not doing the right thing. For not telling Cristiano when I should have, for letting my selfishness take priority.

"Puro, can you get me a …?"

"Your tea is already steeping in a pot on the veranda."

I walked outside and sat down in the old rocking chair, then poured myself a cup of tea. My next task was to search through my messy purse and find the journal entry I'd written on the plane. After finding it I placed it in the envelope at the back of Christopher, then took the hot cup in both hands.

As I finished my second cup, a small amount of Aunt Olive's resolve flashed before my eyes. So I stood up, gave my pendant a squeeze, breathed deeply, and headed out into the vineyard to search for that special piece of Portugal I needed to find in order to tell *my* story.

My feet took me to the chapel. As I entered the beautiful little space, my friend was there. I sat and watched her quietly as she finished replacing the last of the candles. When she was done, she lit a delicate wooden stick and began to sing a lovely hymn. She went on to light three votives, pausing briefly between each one. When she was done, she walked towards the door, stopped, turned, and spoke quietly to me.

"Come," was all she said. Then she held out her hand; I had to follow. We walked together in silence through the rolling hills, over the fields, and down a dirt road. I had never done anything like that in my life, but I felt safe with her. It was an hour before we arrived at her very humble home. The cottage was quaint and solid and the garden was filled with beauty and mystery, just like her. My legs trembled and my heart pounded as we entered, not from nerves, but from pure anticipation.

She put a kettle of water on her old stove and silently sat down beside me. I was not sure what to do but followed her lead. When the coffee was ready, we drank, then she got up and took out an old mill and a beautiful wooden bowl and placed it under the mill spout. She carefully placed scoops of grain into the mill and turned the crank. I could hear the grain in the mill churning, resisting at first, then finally giving in. The scent of the freshly milled flour filled the air. She took my hand over hers and showed me how to grind.

For over an hour she held my hand, making sure I fell into a rhythm. The only sound in the room was the mill. The peace that I felt with her was familiar. It filled my body and left me wanting for nothing. Then she emptied the wooden bowl into a larger crate. It was as if we'd stepped back in time. She squeezed my hand to let me know that we were done with the grinding. Then over the next four hours she walked with me through the remaining steps. I did not need to ask what we were making—it was as if my hands just knew. We took the flour, the yeast, the water, and began. But just as we were going to add the yeast, she stopped and lit a candle and said a prayer. Then we kneaded the dough, let it rise, and pounded it down again. She smiled at me and I knew that we were ready.

She led me out into the back garden where I saw the clay oven. It was then that all the pieces fell into place and I knew where I was and why it felt like home. *How could I have not seen it, sensed it, before? It was her in the market on that first day. She knew I was coming. She'd baked me my own bread.*

We placed our loaves in the oven and then sat and waited. As the bread started to rise and brown, I could smell it, the scent so wonderfully familiar! "Avó." Our eyes met and she held me with one nod. She took my hand and my heart smiled.

"Cristiano." I pointed to my heart as I said his name.

"Cristiano," she responded, placing her hand over my heart. "Maya." She said my name like I was part of her world already. I guess I was.

We sat in the garden for a few more hours, our love for Cristiano transcending everything. When I looked up, the sky had begun to change color. I reached out with one hand and took hers in mine like she had done on that first day when we'd met in the chapel. Her finger stroked my cheek and I knew we were friends—friends beyond language, beyond age, beyond coincidence. She tossed a loaf of bread to me and laughed, then held the garden gate open and shooed me out. The sun was starting to set as I walked back to the inn. The warm bread was the only food I needed that night.

✌

When I entered the lobby, Dalley sat flipping the pages of a magazine. She looked uncomfortable, agitated.

"Hey, where have you been?" she blurted out harshly.

I was taken aback by her tone. Whatever had been going on with her had clearly not been resolved and I didn't want it to touch my beautiful day.

"Nowhere really." I had always hated lying. "I went out this morning looking for project ideas and met a local. We spent the day together learning about Portuguese culture and stuff like that." The truth was easier, even if it wasn't the whole truth. "I'm tired Dalley. I'm going to bed." I paused for a moment and then added with a little more firmness. "Oh, and Dalley, I won't be around much this week. I'll be working on my one-to-one project with the local I met."

The Dam Breaks

Dalley

AFTER MAYA GOT BACK FROM Paris, the next few days were quiet around the inn. We were all supposed to be doing our own thing and preparing for Friday night, but I didn't care about that. The only thing I wanted to do was finish the blog for Joe and get the hell out of Portugal.

Maya was off on a daily secret mission and had stopped talking to me. The only constants in my life were the texts I got from Joe telling me that I had better post something or we would both be out of a job. But she was immovable. She shut me down every time I asked about Paris, kept Christopher with her at all times, and was tight-lipped about her daily outings. My questions were edging on desperate and I got the feeling that she could tell.

As I hit mid-week, I had stopped looking at Joe's messages and started drinking before noon. On Wednesday evening after supper, before I'd popped the third cork of the day, I thought briefly about Maya and how she claimed that a good cup of hot tea could calm the nerves. After ordering my pot of tea, it was delivered beside me with two cups.

Puro placed it on the side table. "No one should ever drink *anything* alone," he commented, then walked away without another word.

I prepared my cup like I had seen Maya do, but this time I hoped her ritual would bring me some kind of peace. I took a sip. It was missing something. I added two heaping teaspoons of sugar and mixed them in. It wasn't half bad. Before long, Maya wandered down the road in the strange, dreamy state she'd been in for days. I thought about Puro's words and how I could make this work for me and end all of this. I just needed to know what she had been up to. I decided to take a chance the moment she set foot on the stairs. "Would you like to join me for a cup of tea?" I asked with a surprising lack of desperation in my tone.

"Tea? You're drinking tea again?" She seemed amused by the idea.

"Yes, I know. Can you believe it? Puro brought it out, steeped and ready."

She looked at me—her face filled with a sense of contentment that I had not seen in her before.

She paused. It looked like she was thinking about it. "Thank you, that would be wonderful." She glided onto the veranda and sat down beside me and poured herself a cup.

I watched her carefully as she took her first sip, and then settled into the chair. "So what's going on with your mystery outings? Have you met yourself a handsome *farmer* now?" I laughed, making sure it sounded like a joke, and then waited.

"No," she chuckled. "One Portuguese romance is all that I want or need, thank you."

"Have you talked with Cristiano since you came back?"

"Only by text. He touches base every day. He was in New York Monday and Tuesday on a layover. Have you ever been there?"

"I have—many times. It's a great city."

"I wish that I could have been there with him. Someday though," she sighed. "He will be arriving home on Saturday morning. He told me that he has a surprise for me." She paused briefly and then began to tell me her story. I knew that if I gave her enough space, she couldn't help herself. I really was too good at my job.

"Actually, I have a surprise for him too." She buzzed with excitement.

"Really? What could you do to surprise him?" I ached to know, but held back my anxious energy.

She tucked her legs up into the chair, took a sip of tea, and began to tell her tale of the last few days, weaving a story that sounded almost too impossible to be true.

It began with the loaf of bread from the market on the first day in Portugal, then meandered over to the rustic chapel and the candle lady she met on the day Maggie left. The strange story continued with loaves of magic bread and how she and the candle lady found their way back to her cottage and began grinding grain and baking in her outdoor oven. Then the pieces came together, and she discovered that the bread woman in the market and the candle lady were the same person. They were Avó, Cristiano's grandmother. I found myself temporarily lost in her world, until my vibrating phone dragged me back and reminded me I had a blog to write. But I decided my next entry was going to be different. I was going to tell her beautiful story of mystery and coincidence. I was going to tell a different kind of truth about Maya Wells.

Her hand reached out to my face. It wasn't until she touched my cheek that I realized I was crying.

"Dalley? Tears? You told me you didn't cry. Are you going soft on me?"

"Maya, if you ever think about starting a new career you are a natural-born storyteller. Thank you for sharing with me. It was beautiful." She leaned over and gave me a hug, then wiped the tears from my face. I felt raw and empty.

"Here's the rest of a loaf I made today, it's still warm." She smiled gently, then handed me the bread, and walked into the inn.

I tried to swallow my guilt, pushing it down with every chunk of bread. But as I finished the loaf, nothing changed, no magic for me.

I wrote the story just as Maya had told it to me. It was the first piece of writing I felt proud of in a very long time. I didn't care if Joe liked it or not.

When my phone pinged, I figured it must have been Joe. I was right. It was him, but the subject line read: 'Brilliant!'

I was very confused.

Dalley … Not sure how these images showed up on the blog, but they're priceless. Our hits and comments have gone through the roof in the last hour. You're Brilliant!

Joe, As brilliant as you think I am, I just posted a story about Maya baking bread with Cristiano's grandmother. What images are you talking about?

… then we may have a small problem. Thought you were playing the bitch and pretending to be Jade. Take a look and see. It's pretty impressive. I'd give her a job. I'll check with legal about where we stand. Well Dalley you sure know how to keep a guy from sleeping, and not in a good way.

My heart raced. "What is he talking about?" A wave of panic and anger crashed over me, causing me to almost choke.

I logged onto the site and he was right. The hits and comments had gone crazy. I toggled back to Friday night, to my last entry when I'd told everyone about Setubal, and Cristiano's father, and the trip to Paris. Then I began reading through all the comments.

Kisses: *That is so romantic that they're going to Paris.*

Bart: *Are you kidding me? The only reason why he would take her to Paris is to screw her. There's no way they are even going to leave the hotel.*

Kisses: *You suck.*

Bart: *Yeah well for his sake I hope she does too.*

My readers' comments didn't shock me, but I had a feeling that things were only going to get worse. My nerve endings bristled as I continued to read.

Daisy: *Bart you are so rude. You're right Kisses. It is romantic, but I hope she tells him about his bio parents. He deserves to know. He has gone through so much.*

Kisses: *You're right Daisy, but it's Paris, if she tells him, it's going to ruin everything.*

Daisy: *Isn't it more important to be honest. If they really love each other that much. She has to tell him no matter what.*

Bart: *You're stupid Daisy.*

Daisy: *You're a caveman Bart. I'm out of here. Good luck this weekend Maya.*

The choking feeling subsided but was replaced with overwhelming nausea. Joe said she used their full names. I swallowed back the bile and continued on my quest to find out what he was talking about.

After searching through hundreds of entries I saw *it*, standing out like it was surrounded in lights:

Jade: *Hi all. I thought you would like to get a little more dirt about all the people that Dalley has been telling you about during her trip to Portugal. Yes, I am the beautiful French model that she spoke about, among other things, and she was right when she said I was stunning. At least she got that part correct. Let's start with the Portuguese lover himself, Cristiano. As you can see in the picture he came to my house in Montreal for a visit Tuesday afternoon. He was only there for a little while, but I gave him a few good reasons to come back. Oh, and then we have Maya and all of the old hags including the grieving mother, Maggie, drinking up a storm after her son's death. Portugal is nice this time of year. But as far as the contest goes, Netuno Wineries was boring and ugly, the rooms at the inn were subpar, the wine average, and the company as you can see, not my caliber of friends. So I left. Oh and the food. Well this French Chef, Gervais, hooked up with this Japanese girl Sachi, one of the contestants if you can believe it, and had her doing his work for him in the kitchen. Well, the food was nothing to write home about. Edible, but forgettable.*

"Oh shit Jade, what have you done?" I stretched my hand over my eyes covering them completely. Part of me hoped that when I looked again the pictures would disappear, but they didn't. Images of Cristiano and Jade took center screen. It looked like they were kissing among other things. "Why was he in Montreal? Oh this is bad, really bad. Jade is all over him in every shot. What the hell are they doing?" I leaned into the computer screen trying to see the image more clearly. It looked like she had her hand in his pocket. "Gross! Maya is going to be crushed. God I hate men!"

The comments that followed ranged from brutal, to hopeful with everything in between.

Daisy: *Screw you Cristiano.*

Bart: *That's my boy. I knew he had it in him.*

Kisses: *I just don't believe it. He would not do that to her.*

Truth be Told: *It is what it is. Maybe she told him the truth about his family and he was mad and wanted to get back at her.*

Color 32: *No... I knew he was too good to be true. All nice guys are. Daisy's right, screw him.*

Bart: *Color 32, I think you are on to something. I'd let you screw me anytime.*

Color 32: *F@*! You!!!*

I continued to scroll down through the comments and arguments that had erupted online and found myself both drawn in and mortified by the base conversation. It was all about us. Our whole group had been flayed and put on display. She'd tagged everyone in the group picture with their first and last names.

Path 67: *So where does Maya fit into this? I bet she doesn't know. Someone needs to tell her before she makes a big mistake and quits her job and moves to Portugal for this asshole. And what about this Dalley Price woman? Where did she get all the info on Maya anyways? There's no way Maya would have told her all that stuff.*

Comet12: *Serves her right. I never liked her anyway. The way she left that guy practically at the altar, I think she gets what she deserves.*

Path 67: *No one deserves what is about to happen to her. This Jade girl is mean and out for revenge. Don't you remember how Cristiano chose Maya over her at the dance club? And then there was that whole thing in the lobby between them on the day when Maggie left.*

Stink 21: *Did you see that pic of them all drinking after Maggie's son died, nice mother.*

Rachel: *I know Stink 21. Maggie and her friends were all laughing and stuff, and you are right the inn is Gross!!! I would never go there. I would have left too, Jade.*

Jade: *Thank you Rachel. Yes it was awful. You should have seen the room that they shoved me into when they discovered that I did not know how to cook like my roommate. They were awful to me.*

Mabel: *Maybe it's not as bad as you think. I don't think that Cristiano would do that to Maya. There must be some misunderstanding.*

Rachel: *Mabel is it? Where did you get that name from? Cristiano is an ass, but he is really hot though. So I think I would forgive him.*

Stink 21: *Yeah, you're right, I'd let him eat crackers in my bed any day.*

My blood boiled as I skimmed over the remaining pictures and comments. Jade had photographed all of us during her stay, and in her tags made us look like sluts, drunkards, or idiots.

I had created the perfect platform for Jade to smash through our lives and it was only a matter of a day or two before everyone at the inn would find out about the blog. Desperation replaced every other emotion in my body.

Trudging upstairs to our room I was barely able to lift my legs with each step. When I entered, Maya was sound asleep holding Christopher tightly in her arms. I was desperate for more answers and hoped that maybe *it* could give me what I needed to settle the anxiety that grew within me. Part of me wanted to save myself and the other part needed to know how Cristiano could have done such a thing to Maya.

Thoughts of Cristiano and Jade plagued me—none of it made sense. I needed to know if Maya had told him about his parents when they were in Paris. I could not figure out what would send him to Montreal to Jade's home? He lied to Maya and told her he was in New York on Tuesday, but obviously he was in Montreal.

I stared at her sleeping peacefully. If I could figure things out before she discovered the truth maybe I could try to repair some part of it. So, I tiptoed closer to her and tried slipping Christopher out of her arms. She tossed a bit and I thought for sure she was going to wake, but to my relief, she rolled over and left him exposed. I snatched him up quickly, then stumbled in the dimly lit room over to my desk and searched for Jade's black file.

Entering my bathroom, I shut the door and sat down on the cold unwelcoming tile floor. As I flipped through Christopher, there was nothing after her last entry. She had not written anything since before her trip to Paris. With disappointment, I went to close the journal but noticed the parchment envelope at the back bulging. My heart skipped as I slowly unwound the string, not sure of what Maya had tucked away within it. My hands trembled as I pulled out what looked like random pieces of paper, but turned out to be so much more than that. As I opened each piece, I held both of their hearts in my hands, Cristiano's poem and letter and Maya's last journal entry. It was sprinkled with her love for him and her regret for not telling him about his bio parents when they were away. I folded their hearts up, tucked them back into the envelope, and wound the string tightly, sealing them back into place.

Why would Cristiano go to Jade's apartment? And what could possibly have motivated her to hijack my blog? It was these questions that inspired me to call her. I found Jade's number in my file and dialed. She picked up on the first ring.

A sticky, slurred voice answered, "Hi Dalley, long time no talk. I was expecting your call sooner. They must have you busy picking grapes out in the vineyard or something," she said sloppily, while her words oozed with wanted superiority.

"Jade, what have you done?" I whispered not wanting to wake Maya.

"Nothing as bad as you," she hissed back, venom leaching out of each word. "*I* was never their friend. *I'm* not the one who started all of this. I just took advantage of the platform you gave me. I couldn't have done it without you. Oh, and using her journal entries, that was impressive."

"I never …"

"Oh, don't even start. I read through the blogs and the details that you gave people. Those were Maya's words and thoughts. I spoke with her enough to know the pathetic way she talked and tried to live her life. I may be a bitch, but you're a fraud in more ways than one!"

I tried to defend myself, but the words were weak and held little impact.

"Dalley, you're such a hypocrite," she laughed. "What you did was *waaay* worse."

At that moment, I wasn't sure if I wanted to kill her, or me. She was right. I was the creator of the nightmare and it was just beginning to unfold.

"I'm pleased our family photo album has made such a splash on the Internet. Honestly though, I'm a little surprised by the amount of traction my addition to your blog has gotten in the last few hours. I think it adds to the drama, don't you?" She sounded so pleased it made me sick.

I decided to take a different approach and swallowed the venom that she'd spewed out. "You're right Jade, I *am* a hypocrite. I'm the one who built the blog and gave you a place to exploit … oh … express your thoughts. But I'm still trying to figure out how you got those shots of Cristiano. They were quite shocking—impressive actually," I said calmly while stoking her ego.

"Oh, that was easy." She embraced the ego strokes and continued. "I had an unexpected visit from Cristiano on Tuesday. I had to think on my feet. Do you know that loser came all the way from wherever the hell he was just to get her pen back? Her stupid, sparkly, blue pen. Who does that?"

Someone who loves a woman with every fiber of his being, I thought to myself. "Yeah you're right, Jade. Who would do that?" I forced myself to sound disgusted.

"The two of them deserve each other. Losers, that's what they are," she spat into the phone.

My pretend calm started to wane. "So nothing happened between you and Cristiano?" I asked, fishing carefully.

"With some careful photo shopping and a couple of shots of me leaning into him, it was easy. I slipped my hand into his pocket. Technology is an amazing thing. Anyway, I wouldn't let that jerk touch me with a ten-foot pole. I just made it *look* that way."

"Oh, so why did you tag the rest of us if this was all about getting back at Maya and Cristiano?

"Actually Dalley, all of you were nauseating to me." She giggled. "No offense."

"None taken," I said, removing the head set from my ear, while I took a deep breath. "You tagged that picture of all of us drinking wine on the first day as *Grieving Mother and Friends?* Maggie's son didn't die until a week after that. That was both cold and impressive," I said, somehow holding back my disgust.

"Oh it was perfect! It was like an all-in-one deal. Great tag and image, and the rest I left to your debased readers. Sometimes you need to start a series of fires to distract your enemy from your real objective. I just got to kill two birds with one stone."

"Real objective?" I had to bite my lip to hide my anger and newly awakened intrigue. "I'm sorry that we weren't able to have a real drink together Jade."

"I know, I wish you were here right now. You could help me finish this bottle of champagne. I'm celebrating."

My instincts told me that whatever Jade was up to, it was about more than just Cristiano and Maya. She had another agenda. I decided bold was best. "You are such a clever girl Jade—what are you up to?"

"Oh Dalley, if I told you, I would be in big trouble. You and your friends can finish up your little contest, but it won't be long now, and

Netuno will be no more." She snapped her fingers and stopped me in my tracks. "In another world maybe we could have been friends. I do like the way you work. I didn't see it coming." Her admiration for what I had done made me sick.

And she was right, this *was* my fault. She just jumped into the chaos I had created and took advantage of it. But during our conversation, she had given me enough information to know that the other part of her plan had something to do with Netuno and that it was bad, really bad.

"Left you speechless?" she slurred on. "Have fun in Portugal while you can," she spoke sloppily and then hung up the phone.

I sat on the bathroom floor, papers strewn around me and made notes from our conversation. Then dialed Joe's number with ferocity, determined to find the answers to all my questions.

"Hi Joe, it's me," I said in a forced whisper. "Any chance we can stop this blog?"

"Not a one," he responded dryly. "Legal said we are good to go. The pics were taken in a public place, and we can't control how people tag the images. She was right though, that pic of you and the mother and your friends? That was cold. Wine tasting just after he died, that's bad even for you Dalley."

If I could have reached through the phone, I would have punched Joe in the face. "Joe, it wasn't like that at all. Clearly the facts don't matter to you anymore."

"The site traffic is up and advertisers are clamoring to get their product on while the getting is good," he explained unapologetically.

"Of course they are," I said, now tired of listening to him make excuses.

"Oh, I had a few minutes to read your bread piece. It was really sweet."

"Thanks Joe ... thanks for absolutely nothing. I quit. Sue me." Defiantly I threw my phone out the bathroom window, and for the first time in years, felt in control of my life. My heart rate didn't start to slow though until I walked back into the room and slipped Christopher onto Maya's bed, near where she lay.

I went back to the bathroom and sat down. I had just quit my job as an impromptu romance blogger and decided it was time to become a real journalist. I was convinced that the starting point was somewhere in Jade's file, and I was going to find out what she was hiding.

44

Convergence

Cristiano

I laughed as I walked away from Jade's Montreal apartment. That vase would have hurt if it had hit me. She definitely did not take rejection very well. I did feel awkward though when she leaned in so close to me and slipped Athena into my pant pocket and kissed me.

I pulled Athena out and held her up to the sunlight. Maya was going to be so excited to see her again. As I hopped into a cab and headed back to the airport, scenes from Jade's apartment played out in my mind. I didn't like the way she'd looked at me and then offered herself. That woman was crazy, but at least I got Athena back for Maya. Saturday seemed so far away. I texted her letting her know that I had a surprise for her. She texted me back and told me that she had one for me too. I decided I couldn't wait until Saturday and began making calls to see if I could fly back for Friday night.

Maya

(WEDNESDAY, LATE NIGHT—LISBON TIME)

I turned over and noticed Dalley standing close to me. She must have thought I was sleeping. Then she walked into the bathroom and closed the door. I rolled over and grabbed Christopher and then searched around in my bed for something to write with. It was dark, but with the light shining from the bottom of the bathroom door, I was able to scratch out a few lines.

Wednesday night late, maybe early Thursday morning.

Over the last few days Dalley's been on edge. Tonight though, something different happened. When I came back she was drinking tea. I sat with her. It felt like she needed a friend.

I told her about meeting Avó and she cried.

It felt good to share our story with Dalley. The time that I've spent with Avó has given me a new way to look at things. She's special; having her in my life has given me the chance to ground myself and realize that no matter what I tell Cristiano on Saturday, it will be okay.

He sent me a text yesterday and he was so excited. He said that he has a surprise for me. What could he possibly do that would be more amazing than Paris?

I guess it's time to tell you about Paris my friend. I don't ever want to forget it.

Jumping out of the car when I saw the Eiffel Tower. The passionate kiss in the café.

Walking the Seine at 2am.

Dancing in the park while the Harlequin played his guitar.

Laughing as I stood nervously in the hotel lobby, wondering if he had changed his mind.

Him showing me the two beds and shaking his head at me.

Discovering I had no pajamas and having to wear his shirt.

The day at le Louvre and the private tour. The purple velvet couch, lunch with Van Gogh, and Pierre La Nou.

The moment when we both thought about giving in to the passion, but simply didn't.

The beautiful dresses that he bought me.

The diamond earrings to match my pendant.

Eating dessert at the top of the world.

My hand on his heart while he slept.

There was no drama, only love. It wasn't until the plane ride home that I let the guilt of not telling him hit me.

I'll take care of things when I see him. Oh so tired. Good night Christopher.

When I opened my eyes again, the morning was in full swing. I had slept in. I lay there for a moment and saw that my journal was still open to last night's page of Paris memories. I looked over it and kissed the page, sealing it with all the love that it held for both of us.

Dalley

(Thursday, 8:30 a.m.—Lisbon Time)

She looked so peaceful in the morning, Christopher open on her bed, pencil still in hand. She must have written the entry after I'd returned him. I had a chance to glance at the first few lines and realized immediately that it held many of the answers my readers and I had about what had happened in Paris. But they weren't my readers anymore. I walked out of the room leaving the entry unread and untouched.

My body felt heavy, like gravity was fighting against me. I could barely take a step forward without seeing flashes of my future. I was going to lose the only group of friends I'd ever had—how selfish was that. At some point I knew it was going to get messy. It was just a question of when.

All the ladies were waiting for breakfast when I arrived in the dining room. "Dalley, you look like crap," Petra offered like a strange gift. I accepted it.

"Yah, one too many last night. Please remind me to call you guys next time I want to start drinking alone." I forced myself to laugh and flicked my hair over my shoulder. I was horrible. I was no friend to anyone. I should have told them right then, but I didn't.

"Dalley, you can always call me. I'm up for a drink anytime," Josie chuckled and raised an eyebrow my way, then changed the subject. "Hey have you seen Maya? I miss that girl. What's she been up to all week? Ellen and I haven't even had a chance to tell her about our trip to the Azores."

I pushed the acid-churning guilt back down into the pit of my stomach and answered, "She's sleeping in a bit today. She's been busy working on her project."

"Well I hope she hurries down for breakfast. I want us to eat together. Dalley, call her and wake her up," Josie insisted.

"No, I think we should let her sleep."

"Oh, she has her whole life to sleep, and only a few days left in Portugal," she pressed on.

I picked up the house phone reluctantly and called up to the room, but there was no answer.

"She must be in a deep sleep," I said trying to get her to drop it.

"Are you calling me a Sleeping Beauty?" I could hear the smile in her tone. I turned around and saw her still sporting that same peaceful look she had had while she was sleeping. She had found her calm. She was a different woman than the one I had met on the airplane. *Just say it. Just start talking and don't stop until they all know. They will forgive you. I can save her, help her.* But I was a coward.

"Yes, Sleeping Beauty, it appears the masses here can't eat without you," I quipped, then shriveled in my seat.

Breakfast was filled with laughter I couldn't hear and food I couldn't taste. People talked about their presentations, but all I heard was a buzzing noise in my head.

"Dalley, what's yours about?" Ellen asked innocently. "Dalley, your presentation. What are you doing?"

The noise ended and I fell back into their world. "Grapes," I remembered Jade said something about grapes. "I'm … I'm learning about harvesting grapes by hand," I said almost convincingly.

"I wouldn't have taken you to be a hands-on-dirt kind of girl," Petra laughed.

"Oh, yeah … I know how to get dirty with the best of them." The table broke into laughter; I felt sick.

"And what about you, Maya? Where have you been sneaking off to?" Petra asked, shifting her curiosity elsewhere.

"Oh, it's a secret—you'll find out tomorrow." She sparkled when she said it, then looked at me and winked. I knew what she was referring to. So did about 3,476,345 other people when I last looked.

Steven

(Thursday, 1 a.m.—Peachland, Canada [Thursday, 9 a.m. in Lisbon])

"Beth, pick up, pick up the God damn phone!"

"Hello? Maya?" Beth answered sounding groggy.

"Maya? Why would you think it's Maya? Was she supposed to call you?" My voice cracked.

"Steven, what the hell? It's the middle of the night?" she growled.

"Actually it's 1:00 in the morning. Have you talked to Maya in the last few days?"

"No, not in the last few. She called me last week. Why, what's going on?"

She was irritated with me, but obviously had no idea what had been happening online.

"What's going on? Oh, let's see. Just a slice and dice of our entire lives over the Internet. You seem to have gotten off easy, but they managed to get my last name, and you wouldn't believe what they are saying about Maya!"

"Steven, what are you talking about? And who are *they*? Did something go wrong with that stupid Facebook page that you started about Maya after the wedding?"

"No, I took that down. That was a mistake. This has nothing to do with that," I said with a note of irritation and shame.

"Tonight I was surfing the net and happened to punch in Maya's name." There was dead air on the other end of the phone. "I can't see you Beth, but I know you are rolling your eyes. So stop it. When I typed in her name the first thing that came up was a reference to *Price's Portugal*. It starts out pretty tame, just a story about a group of eight women traveling to Portugal. They end up at this inn for four weeks cooking and doing photography. A young woman they first called Trina was at the center of the story. She meets this male flight attendant. It goes on and on, talking about her sick mother and failed attempt at getting married, and then all this bullshit about this man she falls in love with. Does any of this sound familiar to you?"

"Oh my God, Steven, I'm on the site right now. This is crazy. Those are pictures of Maya and that must be *him*?" She sounded surprised and impressed at the same time.

"Him? You knew about him? He's real? And you didn't tell me?" I felt angry and betrayed.

"Why? You guys broke up months ago. You have no right to judge her. She can date whomever she likes. Steven, she doesn't love you—she loves Cristiano. For your sake, just let it go. Let *her* go."

Beth's words rang true to what Maya had told me on our wedding day—that she didn't love me. "It took her almost two years to finally say 'I love you' when we were together. So how could she love someone that she just met?" But that didn't matter. I still loved her enough for the both of us.

"Did you see the pictures of the guy who supposedly loves her? He was playing with that model, Jade. I *know* Maya. She is fragile right now. She doesn't know what she's doing. She's going to need someone to help her pick up the pieces when this all falls apart. I can do that. She needs me. I still love her."

"Steven, don't do anything stupid! She doesn't need rescuing. Please stay out of this."

"Beth, she and I were hours away from marrying each other. In the blog it talked about her being depressed. I didn't know. Maybe she really didn't know what she was doing. I have to go to her. I have to be with her right now!"

"Steven, don't go. Please don't go. I'll call her. Then I'll have her call you." Beth tried to convince me to stay, but I had already made my decision and had almost finished booking my flight by the time I had gotten off the phone with her.

"I have to Beth. I don't have a choice. I love her. I just booked my flight and I leave out of Vancouver tonight. I will arrive in Lisbon at 6:30 p.m. Friday evening."

Beth

(Thursday, 7 a.m.—Peachland, Canada [Thursday 3 p.m. in Lisbon])

After the abrupt morning waking from Steven, I called school and left a message that I was dealing with a family emergency and would not be back until Monday. I spent the rest of my early morning poring through the blog, trying to understand what the site was about, and why Maya's entire history and present life were being posted for the world to see. I called Mr. Wells around 6:00 a.m., but he was already up and in full damage control mode. Jordan had been broadcasting the information to whomever she thought would listen. Mr. Wells had made several calls and was trying to figure out what legal footing he had to have the site taken down.

By the time I'd arrived at the Wells' home, my phone was filled with texts, people wondering what was going on with Maya. I realized there was no way of making it disappear. I had hoped Mr. Wells had made some progress, but when he opened the front door, the look on his face indicated he'd had no luck. As I stood in the entry way, Jordan hovered in the stairwell with her phone in hand, happily answering every ping that came in. Her excitement over Maya`s unfortunate situation was disturbing.

"Jordan!" Mr. Wells spoke sharply. "Either turn your phone off or go upstairs. Actually, go upstairs and make sure that your mother is fine. Please do not allow her onto the computer or let her pick up the phone."

"Of course, Dad," she answered back snidely. "I wouldn't want Mom upset by Maya *again*." As she walked up the stairs she snickered, "So Beth, how many times in the course of a year do you need to clean up her messes before *you* dump her?"

"Jordan!" Mr. Wells yelled her name with such intense anger that she stopped laughing and stomped up the stairs without another word.

"Beth, please come in," he said using a forced calm tone. Wearing his lawyer's hat, and leaving Dad behind, he dove right in. "What can you tell me?"

"Have you seen the whole site?" I asked unsure if he had had a chance to view all of the details.

"Humm. Most of it," he said sadly. "I've been going through the entries and it appears that Maya didn't, and still doesn't, know anything about the situation."

"I agree," I said putting my hand on his shoulder. "I think that somehow the woman who started the blog has gotten ahold of Maya's writing and has been copying her journal entries. Maya and I used to read our journals to each other when we were in high school and I know her style."

"I didn't know that she had kept a journal," he responded with surprise and a deeper sadness.

"Oh, she hasn't kept one since she was a teenager, but it looks like she started again when she left on her trip. Miss Price must have found it and used it to her own advantage. What I don't understand is why she would start with pseudonyms, and then just post their full names with the images. She essentially exposed them all, including herself. It just doesn't make a lot of sense."

"Beth what else do you know?" he asked, pushing his feelings aside in pursuit of more information. "We need to get ahold of Maya as quickly as possible."

"I spoke with Maya last week and she was happy. She told me she had met a man and she was good, really good. She said she had learned something about him though, and that she wasn't sure how to tell him. After reading the letter in the blog, it must have been the information about his parents. She loves him Mr. Wells. I've never heard her speak about anyone like that before. She trusts him. There is something else you and Mrs. Wells should know: She isn't planning on coming home. She said she is staying in Portugal."

"For how long?" His reaction was filled with shock and worry.

"I'm not sure, but it sounded like for a long time. Anyways, they are eight hours ahead of us. She told me she turned her phone off so I know the only chance we have to speak with her is to call her at the inn directly. Would you like to call her or should I?"

"I think you should. If she hears my voice, I'm afraid she'll panic and think something has happened to Mrs. Wells. Please try her while you're here," he insisted.

"Does Mrs. Wells know yet? Maya would be devastated if this set her back in any way. She loves her very much."

Mr. Wells smiled warmly at me. "Beth, her mother and I know that. Actually she wrote Judith a letter during the first week of her stay. I think it was the most important letter Judith has ever received. She won't let me read it, but said that Maya is growing up and healing. She keeps it by her bed and reads it nightly."

"Oh! I almost forgot to tell you. I think Steven has lost his mind," I interjected. "When I spoke with him earlier, he talked about wanting to rescue her. I was very blunt and told him she didn't love him, but he is convinced he needs to save her, and has bought a ticket to Lisbon. He leaves tonight. He thinks he can win her back. I tried to stop him but he wouldn't listen to me."

"Yes, Jordan already told me. She supports his plan, unfortunately. Beth, do whatever you have to do to talk with Maya before Steven arrives. I don't want her returning with *him*." Mr. Wells took a breath. "What do you know about this Cristiano fellow? It all looks very bad for him, but I find it hard to believe. If you read all of the other parts of the story, and then add in what Maya has told you, it doesn't make sense that he would cheat on her with this Jade woman. I'm going to try and contact the editor of the blog to see if they can close the site temporarily, but I'm not hopeful." Defeat broke through his voice.

"Don't give up Mr. Wells. I'll track her down. We'll figure it out. I promise."

"Thank you Beth. She's lucky to have you."

"You know Mr. Wells, Maya has been a good friend to me too. She's really special. She just hasn't been able to show many people, but I think that something has changed for her on this trip. She sounded different."

"I know, Beth! That's why it's so important for us to get ahold of this situation. I'm not going to let any kind of scandal ruin the wonderful things that are happening for her."

"Scandal? What's the matter with Maya?" Judith blurted out. She stood on the stairs looking fierce, like a mother bear ready for a fight.

Maya

(THURSDAY, 4:00 P.M.—LISBON [THURSDAY, 8:00 A.M. IN PEACHLAND])

After Avó and I finished grinding grain, prepping loaf pans, and cleaning the garden oven, we dedicated the rest of our day to wandering through the fields, going to the chapel, holding hands, and just being together. Her touch was firm and safe, and her scent reminded me of Cristiano. *She* was home.

On our way back from the chapel, she took me out to a tree in the field. I wondered if it had been the tree where Cristiano sat for those two days after his parents died. It looked like some sort of fruit tree, but it wasn't well.

"Fruit?" I asked pointing at the tree.

"No fruit. Many years, no fruit, but soon," she said confidently. Then she took my hand and we walked back to the house. We made a simple supper and she showed me to my room—Cristiano's room.

Gently she pushed me in and closed the door, leaving me alone in his space. I threw myself on his bed and buried my head into his pillow. I could still smell him. Taking in a deep breath, my heart bounced, as if he had just been holding me in his arms. I laughed at myself and then opened Christopher.

Thursday evening at Avó's house, lying in Cristiano's bed.

Dear Friend,

Thank you for being with me and helping me through the last three weeks. My life has changed and then changed again. They say it takes seven years for you to replace every cell in your body, somehow I think that process has been accelerated. I am a new Maya, every single cell of me. I love me.

Eyes closing, good night. Only two more sleeps until I see him.
M.

Cristiano

(Thursday, 1:30 p.m.—Vancouver, [Thursday, 9:30 p.m. in Lisbon])

I had no trouble switching flights, but in the process of the change I was rerouted through Vancouver. My mother used to tell me that everything happens for a reason, and when I found myself in Vancouver with a few extra hours, I phoned Maggie to see if she would like a visit.

She sounded relieved when she heard my voice. It had been a week since the funeral, and she said that most people had gone back to their regular lives. She was thankful for the peace, as she felt like *other* people just didn't understand what she was going through.

When I arrived in Vancouver it was raining. I flagged a cab and then gave the driver Maggie's address and we began making our way through the wet streets.

When the driver arrived at Maggie's, she was standing in the open doorway. I walked up the stairs and she held out her hand. I could feel the chill on her skin from the early fall weather that had hit the city. She wrapped her arms around me, forever connected through tears, tragedy, and circumstance.

"Maggie, you said on the phone that everyone had left?"

"No, it was not that they left, but more that I sent them all away. They were driving me crazy. Everyone thinks that I've lost my mind because I have been talking with Puro every day, except for Tim. Actually, he hasn't said too much about anything. He went back to school on Monday ... but everything's wrong, he's wrong."

Maggie's voice sounded removed from her body, like she was talking to me, but watching herself at the same time.

"Oh, thank you for arranging the flight for Puro," she said absently. "How is Maya?" Her face lit up as she mentioned her name.

"She is simply the love of my life, wonderful, perfect. *She* makes sense to me."

"I am so pleased for the two of you." She placed her hand over mine. "How are things going with the contest? Is everyone having fun?" She asked changing the subject again.

"I think so. There was a wonderful party in your family's honor last Friday."

"Yes, I know. Puro and I were online, and I heard all the commotion. He took me into the room, and from what I could see it was beautiful."

"Maya wrote a poem, and Sachi baked the most exquisite cake I have ever seen. Here's a picture of it." I pulled out my phone to show her some of the photos.

"Oh my, it is amazing! Puro told me about it, but it was all gone by the time he had taken me into the room." She scrolled through a few more of my pictures. "What a special night it must have been," she said dreamily.

"Oh it was. Maya and I had to leave early though, because I took her to Paris for the weekend."

"Paris, how romantic."

We sat quietly for a moment and the space became heavy with sadness. "How was the funeral last week?" I asked, knowing few people would want to know.

"I have some pictures if you want to see them," she responded with a small surge of enthusiasm.

"I would love to. Thank you."

We walked over to the computer and she sat down. Her email was open. I couldn't help but notice her inbox held dozens of messages and was still downloading more.

"You have a lot of mail coming in."

"I can't imagine who from?" She looked confused.

"Let me see what I can find." I switched chairs with her and looked more closely at all of the addresses. "It looks like they are all being forwarded from PricesPortugal.com? Do you know it?"

"No, I've never heard of it," she said, looking perplexed.

"Let's send all the emails to the trash, but I think we should Google the site, just to find out what we are dealing with. I'm sure it's nothing." I clicked on the link.

The first image we saw when the site opened left me sickened and stunned.

Jade was kissing me and she had her hand in my pocket. The tag read: "*Faithful? Not in this century.*" The second picture on the site was of Maggie and Maya and all of the other ladies drinking wine on the veranda at Netuno. The tag read: "*Grieving Mother and Friends? What a joke.*"

We looked at each other, mortified, not sure what to say to one another, then began scrolling through the entries, trying to figure out what was going on.

"Who wrote this?" Maggie managed to ask, as the two of us fast-forwarded through some of the horrible comments that had been made about her. We toggled back to the top of the blog and there was the author's picture. It was Dalley—Dalley Price. '*Price's Portugal*,' it read.

"Our Dalley?" Maggie asked the question while staring at her picture. She looked winded, like someone had just hit her in the stomach.

I went on to read some of the entries out loud to Maggie, mixing in my interpretations with Dalley's writing.

"The whole thing starts off about the trip in general. At first she only mentions *Trina* and a male *flight attendant*, meeting on the plane and inferred that we joined the mile high club." I smirked knowing the irony in the lie. "Then our date in Montreal. A few days later there's an abrupt change in the writing style." Anger and fear began to grow in my core. "She posted the letter and the poem I wrote to Maya. How could she do that?" I scrolled down farther. "Maggie! She copied Maya's journal entries, word for word in some parts." I felt like I was going to be sick and lose my mind all at the same time. I moved away from the computer to try and get my bearings. I needed to talk to Maya. I called her on our cell. She wasn't picking up and it wouldn't let me leave a message.

Maggie sat down at the computer.

"Dalley not only took Maya's writings, but she scribed *all* the stories that we told each other about our lives. I don't understand, Cristiano. Why would she do that? Why would anyone do that?" She scrolled back to the picture of Jade and I, and her face became distorted. "Cristiano? What's this all about?"

"It's not what it looks like!!" I stammered. "Honestly, I would never cheat on Maya. I flew to Montreal on Tuesday to get Athena back from Jade. She took it when she left Netuno."

"She left? She stole Maya's pen?"

"Yes. Jade left the day after you. Maya told me they'd gotten into a big fight and it got very personal. When Jade left, she took Athena. I knew how much that pen meant to Maya, so when I was in New York I flew up to Montreal to get it back. When I knocked on the door, Jade answered. She had been drinking and threw herself at me. I told her I had just come for the pen and then she leaned in and kissed me and slipped Athena into my pant pocket. I pushed her away and ran. She was so angry that she threw a vase at my head." I pulled the pen out to prove to Maggie that I had only been there for one reason. "I really was there to get Athena back. I would never do anything to hurt Maya. I have been waiting my whole life for her. She is my—everything."

"I know Cristiano. I believe you." She turned back to the computer. "I find it hard to believe though that Dalley and Jade were working together. Dalley really didn't like Jade."

I sat gutted, not knowing what to do next as Maggie went through entry after entry. I couldn't look anymore.

"Cristiano, I found something I think you should see."

"I don't think I can bear anymore of Dalley and Jade's deceit."

"There's a letter here in the blog from Maya to you, dated last week, before you left for Paris. If you are right that many of these entries are from Maya's journal then … Did she read the letter to you?"

"Letter? No. I don't know anything about a letter. That night when we left for the airport I didn't let her go back to her room. I just whisked her away."

"I think you should read it. But you need to be prepared."

Dear Cristiano,

I could hear her voice in my head.

Take my hand. I promise to always be truthful with you and to love you like no one has ever loved you before; to walk with you into the darkness, knowing we will always find light. To bring you joy and laughter when you least expect it and to humble myself when I have hurt you and ask for your forgiveness. I'm not perfect, but with you in my life I strive to be a better me and for that reason alone I could love no one but you … but before we can move forward you need to know something …

I read the letter twice before I could even begin processing what she had written. Within two weeks, I had learned not only that I was adopted, but that my birth parents were together and that I had a brother and a sister—a whole family living just hours from me—my family.

Then I remembered Maya that night in Paris at the airport. She wasn't just sad about me leaving, she had been trying to tell me about my parents. "Oh Maya," I whispered, calling out to her as tears streamed down my cheeks.

Maggie walked back into the room and held me in her arms as I tried to understand what was happening around me.

"What am I going to do?"

"I'll tell you what you're going to do. I'm going to call you a cab for the airport. You are going to text Maya a note. You are going to get on your plane, and you are going to make things right with her. That's what you're going to do!"

"Maggie, I feel terrible for leaving. I came here to help you and …"

"And what?" She smiled. "I got to take a breath and be a mom and help someone I love." Her eyes welled and she hugged me tightly. "Now go and find Maya and don't let anything stop you, not her, not even yourself."

❧

Our flight left from the same gate where I had met Maya just three weeks previously. I smiled as I saw the tea stain on the carpet and could see her kneeling down, hair hanging over her shoulders, and that look on her face: somewhere between giving up and wanting to start over.

We were so perfectly matched.

45

The Handkerchief

Maya

(Friday, 6:00 a.m. Lisbon time—Avó's House)

All it took was a slight tap on the door to wake me. My eyes opened immediately and she peeked into the room.

"Maya, get up!!"

I chuckled as I heard Avó's words.

"*Obrigado* Avó." I gestured to her that I would be down in a minute. I dressed quickly, made Cristiano's bed, and then hurried down the stairs, as I didn't want to make her wait. She had already started the fire in the outdoor oven and had a cup of coffee waiting for me on the table in the garden. The morning was cooler than I had expected, and I stood close by the oven, warming my arms. She gave me an egg tart and a few small sweet buns that were still warm. Clearly, she had been baking since dawn.

After I ate, we went to work. All the flour we'd ground the day before sat resting on the tables, each unmade loaf waiting for its chance to shine. Hours passed as the two of us worked artfully together. My love and admiration for her had grown over the week, and I understood so much more about Cristiano and where he had come from, fully realizing why Jack had never told him about Marcos. Euphemia and Marcos may have been the seeds that started his life, but Avó, Rosa, and Michel were his roots. By late afternoon, we'd finished the last of the loaves and were letting them cool in the garden. I packed my bag and took one last deep breath from his pillow.

We wrapped each loaf like it was a present and then packed them into the large wicker basket that she slung on my back. I could tell she had done it many times, and she showed a sense of relief that it was me who was carrying the load of her magical bread—our magical bread. She kissed me goodbye and sent me on my way. "I love you too," I said as I walked out the garden gate and headed down the path towards the inn.

By the time I arrived, everything in the kitchen was in full swing. Sachi and Gervais were actually smiling and Petra looked like she was trying her hand at another round of Portuguese Seafood Stew. She winked at me when she saw me walk into the kitchen.

"Nice, Maya; very effective look," she teased. I reached up and realized that I was still wearing Avó's hand embroidered handkerchief that she had tied into my hair earlier.

"Okay so are you going to tell me where you've been? Or are you really going to make me wait until tonight? Something is different. You've changed. Not because of *a man kind of change*, but a life one."

She was right. I unloaded my bread and proceeded to tell her the whole story, everything from Jack, to Paris, to Avó. She shook her head in disbelief as she slowly stirred her stew. "You sure know how to keep a girl on the edge of her seat. Are you sure I didn't win the additional bet while you were in Paris?"

"I'm sure." I giggled like a teenager, thinking about our two double beds.

"Oh! Carmo's been looking for you. She said someone's been trying to reach you from home. Also, I wanted to let you know that the Internet has been down for hours. Somehow the local server crashed and cell coverage has been spotty too."

"Did she say who called?" I sucked in a breath of air.

"No, she didn't mention the name. But she did say it was a young woman."

"Oh," I released my breath. "It must have been Beth, my best friend. I called her last week before I went shopping in Évora." I laughed, feeling more relaxed. "Petra, you said that the Internet was down and cell coverage has been spotty all day. Do you know what's going on?"

"No, I just know that my husband has been trying to get ahold of me, and we've been missing each other. Only half of the messages have been getting through and all emails are completely stalled with the server down."

"I had better go upstairs and check the phone that Cristiano gave me. He didn't know that I was away last night and might be worried."

I organized my beautifully-wrapped bread onto one of the tables and left the kitchen. Before heading upstairs, I stopped at the front desk to speak with Carmo.

"Carmo? Petra said that you were looking for me?"

"Yes, things have been a little chaotic around here with the Internet going down last night." She searched through a pile of messages, about thirty-five deep. "Actually, I have five messages for you from a girl named Beth. She said she needed to talk to you, but that was several hours ago. We have been having trouble with cell phones, but the landline at the front desk here is working. The company said that our small grid got slammed with too much traffic last night. We're not sure what's going on, but the repair people think it has something to do with a website. We don't know anything except that things are broken."

The phone rang and Carmo picked it up. She placed her hand over the receiver. "Maya, we only have one line working right now, you'll have to wait. You can try and text, but most messages are undeliverable. Good luck on getting through."

"Do you know when things will be fixed?" I asked, feeling a growing sense of unease.

"The wireless company said everything should be back up and running soon. I'll be happier than anyone. The guests have been beside themselves, not being able to get online for the last eighteen hours, especially Dalley."

"Oh, that makes sense. She has been working a lot online lately. I hope this doesn't mess up anyone's presentation tonight. Puro must be so upset. I know how much he prides himself on things running smoothly around here. Where is he?" My barrage of questions and comments appeared to leave Carmo feeling uncomfortable as she was still holding the receiver in her hand.

"He took the day off and went for a hike," she said hastily, then pointed to the phone, letting me know that she had to get back to work.

My worry began to mount. Beth would never have called that many times unless something was wrong back home. I knew I needed to get ahold of her.

I walked quickly up to my room and turned on my phone from Cristiano. It pinged again and again. There were a dozen missed calls but nothing was retrievable. I jumped from worry to anxious in one frightening, unwanted leap, flirting with panic when I landed. I tried to decipher a few of the texts, but only bits and pieces had come through:

'Maya … mad … Okay call me … Don't worry … Jade. Maggie and Puro …'

None of it made sense. My heart became stuck in my throat. I could barely breathe. I needed to talk to him, to Beth, to someone, but the signal was dead.

My heart rate spiked, and my hands started to sweat. The feeling was getting worse and dread started taking hold like the night before my non-wedding. "Everything is okay," I mumbled to myself unconvincingly while shards of newly-formed panic slashed tiny slits into the new Maya. "I'll talk to both of them in a little while. Whatever it is, we'll sort it out." My body rocked back and forth trying to soothe itself—unsuccessfully.

Dalley walked through the door. She looked frantic. It felt like we were all going crazy. I took a shallow breath.

"Dalley? Are you okay?" I asked. She said nothing, so I kept going. "There are lots of weird things going on around here. I've had multiple messages come in from Beth and Cristiano, but the texts have been scrambled and there are no cell calls going out. And as you know, the Internet is down. Do you know what's going on?"

"Why? Why would I have anything to do with crashing a network?" she snapped defensively.

"I don't know. No reason, I guess. I was just trying to figure it out," I said rebutting her defensive response. "Carmo said that everything will be fixed in the next couple of hours. I need a shower."

As I walked away from Dalley, I noticed her perfectly tanned skin had drained to ashen gray, something was really wrong.

The hot water pushed the rising anxiety back momentarily, but not for long. After showering I grabbed my things and went downstairs to prepare for my presentation, thankful for the distraction. It was simple: music, images, the bread, and my handkerchief.

The dining room was still when I entered, and when Gervais tapped me on the shoulder I jumped.

"Maya? What is it?"

"Oh, Gervais, I'm not feeling well."

"Can you still present?" he asked with an intense look on his face, waiting for only one answer.

"Yes," I smiled half-heartedly; I'll do my best.

"Could you present just before I serve supper? I think your loaves would bridge beautifully with my menu."

"Sure Gervais, just start my music and I will be ready."

Carmo dashed into the dining room looking excited. "Maya, great news, everything is working again."

The embers of my panic reignited and spread.

"Did you manage to get ahold of Beth or Cristiano?"

"No, I'll do that right now." My fingers trembled as I started to text Cristiano.

The phone and Internet has been down here at the inn all day. None of your phone messages came through and I only received partial texts; something about Maggie and Dalley and Jade? Call me. Love you much. (presentations starts soon, call me after 9:00 tonight) I love you.

Hey Beth, the Internet here has been down all day. I'm texting from a phone that Cristiano gave me. Is my Mom okay? I have to do a presentation soon. I'll call you when I'm done.

My head was spinning. I started creating worst-case scenarios. Could my mom have relapsed? Was there an accident? Did I do something to Cristiano? Did he find out? I wanted to scratch the worry out of my head. As the others got started, I stood off to the side, leaning up against the wall so I wouldn't fall over.

Petra had negotiated going first as she was worried about her stew.

Sachi, Ellen, and Josie fell into line after that, with Dalley and then me.

Petra started right on time. Her stew was superb. At the end, she told everyone about how special her time in Portugal had been and how she thought about bringing her children there one day. I smiled.

The presentations continued until Dalley froze on stage, staring at the back of the room, distracted. I followed her vacant gaze that rested upon Petra and Puro, who had just walked back into the dining room. They both looked grim and disturbed.

Ellen helped Dalley off the stage, but before I could find out what was happening, Gervais jumped up and introduced me. The lights dimmed, and my music started. I had no choice but to begin. I tied the handkerchief into my hair, grabbed my bread and started to walk. The melodic music I had chosen to play while the images flashed on the screen filled the space with the tenderness and beauty that I had experienced all week while I was with Avó. I was transported back to her cottage and I could smell her love. The panic released me for a moment.

As my story unfolded, I walked to each table and handed each person a part of me. I encouraged people to open my gift and tear off a piece of bread. That's when I caught movement from the corner of the room. A sharp pain struck my heart. It felt like betrayal. Petra stomped over to Dalley and then Puro walked out. Something was horribly wrong. My hands began to shake, and I dropped my last loaf to the floor. The panic swung towards me like an anvil in my chest—there was no stopping it.

Cristiano

(FRIDAY, 7:35 P.M. LISBON TIME—AIRPORT)

I arrived in Lisbon just after 6 p.m. and got stuck in customs with a new officer who thought I was too jumpy for his liking. One of my friends smoothed things over with the overzealous officer, but I was late, and I had to make up time. I had called ahead and my car was waiting for me at the arrival entrance. When I jumped in, my phone pinged. It was from Maya. I was both relieved and nervous. She hadn't seen the site yet. She hadn't even read my texts. The Internet had been down all day at Netuno. I still had a chance to make it there in time.

Maya

(Friday, 8:53 p.m. Lisbon Time—Netuno)

Then it happened all at the same time. I looked over and there he was. Steven was standing at the back of the room. On the other side was Dalley and Petra—their conversation erupting into a full-blown battle. I purposefully blinked, scrunching up my eyes, and hoping that Steven wasn't really there, and that whatever Dalley and Petra were fighting about would go away. The lights went up and all the attention was focused on the back of the room. Petra raised her hand and slapped Dalley across the face. I held my chest as the pain was so striking that it felt like my heart was being torn in pieces. Josie and Ellen ran towards me and Steven followed too, but I staggered over to Petra who was yelling at the top of her lungs. Dalley was not able to respond as Petra's rant took over the room.

"What the hell have you done Dalley? I have never in all my life met anyone so deceitful and cruel."

Petra's words were horrid. *What was she talking about?* I stood confused as the crowd around us began to grow.

"You took our lives and splayed them all over the Internet! You took Maya's and Cristiano's love and gutted it, and Maggie—well, I can't begin to tell you the contempt I feel. You exposed her and her family in a way that makes me sick to my stomach! You were our friend and you betrayed us."

"So this is the bitch who ruined our lives?" Steven cursed while taking a step towards me.

"Our lives? Steven there is no *our*," I yelled at him. Josie and Ellen moved in closer to me.

"Who are you?" Josie moved to stand in front of me.

"Who am I? I am the man who loves Maya and has come to save her from all of this craziness. I am Steven, her fiancé."

"Steven, I broke up with you months ago and I don't need saving. I don't even know what the hell is going on here." I turned my attention to Petra. "What's this all about?" I grabbed my head feeling like it was going to fall off.

"Where is he anyway?" Steven continued without hearing a word I said.

"Where is who?" I yelled to match the anger in the room.

"Cristiano, Maya. *The love of your life?* He's probably with that Jade girl no doubt."

His words struck me like a startled snake lashing out.

"Steven what are you talking about?" My anger shifted to bewilderment.

"Cristiano, your new *love!* I have proof he was with another woman."

My breaths became short again. "I don't believe it," I sputtered. "None of it! I don't understand what's going on!" I screamed while looking around for someone to explain.

"Do you think I would have come over 5,000 miles if this wasn't real? Maya, I still love you. This is not your world. You should be with me." He stepped closer then ripped the handkerchief off of my head. "This is not you," he yelled holding up a part of my heart. "I can take care of you. I love you. I have always loved you. He does not!"

He pulled out his tablet and touched the screen. The first image that came up was one of Cristiano and Jade. He was kissing her. She was touching him.

"That is not love! He played you, Maya. He's a playboy, and you're a kind girl from Peachland. Come home with me," he said quietly.

Looking around at the crowd, things started to swirl. My knees crumbled and Steven caught me just before I hit the floor.

Cristiano

(Friday, 8:55 p.m.—Standing at the door at Netuno)

When I arrived at Netuno, people were filing out of the dining room like there had been some sort of evacuation. Puro was on the phone when he saw me. He covered the receiver with his palm and yelled, "Cristiano, Maya needs you right now!"

I ran into the dining room and heard *him* declare his love for her— my Maya. Then he showed her his tablet, and she collapsed. I saw him catch her in his arms. She believed him. I had to get out, I had to get away.

"Cristiano!" Puro yelled out and ran over to me as I stumbled towards the door.

"How is that possible? She loves me. She knows I would never do anything to hurt her. I love her," I cried filled with anguish. "She is my home."

"Cristiano, go and talk to her. She's in shock."

"She believed him, she trusts—him."

"Cristiano, I just got off the phone with Maggie. She explained everything. Go back in there right now and tell Maya the truth. She doesn't even know you're here. She doesn't love that man. She loves only you."

Puro's words bounced off me. All I could see was Maya in *his* arms, when it should have been me holding her. I should have been there to catch her.

"Puro, I've let her down. I didn't give her enough reasons to trust me, to love me enough."

"That's not true," Puro implored with desperation. Then his face and voice softened. "Don't do this Cristiano. I can see it in your eyes. Don't run. It won't solve anything."

"Please give this to her." I handed him the box and walked out the door.

Maya

"Cristiano!!! Cristiano!!!" Puro cried from the lobby.

Pushing Steven away from me I scrambled out of his arms and ran to the front door.

Puro grabbed me. "Maya! Maya, listen to me. It's all lies. It wasn't his fault. They did this, both of them—Dalley and Jade."

"Maya," Puro said quietly as I stood confused, trying to comprehend what had just happened. "Let me explain. Dalley has been writing a blog about you and Cristiano and the rest of us. She stole entries from your journal and posted them on her site. Somehow Jade got involved. Cristiano returned early to try and sort things out."

"She did what? Dalley's my friend. I told her everything." I stopped. "Cristiano was here. He saw me in Steven's arms, didn't he?" My breath hitched.

"Yes." He paused, then handed me a small box. "He asked me to give this to you."

I tore open the wrapping and inside lay—Athena. No one needed to explain anything else. By that time Steven had entered the lobby and tried to interject again.

"Maya, a cheap sparkly pen isn't going to change the fact that he cheated on you." He spat the words out at me.

Looking at him I responded calmly, my anxiety and panic incinerated by truth. "Actually, it does." I pushed a stray piece of bang from my face and tucked it behind my ear. "Go home Steven." I smiled gently and whispered the next part so as not to cause him further embarrassment. "I told you before, I don't love you and I'm not the same girl from Peachland that you knew." I took back the handkerchief that he still held in his hand and tied it into my hair. "I love Cristiano. He is my future." Strength and confidence rang true in my tone.

The dining room fell silent as I walked through the door. All eyes were on me as I stepped towards Dalley. Athena buzzed noisily in my hand egging me on, demanding retribution. My newly formed fist tightened and without thinking I hit Dalley square on the chin, sending her backwards into the wall and knocking her out cold.

I ran out of the inn after Cristiano, sprinting down the road until my muscles ached and my heart could take me no farther, then stopped and let the darkness and the dust settle around me. Pain leaked into my chest. I offered my heart up to the stars, but it was the night sky who answered. A wave of emotion rolled towards me and without hesitation I dove in. When I finally came up for air, my head was clear, and I was ready—ready to fight for love and for me.

Epilogue

Puro

I STOOD ON THE VERANDA and watched Maya race down the dirt road after Cristiano. There was a ferocity in her step that made me believe Maya was not going to let him run away from his life or step out of hers without a fight. She was not the same person who had walked through Netuno's doors at the start of the contest. She had changed—we all had changed.

But I believed that Maya would bring Cristiano home, no matter where she had to go or what she had to do to find him.

When I stepped back into the lobby, Josie, Ellen, Sachi, and Petra were sitting down, each holding a glass of wine. Their chatter minimal at first as they pored over Petra's computer, reading through *Price's Portugal*, letting out numerous sighs and gasps, expressing their horror at the blog, and all that Dalley and Jade had done. When the second bottle was almost empty, the conversation shifted from dismay into what sounded like a battle plan; but was interrupted when they saw Dalley on the stairs with her luggage. Petra stood first, followed by the rest of the ladies. Dalley set her suitcases down and moved towards them, looking dejected, her face swollen and bruised. Rummaging through her purse she pulled out a black file and tried to explain herself to them, but they turned away, not willing to listen.

Exasperated, she tossed the file into the air, grabbed her bags and marched towards the doors. The folder landed on the wooden table with an unnatural crack that startled us all and left me feeling like Cristiano was not the only person in trouble.

Acknowledgements

(SUPER SPARKLY THANK YOUS)

Launching a 2nd edition of The Girl in the Peach Tree four years after its original release took a lot of courage and support from my family, friends and colleagues.

Many thanks to all the people who encouraged me to look at the manuscript through my new life lenses as it truly helped shape the story in so many remarkable ways.

I want to thank my amazing uncle Wally Oucharek who painted the original cover art for the 1st edition of the book in 2016, and Nada Orlic, the newest member of my team, who redesigned the cover for the 2nd edition.

For my cousin Jennifer who read the roughest of drafts many years ago and to my beta readers, whose honesty and heartfelt feedback was truly humbling.

For my husband, Brian, who served up endless cups of coffee, tea, and love throughout the writing of the 1st and 2nd editions, and for my son: a remarkable young man who understands what it takes to achieve one's goals.

And a special continued thank-you to my original editor, Stephanie Brennen, who dove into my story so many years ago without hesitation.

She walked through the manuscript with a pink marking pen using it like a magic wand.

And a final thanks to my number one fan, Auntie Delores, and to all the readers of the original Girl in the Peach Tree. It has been moving to hear the different stories of how Maya's and Cristiano's lives affected so many people in different ways around the globe.

Truly Thankful,

Michelle

BAREFOOT IN THE DIRT

The Vinho Verde Trilogy

❧

Book II

Prologue

Maya

As long as I was moving, I was closer to him. Stride after stride, my feet pounded into the dirt, my pain fueling each step. Then out of nowhere, a car came up from behind. It all happened so fast. I heard the brakes screech, and at the last second the car swerved, barely missing me. I fell to the ground, filled with rage, my heart hammering in my chest as if it were going to explode.

The brake lights flashed, and the car stopped.

"You picked the wrong person to run over tonight!" I screamed, trying to catch my breath as I waited for the driver to get out of their car. I heard a female voice yell sorry from her open window.

Before I could even think, obscenities came tumbling from my lips. The car sped off leaving me sitting on the side of the road with only my soured tongue and wounded heart to keep me company. It was in that moment that my fury turned to hysteria. I had never told anyone to 'f' off before in my life and it felt good, better than it probably should have.

As my breath slowed, and I sought out the stillness of the evening, the calm returned. Being angry seemed far more productive, but anger took energy and I had nothing left. There I was, barefoot and a long way from the inn, so I stood up and started back. I had only walked a few minutes when I heard a car approaching from behind.

I was prepared for a fight but when the window rolled down, all I saw was a scruffy looking man smiling back at me. After a brief interaction, he realized I was not a local, then asked if I needed a lift. I hesitated, distracted by his unruly black hair. He laughed like it was not the first time his hair had upstaged a conversation, then pulled it back in a ponytail, flashed me a badge, and shrugged good-naturedly.

At that point, I threw caution to the wind and broke yet another life rule: I got into a car with a stranger. He carefully studied my face, glanced down at my dirty feet, then without another word, drove me back to Netuno and dropped me off at the inn.

1

Shards of Glass

Cristiano

I STOOD IN THE BLACKNESS of the night at the side of the road, not sure where to go or what to do. The only thing left of me was a tinder-dry shell. My heart raced and the muscles in my chest tightened like someone was knocking flint rock together. And then it happened. An unstoppable rage exploded in my heart; it was just the spark I was waiting for.

I never thought I could feel hate but, in that moment, I hated everyone: Jack for not telling me *my* truth when I was a teenager; Avo, for revealing my adoption in a letter twenty years too late; my birth parents for giving me up; my mom and dad for dying in the plane crash in Egypt; and Maya, for making me think I was worthy of being loved.

Fire raged as I got back into the car and it was only when I arrived on Jack's beach in Setubal that I took a breath. It was like breathing in shards of glass. It reminded me of the pain I used to feel, almost like an old friend coming back for a surprise visit.

I started yelling his name as I ran down the darkened path. Then I tore open his flimsy door and roused him out of bed.

"Cristiano? Is that you? What the hell are you …?"

I didn't give him a chance to finish. I pulled back my fist and hit him. Jack was unconscious before he smashed through his cot.

I searched through his things like a mad man until I found his phone. I needed to find my birth parents, to find out where I really came from. I combed through his contacts, finally finding them under the last name of Tavares: Marcos and Euphemia Tavares. Cristiano Tavares? Cristiano Lazaro? I had no idea who I really was, but I was not going to stop until I found out.

❧

The drive towards Porto, their hometown, was just a few hours. I usually loved driving, but with my emotions raw and anxiety high, I slowed down to a snail's pace and broke into an unwinnable argument with myself.

"It's the middle of the night. What am I going to do? Knock on their door? I would never get a second chance with them if I descended on their home filled with this much anger. Marcos would call the police. I know I would. Besides, my brother and sister don't even know I exist. I'm just a stranger looking for answers. They'd think I was crazy. Maybe I am. Look what I did to Jack. Oh my God, I knocked him out cold. He could be hurt."

I pulled into a service station in Aveiro. I had heard of the town before but had never been. People said it was like the Venice of Portugal. Maya would have loved it. Aveiro was beautiful just like her. My heart twisted, then sank when I thought about her. All I could see was her in *his* arms, but it didn't make sense. None of it made sense.

"Do you really believe I could be unfaithful to you?" I asked looking up into the sky. "Maybe I should call her? No! I can't. But I do need to talk to Jack."

I reached for my phone—it was gone. The last time I used it was just after I landed and listened to Maya's message while driving to Netuno. "She told me she loved me …"

The gas attendant sold me a burner phone that was only good in Portugal. I dialed my number. It rang once, then twice.

"Hello?" The voice sounded groggy like the person on the other end had been sleeping.

"Jack? Is that you?" I asked hesitantly.

"It depends. Are you going to hit me again? I think you broke a tooth. You sucker punched me. I was right in the middle of the most awesome dream," Jack responded, sounding relatively unphased.

"That's all you have to say. I knocked you out, broke a tooth, tore your place apart, and you're mad at me because I disrupted your dream?"

"No, I'm not mad at you. I expected you to be upset—maybe not break-my-bed upset, but …"

"Yeah, I'm sorry about that Jack. I'll buy you a new one."

"No, it's okay, maybe I should sleep on the floor as punishment for not telling you about Marcos myself."

"Yeah, you do deserve to be punished, but you don't need to sleep on the floor," I sighed. "Why don't you go and stay at my place in Lisbon until you get a new bed? I won't be back for a while. I'll call Mrs. Dutra and let her know you're coming."

"I never said I was going to stay at your place."

"When have you ever turned down a free anything? Just go and have a good time in the city."

"What do you mean you won't be back for a while? Please tell me you're not going to do something more stupid than beating up your best friend."

"You're my best friend?"

"Yeah, at least I thought I was."

I paused. "Jack? What *were* you thinking? Why didn't you tell me about being adopted when you figured it out?" Then I had to ask, "Maya's letter—was it all true?

"I don't know anything about a letter, but when I told her about Marcos, she was very upset and insisted you had to know the truth."

"I have two questions for you: Firstly, why didn't you tell Marcos about my parents' death when he came to see me surf that first day? And …" I paused, feeling my chest tighten and my eyes fill, "why didn't he stay?"

"I don't know why he didn't stay. And I thought I had a good reason not to tell him about your parents. But Cristiano, the stuff with Marcos happened a long time ago, there is nothing I can do to change things, and truthfully … I don't think I would," he said defiantly. "When he came to see you and confirmed my suspicions about being your father, I thought briefly about telling him everything, but you were just starting to pull your life back together. I was worried about you." He paused. "In the end, everything worked out though. You have Maya and Avo and me," he laughed. "You have everything you've always wanted."

"Right, I have everything I've always wanted," I spat back painfully. Jack's words reignited the anger and I had to stop talking before I said something I would regret.

"What's going on Cristiano? What did you do? Is Maya okay? Cristiano? Where are you?" Jack asked with uncharacteristic concern breaking through.

"Jack, I have to sort some things out and I need to start at the beginning."

"And where is that Cristiano?"

"Your phone said my family lives in Porto. Sounds like a good place to start."

"Cristiano? Like I said, don't do anything stupid."

"Sure Jack, whatever you say because you know so much about being smart."

"You're a real jerk, you know?" he said coolly.

I winced, knowing he was right but couldn't admit it. "Mrs. Dutra will have the key. I have to go."

"Cristiano?" Jack paused. "You know she loves you, right?"

"Mrs. Dutra?" I asked dryly.

"No, you idiot, Maya … Maya loves you."

Author's Note

THERE ARE NO GUARANTEES IN life, but I believe that if you follow your heart and try your best at any task, happiness is not far behind. I am not saying the road to accomplishing your goals is easy; sometimes it is so hard you just want to quit. But when you do make the decision to keep going and wipe the mud out of your eyes, you are a stronger person for it. I know this because I've lived it. I've lived through the death of both my parents four months apart; a diagnosis that left me in pain and waiting months for surgery; COVID-19 which left our world upside down, and having to say goodbye to Lily, my ten-year-old golden doodle and writing partner. When I look back, the one action that kept me going each day through all of it was my writing—being able to dive into something I loved in spite of all the loss and pain.

As I move forward in my writing career I invite you to join me on my website www.michelleoucharekdeo.com and subscribe to my mailing list as well follow me on Instagram @moucharekauthor and Facebook @michelleoucharekdeoauthor where I share my journey of writing, gardening, and painting, along with a few good recipes.

Michelle

Lily Girl
April 27, 2020.